OUT OF THE
ASHES

TOM CLANCY'S OP-CENTER NOVELS

ALSO BY DICK COUCH

NONFICTION

Tom Clancy's
OP-CENTER

OUT OF THE
ASHES

CREATED BY
Tom Clancy and Steve Pieczenik

WRITTEN BY
Dick Couch and George Galdorisi

St. Martin's Griffin ⚑ New York

TOM CLANCY'S OP-CENTER: OUT OF THE ASHES. Copyright © 2014 by Jack Ryan Limited Partnership and S&R Literary, Inc. All rights reserved. Printed in the United States of America. For information, address St. Martin's Press, 175 Fifth Avenue, New York, N.Y. 10010.

www.stmartins.com

Designed by Omar Chapa

Library of Congress Cataloging-in-Publication Data

Couch, Dick, 1943–
Tom Clancy's Op-center : out of the ashes / written by Dick Couch and George Galdorisi.
        p. cm.—(Tom Clancy's Op-center)
    ISBN 978-1-250-02683-5 (trade paperback)
    ISBN 978-1-250-06401-1
    ISBN 978-1-250-02682-8 (e-book)
    1. Terrorism—Prevention—Fiction.   2. Undercover operations—Fiction.   3. Suspense fiction.   I. Galdorisi, George, 1948–
II. Clancy, Tom, 1947–2013.   III. Title.   IV. Title: Out of the ashes.
    PS3553.O769T66 2014
    813'.54—dc23

                                                            2014008057

St. Martin's Griffin books may be purchased for educational, business, or promotional use. For information on bulk purchases, please contact Macmillan Corporate and Premium Sales Department at 1-800-221-7945, extension 5442, or write specialmarkets@macmillan.com.

First Edition: May 2014

10 9 8 7 6 5 4 3 2 1

Decades ago, Winston Churchill famously said, "We sleep safely at night because rough men stand ready to visit violence on those who would harm us." More contemporaneously, in the 1992 film, A Few Good Men, *in the courtroom dialogue, Colonel Nathan Jessup (Jack Nicholson) responds to an aggressive interrogation by Lieutenant Daniel Kaffee (Tom Cruise) with, "We live in a world that has walls, and those walls have to be guarded by men with guns . . . Because deep down in places you don't talk about at parties, you* want *me on that wall. You* need *me on that wall."*

This book is dedicated to the selfless men and women—in and out of the military—who toil and sacrifice in obscurity so we may sleep safely at night. They receive no medals or public recognition, and few know of their risks, dedication, and contributions to our security. They endure lengthy—and repeated—deployments away from their families. Yet they stand guard "on the wall" for all of us, silently, professionally, and with no acclaim.

ACKNOWLEDGMENTS

In 1996, then-first lady Hillary Clinton wrote the book *It Takes a Village*. Reviving Tom Clancy's Op-Center series was a momentous undertaking and it took a village of family, friends, colleagues, and others we reached out to in order to make *Out of the Ashes* a book that could live up to our expectations—and especially to the expectations of readers of the twelve previous Op-Center books—as well as our new Op-Center readers. Many thanks to the following who contributed their time and talent so unselfishly: Bill Bleich, Anne Clifford, Ken Curtis, Melinda Day, Jeff Edwards, Herb Gilliland, Kate Green, Kevin Green, Krystee Kott, Robert Masello, Laurie McCord, Scott McCord, Rick "Ozzie" Nelson, Bob O'Donnell, Jerry O'Donnell, Norman Polmar, Curtis Shaub, Scott Truver, Sandy Wetzel-Smith, and Ed Whitman.

Additionally, *Out of the Ashes* would not have been possible—nor would it have been produced so professionally—without the expertise and persistence of our agent, John Silbersack, our editor, Charlie Spicer, as well as Mel Berger, Robert Gottlieb, Madeleine Morrel, April Osborn, Matthew Shear, and Anna Wu.

AUTHORS' INTRODUCTION

The Muslim East and the Christian West have been at war for over a millennium. They are at war today, and that is not likely to change in the near future. As Samuel Huffington would put it, the cultures will continue to clash. At times in the past, the war has been invasive, as in the eighth century, when the Moors moved north and west into Europe, and during the Crusades, when the Christian West invaded the Levant. Regional empires rose and fell through the Middle Ages, and while the Renaissance brought significant material and cultural advances to the Western world, plagues and corrupt monarchies did more to the detriment of both East and West than they were able to do to each other.

In time, as a century of war engulfed Europe and as those same nations embarked on more aggressive colonialism, the East-West struggle receded into the background. The nineteenth-century rise of nationalism and modern weapons technology in the West resulted in an almost universal hegemony, while the

East remained locked in antiquity and internal struggle. The twentieth century and the developing thirst for oil were to change all that.

The seeds of today's East-West conflict were sown when Western nations took it upon themselves to draw national boundaries in the Middle East after the First World War. The infamous Sykes-Picot agreement, which clumsily divided the Middle East into British and French spheres of influence, created weak-sister countries such as Syria, Iraq, and Lebanon, all but ensuring permanent turmoil. After the Second World War, Pan-Arab nationalism, the establishment of the state of Israel, the Suez crisis, the Lebanese civil war, and the Iranian revolution all drove tensions between East and West even higher. While the competition for oil and oil reserves remained a major stimulus, long-standing Muslim-Christian, East-West issues created a catalyst that never let tensions get too far below the surface—and then came 9/11.

The events of September 11, 2001, and the retaliatory invasions that followed, redefined and codified this long-running conflict. For the first time in centuries, the East had struck at the West, and delivered a telling blow. Thus, from Afghanistan to Iraq to Yemen to North Africa and into Indonesia, Thailand, the Philippines, and beyond, the struggle has now become worldwide, nasty, and unrelenting.

Surveys taken just after 9/11 showed that some 15 percent of the world's over 1.5 billion Muslims supported the attack. *It was about time we struck back against those arrogant infidels,* they said. A significant percentage felt no sympathy for the Americans killed in the attack. Nearly all applauded the daring and audacity of the attackers. Many Arab youths wanted to be like those who had so boldly struck at the West.

As the world's foremost authority on the region, Bernard Lewis, has put it, "the outcome of the struggle in the Middle East is still far from clear." For this reason, we chose the Greater Levant as the epicenter of our story of Op-Center's reemergence.

Dick Couch   *George Galdorisi*
Ketchum, Idaho   *Coronado, California*

PROLOGUE

Long before the events of 9/11, even before the first attack on the World Trade Center, America has been under siege by the dark forces of terrorism. Radical Islam, technology, and repressive regimes in oil-rich nations had encouraged the disenfranchised to seek new and more deadly ways to bring harm to our nation. The attacks of 9/11 demonstrated to the world that America was vulnerable. However, in response to those attacks, an aroused America proved it could strike back.

The incursions into Iraq and Afghanistan, while only modestly successful in stabilizing those nations, took a fearful toll on the senior leadership of al Qaeda and their franchises around the world. The world's most formidable terrorist group was decimated to the extent that Americans began to look at the attacks on New York and the Pentagon as a one-time event. Such an attack on our soil had not taken place before, and it hadn't happened since. Perhaps those trillions of dollars spent in the Global War on Terrorism had not been wasted after all. The U.S. military and intelligence communities could rightfully take credit for pushing the terrorists back into the shadows, but there had been another force at work—one that operated in the shadows as well.

Before 9/11 and for several years afterward, our nation was protected by a quiet, covert force known as the National Crisis Management Center. More commonly known as Op-Center, this silent, secret mantle guarded the American people and thwarted numerous threats to our security. The charter of Op-Center was unlike any other in the history of the United States, and its director, Paul Hood, reported directly to the president.

Op-Center dealt with both domestic and international crises. What had started as an information clearinghouse with SWAT capabilities had evolved into an independent organization with the singular capacity to monitor, initiate, and manage operations worldwide. They were good; in fact, too good. Budgets were tight and cuts had to be made. There also was the vaunted U.S. Special Operations Command to deal with terrorists. So Op-Center was disbanded, but the need for Op-Center remained.

For America in the second decade of the twenty-first century, Op-Center was becoming little more than an increasingly distant memory and even those who had taken issue with Op-Center's disestablishment were finally moving on. However, the nation was about to learn just how dangerous it was to do away with this valuable force and the awful price it was about to pay. Just how much Op-Center was needed was about to be demonstrated.

PART I

THE DIE IS CAST

CHAPTER ONE

New York City
(September 6, 2230 Eastern Daylight Time)

He didn't particularly like being in America, and especially didn't enjoy being in New York City. However, Abdul-Muqtadir Kashif was above all else a businessman and this was business.

Kashif was Arab, wealthy, and, from outward appearances, quite Westernized. He was in his midfifties, slim, fit, well-educated, and sophisticated. His eyes were alert but not predatory, and he had a disarming smile. Kashif wore his hair stylishly long but well barbered and kept his goatee and mustache neatly trimmed. He was Kuwaiti by birth and citizenship, but he kept elegant, if not lavish, homes in Paris, London, and Mumbai as well as a primary residence in Kuwait City. He had but a single wife and three children, all girls, who he shamelessly spoiled. He read the Koran often and found the teachings of the Prophet made for an ideal guide for a good and productive life, yet, by and large, he rejected any literal interpretation of the book. Abdul-Muqtadir Kashif was one of those men who his London and Parisian acquaintances never seemed to see as an Arab or a

Muslim. If they did, they were quick to comment, "That Abdul, what a splendid fellow. Why can't more of them be like him?"

He permitted himself the indulgence of bringing his wife, Jumana, along on this short, three-day, business trip. It hadn't been his idea. Somehow she found the shopping in New York superior to that of even London. What harm could come from making her happy by allowing her to busy herself trolling through the high-end boutiques on Fifth Avenue while he hammered out a business deal? Her chauffeur and escort would look out for her.

That same chauffeur had delivered them from their hotel, the Intercontinental New York Barclay, to the penthouse condo of his new business associate, who was hosting a small dinner party in their honor. They had bid their host good-bye and were riding in the swiftly descending elevator when Jumana turned to Kashif.

"My husband, it is such a beautiful night, and our hotel is only a short walk away. Would you just dismiss the chauffeur? We can enjoy an evening stroll together."

Kashif did some quick mental calculations. It was a mere eight blocks walk to East 48th Street where the Intercontinental enjoyed a prominent location between Park and Lexington Avenues. What harm was there if it pleased her? She had, as she always did, charmed his new business associates. It was their last night in New York, a beautiful Sunday night with a full summer moon, and he was feeling exceptionally good about the deal he had struck. Perhaps being in America wasn't so bad after all.

"Of course, my dear. It is a lovely evening."

As they exited the building Kashif dismissed his driver

and they set out walking south on Seventh Avenue. Jumana pulled her hijab tightly around her head, feeling the need for more modesty walking the streets in an American city than she might elsewhere. Abdul-Muqtadir Kashif was happy they had left the dinner party a bit early. The oafish American men there talked about little else than the opening of their football season that weekend. They were even rude enough to keep incessantly checking their smart phones for the progress of one of their hometown teams, the "Giants," who, apparently, would have to save the city's honor that evening in their Sunday night game. Their other team, the "Jets," had lost badly earlier in the day.

As they approached 48th Street and prepared to turn east to reach the Intercontinental, Kashif saw commotion ahead as a number of men poured out of a sports bar. The sign on the bar read TONIC. *How apt,* he thought as he pulled Jumana close to him. They quickened their pace.

Then he heard them.

"He choked! They had them. Then he throws an interception. What a piece of meat. They need to get rid of him."

"He's a complete fraud. God, this is going to be a long season."

"What a punk."

"The Giants suck so bad!"

More men tumbled out of the bar, all obviously inebriated and clearly angry their team had lost.

He pulled Jumana closer and accelerated their pace even more, intending to give the swelling crowd of men a wide berth. Their language was growing fouler and they were now pushing and jostling each other. *What juveniles. America is as decadent as many of my friends say it is.*

Kashif thought about crossing 7th Avenue to avoid these contemptible men entirely, but the traffic was heavy even at this time of night. Turning around and walking back north was not an option he considered. He didn't run from scum.

As they walked close to the curb to avoid the crowd of agitated fans, a large man on the outside of the pack bumped into Jumana.

"Ouch," she said instinctively as she fought to keep her balance, still clutching her hijab.

Reflexively, Kashif stuck out his left hand to fend the man off as he tried to steady his wife with his right.

In his drunken stupor the man fell to the ground. "Shit," he cried.

That got the attention of some of the other men and they tried to pick him up. Instinctively, Kashif attempted to go around the crowd, but instead he bumped into another man.

The man pushed back at him, looked at Jumana, and shouted, "Hey, watch it, you fucking ragheads."

"You watch your mouth," Kashif protested.

By now, the other men had been attracted to the commotion and surrounded Kashif and Jumana.

"Back off! You're in *our* country, you stinking Arab. She part of your harem?"

"Get out of our way or I'll call the police," Kashif yelled as he pulled Jumana in a tight grip and he tried to push their way through the now roused pack of men.

"Good luck with that, camel jockey," another man shouted.

From behind Jumana, a man grabbed her hijab. "So, let's see what's under here. What you hiding there, bitch?"

Kashif wheeled and threw a right roundhouse punch and staggered the man.

That was all it took. With one blow another man knocked Kashif to the ground. Jumana tumbled down with him. The enraged mass of men began stomping the two Kuwaitis. Fit and agile, Kashif was able to fend off many of the blows with his arms. Jumana was not so lucky. The men continued to stomp them, cursing and swearing at the two now-helpless people.

Suddenly, one of New York's ever-present yellow cabs screeched to a stop right at the curb and the driver began honking his horn while shouting, "Hey, stop. Get the hell away from them."

"Mind your own business," one of the men shot back.

"I said, stop it!" the cabbie replied as he emerged from the cab, a gun in his right hand and a cell phone in his left. That he was white and overweight, and wore a Jets sweatshirt, meant nothing; all they saw was the big automatic. That was all it took for the men to turn and run.

The Good Samaritan rushed over and helped Kashif lift himself up. Jumana remained inert on the ground, a pool of blood spreading from under her head.

It had all been a blur for Abdul-Muqtadir Kashif. A New York Police Department cruiser had appeared minutes after the cabbie had called 911. Shortly after that, an ambulance had arrived.

The EMTs placed Jumana on a gurney, started an IV, and put her in the ambulance. Lights flashing and siren blaring they raced south on 7th Avenue and east on 31st Street to reach the New York University Langone urgent care center on 1st Avenue.

Despite his protests, the doctors would not let him in the OR. He was put in a waiting room for those who were with critically injured patients. There he sat for over three hours, the worst three hours of his life, but the next few minutes were about to be more awful than those hours.

"Mr. Kashif?" the man with the green scrubs asked softly. He had coal black hair, soft brown eyes, the smooth olive skin and broad handsome features that marked him as of the upper caste. It was 0430, and in his state Kashif saw only the physician.

"Yes, yes, Doctor?"

"Sir, your wife will be wheeled into ICU recovery in a bit, but it may be some time before you can see her. Does she have an advanced directive?"

"Advanced directive?"

"Yes, an advanced directive. Sir, your wife has severe internal injuries and major head trauma. We've already removed her spleen and she has at least four broken ribs. I'm sorry, sir, but you must be prepared for the worst."

Abdul-Muqtadir Kashif just gasped, but what would follow would be worse.

"Sir, would you sit down, please?" the doctor asked, gently taking Kashif's arm and helping him into a chair.

"Mr. Kashif, I'm sorry to say your wife has suffered major head trauma and is in a deep coma. We have taken an initial

MRI and based on those results we've woken up our chief neurologist and he'll be arriving in less than an hour. We'll know more then, but I can't tell you with certainty your wife will ever wake up. That's why I asked you if she had an advanced directive—in the event her injuries are irreversible."

"I want to see her."

"Sir, you can't see her. She wouldn't know you were there anyway, and she's surrounded by doctors, nurses, and life-support equipment."

"Please, I want to see her," Kashif implored.

Something in his pleading eyes moved the doctor. "Only through the ICU glass, all right?"

"Yes."

Kashif hardly even remembered the doctor steadying him as if he were a tottering old man as they walked the short distance to the ICU room that contained his once-vibrant wife.

His eyes went wide with horror at the sight of Jumana. He broke free from the doctor and ran back the way he had come, weeping bitterly. The doctor followed closely behind.

Kashif collapsed in a chair in the waiting room, still sobbing openly, as the doctor sat down with him, putting his steady hand on his shoulder. "Sir, is there someone we can call for you?"

"No."

"Are you staying nearby?"

"Yes."

"Sir, can I get you something; a sedative perhaps?"

"No. No. I just need to make some calls. You've been very kind. I will be all right here."

Reluctantly, the doctor had left Kashif alone in the waiting area. An hour had passed and Kashif had sat doing nothing but thinking. He knew he should call his oldest daughter, now sixteen, back in Kuwait City, tell her what had happened, and have her break the news to her two younger sisters. Yet what news? That their mother might be a vegetable for the rest of her life? He couldn't find the right words, so that call would have to wait.

Kashif felt the bile building and his rage simmering. He had led a good and righteous life and followed the teachings of the Prophet—to a point. What had just happened to them would not stand. Their life had been so blessed. Now it was all but ended and ended by drunken Americans angered by nothing more than the fact their sports team had lost. This was worse than Europe and their stupid soccer! They needed to pay and they needed to pay as dearly as he was now paying.

Most Americans shared the misconception that all Arabs who had wealth were distant cousins of some Middle East monarch, but Abdul Kashif was more than just another wealthy Arab, though few who knew him thought of him as anything more. He was too quiet, too reserved, and not showy as were most Arabs who had money. Kashif had taken his family's modest funds, his degree in finance from the London School of Economics, a work ethic that would have won approval from Warren Buffett, and the underworld connections of an unsavory uncle from his wife's side of the family, and had amassed a considerable fortune. It now amounted to several hundred million dollars. He was wealthy and now, for the first time in his life, he was consumed with rage—rage and the desire for revenge.

Some Arabs with the financial resources of Abdul-Muqtadir Kashif contributed to radical Arab causes. Those who did secreted these funds to Arab charities from which a good portion of the money found its way into the offshore accounts of those who ran the charities. Those monies that did find their way to a serious terrorist organization like al Qaeda in the Arabian Peninsula were used by Arabs aligned with AQAP to kill other Arabs. Kashif had no intention of spending his hard-earned money that way.

While he was consumed by rage and the need for revenge, he was not blinded by it. If America was to be punished for what had just happened to him and his beloved Jumana, then it needed to be done professionally and with some precision. A strike like the one Osama bin Laden and Mohammad Atta had brought about on 9/11 was no longer possible. The Americans were too well prepared to allow a repeat of that event. *However, there had to be a way,* Kashif thought. He was a businessman, and there was always a way.

He picked up his cell phone and called a particularly capable and discreet Lebanese who sometimes worked for his wife's uncle and arranged for him to fly to New York. With that single call, he had set in motion the events that would once again bring America to its knees.

CHAPTER TWO

Aboard Eva Air Flight BR0017
(November 9, 1330 Eastern Standard Time)

Azka Perkasa sat in the midlevel comfort of his business-class accommodations. When the flight attendant came by with the drink cart, he asked for tea. The attendant was polite and demure, and he lowered his head in thanks for her kind attention and service. He had left Washington's Dulles Airport early Sunday morning on a direct flight to San Francisco. Now he was flying on an Eva Air 747-400 that would take him from San Francisco to Taipei and then on to Kuala Lumpur. He was glad to be on a Taiwanese carrier and even more glad to be out of American airspace. He almost always flew coach class, as his current occupation dictated that he keep a low profile, but after what he had just accomplished, he felt that just this once he could allow himself a small pleasure.

Perkasa was Indonesian by birth, Chinese by ethnicity, and Christian in his upbringing and education. His paternal grandfather had left Hong Kong under a cloud of shame his parents refused to talk about. They settled first in Jakarta, but following yet another business reversal, moved to the West Java city of Bandung. His family was poor to the point of despair, and Perkasa and his three sisters had grown up with barely enough to eat. Being both poor and Chinese caused his family to be shunned by both the small but affluent Chinese minority and the Javanese majority.

At the mission school, he proved to be an exceedingly bright student. He studied hard, kept to himself, and vowed that he would someday not be poor and hungry. When a typhoon destroyed their home, he left without a word and headed back to Jakarta. There he found work as a janitor for an American firm of consulting engineers who designed the skyscrapers that seemed to be springing up everywhere in the capital city. There he was noticed, trained as a clerk, then as a draftsman. Finally, one of the senior engineers said, "This Azka is a bright lad. Let's get him to the polytechnic. Might even put us in a good light with the locals come contract time."

He again excelled in school, but he would always be one of *them*, a token local; he would never be a partner and never see the inside of the boardroom. He wanted more, much more. One day, seemingly out of the blue, a rival firm just down the street from his approached him with an offer of cash for information about a bid his firm was about to submit on another high rise; specifically, the amount of the bribe his firm had offered to the building authority. He gave them the information without hesitation and pocketed the money.

Shortly thereafter, the same firm came to him demanding more information. This time, instead of offering payment, they said they would inform on him if he did not comply. Azka reluctantly agreed to do their bidding, but before he did what they asked, a large explosion ripped through the offices of that firm during working hours, causing great loss of life. When the blast took place, he was in his cubicle, calculating the load bearing of the I-beams on one of his firm's projects. He felt the slight movement as the pressure wave passed, smiled to himself, and continued with his calculations. Later that month, he resigned his position with the American engineering firm; he had found a new calling.

The life of an ethnic Chinese in Jakarta with no family was an isolated and lonely existence. Yet Azka didn't mind; he had his work, although that work took only one or two weeks every few months. He had discretely made contact with an element of a Singapore triad operating in Jakarta. With only a post office box that served the interests of all concerned, Azka had a new employer, and one that paid well.

Azka was physically a slight man, partly from his ancestry and partly from his lack of a proper diet when he was a child. He had regular features, a pronounced overbite, and a lazy left eye that was the result of a bout with scarlet fever that had gone untreated. *One day soon,* Azka told himself, *I will be wealthy enough to leave this place and purchase a better life.* Aside from his intellect and training, he had another advantage to aid in his new calling. He was a man totally devoid of compassion or conscience. Finally, his day had arrived and he *would* be wealthy.

When Azka took the job, Abdul-Muqtadir Kashif, through his Lebanese intermediary, had assured him US$10,000 for every American life he took. He hoped to earn close to US$20 million from this venture. It was not as much as the Americans paid to *their* contractors, like Blackwater and Triple Canopy, but it was still a tidy sum. The contracting of mercenaries had worked well for the United States. Was he not entitled to his share in this killing-for-hire business?

Azka looked at his watch; it would not be long now, minutes perhaps.

CHAPTER THREE

Lincoln Financial Field, Philadelphia, Pennsylvania
(November 9, 1415 Eastern Standard Time)

Meagan Phillips didn't really like football, but her father had taken each of her two older brothers to Eagles games before, and now it was her turn. *Her* daddy was taking her! A high school history teacher, Charlie Phillips couldn't afford to buy Eagles football tickets often, but when he could, he had always taken one of his boys. Now he was finally taking Meagan. She was ecstatic.

"Meagan, do you see that big board up there with all the lights?"

"Uh-huh."

"That's the scoreboard. It tells us what the score is, how long there is to go in the game, who has the ball, and things like that."

"Does it say who is going to win, Daddy?"

"No, Meagan, it doesn't. We don't know who is going to win. That's why we cheer so hard for the Eagles, because we want them to win."

"Uh-huh."

Charlie's two sons both played Pop Warner football, and they had coached Meagan on how much fun she'd have at the game with her daddy. Charlie *was* making it fun. It was barely into the second quarter, and they'd been to the concession stand fifty feet behind them twice and to the potty once, and had bought pink cotton candy from a roving vender. Charlie hadn't fussed at Meagan because she had spent most of the game hunched down in her seat playing a video game and munching her goodies. After all, she was only five.

"Now, Meagan, when everyone gets up and cheers, you wave that big foam finger I bought you."

"Like this, Daddy?" Meagan replied as she waved the midnight-green Eagles finger from side to side.

"That's it, Meagan! I know the Eagles are going to win now," Charlie replied with a chuckle.

They divided their attention as they had before—Charlie to the Eagles, down a touchdown but driving toward the end zone, and Meagan to her video game.

Minutes later, Charlie Phillips leapt to his feet as the Eagles receiver snared the pass in the corner of the end zone. "Touchdown, Meagan!"

Meagan stood up and started to wave her foam finger, but then dropped it and whipped her tiny hands over her ears. "Daddy, it's so loud. Everyone is yelling."

"It's OK, Meagan," Charlie replied, bending down and cuddling his daughter. "Everyone is just so excited, that's all. Tell you what. Next Eagles touchdown we'll celebrate and buy some more cotton candy."

"I want blue this time, Daddy."

"Blue it is."

Meagan returned to her video game and her Twix bar as the Eagles kicker punched the ball through the uprights for the extra point. Charlie Phillips sat back down and congratulated himself on his decision to bring Meagan to a game. She *was* having fun.

"Daddy?"

Meagan felt her seat vibrating, then shuddering, then heard the sound. Her senses were alert. Something was different, something was wrong. The sound was louder, much louder, than when the people were cheering a few moments ago, and now the stadium was shaking.

"Daddy?"

The sound was deafening, more like a thunderstorm than an explosion, more like a subway entering a station than a bomb, piercing the air above the cheers of sixty-five thousand fans.

"Daddy!"

Meagan's senses caused her to finally look up. She followed the turned heads of the people around her as they looked back behind them. There they saw smoke, flame, and debris as an entire section of seats in the deck above and behind them collapsed, raining down concrete, seats, other debris, and *people*!

"Daddy!" Meagan shouted as she reached for her father's arm, not knowing what was happening. Her brain was in sensory overload with the acrid smells of fire and chemical accelerants now overwhelming her.

A split second later, Meagan's world was destroyed.

A large piece of concrete smashed into the top of Charlie Phillips's head, shattering his skull. Her daddy's blood, tissue, and brain matter flew over Meagan's head. Then he collapsed on top of Meagan.

"Daddy, Daddy, Daddy!" Meagan cried as she shook her father's inert body, squirming to try to free herself, his weight crushing her.

New sounds, the screams and shrieks of the wounded and dying, pierced the air. Then it was the increasing crescendo, feet stomping on concrete, fans stampeding toward the exit tunnels, their frantic footfalls growing ever louder.

Panicked fans near them pushed, shoved, and stepped on each other, their panic rising. The dust still had not settled from the collapsed section of the upper deck of the stadium that had fallen onto the section below. It was right behind where Megan Phillips now lay trapped underneath her father's lifeless body, sobbing inconsolably, the smell and stench of death overwhelming her, her father's own blood now oozing onto her.

"Little girl, come on, it's not safe, we have to go!" said a young woman as she lifted Charlie Phillips's limp body off of Meagan. The Good Samaritan grabbed the little girl's left forearm and tried to lead her away.

"NO! My daddy, my daddy!" Meagan cried as she tried to pull her father upright, her efforts futile, the blood pooling up, the life already drained from him.

The woman was torn; her two friends were shoving their way toward the exits, stepping over many bodies like those of Charlie Phillips who had been killed by falling debris. She was scared beyond words, but she didn't want this little girl crushed in the stampede.

"Please, we'll come back for him," she said as she knelt down and tried to coax Megan to come with her.

"My daddy, my daddy," Meagan wailed.

Suddenly, there was deafening noise from across the stadium. The young woman looked up to see a section of upper-deck seats collapsing onto the lower section, raining concrete, seats, and people, scores of people, down onto the section below.

"There has been a terrorist attack. There may be more attacks. Please evacuate the stadium now. More attacks are imminent. Please leave the stadium. There has been a terrorist attack. There may be more attacks. Please evacuate the stadium now. More attacks are imminent. Please leave the stadium . . ."

The announcement droned on and on, and as it did, more fans fled toward the exits.

A big man stampeding for the exits knocked down the young woman and Meagan with her. As Meagan looked down, she saw a severed hand covered in blood, like that of a mangled store mannequin. She began to shriek uncontrollably, now clutching the woman beside her.

"There has been a terrorist attack. There may be more attacks. Please evacuate the stadium now. More attacks are imminent. Please leave the stadium. There has been a terrorist attack. There may be more attacks. Please evacuate the stadium now. More attacks are imminent. Please leave the stadium . . ."

The woman scooped Megan up in her arms and joined the thousands of panicked fans as they continued to empty out of

Lincoln Financial Field. They were running for their lives, running for their cars, running anywhere away from what had just happened.

This deadly scene played out not just at the Eagles' Lincoln Financial Field, but nearly simultaneously in three other NFL football stadiums on that Sunday afternoon in November. The final attack, one that went down as planned about ten minutes after all the others, occurred at FedEx Field in suburban Landover, Maryland, home of the Washington Redskins.

Yet, while numerous panicked fans made for the exits thinking only of themselves, there were also heroics. At the Meadowlands, a biker covered with tats and dressed in Harley leather carried a bleeding woman toward the exit, moving only as fast as his heavy load would let him. At the M&T Bank Stadium, a Ravens fan used her scarf as a makeshift tourniquet to stanch the bleeding of a severely injured fan's leg. At FedEx Field, a Redskin fan in full "Hog" regalia threw an injured teenager over his shoulder and slowly carried him to the exit.

The explosions were restricted to just those four stadiums, but not the panic. In five other stadiums across the nation, there was nothing *but* panic. Once the people in the stadiums where the explosions occurred reached safety, they tweeted about the attacks, and fans in other stadiums picked up these tweets. Then the announcing systems in *those* stadiums began to drone, "There have been terrorist attacks in several NFL stadiums. An attack in this stadium is imminent. Please evacuate the stadium now. There have been terrorist attacks in several NFL stadiums.

An attack in this stadium is imminent. Please evacuate the stadium now." Fans immediately rushed for the exits, and many
were trampled in the process.

The death toll was substantial, and while not rivaling the
numbers killed on 9/11, the fact that Americans were attacked
in multiple cities, and simultaneously, in many ways induced a
new, and in some ways deeper, angst. The nation was shocked
and gripped with fear.

Throughout the nation, but especially in the national capital region, watchstanders in the White House Situation Room, the
National Counterterrorism Center, the Pentagon, the Department of Homeland Security, the various three-letter agencies, and
elsewhere attempted to make sense of the attacks and deal with
the ensuing chaos. They all sought to take action. But for the
moment, there was nothing to do.

Trevor Harward, the president's national security advisor, stood
outside the Cosmos Club on Massachusetts Avenue in Northwest
Washington, D.C., waiting impatiently for the valet to bring his
car around. He and his wife had been having brunch with
friends in the club's elegant main dining room when the watchstander in the Situation Room had called him. The conversation
lasted no more than 30 seconds, time enough for him to turn
white as he rose from his chair. "I've got to go. Please excuse us,"
was all he said as he headed for the door with his wife in tow.

"I need to get to the Situation Room now," he said to his
wife as he looked right toward 22nd Street Northwest, craning

his neck searching for his black Mercedes E550 4Matic sedan to come into view. "I'll drive, jump out, and then you take the car home. I'm going to be there a while."

Harward jerked the driver's door open before the valet could open it himself and shouted to his wife, "Get in." The tires squealed as Harward mashed the gas pedal and the car bolted away from the curb and headed southeast toward DuPont Circle. He had the Mercedes going seventy by the time they passed the Embassy Row Hotel, just a block and a half from the Cosmos Club.

"Slow down, you're going to kill us," his wife shouted as she clutched the car's dashboard.

"Slow down—I wish! We've just been attacked, the president's on the West Coast, and the fucking vice president is playing golf at the Congressional Country Club way the hell up in Potomac. I'm it for now!"

Harward powered the car into DuPont Circle's inner loop at breakneck speed, simultaneously punching the accelerator and riding the brake, the Mercedes' squealing tires startling the small groups of men playing checkers in the shadow of the fountain on this mild fall Sunday. Suddenly, he realized he was in the inner loop and couldn't turn down Connecticut Avenue. "Hold on," he yelled to his now panicked wife as he jerked the car's wheel and lumbered over the curbed barrier separating the circle's inner and outer loops.

The Mercedes thudded over the barrier and came down hard on its shocks. Horns blared and Harward narrowly missed a minivan.

"Slow down, Trevor; slow down for God's sake."

Harward ignored her and stared straight ahead as he pointed the car down Connecticut Avenue. Now sweating profusely and cursing at the cars he had to maneuver around, he barreled ahead at close to ninety miles per hour. Harward slowed, but didn't stop, as he blew through a red light.

"Trevor, you're going to kill us. Damn it!"

He continued to stare straight ahead. The sixty-year-old Harward looked the part of a creature of Washington who'd been beat down into submission after decades of too much responsibility and not enough control over policy or his life. Packing 230 pounds on his five-foot eight-inch frame, he was obese. His fashion sense was decades in the past; he was prepped out in his Brooks Brothers blue sport coat, tan cuffed pants, crisp white polo button-down, and blue club tie.

"Get on your iPhone and try to find out something, anything!" he shouted at his wife.

His wife refused to release her death grip on the car's dash to look into her lap, convinced Harward was going to kill them both.

Harward slowed only slightly as he passed the Farragut North Metro station, and turned right onto 17th Street, now heading due south. He was almost there, only a few blocks from the White House and the West Wing.

As he approached the Corcoran Gallery on his right, Harward slowed and turned hard left on E Street Northwest. He screeched to a halt at the security checkpoint. The uniformed Secret Service guards had been alerted he was coming. He flashed his creds.

"Mr. Harward."

"She's with me," he snapped at the guard, jerking his head toward his ashen-faced wife. "She'll drop me here at West Exec and then take the car away."

"Yes, sir."

The guard let the recessing barrier down as Harward drove into the White House complex. He turned left at Lower West Exec where another uniformed Secret Service guard opened a tall iron gate and waved his Mercedes through. There, he slammed on the brakes, jumped out of the car, and made a beeline for the West Wing entrance. He left his wife sitting in the passenger seat. He never looked back as he ran, wheezing and coughing as he did.

His wife sat in the passenger seat, shaking and breathing heavily, looking like a shell-shocked soldier. After several minutes the color finally returned to her face and she got control of her shaking. Then with as much dignity as she could muster, she walked around the Mercedes, got into the driver's seat, and slowly drove away.

Aboard Air Force One, President Wyatt Midkiff put the phone back into its receiver, hoping his chief of staff didn't notice his hand trembling. He did, though, and Midkiff knew it. *OK. Take a breath. Relax. You can manage this. Just breathe; just breathe.* The physically imposing, polished, and measured Midkiff felt he might be losing it. *God in heaven, how am I going to get through this?*

Less than a year into his administration after four terms as the junior senator from Florida, Wyatt Midkiff had developed a

well-deserved reputation as a smooth operator and for grace under pressure, but he *was* losing it now. "All I want is information, any information, and I've talked with my National Security
Staff and with half my cabinet but no one knows squat. Where
are we now?"

"Mr. President, we're over Nebraska, and we should be
landing at Andrews in a bit less than two hours," his chief of
staff replied. "That is, if we are still going to Washington—"

"'If'? What do you mean, 'if'?" the president interrupted.

"Mr. President, one of the attacks was at FedEx Field. There
could still be a threat."

"You're my chief of staff, for God's sake! Do you really want
me to make up some lame excuse for why I was afraid to go back
to the White House? That didn't work out so good for George
W. Bush in 2001, now, did it?" His chief of staff knew it was a
rhetorical question, so no response was required, or desired. "The
last report I got was there have been almost a thousand deaths.
You hear anything more?"

"No, Mr. President. It's predicted to go higher, though.
Emergency services in all those cities are still taking victims to
trauma centers."

"And I'm told there were many victims at stadiums where
there weren't attacks, but just bogus announcements to evacuate
the stadiums."

"Yes, Mr. President, there were hundreds killed and injured
in the stampedes to escape from those stadiums. The reports
were that there was mass hysteria."

"Well, I'm the president of the United States, and I'm going back to Washington immediately to end the hysteria, and to find out who did this."

"Yes, Mr. President, I understand. Now, here's the draft of your statement to the nation when you disembark at Andrews I had the press secretary put together—"

"I'm not ready for that yet. Get me the national security advisor on secure."

Moments later, Trevor Harward was on the line. "Trevor, give me an update." The president was now more settled and was all business.

"Mr. President. I'm here in the Situation Room. The vice president just arrived at his residence and he should be here shortly. Now, here's what we know so far," he replied, giving the president little more than he already knew.

Midkiff just shook his head. "We'll be at Andrews in less than two hours. I want to meet with you and a small group from FBI, Homeland Security, and whoever else you need to assemble to help me sort this out. We'll meet in the Situation Room."

"Yes, Mr. President."

"Make this a small, select group, Trevor. I don't need to see everybody who wants face time."

Next he called his vice president, who had had his security detail take him from the Congressional Country Club to his quarters on the grounds of the U.S. Naval Observatory on the southeast corner of Massachusetts Avenue and 34th Street. Fastidious to a fault, the vice president had decided he needed to change out of his golf attire before heading to the Situation Room. Midkiff instructed him to make a brief statement and a plea for calm until he could get back to Washington and address the nation.

Only weeks earlier, he had told the vice president he thought the crisis-management exercises his staff had insisted on were a waste of time. Now he was glad they had persisted.

It was in the middle of the leg from San Francisco to Taipei that Azka Perkasa slowly awoke from a deep sleep. He sensed something was different. At once all his senses came alert, and then he relaxed. There was a general stir about the cabin as people logged onto their PCs, smart phones, or sat glued to the seat-back monitors, where news bulletins had replaced all in-flight programming.

"I can't believe it," the man sitting next to him said with a pronounced Australian accent. "Those fuckin' towel heads are at it again!" A moment later he turned toward Azka. "Sorry mate, no offense meant."

"None taken," Azka said in his nearly flawless English. He flicked on his own small screen. He watched as the scenes went from news anchors to emergency crews at work to twisted concrete at several football stadiums. He permitted himself a grim smile when the vice president of the United States promised that those responsible would be brought to justice.

Azka Perkasa could imagine the multitiered security services of America and her allies looking for swarthy, dark-skinned men with shadowy beards or those dressed in non-Western clothing. It would be a difficult few days for those who were male and in their twenties or thirties from Mexico, Argentina, or India. Anyone traveling who seemed the least bit nervous, for reasons ranging from fear of flying to not having a green card, would be detained and questioned. He knew the American law enforcement and intelligence agencies, all capable at what they did, would soon know *what* had happened, but, he was equally confident, they would never know *who*.

His plan was simple in concept and not complex to execute, for a person with the right skills and resources. He had secured a truck and then applied the logo of the beer distributor that had the contract to supply beer to all thirty-two NFL teams. Over the course of the week, he had delivered kegs loaded with C4 and armed with a sophisticated timing device to selected concession stands, those that were tucked under higher level sections of seats, in the four NFL stadiums he selected. He took pains to ensure his special kegs were stored behind the ones that would be used first. He had then hacked into the PA systems of the stadiums he chose, timing his announcement to begin immediately after the explosions in four of the stadiums, and later in the five stadiums where no explosion occurred. His engineering training at the polytechnic, as well as all those years slaving away as a junior civil engineer working for peanuts compared to what the white expats working right beside him were making, was finally paying off.

The Aussie next to Azka glanced at his seatmate. *The world is going to hell and this little wog has gone back to sleep.* What he didn't know, and couldn't know, was that he was looking at the new face of terrorism.

CHAPTER FOUR

The White House Oval Office, Washington, D.C.
(November 10, 0930 Eastern Standard Time)

After what he admitted was a less-than-inspiring address to the nation after he landed at Andrews the night before, and after only three hours of fitful sleep, the president met with a select group of his national security principals in one of the White House Situation Room's two secure conference rooms. The three-letter agencies were well represented. After forty minutes of blank looks and little information, the president dismissed them abruptly—something the normally courteous Midkiff rarely did. Almost as an afterthought he asked Trevor Harward to remain behind.

"Trevor, am I being too rough on them?"

"No, Mr. President. We all let the nation down. We need to fix what's broken."

"But what I heard was we had bits and pieces of this information but no way to collate it so we could take action. In essence we were too slow. Is our system broken that badly?"

Trevor Harward had spent his life in the national security

world. He knew the president counted on him for answers. This wasn't the time to dance around the issues.

"Mr. President, the system works, but it just doesn't work fast enough. The intel part works pretty well, given all the humans in the loop, but there's a lot more that could be done with automation, high-power computing, smart digital agents, and decision-support algorithms. We also need an operations-response element that can work quicker, across all rice bowls, and that can break through choke points. This entity would need to be able to work internationally and nationally, and probably outside of legal channels when necessary."

"Then it's not an issue of just telling everyone to 'work harder' or 'do better,' is it?"

"I'm afraid not, Mr. President."

"All right, Trevor. You briefed me on this when we started this journey together. I didn't think we'd ever be here, but we are. Get me the Op-Center file."

"I'll do that, Mr. President, but you do know what that might entail and where it could take us?"

"I do, but do you feel we have an alternative?"

"I don't, Mr. President. I'll have it on your desk within the hour."

Half a world away, Abdul-Muqtadir Kashif waited impatiently. He had instructed the Lebanese to have Azka Perkasa call him on a disposable cell phone once he reached his final destination. He had never met Perkasa, nor did he want to. The Lebanese had found him and negotiated his price, but Kashif wanted the first-person assurance, to say nothing of the satisfaction, that the deed was done. He also wanted to be certain Perkasa was well away from America and from American authorities. As agreed, just a few words would be exchanged.

"I am home," Perkasa said.

"Just so," the voice at the other end replied.

"Have you wired the funds yet?"

"I have instructed my agent to do so, as was agreed," Kashif said, making no attempt to hide the annoyance in his voice. Who was this . . . this . . . hired man to question him?

The line went dead as Kashif clicked off his cell phone and climbed the steps to look in on his wife, now monitored by one of their full-time, in-home, caretakers.

"How is she?"

"No change, but she's resting comfortably," the woman said as she stood next to the hospital bed where the unmoving Jumana lay.

Abdul-Muqtadir Kashif walked back downstairs and turned on a news channel. The news was the same as on all channels— the attack on America. He felt no joy, just sadness for his wife, for those who would have to tend to what was left of their shattered families as he was doing, and for himself. He felt sadness, but no regret.

CHAPTER FIVE

National Counterterrorism Center, Liberty Crossing,
Virginia
(November 11, 0830 Eastern Standard Time)

Much had changed in the wake of the U.S. invasions of Afghanistan and Iraq, and then the Arab Spring. While there was some general stability in the Middle East in the twentieth century, that had changed dramatically in the twenty-first century. In retrospect, one would have thought the ouster of Saddam Hussein, Muammar Gadhafi, and Hosni Mubarak would have created a more stable region. But it hadn't. There were new leaders with new agendas, but there was still revenge, religious tension, and greed. The only true winners in this new order were the transnational terrorist groups, which now operated openly and often with near-impunity. The national intelligence community's job was to ensure one of these groups didn't attack America. They had failed.

The director of national intelligence, Adam Putnam, strode into his conference room at the National Counterterrorism Center, the NCTC, at Liberty Crossing in McLean, Virginia.

The leaders of the nation's intelligence agencies were assembled in the director's conference room on the first floor of the NCTC. His job was to coordinate the efforts of these sixteen diverse agencies. The president didn't say it in so many words in the Situation Room, but Putnam knew the score. He had failed.

"Ladies and gentlemen, you all know why you are here. We've been attacked again. I brought you here because I want to hear directly from each of you. Nine-eleven was clearly a one-of-a-kind attack unlikely to be repeated in the short term. Not so this time; our nation is gripped with fear, wondering when, not if, the next attacks will occur."

The men and women arrayed around the table were weary; they had been searching for answers but had none. Putnam listened, his impatience growing. He'd heard from everyone. He still knew nothing and he knew that wouldn't be good enough for the president.

"Look, folks, our fellow citizens spend well north of $80 billion on intelligence every year. We've just endured attacks in several American cities that have killed well over a thousand of those citizens. The nation is in a virtual fetal position bracing for the next attack. There will not be another attack. Are we clear on that?"

Less than fifty miles due east of the National Counterterrorism Center, at a corner table in Miss Shirley's café in Annapolis, Maryland, Paul Hood, former director of Op-Center, and General Mike Rodgers, his deputy director, met for breakfast. Hood was living in a waterfront home on Weems Creek near Annapolis and consulting for senior officials in several U.S. intelligence agencies. Rodgers was living on Capitol Hill and was vice president of a successful international business consultancy.

The two men were a study in contrasts. Paul Hood wore a smart, but inexpensive, blue blazer, tan pants, a buttoned-down blue shirt, a Talbot's club tie, and tassel loafers. His outfit was often jokingly called the "uniform" in the typically anonymous intelligence community. Rogers, in contrast, was attired in an expensive blue suit, a crisp white shirt, an Ermenegildo Zegna woven silk tie, and Tanino Crisci black wingtips. Rogers was at home in the corporate boardrooms he now frequented.

Both men were plugged into the intelligence and defense communities sufficiently to know what the president and his advisors were wrestling with. It didn't take an epiphany for them to understand why these attacks had not been prevented.

"Hell of a thing, these attacks," Hood began.

"Yeah, to say the least."

"You know anyone personally who died at FedEx Field?"

"Yes, actually two people," Rodgers replied. "Good friends. Both former general officers. One working for General Dynamics and one for Northrop Grumman. Tragic. You?"

"No. No one, thank God."

"Good."

"Thanks for coming all the way out here, Mike. I needed to talk with you in person. Your consultancy still going well?"

"Yeah, but it's too much damn traveling. I don't care how you slice it, even in business class, the red-eye sucks. I'm getting too old for this shit."

"No, Mike, you're a warrior. You could do it in a troop seat on a C-130."

Rodgers just shook his head and smiled. It had been years since they worked together, leading Op-Center. Both men were quietly proud of what they had accomplished. They had saved lives. Hell, they may have even saved the nation.

"Mike, I got a call from the president's national security advisor yesterday evening. It wasn't a secure line so he was couching what he said, but he wants me to come in and talk to the president. He hinted they're thinking about standing up Op-Center again."

"Whew," Rodgers exhaled. "What did you tell him?"

"I told him what you'd tell him. If the president wants to talk with me I'm happy to do my duty."

"We did our duty, Paul, but they shut us down."

"They did, Mike. Now these are different times and different dangers. I need to at least talk with him, but I wanted to get your counsel first."

Both men knew it wasn't in anyone's interest to slam the prior administration that had disestablished Op-Center. For the two of them, as well as for their loyal staff, it was a cataclysmic event when Op-Center was stood down. For Hood, it was a professional body blow, and one he didn't see coming.

Both Hood and Rogers had bitter feelings toward the director of national intelligence and the secretary of defense who conspired to have the previous president close down Op-Center. And they also recognized more than a decade without any attacks on the American homeland, along with the nation's eco-

OUT OF THE ASHES

nomic crisis, made Op-Center a budgetary target. However, that was in the past.

It took a while for Rodgers to frame his thoughts. He knew even talking about reestablishing Op-Center wasn't a trivial thing, and he understood Paul Hood well enough to read his former boss's body language—he was conflicted.

"Sure, boss. I'd talk with the president, but I'd lay out all the facts as to why and how they shut us down last time and then I'd get ironclad assurance that he and his successors will never let that happen again. I'd make them court you big time."

"That's good advice, Mike, and goes with my line of thinking."

"How soon are you going in?"

"Next day or two, I think."

The two men continued to talk and as they did, Mike Rodgers helped Paul Hood weigh the issues that would be involved in recreating Op-Center. What Hood didn't tell him, wouldn't tell him, was that if there was going to be a new Op-Center, he couldn't lead it.

Later that day, Trevor Harward sat at his desk in the West Wing. He had slept barely four hours in two days. His shirt was rumpled and his finely tailored suit trousers looked like sweat pants. It was a few minutes before noon and he had been in meetings for most of the last seven hours—and all for nothing. He had met with his core National Security Staff and ranking officials from State, CIA, FBI, and the National Counterterrorism Center—*the best of the best. All of them had theories; none of them had a shred of proof of who had done this or why. We know nothing more now,* Harward had to admit, *than we did just after the attack.* They were beginning to piece together the how, but not the why or the who. The national security advisor was frustrated beyond all measure.

The meetings had all been videotaped and in some cases monitored by selected military and civilian officials who could not be present. This encrypted video feed had also found its way to a study in a small but tasteful brownstone in Georgetown. It was the study of Gamal Haaziq. Haaziq was cleared for this information; in fact, his security clearances were about as high as was possible for an Egyptian-born U.S. citizen who was a tenured PhD in Middle Eastern Studies at American University and a practicing Muslim. Beyond all that, he was the most informed individual Harward knew in or out of government—and the smartest. Harward's reverie was broken by the buzz of his intercom.

It was one of his senior aides. "Sir, Dr. Haaziq is on the line for your twelve o'clock VTC."

"Thank you," he replied into the desk speaker. "Tell him I'll be just a minute."

Harward glanced at his watch and saw the digital readout was exactly 1200. On his other wrist, his heart monitor said 130. It was the stress. He cinched up his tie, smoothed his hair, and clicked on the desk screen that opened the secure video-teleconference channel to connect him with Haaziq.

"Gamal, good morning, or rather good afternoon. Thanks for meeting with me."

"Good afternoon, Trevor," Haaziq replied with only a trace of an accent. In contrast to the disheveled Harward, the Egyptian was the picture of an urbane Arab, with strong dark features, full lips, and thick, well-cut silver hair. "Forgive me an observation, my friend, but you look terrible. Even in these times, you must attend to yourself."

Despite his state, Harward was touched by his concern. "Thank you, Gamal. Perhaps the best medicine for me is for you to tell me something useful—something I can pass along to the president. I assume you VTCed into this morning's meetings?"

"I did. Your excellent staff, and the others, they are all good people, but as you know, they have not a clue about who did this or why they did it."

Harward nodded wearily. "Nor do I. That's why I hope you can help us, for we seem to be at an impasse."

Gamal Haaziq had extensive contacts throughout the Middle East. He had been an outspoken critic of the policies of the United States and of the moderates in the Muslim world who refused to condemn acts of terror or to denounce the extremists who committed them. Both, he maintained, were responsible for the cycle of distrust and violence. Yet he was an American citizen and a patriot. Harward had come to like and trust the man. If there was a group or entity responsible for the stadium bombings, Haaziq's contacts might have that information.

"I'm sorry not to be able to help you with this, Trevor, but I can tell you nothing. I wish I could. I've spoken with those who would know if there were an organization or splinter group responsible. They have said nothing and I believe they know nothing."

Harward sighed and visibly slumped in his chair. "So can you tell me anything?"

"Only that this is nothing like 9/11. This is very different, and in my opinion, has nothing to do with al Qaeda or one of the al Qaeda Central franchisees. Given the sophistication of this attack and the lack of information out there, I think you are dealing with a very small group or even with only one or two individuals. I also think whoever did this is extremely well resourced. I recommend that you follow the money behind the act and that you look at revenge as motive for this."

Revenge, mused Harward. He thanked Haaziq and broke the connection.

CHAPTER SIX

The Syrian Desert
(November 12, 1630 Arabian Standard Time)

Half a world away, while the forces unleashed by the Arab Spring had significant impact, and that effect was still playing out, one thing that hadn't changed was the developed and developing world's thirst for oil. Deep in the vast Syrian Desert, massive vehicles of all kinds kicked up a tsunami of sand and dust as they maneuvered over the flat and rocky desert surface and an army of workers of multiple nationalities labored under the supervision of a small team of Saudi engineers.

It was barely organized chaos as the polyglot of foreign nationals driving the trucks, cranes, bulldozers, and other huge vehicles had no common language so they maneuvered around each other as best they could by liberally using their horns and flashing their headlamps. The pace wasn't just intense; it was frenetic and even manic.

The Saudi foreman managing the work crew putting the enormous pipes on their mountings urged his work crew on. "You can do it! The prince was here two days ago and promised us a bonus if we got just two kilometers ahead of schedule. We can get that far ahead by tomorrow morning if we just keep at it for another four or five hours."

The weary men bent to their task. They had been working hellish hours in the desert sun for months with little respite. Yet the money was good and the Indians, Pakistanis, Filipinos, and Indonesians who formed the bulk of the labor crew needed the money, so they said little, continued to work, and sent the majority of their earnings home. They didn't understand why the Saudis were building this pipeline, or why there was so much urgency to construct it so quickly, nor did they care. However, those in Saudi Arabia's elite understood why.

Saudi Arabia had long been the kingpin in the oil world, but that was changing. The United States had helped rebuild Iraq, and that nation was now a major oil producer, as were Iran, Kuwait, and Russia. Saudi Arabia was no longer the big kid on the block, just one of many. Even the United States, thanks to shale oil gas, was predicted to be a net oil exporter as early as 2020.

Saudi Arabia had a unique disadvantage in that all of her oil went to ports on either the Red Sea or the Arabian Gulf. Intermittent violence over the years, and especially the uncertainties the popular uprisings of 2011 unleashed, had made it too risky to depend solely on getting her oil through the narrow choke points of the Strait of Hormuz, the southern terminus of the Red Sea, or the Suez Canal. Additionally, the Saudis recognized if Iran ever followed through on its frequent threats to mine the Strait of Hormuz, Saudi Arabia's economy would be crippled.

So the Saudis had made a decision to construct a multibillion dollar pipeline through Jordan and Syria to get their oil to the Mediterranean to meet the energy demands of Europe, especially the now-recovering economies of Eastern Europe. Saudi Arabia had paid Jordan and Syria a fortune up front to allow construction of a pipeline and passage of oil.

Now, in one of the biggest energy construction projects ever, the Saudis were building a massive pipeline from their richest fields in the eastern part of their country across their nation, through Jordan and Syria, and to the Mediterranean. Saudi prince Ali al-Wandi, the nation's deputy oil minister, was personally supervising all aspects of the pipeline's construction. His executive helicopter was a frequent sight along the pipeline route and he made it well known to the managers, foremen, and workers he was the one who approved performance bonuses.

"As soon as we finish this section, we'll set the pipe on the foundations we've already put in place up that berm," the foreman said to his Filipino crew chief.

As the foreman spoke, an eighteen-wheeler with oversized tires drove up the berm with its burden of large-diameter pipes strapped one on top of the other. The driver downshifted as he neared the top of the berm, but as he did he turned the wheel ever so slightly to the left. The wheels of the big rig started to lose purchase, then spin. Two hundred yards away, on the rocky desert floor below, the foreman saw it first and shouted into his hand-held radio.

"Turn right; turn right, you're in danger of tipping over!"

In the cab of his truck, the panicked driver tried to comply.

He jerked the wheel to the right and downshifted again, but the wheels just spun more rapidly, gravity took over, and the over-loaded truck reached the tipping point.

"Get out of the way, get out of the way now!" the foreman shouted at the workers setting the pipe on its mountings below where the truck was now tipping over.

Slowly, then more rapidly, like a mortally wounded ship slipping beneath the waves, the truck crashed over on its left side. As it did, the straps holding the pipes on its back gave way and the pipes started tumbling down the hill.

Below, the dozens of men in the panicked work crew began to run. It was no use. The massive pipes crushed man after man as they cascaded down the hill and across the flat desert floor.

When all motion had finally stopped, a half dozen workers lay dead and many more were crying out in agony. Throughout the work camp alarms went off and others rushed to help the wounded.

The foreman, who had taken shelter behind a small dune and was unharmed, reached into his pocket and pulled out his Thuraya XT-Dual Satellite Phone and called Prince Ali al-Wandi.

Paul Hood sat on his back porch looking out onto Weems Creek, wearing a North Face fleece vest to ward off the Novem-ber chill. He considered his upcoming meeting with the presi-dent. He knew he couldn't lead the new Op-Center and he also knew Mike Rodgers's complex business connections meant he couldn't lead it, either.

Hood was enough of a patriot that he knew he needed to do

more than just validate what Trevor Harward had hinted at, that the president thought he needed to reconstitute Op-Center. He knew he needed to come up with a leader to recommend to the president. As he searched his mental Rolodex one name rose to the top.

Five days later, on Monday morning, the NFL commissioner assembled his core staff in his expansive office at the NFL headquarters on Park Avenue in New York. They had braced for the impact of canceling all NFL games the day before. The commissioner anticipated an angry backlash from disappointed fans. However, as his staff briefed him, he was surprised to learn that far from a backlash, fans were e-mailing and tweeting the NFL, thanking the league for canceling Sunday's games. Nevertheless, what his director of operations was about to tell him would shock him even more.

"Morning, Commissioner."

"What ya got, Ops?"

"This started last Monday, but has accelerated over the past week. Our owners are reporting their season ticket holders are dumping their tickets on sites like eBay and StubHub as fast as they can. Not only that, but they're offering them at a discount, often a deep discount."

"And are people buying them?" he asked.

"No, not really. Legal has more."

"Judge?" he said, turning to his senior in-house lawyer.

"Not sure how to tell you this, but we've sniffed out at least two, and maybe three, class-action suits that are signing up people as fast as they can. They plan to sue us for failing to provide adequate security at our stadiums."

"You're shitting me!"

"Wish I was."

His number two, the deputy commissioner, chimed in. "Look, all this got worse last Wednesday night, right after the president addressed the nation in prime time. Everyone was frightened before that, but after his address the entire country is waiting for the other shoe to drop and the next attack to happen. We need to talk about canceling the rest of the season."

"I know, I know . . . but not yet. Yeah, I'll say he bumbled questions. What the hell was he thinking telling the nation not only that we weren't sure who was behind these attacks, but we also didn't have a clue about where they came from? One of our interns could have handled that better!"

"We all know that, Commissioner, but what do we do now?"

CHAPTER SEVEN

The White House Complex
(November 19, 0930 Eastern Standard Time)

Paul Hood stepped out of the presidential limousine that had brought him from his home in Annapolis. It had been years since he had walked on the White House grounds, and a sea of memories washed over him. The national security advisor's assistant had cleared Hood, as well as another visitor, onto the White House compound. That visitor was now waiting in a small office in the Eisenhower Executive Office Building.

He was as prepared for this meeting as he possibly could be. At the last minute, he had learned the national security advisor would sit in on their meeting.

"Paul, thank you for coming," Wyatt Midkiff said as the president's secretary ushered Hood into the Oval Office.

"Mr. President, thank you for asking me to come in."

"I'm eager for this meeting, Paul. I believe you know my national security advisor, Trevor Harward."

"Yes, it's been years, but nice to see you again."

The pleasantries over, the three men sat down in the Oval Office's conversational area. The president spoke first.

"Paul, we all know why we're here. We've had a terrible national tragedy. Trevor's staff has given me a thick file on Op-Center, but I have to tell you, I haven't yet decided what to do. I wanted to hear your thoughts and then perhaps the three of us could consider how we might move forward." The president paused, searching for just the right words.

"Our entire intelligence and national security communities seem to agree on but one issue: No one agency is at fault. So, by that, I've had to conclude they all are at fault. These attacks go well beyond any failures by a single individual or institution, and there's more to this than just failing to connect the dots." Midkiff paused for emphasis. "And God knows, Congress has raked me and my national security leadership over the coals over these attacks. And they may be right. If no one failed to do their job, and if the system doesn't work, then I am to blame. I'm the president, and so it's up to me to get it fixed. It seems we just didn't have the . . . have the . . . how do you phrase it, Trevor?"

"We didn't have the predictive intelligence and the ops-intel fusion, Mr. President."

"Ah, thank you. Yes, terms I've become increasingly familiar with over the past several weeks. Do you agree with me thus far, Paul?"

"Absolutely, Mr. President."

"And I think, as Trevor and my director of national intelligence have suggested, while our systems may have worked in the past, they didn't work fast enough to stop these recent attacks. We've got large, capable organizations staffed by hardworking professionals doing their best to ensure our national security. Yet they all have their limits, to say nothing of their statutory and legal frameworks. Have I put this about right, Trevor?"

"Yes, Mr. President."

"So I think we generally agree we need something new, and someone I can call on when the normal instruments of national security can't move fast enough or in the right legal channels to get the job done. We probably need a more alert, anticipatory, and predictive system that can see these things coming so we have the time to take action. I think that's where you come in, Paul."

"I'm at your service, Mr. President."

"Thank you. The national security advisor and I have reviewed the Op-Center file and discussed the possibility of reestablishing Op-Center, or something like Op-Center. I think we are of the opinion that if Op-Center had been around these attacks might have been prevented. Of course, we'll never know for sure, and hindsight is always twenty-twenty, but we are of a mind to consider standing up an Op-Center-like organization."

Midkiff paused and measured Hood carefully. "In addition to reviewing the file, I've had my staff give me a crash course on Op-Center's history and especially its past successes. As you probably know, in my years in the Senate, national security wasn't my primary focus, so I really didn't fully know what you and your organization accomplished over those years. Now I feel I'm at least a bit caught up. If we believe it might be advisable to re-create an Op-Center organization, how should we move forward?"

The three men embarked on an earnest discussion focused on reestablishing Op-Center to deal with just the sort of between-the-seams challenges and intelligence shortcomings that had failed to anticipate and prevent the attacks on the NFL stadiums. The men agreed it was the right thing to do.

The president was of a mind-set, and Paul Hood found it difficult to disagree, the new Op-Center would need to have a new look and function differently than the old one. The objectives of its operation would remain the same: It had to take on issues and challenges no other agency or agencies could, but there would be substantial differences. These differences had to do with speed and execution. The goal was the same: to protect American citizens at home as well as American interests around the world. The men discussed a host of details, and after almost an hour of intense discussion, they had resolved most of the hard spots and agreed in principle on their plan.

"So, Paul, the next question is who should lead Op-Center? As you might imagine, this is a huge assignment, and having the right Op-Center director stand it up again can make or break our efforts. We have discussed this in great detail here, and I think—we think—you're the right man for this assignment."

There was a long pause, and the president could see Paul Hood was struggling with what he was about to say.

"Mr. President, I'm honored, first of all, by your commitment to reestablish Op-Center, and second, by the high honor of offering me this position." Hood was silent for several moments.

Finally, and a bit abruptly, he said, "Sir, may we have a moment alone?"

Trevor Harward had been around the block, and he saw Wyatt Midkiff was struggling with how to respond. He offered a way out. "Mr. President, we're running a bit over time, so I'll just step out and ask your secretary to adjust your calendar."

"Yes, Trevor, thank you."

When the door closed, the president stared at Paul Hood. "Paul?"

"Mr. President, again, I am honored by your confidence in me. However, I cannot accept this assignment."

"Paul, I'm not offering this to you to make you feel good. Believe me, we discussed this at length before you arrived. My national security advisor and I have vetted several potential candidates, and I assure you that you are our consensus choice. We *need* you, Paul."

There was again a long silence before Hood continued. "Mr. President, I would like to do this, believe me. Unfortunately, I'm afraid I've recently been diagnosed with amyotrophic lateral sclerosis."

Now it was Midkiff's turn to pause as he digested what Hood had just told him. ALS—or Lou Gehrig's disease—had no cure, and people with this condition deteriorated rapidly and often quite dramatically. "Oh, Paul, I am so sorry!"

"Thank you, Mr. President. At the moment I seem to be doing just fine, but there's just too much at stake if I'm not a hundred percent tomorrow, next week, or a month from now. As I suspect you might know—and trust me, Mr. President, I now know vastly more about this condition than I ever wanted to know—the problems arise when your physical abilities begin to degrade. The difficulty is, they degrade rapidly and often unpredictably. I'm afraid I need to give this condition my full attention."

The president searched for something soothing to say. "Paul, perhaps you could just get things moving, gather a strong cast around you, and then hand over the reins to someone else later."

"Thank you, Mr. President, but as I said, there's too much at stake here, and right now my attention is on coping with this condition as best I can."

The president paused again. "Paul, I know you're a patriot; this difficult decision you've just made only confirms that. If there were any way that you thought you could do this, I know you would. So I respect your decision."

"Thank you, Mr. President."

"But to be honest with you, we were counting on you doing this. I don't know how else to ask this, but if not you, who?"

"Mr. President, I hope you don't think this is too forward of me, but I may have just the right man for this assignment. And he's right across the street waiting in the Eisenhower Executive Office Building. Do you have time to meet him right now?"

Wyatt Midkiff sat back and considered for a long moment the need to move and move quickly, Paul Hood's condition, and the nation's vulnerabilities. Then he stood up, walked to his desk, and punched the button on his phone that connected him to his secretary.

"Alice, clear my calendar for the rest of the afternoon and ask Mr. Harward to come back in here."

The president turned back to Hood. "All right, then, Paul, let's meet your man."

"I'll have him here in a moment, Mr. President."

Trevor Harward rejoined the president and Paul Hood. Midkiff sought to skate around the issue of Hood's condition, but he would have none of that. He restated the reasons for his inability to serve and moved on to his nominee for Op-Center director. Hood assured both men the individual he had sought out was eminently and uniquely qualified to lead a reconstituted Op-Center. He handed the president and Harward a brief biographical sketch. They discussed the Op-Center designee's qualifications, and neither the president nor his national security advisor could fault Hood's logic, or the man's qualifications.

The president did recall the man, if a bit vaguely, from his time in the Senate. A four-star Navy admiral leading first the United States Pacific Command, and subsequently the United States Central Command, could never operate completely below the radar of a U.S. senator, even one who was not focused directly on foreign policy or defense matters.

"I do recall the admiral had impressive credentials and was always well thought of. I seem to remember his name being mentioned as a candidate for chairman of the Joint Chiefs of Staff," Midkiff offered.

"He was," Hood replied, "but your predecessor chose someone else."

"Was that all there was to it?" the president asked.

"There was an issue when he was Central Command commander," Trevor Harward added.

"Mr. Harward has it right, Mr. President," Hood replied. "There was an incident, one not well publicized, where he was ordered to conduct a strike on a small city in Afghanistan because al Qaeda operatives were thought to have seized control of the city. He told the president and his secretary of defense the strike would cause massive civilian casualties but was ordered to do the strike anyway. He refused."

"Bet that went over well with my predecessor," the president said.

"I've never asked him to tell me the full story, Mr. President, but from what I hear the president finally recognized the wisdom of what the admiral recommended and never found cause to relieve him of his duties. Still, his secretary of defense never got over it and did everything he could to sandbag the admiral's candidacy for the chairmanship. He was eased out of his tour as Central Command commander five months early and retired as one of the most accomplished, and honored, flag or general officers I've known in my lifetime." Hood paused before continuing. "I trust him, Mr. President. Along with his leadership and managerial qualities, he's a man of immense integrity. I think that's an important attribute for the man to whom you will be delegating this much power."

"That's a strong endorsement, Paul," the president replied, "and a sobering one. But tell me this. What qualities do you think he has that make him the right fit for Op-Center?"

"Mr. President, he puts service above self, will do what is right for the nation, and will never lie to power. I will submit to you, sir, this relationship between you and your new Op-Center director has to be built on trust. He may often have to move quickly, do what he feels needs to be done, and inform you or Mr. Harward after the fact. For this to work, you will have to trust him."

Chase Williams waited at the secretary's desk, anticipating the doors to the Oval Office would open at any moment. He had surrendered his cell phone at the entry of the West Wing and held only a thin Bosca black leather portfolio.

"Admiral, the president will see you now," the president's secretary said. "You can go right in."

Williams opened the door to the Oval Office and strode toward the president's desk. Wyatt Midkiff was already out in front of his desk to greet him.

Midkiff immediately sized Williams up as a man who didn't appear intimidated walking into the Oval Office. The six-foot-tall, 170-pound Williams was attired in a Brooks Brothers blue suit and a red and white club tie. *Fashionable, but not trendy,* Midkiff found himself thinking, and noted Williams didn't carry himself in the rigid way some former military officers did.

The president prided himself on his ability to size people up quickly and accurately. *Confident, self-assured, but not full of himself* was his initial assessment.

"Admiral, welcome," Midkiff began. "I know you know

Paul, but I don't believe you've met my national security advisor, Trevor Harward."

"A pleasure, Mr. Harward."

"Likewise, Admiral."

"Well, let's get to it, shall we?" the president said as he gestured for the three men to sit in the conversational area in the center of the Oval Office. "Admiral, candidly, I have to tell you this is quite a surprise. Other than a brief biographical sketch Mr. Hood provided us, we don't know a lot about you. Can we assume you're here because you might be interested in the job as Op-Center director?"

"A job," Williams said reflectively. "I think we all agree that what we're talking about is something more than a job. If there is a way I can continue to serve my country, then I'd like to learn more. I have Paul's perspective on this. Now I'm here to listen to what you have in mind."

Midkiff considered this. The man had said it without flourish or smugness; it was an honest statement of his position. "Yes, well, Admiral, as you probably know, our analysis of recent events has convinced me we have a missing piece in our national security apparatus. We believe we need to reconstitute something like Op-Center that Paul here used to run."

"Yes, Mr. President," Williams replied neutrally.

"Paul has told me he's not the right person to lead this new entity, but he recommends we consider you for the, ah, the position. Are we all on the same page thus far?"

"I believe we are, Mr. President."

"Good. As you know, I was a bit surprised when Paul declined the job and then had you waiting, ready to meet with me. What are your thoughts about how we should proceed?"

"To begin with, Mr. President, I think you should tell me what your expectations are," Williams replied. "In the military, we always begin with a clear understanding of the commander's intent, and I should like to know what that is."

Wyatt Midkiff had been a politician for more than three decades. Almost without conscious thought, he continued to size up Williams. Outwardly, the admiral was disarmingly average and would not stand out in a group of senior executives or government officials. Yet it was impossible to miss the man's focus and strength. Above all else, the president was immediately taken by his quiet intensity and especially his ability to *listen*. To his surprise and chagrin, Midkiff felt Williams could almost anticipate what he was thinking—his concerns, his apprehensions, and even his reservations. By any measure, Midkiff sensed, this was a formidable individual, one not to be underestimated, and certainly not one to be misled or toyed with.

"Yes, all right then," Midkiff replied. "I think we agree our current organizations are unable to anticipate and, more importantly, prevent attacks like the ones that occurred earlier this month. And Trevor here and his staff have suggested we reconstitute something like Op-Center to work in those areas where our current organizations can't often go or can't be effective. Trevor, do you want to jump in?"

"Thank you, Mr. President," Harward replied. Turning to Williams, the national security advisor was now equally direct. "Admiral, Mr. Hood and I thought it best if at some point we left you and the president alone to have this important conversation one-on-one, but first, I wanted to weigh in as national security advisor."

"Yes, Mr. Harward, I'm listening."

"We're all familiar with Op-Center's enviable record under Paul's guidance. Yet all institutions have their successes and failures. I think we'd all be naive to think the organizations involved didn't sometimes get into turf wars. Those turf wars did arise between the intelligence community, Defense, and the old Op-Center. Would you agree with me on that, Paul?"

Hood's antennae were up; he didn't know where Harward was going with this.

"I think that's fair, though as I recall, you may not have been privy to all that went on when Op-Center was called on," Hood offered.

"All right, I may not have, but my point, gentlemen, is as the president's national security advisor, I and my staff have the primary responsibility to advise the president on *all* matters impacting the security of our nation. While the president will always have the final call, I would hope we use Op-Center only in those special circumstances where it's specifically appropriate, within its charter. I would hope you don't have in mind that Op-Center would be the first responder every time there's a national crisis."

The president didn't mind his national security advisor standing his ground, but he didn't want this to start out as an adversarial relationship.

"Trevor," Midkiff said, "you know we'll be mindful of that.

I'm certain the admiral's thirty-five years of military service have left him with a well-nuanced view of when the normal levers of national power are sufficient and when we need to turn to Op-Center in a crunch. Admiral?"

"You are both right, Mr. President. I think we all recognize and respect Mr. Harward's position as your primary advisor on all national security matters. I agree with him and believe we all view a reconstituted Op-Center as an instrument you would use only when the situation called for it." Williams paused for a long moment, and then continued. "So I'll say this carefully, Mr. President, and forgive me for being so blunt, but if I take this assignment, I work for you, period. I respect your position as national security advisor, Mr. Harward, but if I think there is an issue for the president's attention and his attention alone, I will make that known to him—directly, and only to him."

Trevor Harward, normally quite good at concealing his emotions, was visibly taken aback. He had not expected this. He sat forward, clearly taking issue with what Williams was proposing.

"Mr. President," Williams continued, "if you wish to put the national security advisor in the picture, I will accept that, but I want to make it crystal clear that I won't work *through* Mr. Harward. I have no issue in working with him, but only at your direction."

There was an uncomfortable silence, and Wyatt Midkiff knew he was the only one who could break it.

"Yes, well, I think that captures it appropriately, Admiral. I would expect you to come directly to me, and I'll make the call when Mr. Harward and his capable staff need to become involved." The president knew his national security advisor's feathers were ruffled, but at the same time he was becoming increasingly comfortable with Williams. "Gentlemen, as you suggested earlier, Admiral Williams and I need to spend a few moments one-on-one while I consider him for this assignment. Let's table this, and other agency relationships, until the two of us have had a chance to talk."

"Yes, Mr. President," Harward and Hood said nearly simultaneously as they rose and left the Oval Office.

The president waited several moments after the door to the Oval Office closed. Wyatt Midkiff's initial assessment of Chase Williams had left him with a positive impression. Now it was time to dig deeper.

"Admiral, well, here we are, alone at last. A meeting I didn't anticipate but one you clearly did. I must confess I feel you have me at a disadvantage."

"I assure you, Mr. President, I didn't come in here with an elaborate pitch for why you should select me to lead Op-Center. I came here to listen. I'm sure you have a long list of exceptionally well-qualified candidates who could serve in this capacity."

"Perhaps so, but none of them have Paul Hood's recommendation. Paul's not a politician; he's a patriot. He says the same of you. Tell me, Admiral, have you and Paul known each other professionally?"

"No, Mr. President. I was aware of Mr. Hood's service as Op-Center director years ago when I was serving on the National

Security Staff as a Navy captain. But I was pretty far down the food chain then, so we had no direct interaction."

"I see. So because you've served on the National Security Staff before, I'm sure you appreciate Mr. Harward's position."

"I do, Mr. President. For my money, he's got one of the toughest jobs in government, especially during these challenging times."

The conversation continued for forty-five minutes, the two men measuring each other, discussing national security, sharing ideas regarding what Op-Center should look like, and when it should and should not be called into action. They talked about issues from staff size to possible locations for Op-Center to relationships with the rest of the executive branch. They also were in general agreement Op-Center's initial focus should be to deal with international crises, nipping potential attacks on the United States far from America's shores.

The president wanted to know more about Williams's background and he learned a great deal. Chase Williams was a military brat, the son of a career Marine Corps officer and a schoolteacher. He was a middle child with one older brother and one younger sister. He chose the Naval Academy and graduated third in his class. His class standing afforded him immediate graduate-education opportunities, but he turned them down. Instead, he chose to go directly to sea duty because, for Williams, going to sea and leading sailors on a Navy destroyer was the purest form of naval service. More than that, he understood the privilege of service; this was where he felt he could serve best. He loved his nation, his Navy, and his enlisted sailors.

Those priorities guided him as a young ensign and as a four-star admiral.

Their discussion ranged from the professional into the personal. Though Williams was a widower, he and Midkiff both were grounded in traditional marriage, had grown children, and relished the prospect of grandchildren. Neither played golf, and both were voracious readers of historical biography.

The longer the conversation went, the more Wyatt Midkiff came to recognize the qualities Chase Williams brought to the table and could bring to Op-Center. Yet while the conversation was amiable and professional, the two men had not addressed some thorny and difficult questions.

"Admiral, I understand that you crossed swords with my predecessor while you were at Central Command. I know the barest outlines of that incident. Is there anything more you'd like to add?"

"What happened is a matter of record, Mr. President. I was given what I judged to be an unlawful order. I refused to carry it out. That's part of my officer's oath."

"Your officer's oath?"

"Yes, Mr. President. As you probably remember from your naval service, when enlisted men or women join our military, reenlist, or get promoted, they take an oath, part of which includes 'and obey the orders of the president of the United States and the officers appointed over me.'"

"Yes, well, that sounds reasonable," Midkiff replied, doing nothing more than trying to be an active listener.

"It does, Mr. President. However, as you also likely recall, the officers' oath contains no such language, only that the officer will 'support and defend the Constitution of the United States.'"

"And I suspect you're going to tell me why, Admiral."

"Two words, Mr. President. My Lai. Vietnam in 1968. Soldiers of Charlie Company murdered more than three hundred Vietnamese villagers. Their company commander was Captain William Calley. At his trial, Calley's defense was he was just following orders."

"Yes, Admiral, I'm aware of that history. And so you refused to follow your president's orders?"

"I did."

"In hindsight, was there anything either of you could have done to defuse that situation? I'm asking not out of curiosity, but just to be sure we begin our relationship on the right foot."

Williams paused to carefully frame his words. "Sir, some things can be anticipated in advance, others not. They have to be defined in practice. Like William Calley's platoon sergeant, I was given an order to kill civilians—a large number of civilians. Not without some serious consideration, I felt was the order was unlawful. I did what was required in such situations. I first respectfully and privately pointed out that this was, in fact, an unlawful order. I then tried to get the order rescinded. When that was unsuccessful, I had but one option: I refused, openly and respectfully, to carry out the order."

"And that's why you're being as blunt as you are in this office, especially with my national security advisor?"

"I don't intend to be blunt, Mr. President. I'm respectful of your office and of the tough job your national security advisor has. But, Mr. President, if I may be direct."

"By all means."

"What happened to me notwithstanding, the U.S. military has centuries of tradition. It also has an enormous body of directives spelling out roles and responsibilities, command relationships, statutory and regulatory rules, and authorities laid out in the U.S. Code and military regulations. Other than on the battlefield, there is little that is opaque."

"Yes, I'm following you, Admiral. I've learned a great deal about the military as commander in chief."

Chase Williams couldn't miss the fact that the president was sounding a bit wounded. He softened his tone. "I know you have, Mr. President. As an outsider looking in, it appears to me you have a strong and professional working relationship with our military leadership. And I would offer that part of what makes that all work are the clear-cut roles and responsibilities I just mentioned. So all I'm saying, Mr. President, is that before you and I embark on a mission to reconstitute Op-Center, the most important thing we need to do is to clarify our relationship, even to the point of where we may find ourselves in disagreement."

"In protecting our nation, we may have to kill people. There may be collateral damage and unintended consequences to our actions. There will always be three considerations on the table. The first is the safety of America—the mission. The second is the lives of innocents and those affected if and when we take action. And, finally, the lives of those who will go into harm's way in our service. Regarding the role of Op-Center, you and I, Mr.

President, will be responsible for balancing those three things within the bounds of our duty, our judgment, and the constraints of the Constitution."

In that instant, President Midkiff knew what Paul Hood had known all along. This was the right man for the job. Williams's reference to "when we take action" and "our duty" were not lost on him. He and Chase Williams were entering a partnership and a course of action that was at once dangerous, uncertain, and necessary. The president also now knew what Paul Hood had meant when he had talked about trust.

Midkiff exhaled deeply. "Admiral, I understand and I agree. We should have no confusion regarding what I expect of you, what you expect of me, and what we both expect of Op-Center. I know we'll have further discussions like this, but if we move forward with this understanding, then I think we can both carry out our duties."

Without conscious thought, both men extended their hands. Their eyes met as each gripped the other's hand firmly.

After a comfortable silence, Williams spoke first. "Thank you, Mr. President. I appreciate your understanding and your confidence. With your permission, I do have one remaining order of business."

"Yes?"

"I don't need anything in writing, although I suspect there are others who will. So I'll leave that to you. What I'd like from you is a simple statement of what you want me to do. What is your command guidance, or, as my Army and Marine Corps colleagues would say, what is the commander's intent?"

Midkiff could now answer without hesitation. "Admiral, I want *you* to lead Op-Center, and I want you to be single-minded in your devotion to protecting this nation and its citizens. I can't put it more plainly than that. And as you stated, you will report directly to me."

"Very well, Mr. President. Is there anything else?" Williams asked with just a touch of finality in his voice.

Wyatt Midkiff paused to study the man. *Is it really that simple for him?* he found himself thinking. *Protect the nation. No agenda. No maneuvering. No power play.* For the president, it was rare in his political experience. It was, Midkiff reflected, most refreshing. "There is just one thing, Admiral. Will there be a role for Paul Hood in your organization?"

"When Paul first sought me out for this role, I asked him if he would be willing to serve as a consultant. He has assured me he would, as long as"—here Williams permitted himself a slight smile—"it was as an unpaid consultant. He has also made me fully aware of his condition, and we both feel it should not prevent him, at least for now, from serving in that capacity."

Midkiff nodded. "How long will it take you to get Op-Center up and running?"

"Mr. President, I would like to give you a definitive answer right now, but I do need to study this and get back to you. Can you allow me four to six weeks to give this the care and attention it deserves? Then I can give you a plan and the way ahead."

"That's more than fair, Admiral," the president said as he rose. "Let's invite the others back in. They've been standing out there, no doubt keeping my secretary from doing her work."

Harward and Hood were anticipating the president would evaluate Williams and agree to consider him to lead Op-Center. Both were surprised when the president himself pulled open the door to the Oval Office and said, "Gentlemen, meet the new Op-Center director. Let's get to work."

CHAPTER EIGHT

Capitol Hill, Washington, D.C.
(December 2, 0815 Eastern Standard Time)

It had been three weeks since the NFL stadium attacks, and the nation was slowly returning to normalcy. In the wake of the president's ineffective news conference, the White House had worked tirelessly, and with some success, to put the nation at ease. The run-up to the Thanksgiving holiday helped. Americans can stay away from the malls only so long, and the retailers began to welcome the Christmas shoppers. If there was any beneficiary of the attacks, it was online merchants. A great many Americans still felt safest in their homes. Enhanced security at places where the public gathered was having a positive impact. The NBA was moving forward with its season, and the NFL had reached a tentative decision to resume the season this month, but with greater visible security at its stadiums.

On Capitol Hill, Congress continued the inevitable hunt for the guilty. The administration controlled neither house of Congress, and it was open season on the president's national security leadership. Top leaders from the intelligence community,

Defense, State, Homeland Security, and Justice were called before a wide array of committees, thoroughly grilled, and sent away to "clean things up." Then, with the committee leaders' posturing complete, as suddenly as they had begun, the hearings played themselves out. While the nation and Congress were moving on, the executive branch remained on point with a single message: This would not happen again.

Three hundred miles south-southwest of Capitol Hill, two men were focused on their mission and on their men. Major Michael Volner, United States Army, and Master Gunnery Sergeant Charles Moore, United States Marine Corps, had been together for close to three years. Volner was young for a major and old for a troop commander at the Joint Special Operations Command. Moore was a seasoned veteran of indeterminable age. Volner came to JSOC from the 75th Rangers; Moore from the Marine Corps Special Operations Command. The two stood together on the catwalk of one of the shoot houses at Fort Bragg, North Carolina.

This shoot house was a single-story facility with walls and movable partitions of heavy-rubber, bullet-absorbent material. Below Volner and Moore on the catwalk, their special operations troop ran standard room-clearing drills, moving from room to room like laboratory mice in a maze.

"Clear left!"

"Moving!"

"Clear right!

"Moving!"

"I'm down!"

"Coming up!"

The work in the house was proficiency drill for these veteran shooters. The game was initiative-based tactics or IBTs—moving and shooting, or not shooting, depending on the threat and the target. The teams progressed like members of a ballet company as they went from one room to the next, adjusting and readjusting their formations as needed. Down on the floor of the house, paper targets depicting swarthy men holding guns, or coffee cups, were shot or not shot depending on the threat posed. The troop worked in fire teams of four to six shooters. It was primarily a drill for the team leaders, but depending on the flow of the action, anyone on the team could be the lead shooter through any given door. It was full-on, close-quarter, live fire and movement.

"They've done this dozens of times," Moore observed, "but they never seem to get tired of it." Thanks to their Peltor Tactical Pro MT15H7B sound-canceling headphones the two senior leaders could speak in normal conversation in spite of the shouting and shooting below.

"That's a good thing, because there's a strong chance we'll be doing a lot more training and a lot less operating. We're just not the flavor of the month—and may not be for some time."

Volner was referring to the shift in the focus of special operations to indirect action—the training of foreign soldiers and the embedding of American special operators with partner-nation forces. Volner's troop, like all of the JSOC strike elements, was a direct-action team. If a good direct-action mission did come along, it could easily go to another troop, although Volner knew, as did his Master Guns, theirs was the top-rated troop among the JSOC special mission elements. *That might count for something,* Volner reasoned, *but probably not.*

"Of course," Volner continued, "I'm kinda stuck here. You, on the other hand, could always get out and write a book. I can see it on the shelves, *Master Guns Moore Tells It like It Was.*" Master Gunnery Sergeant Moore was also a tactical intelligence specialist and had been on the raid into Pakistan that led to the killing of Osama bin Laden. He led the site exploitation effort on that famous SEAL raid.

Moore rolled his quid from one side of his mouth to the other and considered this. "Sir, if I write a book, you have my standing permission to kick my ass up between my shoulder blades and then shoot me. I'm not some blabby-mouthed Navy SEAL."

"I'll take that under advisement, Master Guns."

"You do that, sir. Meanwhile, let's go down and see if one or two of those fire team leaders will let us in the stack. We got nothin' else to do."

Volner grinned. "Maybe, if we ask them politely."

In a special operations assault, the key kinetic leaders were the fire team leads. The troop commander and the troop senior sergeant seldom had their guns in the fight. The troop sergeant managed the fight and coordinated the movement of his fire teams and the blocking elements. His troop commander was on two, and sometimes three, radios. He monitored the fight, coordinated the air assets, and kept higher headquarters informed.

Both carried the responsibility for the fight, but they were seldom directly engaged. They ran the radios and stayed with the big picture. They could make adjustments and give direction, as a fight seldom goes as planned. Volner and Moore made their way down from the catwalk, each to a different fire team.

"Sergeant First Class Jamison," Volner said to his alpha team leader. "Mind if I jump into the stack for a run or two?"

Jamison, a lanky former Special Forces A-Team sergeant, pursed his lips as he thought about his major's request for a moment. "OK, Charlie, take a break." Turning to Volner, he continued. "Major, you'll be number four on the first door for this pass. And sir, I'd consider it a personal favor if you didn't shoot one of my men."

"Roger that, Sergeant," Volner replied as he took his place in the file.

CHAPTER NINE

The president was not surprised, but his confidence was validated, when Chase Williams contacted him six weeks to the day after their initial meeting. He had cleared his calendar and waited for their early afternoon meeting. It was a blustery January day, yet the president, as was his custom, was in a crisp white shirt, tie loosened, and his sleeves rolled to his forearms.

"Admiral, welcome."

"Thank you, Mr. President. I trust you and your family had a wonderful Christmas holiday."

"We did manage to break away and spend some time at Camp David. I know your wife passed away some years ago, but were you able to spend some time with your children?"

"Yes, thank you for asking. Our daughter invited us to her home in the Hollywood Hills. Our son managed to wrangle a week off from Goldman Sachs and got out of Boston just hours ahead of the blizzard that hit the Northeast days before Christmas."

"Good, that's great to hear. So here we both are, Admiral, reasonably relaxed and refreshed."

"Yes, Mr. President. And sir, if I may, can I ask that you call me Chase? Some people like to wear their former military rank to the grave. I'm not one of them. If you're OK with it, Chase would be better."

"Fair enough. Chase, then. So how should we proceed?"

"Mr. President, I've studied the issues we discussed and consulted with a small circle of friends and associates I trust implicitly and have come to some tentative conclusions. I think what I'm about to present to you will both frame our concept of operations for Op-Center and provide you with the confidence it can serve you and our nation's interests."

"I'm eager to hear what you have to say."

"Thank you. First of all, Mr. Harward was right in what he said when we met here six weeks ago. Op-Center shouldn't be the first thing that comes to mind when there is a crisis."

"Good. I'm glad we agree on that."

"I think, Mr. President, it's important to give credit where credit is due. In the decade following 9/11, our traditional intelligence and security services became superb at finding and killing terrorists. Our conventional intelligence collectors and military capability were up to the task of containing the threats from Iran, North Korea, China, and Russia as they made attempts to export militarism or expand their spheres of influence, but things have changed."

"I know they have, but how do we deal with these new threats?"

"As a start, Mr. President, we identify them for what they are. The available evidence we have thus far strongly suggests these stadium attacks weren't the work of some agitated jihadists. This was a professional hit. The terrorists have taken a page from our use of contractors to support the U.S. military and have begun to contract out terrorism. Our current intelligence agencies and our military are superb at what they do. However, a decade of war in Iraq and Afghanistan, the focus on counterinsurgency, and the major budget cuts to our military capabilities have left us a step behind today's emerging threats. This is especially true when it essentially becomes terror for hire."

"So how do we get ahead of the power curve?"

"Do you remember the movie *Top Gun*, Mr. President?"

"Do I ever."

"Remember Maverick's saying, 'I feel the need—the need for speed'?"

"Yes. That was kind of an unforgettable line."

"That's what we need. More speed. We need to turn inside the new threat's OODA loop."

"OODA loop?"

"Sorry, Mr. President. I'm still excising military acronyms from my vocabulary. OODA stands for 'observe, orient, decide, and act.' It was a brainchild of Air Force Colonel John Boyd, and, as you might guess, its first application was to fighter tactics."

"Come to think of it, I believe I've at least heard the term before."

"I suspect you don't need or want a full tutorial on this, Mr. President, but boiled down to its basics, the OODA loop concept says all decision-making occurs in a recurring cycle of observe-orient-decide-act. Any entity, whether an individual or an organization, that can process this cycle quickly, observing and reacting to unfolding events more rapidly than an opponent, can thereby 'get inside' the opponent's decision cycle, get inside *their* OODA loop, and gain the advantage."

"I think I see that. It's a simple but elegant concept. So how do you see it applying to Op-Center?"

"It's just this. As superb as our intelligence and military organizations are, there are several problems that come with their territory."

"Go on."

"First, there's our intelligence community, our IC. It does a fine job in many areas, but it's just not structured for rapid intelligence collation. It can't get inside the new, professional terrorists' OODA loop. There is simply too much lag time between when the information is collected as raw intelligence, analyzed, and converted into actionable intelligence. We collect plenty of intelligence; we can and do capture almost everything we need to take action. The problem lies in speedy processing of that information and focusing on anticipatory intelligence."

"Anticipatory intelligence?"

"Yes. We need to build intelligence algorithms that use what we know or can surmise to anticipate what might happen next. To use a well-known sports metaphor, it's roughly analogous to 'skating to where the puck is going to be, not where it has been.'"

"So are you proposing we restructure our intelligence community? I know Adam Putnam is a good man, and he'll be responsive."

"No, I'm not. The IC does so many things well that you'll lose far more than you gain if you turn them upside down and shake them real hard."

"I see. So what are you proposing?"

"I'll get to that in a moment, Mr. President, but there are two parts to this, and we need to discuss the military side also."

"Fine."

"Again, in the same vein as what I just said about the intelligence community, our military is the finest in the world and it is battle-hardened. There are so many things it does superbly; we should not fiddle with what it does."

Williams paused for a moment.

"However, Mr. President, there is a problem with how we conduct proportional military response today. Even our Tier One special operations elements need time, permissions, and information before they go out the door. Quite often tactical, theater, congressional, and even political issues get in the way, and it takes time to go up the line for a launch-the-strike order. This also applies to the prepositioning of forces early on in anticipation of a strike. Unfortunately, the way our military must work prevents them from getting inside these new, professional terrorists' OODA loop."

"So how do you see Op-Center moving faster than the terrorists?"

"The concept of operations I have for Op-Center is structured to get inside the new professional terrorist threat. I'll ask just two things from you, Mr. President, and I think these are things on which you'll want to get buy-in from your intelligence community and your military leadership."

"What are they?"

"First, I'll need Op-Center to have access to *all* intelligence feeds, and in real time. I'll need unimpeded access. If it flows to Mr. Putnam's National Counterterrorism Center, it flows to Op-Center."

"If we agree to do that, what will you do differently than what they do at the NCTC?"

"Mr. President, we're facing a situation where, as good as the intelligence community analysts are, a human in the loop actually slows things down and all but guarantees failure. To make Op-Center work to defeat today's threat, I need to hire bright minds from Silicon Valley. Then I have to have them build collation architecture with the right sensitivities and algorithms that can electronically filter all raw intelligence data and distill a problem faster than even the best analysts. It's the only way we can generate the anticipatory intelligence we need to get inside any plotters' OODA loop."

"You're not talking about 'automating' our intelligence, are you?"

"No, I'm not. There will always be a human at the end of the process. We just need to adapt what Google, Amazon, and eBay do so well. I can build a 'Geek Tank' that can get us anticipatory and actionable intelligence quickly enough so we can respond before a terrorist strikes. I'll have to hire the best talent available and we'll need to pay them what they're worth in the competitive marketplace. I don't anticipate it will be cheap."

"I expect it won't be, however, it sounds like it's worth a try and we do need the best minds we can bring to the problem. Yet how will you solve the issue you described regarding how fast our military can respond?"

"I know our military is stretched thin as it is, so I need to be economical with what I request. I propose that Op-Center have a dedicated Joint Special Operations Command element that will allow it to conduct platoon-sized operations supported by ground enablers and aviation components that are completely under expeditionary command of Op-Center. If the Special Operations Command commander can put this in place, and brief all combatant commanders that when this special JSOC unit is operating in their area it must receive the appropriate amount of support and operational security it needs, I think we can have a military unit that can get inside the enemy's OODA loop."

"That sounds like a reasonable request."

"Nevertheless, there's one more thing. I will need to have authority to surge this group into theater when there is even a hint they may be needed. There will be false alarms, and we may well surge this unit a half dozen times without having them see action, but that's the only way they can be on-scene to deal with a short-fused crisis."

"If it's a small enough footprint, I think we can make that work."

"Thank you, Mr. President, and per what we discussed during our initial meeting, my primary focus with Op-Center will be on external dangers, reaching out beyond our shores to nip the threat in the bud before it reaches our soil. In the military we call this 'shooting the archer instead of the arrow.'"

"Yes, I'm familiar with that term."

"As you know all too well, sir, the prohibitions against using military forces on U.S. territory are well established in law and practice. However, if we get actionable intelligence on a threat within our borders we will pass that to the attorney general and the FBI director and they can bring their Critical Incident Response Group to bear. I've already established a dialogue with both your AG and FBI director and they are receptive to this."

"Good, Chase. I appreciate you taking that on. And I agree, let's have Op-Center focus outward for now."

"Then my final request is this, and I'll say this carefully, sir. I have picked Paul Hood's brain extensively, and part of the reason the old Op-Center ultimately failed was, personalities aside, it presented a threat to the intelligence community and to the Pentagon. You have the authority to revive Op-Center. However, if you want it to *succeed*, you're going to have to get your national security team, your intelligence community, and your military chiefs on board. I can't do that, sir. Only you can."

Midkiff considered this. He knew Williams was right, but it was easier said than done, even for the commander in chief. "I think you're on the right track, but give me some time to think about just how to go about this."

"I understand, Mr. President. Here is a memo that captures the concept of operations for Op-Center. It contains everything we just discussed, and the mechanics for putting these procedures into place."

"Thank you for this. I'm virtually certain we'll get the kind of buy-in you want. Once we do, how soon do you think you can get Op-Center up and running?"

"If you have the resources, give me just three months and I can have a skeleton organization going. In eight to ten months we can be fully functioning."

"I know this is an ambitious undertaking. I've already consulted with the House and Senate majority and minority leadership. None of them want to see attacks like these happen again. You won't have a blank check, but move forward aggressively and let us worry about resourcing Op-Center."

"Thank you, Mr. President. I appreciate your vote of confidence. It's three months and eight to ten months, then—less if I can make it work. And I'll try not to give you sticker-shock over my hires for the Geek Tank."

"That's an ambitious timeline, Chase, and I'll hold you to it. As for your Geek Tank, get the best minds you can working on this. We can't give them stock options, so pay what you must to get them on board."

Their meeting complete, the president walked Chase Williams to the door of the Oval Office. Williams had done his part. Now it was up to Wyatt Midkiff to do his.

Late that night, forty miles southeast of the White House, near Mechanicsville, Maryland, there was no moon, few stars, and enough low fog to obscure almost everything on the ground.

"Altitude, altitude!" the crew chief shouted to her pilot as he brought their UH-60 Black Hawk helicopter into a hover over the warehouse. She was a veteran with thousands of hours in the air, yet her voice had an urgent screech to it.

"Got it," the pilot replied into his lip mic as he pulled collective and stabilized the bird in an eighty-foot hover over the roof of the massive building. *Stay on the instruments,* he said to himself, willing himself not to look out into the inky blackness surrounding their helicopter. *Don't fight the controls. EASY with it.*

"Now!" he said, working to keep the emotion from his voice.

The crew chief turned in her seat and looked back into the cabin where eight members of the FBI's Critical Incident Response Group waited for the signal. The HRT—Hostage Rescue Team—all wore black coveralls, Kevlar helmets, and their faces were either blackened or hidden by balaclavas. The team's primary weapons were the same, the Special Operations Peculiar Modification M4 carbines with SU-231 EO Tech holographic sights and LA-5 IR lasers/pointers. The FBI armory had newer rifles, but most on the HRT team were former special operators or SWAT veterans, and the SOPMOD M-4 was what they were used to and what they were comfortable with. Their secondary weapons strapped to their thighs ranged from Glocks to SIG SAUERs to a 1911 .45. They wore body armor and Rhodesian vests with an impressive array of urban assault gear. All had PSC-15 night vision goggles.

She pulled an infrared light from her torso harness and, leaning from her cabin perch, signaled the ground, moving the light in a circular motion. As she did, the assault team in the back of the Black Hawk kicked out two hundred-foot-long, four-inch-thick braided nylon fast-ropes. Seconds later, four HRT members slid down each length of rope and landed on top of the warehouse. They were like drops of oil coming down a string. The last man down brought a section of climbing rope.

As the team on the roof signaled all clear, the pilot pulled collective and lifted the Black Hawk into the dark sky above.

On the roof, the team leader split his men into two groups. He took four other men with him as they scrambled down the climbing rope to the ground while his number two led two other men to the one skylight on the roof.

On the deck, the team leader positioned two of his men in front of the main warehouse door. A third man put a small explosive strip-charge on the door, ready to breach the door at his leader's command. When the two men nodded they were ready, he whispered into the boom mic of his squad radio, "Now."

"Now," repeated his number two on the roof.

On the ground level, the door blew back into the building. The team poured into the room, sweeping the interior with their M4 rifles. They then began the well-choreographed actions of clearing the first room and moving on to the next, and the next.

On the roof, the number two man lifted the skylight and tossed in two flash-bang stun grenades. Immediately following the explosions, the second team kipped through the opening and dropped to the floor of the room below.

Inside the warehouse it was twenty seconds of measured

violence as the teams moved from room to room—shooting, clearing, and marking bodies of the fallen. Then calls of "clear" came from various points inside the building.

The chattering of the rotor blades grew louder as the Black Hawk descended into the vacant parking lot adjacent to the building. As the crew shut down the bird's engines and the blades began to coast to a stop, shrill whistles blew from inside and outside the building. Then came the loud announcement, "Exercise over—EndEx, EndEx."

The exercise coordinator walked up to the team lead. "Congratulations, you killed the terrorists and also half the hostages."

They all knew it would be a long debrief back at the Quantico CIRG team facility.

CHAPTER TEN

The White House Oval Office, Washington, D.C.
(January 14, 0900 Eastern Standard Time)

Wyatt Midkiff sat in the Oval Office. He was anticipating a meeting he knew he needed to have, but one he was not looking forward to.

He had used his considerable political and social skills over the past six weeks to calm his national security advisor's concerns. Yet he knew Trevor Harward was still anxious about this new venture. Punctual to the minute, Harward entered the president's office at precisely 0900.

"Morning, Mr. President. How did your meeting with Admiral Williams go?"

"It went well, Trevor; actually, better than expected. I asked the admiral—and by the way, he prefers being addressed as Chase—to draft up a memo capturing what we discussed and get it to you by the end of the week. I think we are ready to move forward with Op-Center."

"That's good, Mr. President. I think it's something we both believe the nation needs."

"I agree, Trevor. However, you're my national security advisor, and I want to ensure we both come to an understanding regarding the way we want to use Op-Center and the relationship I'll have with Chase Williams."

"Mr. President, I appreciate you raising this. I admit I initially found Chase's directness and insistence that he come directly to you when he felt the need a bit off-putting. However, as you and I have talked about this over the past six weeks, I recognize you should have the option of communicating with him, and only him, directly if the situation demands it."

"Give it to me straight, Trevor; I sense you still have reservations."

"Mr. President, I've served in this town for a long time. As you know, I have considerable experience in national security matters from tours in the Pentagon, State, the National Security Council, and elsewhere. I was pretty well plugged into some of the missions the old Op-Center was called on to do."

Harward paused to frame his next words carefully.

"When you recruited me, Mr. President, we agreed that due to the stakes involved, there had to be complete trust between us in all we did—"

"And we have had that in our time together, haven't we?" Midkiff interrupted.

"Absolutely, Mr. President, and I'm honored by the trust you've placed in me. Yet I'm your national security *advisor*. At the end of the day, all I bring you is advice—well-reasoned and well-staffed advice—but advice nonetheless. In the final analysis, that's all it is."

"But Trevor, don't minimize your importance to my administration."

"I'm not, Mr. President, but I am most certainly motivated to protect you as well as advise you. Once you put Op-Center in motion, it will begin to do things I believe we both want done. When needed, you will likely give Chase Williams broad discretion and freedom of action. That authority will sometimes allow him to act first and inform you after the fact."

"Well, yes, I think we agree on that."

"Then that becomes the critical question. Do you, as president, trust Chase Williams with the broad discretion and freedom of action he needs to have as Op-Center director? Are you certain he will be thoughtful and discreet as he takes action? This is important, Mr. President, because without putting too fine a point on it, his actions could make or break your presidency."

There was a long silence, and Harward could tell the president needed a moment to weigh the full import of what he had just told him. As for Midkiff, he was moved. As with all good politicians, he was inspired by the loyalty and selflessness of a hardworking subordinate.

"Trevor, first of all, thank you for that courageous and forthright analysis, and while I have never framed it the way you just did, I have indeed thought about this and thought about it deeply. I do trust the man. I trust him to do the right thing for our nation."

"And for your presidency?" Harward asked.

Midkiff smiled. "Can the two be separated?"

"Then let's move forward, Mr. President."

•   •   •

The call between the secretary of defense and the commander of the United States Special Operations Command had been brief and to the point. It had not been preceded by the countless hours of staff work by each of the respective staffs that typically lead up to such calls between two senior national security principals.

The president had directed his SECDEF to deliver a measured, but firm, message to the SOCOM commander. Op-Center was being put back into operation and the new Op-Center director needed one of SOCOM's JSOC teams under his exclusive operational control. The secretary of defense told him the Op-Center director would visit him at SOCOM headquarters in Tampa within the week and that the president expected him to have a JSOC team ready to second to Op-Center by then.

Armed with his mandate from the president, Chase Williams sat at his desk in the Eisenhower Executive Office Building with an Excel spreadsheet in front of him.

In the six weeks since the initial meeting with the president, Williams had worked nearly around the clock. In addition to developing an operational blueprint for Op-Center, he had been working on a short list of the talent he would need for the new organization.

He had promised the president he would have a skeleton organization up and running in three months. He had some phone calls to make.

CHAPTER ELEVEN

Central Command, Commander's Office, MacDill Air
Force Base, Tampa, Florida
(January 19, 1400 Eastern Standard Time)

"Would you like some more coffee, Admiral?"

"Thank you, but I'm just fine."

Chase Williams had been waiting in the outer office of the Commander, United States Special Operations Command for just under twenty minutes. It was unacceptable by any standard, but the SOCOM commander was making a point. *So be it*, Williams thought. *I've certainly come down here to make mine.* After a few more minutes, the attractive and aloof gatekeeper lifted the receiver. She listened for a few seconds and then replaced it.

"The commander will see you now."

Williams rose and made his way into the general's office. He stepped inside just as General Mark Patrick eased himself from his chair and walked around the desk to greet him.

"Admiral Williams, sorry to keep you waiting. Welcome and please have a seat." He returned to his desk and picked up the phone. "Tracy, please hold all calls with the exception of the

Southern Command commander. I'll speak with him." He glanced over at Williams. "That's a call I have to take." He replaced the receiver and took a seat, seemingly to now afford his guest his full attention. "Now, Admiral, what can I do for you—oh, and can I get you some more coffee?"

Williams leveled his gaze at the SOCOM commander for a full twenty seconds before he replied. "First of all, General, I've had quite enough coffee. Secondly, you may call me Mr. Williams. Unlike you, I'm no longer on active duty, and it's a title I relinquished when I left active service. Thirdly, when this meeting was scheduled, I asked that your Joint Special Operations Command commander be present. I see he's not here." Patrick moved to speak, but Williams forestalled him with a raised hand. "And finally, you know exactly why I'm here. I sent you a service support request that was explicit and detailed, both in the force composition and the command relationships that will govern my operational control of these assets. Are you telling me you don't have that request or are not prepared to discuss it?"

"Well, Admiral, or Mr. Williams, if you prefer, this is highly irregular. My JSOC commander had a previous engagement, so I took the liberty of excusing him from this meeting. As for the transfer of operational control of SOCOM and JSOC assets to you that's, ah, well, I'm not sure that's advisable, or if it's even legal."

This time, Williams waited even longer before speaking. When he did, he seemed to soften. "General, I've been a type commander and a geographic combatant commander—twice. So I can understand the parochial and even the personal issues that go with releasing your people to the authority of someone else who intends to put them in harm's way. And I have great respect for your position and your time; that's why I sent that request, which is nothing short of a formal operational tasker, to you personally. Also, General, I didn't summon you to Washington; I came to you."

Williams leaned in toward Patrick and hardened his tone. "As a direct representative of the president and in keeping with current executive practice that is well within the guidelines of congressional oversight, I think you know I'm on firm legal ground. As for the 'advisability' you referred to, that is noted, and with due respect, it's above your pay grade. Now, per the request you've had for a week and that I know you've read thoroughly, I want a full troop of JSOC commandos put solely under my direction with the orders and authorization to train and act exclusively at my discretion. I will want those designated assets at the 160th Special Operations Aviation Squadron and the 1st Special Operations Wing also fenced so they come under my authority and mine alone." There was another long pause while the two men stared at each other. "Now, I understand this is an unusual request, but when you give it consideration, it's not unlike the arrangements you have with the geographic combatant commanders and your theater special operations commanders. You send them assets, you support those assets in theater, and they, not you, employ them in accordance with standing theater guidelines and host-nation agreements. With the exception of stateside training authority, I'm simply another end user."

The SOCOM commander had turned several shades darker

and started to speak, but again, Williams silenced him with a raised hand. "Now, sir," he continued with more steel in his voice, "you have two choices here. You can comply with this request and we can discuss how you would like me to deal with your subordinate commanders for the transfer of these assets, and we'll do this with no interruptions, from the Southern Command commander or anyone else. Or, if you feel this is simply beyond your statutory or moral obligations as the SOCOM commander, you can resign. It's not an easy thing, I assure you, but we all have to act within the constraints of our conscience and how we see our duty. There is a third alternative; I can simply have you relieved, but that serves neither your nor my interests, or our obligations. So, General, what's it going to be?"

After a long moment, Patrick picked up the sheet of paper lying on his blotter and studied it. "You feel you need a full troop?"

"I do," Williams said politely. "I will need a platoon-sized element on immediate standby and a second element in a lesser recall status. You know better than I the toll it takes on men and their families if they are kept on immediate flyaway status. So yes, I'll need a full troop."

"You'll get what you need, Mr. Williams," Patrick said, the tension in his voice palpable. "And I hope to God you know what you're doing," he continued as he rose abruptly, walked to the door, and opened it.

Williams walked out without another word, and no handshakes were exchanged.

• • •

A week later, Chase Williams handed the guard his credentials at the gate of the National Counterterrorism Center compound at Liberty Crossing, near McLean, Virginia. He had been here many times during his years in uniform, and he declined the guard's offer of directions. Inside the compound, he drove the short distance to NCTC's headquarters building and parked in a space marked "Op-Center Director." *Nice touch*, he thought.

NCTC's deputy director was on the curb to greet him. "Admiral, welcome. Mr. Putnam is expecting you. I'll escort you to his office." *Better touch*.

"You all have been a bit busy over the past several months, haven't you?" Williams asked the deputy director as they entered the imposing six-story building.

"We're up for the challenge, Admiral. Mr. Putnam has had the intelligence community in overdrive working to get to the bottom of who did this to us."

Built on the foundations of the CIA's Terrorist Threat Integration Center, with bullet- and blast-proof external windows cast to standards set after the Oklahoma City bombing, the NCTC looked like a fortress, and it was. The deputy director led Chase Williams past office after office with coded locks, each office essentially a vault, where the NCTC staff worked to fulfill its mission to lead the nation's effort to combat terrorism at home and abroad. That was their mission, but they had failed.

As Chase Williams entered Adam Putnam's spacious office, the director of national intelligence rose to greet him as the deputy director closed the door, leaving the two men alone.

"Chase, it's nice to see you again."

"Likewise, Adam."

"The president's given you a huge assignment, and we're here to help in every way we can."

"Appreciate that."

Chase Williams reflected on his years-long relationship with Adam Putnam. When he had heard Putnam was selected as director of national intelligence he was cheered that the intelligence community—the IC—had gotten it right. Putnam was one of the most capable and least territorial professionals he knew. He understood Putnam was doing all he could to ensure the nation's intelligence agencies sniffed out potential attacks on Americans at home or abroad and he also knew he felt a sense of professional failure over the "NFL attacks."

"You mentioned you'd met with Trevor Harward and the national security staff," Putnam continued. "They think they've teased out a motive for these attacks?"

"They may well have. First, I'd like to thank you for putting Op-Center on all your intelligence feeds. We're still getting staffed and organized, and truth be known we don't yet have the capacity to use all you're providing, but we will in time. In the meantime, I appreciate your willingness to make our endeavor to track down whoever attacked us a team effort."

"I didn't anticipate we'd have any issues, Chase. We in the intelligence community let the nation down. You and your organization will go a long way to ensuring this doesn't happen again."

With that, the two men embarked on an extended conversation regarding what they knew and what they still didn't know.

Williams shared what he had gleaned from Trevor Harward and what the national security advisor had learned from Gamal Haaziq. They were in general agreement to focus their efforts in keeping with a motive of revenge, a line of investigation they had yet to mine. Putnam agreed to have his analysts take the lead on running this to ground while Williams got his Geek Tank up and running on all cylinders. While they both recognized that the nation, and especially the president, wanted answers and wanted to avenge the NFL attacks as soon as possible, they both knew they would embark on work that was often painfully slow and deliberate.

The meeting complete, Williams rose to leave. "Adam, we're going to get this done."

"We will, Chase. I know we will."

Twenty miles due south of where Chase Williams and Adam Putnam were hammering out their long-term working relationships, two other men were also trying to make things happen—and just as quickly. "I want your two bulldozers down there. Trench it out another four to five feet and then we can pour the next two columns we need to build."

"Got it," the foreman said to the project manager.

"Will your team have any problem working overtime for a few hours? We're paying time and a half."

"I think they'll go for it. But I'm kinda worried they'll burn out and somebody will make a dumb-ass mistake and get someone hurt or killed. This pace has been kind of brutal."

"That's why we pay up for foremen with your experience," the project manager replied, raising his voice to be heard as the massive dump truck thundered by.

The foreman grinned. "Thanks, but it's still not an easy build. I'll keep a sharp eye out, and we'll do our best to balance the schedule and safety."

"That's the Hitte spirit!"

Hitte Construction had secured a lucrative contract to build a basement under the National Geospatial-Intelligence Agency, the NGA, in Fort Belvoir North and the project manager would receive a substantial bonus if the massive construction project was completed early. He needed to push his team and push them hard. They hadn't told him why they were building this basement under the NGA. All he had heard were rumors it was for an "important new organization."

"So why the hell is this such a rush job? This is the government, after all, isn't it," the foreman asked.

"Hey, that's way above my pay grade," the project manager replied. "They don't pay us to worry about that shit."

Two days after his meeting with the director of national intelligence, Chase Williams sat in a small meeting room on the JSOC compound at Fort Bragg. He felt his business with JSOC called for a personal visit. The first of his two scheduled meetings had gone far better than the one with General Patrick at SOCOM headquarters just a few days before. The JSOC commander, a former 75th Ranger regimental commander and now a lieutenant general, had known exactly why Williams had come and what he needed. Far more than the SOCOM commander, he knew what it was to send men into dangerous and difficult situations. That was his job—had been his job. He also knew his primary role now was to assess, select, and train men for this most difficult of direct special operations tasks, not to command them in combat or even to select their missions. This didn't mean he didn't have his concerns. "I've given you one of my best troops, Admiral," he told Williams. "If you get them hurt or killed, I will be the one to break the news to the families. I've had to call on recent widows and it's something I'd like to avoid. You have your responsibilities, sir, as do I. So please, take care of *our* men."

Now Williams waited for the troop commander and his senior enlisted advisor. The room was Spartan, just a small conference table, padded chairs but not comfy swivels, and a complex ceiling-mounted audio-visual projector. The coffee was in a plastic foam cup and it was lukewarm, but for the new Op-Center director, it somehow felt just right. The door opened and two men of medium height and starched battledress utilities stepped into the room. Williams himself was dressed in chinos and an open-collared Oxford shirt. He rose to meet them. Once introductions were made, the three seated themselves at the table.

"I understand you may have some work for us," Major Mike Volner began.

"I just may," Williams replied. "Tell me, have you been briefed on my organization or why you were seconded to me?" Volner glanced at his senior sergeant and both men shook their heads. Williams smiled. "Well, this will take a bit of explaining.

Before we get to that, I'd like to learn more about each of you. If you would, Major, perhaps you could tell me something about yourself."

Williams had been the given the files on these men, as well as the rest of the troop, but he wanted to hear it directly from them. Major Michael Volner was five feet ten inches tall and weighed 160 pounds, trim but not noticeably athletically built, with brown hair and brown eyes. If unremarkable in appearance, his background was anything but that.

Following the bitter divorce of his parents when he was twelve his father, a college professor, left the country only to be killed as a bystander of a car bomb four years later while teaching in Pakistan. His mother, a stay-at-home mom, fell prey to the ravages of solitary drinking and prescription pain killers to the point of being institutionalized. Raised from fourteen on by his maternal grandmother, he felt adrift and alone. His grandmother recognized his keen intelligence and little need of others and decided not to change him, but strengthen his existing traits. She taught him contract bridge at an early age and played with him as her partner in regional tournaments. He became a prodigy, able to accurately assess multiple possibilities, gifted with unbelievably quick decision-making abilities, and an almost unbeatable opponent. He also learned to read people as well as cards.

At sixteen he became fascinated with free-form rock climbing. He frequented various climbing sites and he watched and learned without formal training. Every weekend he climbed alone, perfecting his technique and building tremendous core strength. He trained and taught his body to perform remarkable feats. Volner attended Brown University on a scholarship and entered the Army right out of college. He was not a born leader, but became a leader by example. He readily took to military life and made the most of the professional and tactical training the Army afforded its infantry officers. The Army also taught him what his grandmother did not: To be a leader, you must first be a team player, and you must care for the men you lead. Volner had been both a platoon commander and a company commander with the 82nd Airborne and the 75th Rangers. Now he was a JSOC troop commander, or what in previous times had been called a Delta Force Team Leader.

If the major was something of a smooth article, his senior sergeant was not. Master Gunnery Sergeant Moore was similar in stature, but thicker. He was older and his craggy features were capped with a dense thatch of salt-and-pepper. He bore an uncanny resemblance to the late actor Dennis Farina, something he quietly cultivated. Moore was bred for the Marine Corps. He was born at the Naval Hospital at Camp Lejeune, North Carolina, and shuffled from one Marine base to another until he was old enough to enlist. His father waded ashore with the 7th Marines of the 1st Marine Division in Vietnam in 1965. His grandfather was wounded twice at Guadalcanal and killed in action on Saipan. Two of his great uncles were at the Chosin Reservoir; one made it back. His great-grandfather was with Gunnery Sergeant Dan Daily at Belleau Wood. Moore's Marine roots were in Battalion and Force Recon, and he was one of the plank holders of the Marine Special Operations Command he helped to establish in 2006. After five combat deployments with MAR-SOC, he migrated to JSOC. In one capacity or another, Master Guns Moore had been in continuous combat rotation for over a decade and a half. He was fluent in Arabic and Farsi.

Most field and senior grade officers in the Army or Marine Corps found it hard to contemplate an officer and an enlisted man with this seniority leading a combat unit that was barely half the size of a company. Yet, as Williams had recently come to understand, all that seniority and experience came into play when planning a special operations, direct-action mission. When the need arose, he would task these men with just such a mission. They would study the task given them, then plan and carry out the operation. Careful attention to training and tactical execution helped; combat experience in special operations was essential.

These were men who were not comfortable talking about themselves, but Williams drew them out. It was Moore who finally brought up the task ahead.

"Sir, I appreciate your interest in us, but can you tell us something about what you have for us, and how you think we can be of service?"

So Williams did. He gave them a short version of the old Op-Center, which they had heard about but knew little of, and a complete breakdown of what he envisioned for the future. "There may be long periods training and operational inactivity," he concluded, "but when the call comes from Op-Center to you, you will have to be quick, professional, and I can assure you, it will be important—and most probably, dangerous. There may be a great many flyaways and prepositioning with no action. Each time you will have to move out smartly and come up with a workable plan in short order. Yet, when you are committed to an operation, it will likely be of crisis proportions. Sound fair enough?"

The two veteran warriors exchanged a glance and nodded in unison.

"Your primary liaison with Op-Center will be a retired Army man named Hector Rodriquez." At the mention of this name, both men paused, then broke into broad smiles.

"Sergeant Major Rodriquez is on your team?" Moore blurted.

"He is," Williams said with a straight face. It was a card he had waited to play until now. Rodriquez was a former JSOC command sergeant major. This drew a low whistle from Moore, and both men seemed to visibly relax at the mention of his name.

"Uh, I don't know about your schedule, sir," Volner said, "but would you like to meet the rest of the troop?"

Williams looked at his watch and took out his cell phone. He hit the speed dial and it was answered immediately. "Captain, I'm going to be a little longer than planned. Can you delay our take off for another hour or so? . . . Excellent . . . I'll let you know and thank you." Then, turning to Volner, he said, "Major, I'd be honored to meet your men."

CHAPTER TWELVE

Azka Perkasa's Condo, Kuala Lumpur, Malaysia
(August 22, 1015 Malaysia Time)

It was late summer, and Azka Perkasa was at his computer in the home office of his Kuala Lumpur high-rise condo, surfing the Web. He was looking at vacation rentals in Bali. He had recently found some joy in the purchase of relationships from an upscale, discreet service he used on occasion. Once he had confirmed a property on Bali and rented the time and space on Net Jets, he would contact the service and rent a woman for the week. If she didn't work out, he would simply send her home on a commercial flight. The engineer in Perkasa liked both the impersonal nature and privacy this kind of arrangement afforded him. Like any man he had needs, but no one needed to know of his personal life or how he made his living—certainly not some woman retained only for pleasure. Be that as it may, this was not entirely the case.

Someone did, in fact, know about Azka Perkasa and his personal life—and a great deal more. Over the course of the past several weeks, he had come to the attention of a bespectacled man in a small, sparsely appointed office crammed with computers, cables, and keyboards. The office was in the basement of the National Geospatial-Intelligence Agency, and still smelled of fresh paint and drywall paste. It was Op-Center's new, but still under-construction, headquarters, and the man's name was Aaron Bleich. He had been one of Op-Center's first hires, and his services cost the new organization more in annual salary than the president, with a substantial up-front signing bonus. Yet in the multifaceted world of information, Aaron Bleich was worth his weight in gold—literally—and he was the first of his kind to be hired by Op-Center. He was given the equipment he demanded and put in a room with a single mission: Find who was responsible for the stadium bombings. This he had done. With official, and some nonofficial, access to law enforcement and intelligence-agency databases, he had, in his words, "laid hands on" his beloved suite of computers and found Azka Perkasa. Next, he traced and documented his movements back to and before the bombings. Just as soon as he knew, Chase Williams knew.

Perkasa's condo was on the forty-fourth floor and looked out over the expanse of the extended port area and the Strait of Malacca. There was a smog-induced haze that partially obscured the Aerospatiale helicopter that was hovering a half mile offshore. The helo was draped in civilian markings, but it was the property of the Grup Gerak Khas—the 10th Paratroop Brigade of the Indonesian Special Forces. It was a crack force trained in part by the 1st Special Forces Group. The Grup Gerak Khas was partial to the Green Berets from Fort Lewis in Washington State, and posed no questions when asked if a sanitized helicopter could be made available for a few hours. Earlier that day, an unmarked, extended range Gulfstream V had landed at Kuala Lumpur International and taxied to a remote hangar. Two pilots from the 160th Special Operations Aviation Regiment and two snipers from the Op-Center JSOC troop stepped from the Gulfstream and quickly boarded the fully fueled French helicopter. They took off immediately.

If Azka did not clearly see the helo from the perch in his condo, the shooter behind the stabilized optics saw him. The optics were married to a CheyTac .408 rifle with a point-designated sighting system. After the target had been identified by the system's laser range finder and target designator, the weapon would not fire unless the gun was on target—precisely on target. Once the shooter had identified his target, Azka's head, and pressed the trigger, he wavered around a bit until the crosshairs momentarily rested on the Azka's lazy left eye. The CheyTac bucked, and two seconds later a 210-grain round came through the plate glass and into Azka's right nostril. Still traveling at twenty-four hundred feet per second, the heavy slug tore into his skull, causing it to explode and paint the inside of his home office with cranial tissue and brain matter.

His body was found later that day. By that time, the Gulfstream, the two shooters, and the two pilots were out over the Indian Ocean, well on their way to a fueling stop at Diego Garcia.

Chase Williams was standing on the tarmac at Pope Air Force Base shortly after sunrise when the JSOC team emerged from their aircraft. Major Mike Volner let his weary troop disembark first and was last off the plane. While only a portion of the team were used to make the airborne hit on Perkasa, Volner had taken his entire troop downrange to set up the necessary coordination and command and control

Williams shook hands with each of the team members, and then paused to speak with Volner. "Well done, Major. I read your reports but am looking forward to you debriefing my staff in person. You carried this out superbly and we're all enormously proud of you."

"Thank you, Admiral. It was a great team effort. The intel your Geek Tank provided was spot on, the Pacific combatant commander gave us everything we needed, and we couldn't have asked for better support. We'll be standing by for our next assignment. And sir, if you don't mind me saying so, thank you for coming all the way down from Washington to meet us. I know you're busy and this was an unexpected surprise."

"I'm never too busy to recognize a job well done, Major. We may not be far from pinning down the location of the bastard who perpetrated these attacks. I'd like to give your boys the R&R they deserve after what you've just accomplished, but I'm going to have to ask you to keep them on twenty-four-hour standby."

"We can do that, Admiral. I'll give them the afternoon and evening off once we get back to Fort Bragg. Any idea where we'll be heading for our next mission, sir?"

"I can't tell you for sure, but I think you might want to break out your desert camis."

"Works for me, Admiral. We'll be ready when you call us."

· · · ·

The next day, Chase Williams assembled his skeleton staff in the basement of the National Geospatial-Intelligence Agency. He complimented them on their efforts in orchestrating the hit on Azka Perkasa and thanked them for how quickly they had gotten Op-Center up and running.

That done, his face hardened, and he was all business. "Ladies and gentlemen, I'm going to give it to you right between the running lights. Our JSOC team performed superbly and did everything we expected of them. We all should be proud to work with pros like Major Volner and his troop."

Williams paused to frame his thoughts.

"That said, we need to mine the lessons learned from what just happened. Getting our team surged into theater was not a smooth operation. Not all the gear they needed got to them in time and they had to do work-arounds to make their mission succeed. Getting them back here wasn't much better, and we could have reunited them with their families a day sooner if we'd been on the ball."

Heads nodded. The staff knew where they had fallen short.

"I think we're finding the limits of the talent we have onboard Op-Center right now," Williams continued, his tone softening. "There are certainly areas where I'm out of my depth, and I think it's also clear the kind of folks we should hire as we continue to staff up. Now, here's what we need to do to get ready for our next mission."

Once Aaron Bleich had a complete profile of Azka Perkasa, it did not take him long to connect him to Abdul-Muqtadir

Kashif—and Kashif's role in financing the bombings. There were just enough phone calls and money wire transfers to connect Kashif, the Lebanese, and Perkasa. As good as he was, Bleich had to admit that luck did play a part in his success. While Kashif and Perkasa had been circumspect and careful to a fault, save for the short phone call between Perkasa and Kashif, their Lebanese intermediary had been sloppy, even cavalier, with his phone and e-mail communications. It was just enough to finger Kashif.

Shortly following the death of Perkasa, of which he had no knowledge, Kashif was with his wife's father's brother in a warehouse outside Beirut. He was checking the false loading documents for a shipment of goods from Marseilles that would arrive by shipboard container the following day. Kashif normally did his best to stay away from the working end of this part of his business, but sometimes he had to make himself visible for the sake of appearances.

This uncle was a scoundrel by any measurement, yet Kashif genuinely liked the old smuggler. He had a sense of himself and of their enterprise he found refreshing. The old man was smart, and Kashif knew no small amount of what he had accomplished financially was due to the help and guidance of this wily relative.

Kashif was impressed by the way his uncle worked the dozen men in the warehouse, giving his foreman suggestions rather than orders. He sensed these men had worked for his uncle for quite some time. Suddenly, the old man cocked his head, as if he sensed something rather than heard it. He turned to the foreman.

"What is that truck doing there in the back, behind that stack of lumber?"

"Ah," the man replied, "it's the consignment of fertilizer that was delivered this morning."

"I didn't order any—"

It wasn't a blinding flash, and the sound was more of an angry gray WHUMP than an explosion. Yet, it leveled the building. Surprisingly, there was only minor damage done to the surrounding structures. Yet, everyone in the warehouse perished. Some fourteen men were killed, but only those few with dental records were identified. One was a wealthy Arab businessman, and the authorities wondered just what he might have been doing there.

At Rafic Hariri International Airport outside Beirut, two men with impeccable Canadian passports boarded a flight for Cairo. One of them was a middle-aged man who bore a striking resemblance to Dennis Farina. In the troop commander's office at Fort Bragg, an anxious Major Mike Volner waited, cell phone in hand. It was a throwaway and untraceable, except for the likes of someone like Aaron Bleich. He did not have to wait long.

"Yes," he said after the first ring.

"It would seem the flight is on time."

"Fine, and thanks for the call."

Volner closed the phone and took a deep breath. Then he dialed a number on the secure phone on his desk. Chase Williams was sitting in his new office, which was still under construction, and answered immediately. He, too, had been waiting by the phone. The Op-Center director listened a moment, then permitted himself a smile—one of satisfaction and relief.

• • •

The elimination of Azka Perkasa and Abdul-Muqtadir Kashif was still a well-kept secret in government in the few weeks since Op-Center had made their two surgical hits. The Op-Center staff and their JSOC team had been asked not to reveal the hits had been made—that would be done "at the national level" in short order.

As with the hit on Perkasa, the takedown of Kashif had generated more lessons learned that Chase Williams and his team were still digesting as they continued to build up the Op-Center staff. These two hits had been done essentially "on the fly" by leveraging the intelligence Adam Putnam and his National Counterterrorism Center were able to provide, by turning loose Aaron Bleich, and by employing the JSOC team with the talent they brought to the table.

While Williams was proud of what both teams had accomplished, he knew it would not be good enough to carry out the Op-Center mission for the long haul. They weren't there yet, not by a long shot. He had to keep recruiting, he had to keep building, and he had to keep training. However, for now, he had a memo to write to the president.

CHAPTER THIRTEEN

Washington, D.C.
(September 6, 1115 Eastern Daylight Time)

Chase Williams reported the deaths of Perkasa and Kashif in a short, cryptic memo to the president. It was in the format and protocol of Williams's own design for communications that were to be strictly between him and the president, and no one else. The infrequent communiqués were coded simply "POTUS/OC Eyes Only." These memos were never more than a single page, as was this one, and omitted nothing.

President Midkiff, in his reply, offered that strikes like these into foreign nations, and with the accompanying collateral damage, might be called to his attention *before* such events took place.

The next POTUS/OC Eyes Only from Williams was short and to the point. "Mr. President: There is no sense in both of us losing sleep over the innocent loss of life in doing what has to be done. Unless you direct otherwise, I will proceed as before unless there are strategic implications. CW."

Midkiff pondered Williams's reply. After a few moments

he raised his eyebrows, pursed his lips, and slid the memo into the shredder.

Several days later, on September 9, a day selected because it was ten months to the day since the NFL attacks, President Midkiff sat in the Oval Office under the hot tungsten-halogen lamps as cameras rolled for his address to the nation. The Washington press corps had not been able to sniff out the reason for the prime-time address, and the White House press secretary had been vague, saying only that it was a national security matter.

"Three, two, one . . . rolling, Mr. President."

"My fellow Americans, good evening. Tonight I can tell you that the perpetrators of the unprovoked attacks against our citizens on November 9 of last year have been brought to swift justice. There has been no internment in prison, there will be no trial. We will not have to listen to them hold forth about their 'cause' or their attempt to justify what they did. They have simply been identified, and we have eliminated them."

The president was all business, not a hint of a smile or any other emotion other than *purpose* on his face. He went on to tell the American people in graphic detail just who was responsible and the violence that accompanied their summary judgment.

"Tonight we are serving notice to anyone, or any nation, who would cause our citizens harm. We have no patience, no compassion, and are not interested in whatever sick purpose might propel you to attack us. If you hurt our citizens, we will chase you to the ends of the earth and hunt you down and kill you. And it won't take us a decade to do it."

"This closes a tragic chapter for America that began exactly ten months ago. We have made substantial changes to our national security structure to ensure this does not happen again. May God bless our citizens killed on November 9, may God bless their grieving families, and may God bless America."

As the cameras faded out on the president and the network talking heads took over, America, and the world, recognized a new chapter had begun. What they didn't know, nor would ever know, was that Op-Center was up and running. Azka Perkasa and Abdul-Muqtadir Kashif had thought they had moved on from the events of November 9, but a team of bright and persistent analysts had carefully sifted through the e-mails, voice mails, and fund transfers to link them with the date and the crime. They were the first to feel the reach and finality of the new Op-Center. As the president got up from his chair after his announcement the first hand he shook belonged to Chase Williams.

PART II

EMERGENCE

Fifteen Months Later . . .

CHAPTER FOURTEEN

*Op-Center Headquarters, Fort Belvoir North, Fairfax
County, Virginia
(February 11, 0830 Eastern Standard Time)*

Admiral Chase Williams emerged from the elevator in the basement of the headquarters of the National Geospatial-Intelligence Agency, the NGA, in Fort Belvoir North, in Fairfax, Virginia, for his weekly meeting with his core staff. This location enabled the new Op-Center to have access to NGA's products and personnel, secure movement of data, and supersecure spaces, all key assets in information-based war fighting. The site they had chosen was ideal—it was close enough to the Beltway for Williams and the Op-Center staff to get to the White House, Pentagon, CIA, FBI, and National Counterterrorism Center—but it was still a bit off the beaten path.

While Chase Williams had moved out quickly once he was given the job as Op-Center director, assembling a staff and devising an effective concept of operations for the new Op-Center had taken some time. While there were still a few holes to fill, the core staff was largely in place. Also, as part of establishing Op-Center, special relationships were established with the Joint Special Operations Command, the JSOC, as well as with the FBI.

The president had used significant political capital to get Congress to agree to re-create Op-Center. Then there was funding to put in place, hiring authorities to set up within the Office of Personnel Management, and relationships to establish with other organizations inside the executive branch. Finally, there had been the matter of selecting a location and then actually constructing the new Op-Center.

While the reasons for selecting a basement underneath the National Geospatial-Intelligence Agency, constructed from scratch because there was no unused basement in existence, were sound, the actual construction project, like many things done in government, took longer than it should have. During that time, Op-Center had been able to put notches in its belt by eliminating Azka Perkasa and Abdul-Muqtadir Kashif. Fortunately, there had been no major "seam crises" that required Op-Center's attention.

"Boss, we're ready to begin if you are," Anne Sullivan, Op-Center's deputy director, began.

"Great," Williams said. "Looks like you have the usual suspects assembled."

"All mustered, boss," Sullivan replied, a bit of brogue in her speech, a leftover of her early years growing up in East Belfast. "I've asked Roger to kick it off with an intel update."

Early in his tenure as Op-Center director, Chase Williams had told the staff to not address him as "admiral." Sullivan, a career civil servant and retired senior executive supergrade—and the first person Williams hired—had settled on "boss" as a way to address him, and it had stuck.

As Op-Center's intelligence director, the N2, Roger Mc-Cord, rose to begin his briefing. Williams chided him, "So, Roger, I see you've managed to make it all the way in from Reston once again without wrecking your Harley."

"Barely, boss, barely 'cause I think it was your Beamer that almost ran me into a ditch during the merge onto Heller Road," McCord replied, smiling.

"Perhaps," Williams said with a straight face, "but there are a lot of BMWs in this town."

If Williams had a persistent habit, it was to begin meetings on a light note. He also tended to joke with the Op-Center staff with military backgrounds just a bit more than with the others. McCord was a former Marine who commanded the Intelligence Battalion in the Marine Special Operations Command, or MARSOC, and had been a company commander in Fallujah and a battalion exec in Ramadi prior to that. Wounded twice, the second time leaving his right leg so torn up it ended his combat career, he was allowed to remain on active duty while he stood up the MARSOC Intelligence Battalion. Williams figured if anyone on the staff could take some gentle ribbing it was McCord, and he was right.

"Fair enough, I'll try to be a little more careful next time," Williams continued, shaking his head. McCord could give as good as he got, and that pleased him.

"All right, I'm just going to throw up a few slides to recap our discussions over the past month regarding what's going on in the Mideast. No action for Op-Center anticipated yet, but we're following this closely to stay ahead of the problem."

"Excellent. You and Brian are still having your subgroup meetings on this twice a week?" Williams asked.

"We are, boss. Brian's chairing them. I'll let him give you a quick recap before I get rolling."

Williams looked over to his operations director, the N3, Brian Dawson. The man was a wall, six feet four and a hard 225 pounds. Dawson was a recently retired Army colonel and former commander of the 5th Special Forces Group.

"We've kept you up to date regarding the way the United States is surging forces to the Middle East," Dawson began, speaking in precise, almost clipped terms. "The *Truman* carrier strike group is leaving on their rotational deployment six weeks early. The Air Force is surging bombers into theater to just about everywhere we have basing rights, and the Marines are keeping one of their expeditionary strike groups in the Central Command AOR and extending their deployment for at least another month," he said, referring to Central Command's, or CENTCOM's, Area of Responsibility. "There's an enormous amount of churn in the Middle East right now and as you know, most of it is focused on the threats Iran is making against Iraq. The way we see it, this surge is designed to reassure Iraq and to make Iran think twice before carrying out any of their threats."

"I see," Williams replied. "The tension is worse, way worse, than when I was CENTCOM commander, and I can see why we want, and need, more presence in CENTCOM."

If there was one person on the Op-Center staff who thought

like Chase Williams, it was Dawson. A West Pointer with massive contacts in the Pentagon, at CIA, and at State, he had been one of the youngest colonels in the Army and been deep-promoted numerous times. Operationally, he was rock solid. He left the Army before the selection board convened to consider him for his first star. Dawson said he wanted to go out while he was on top, and the top for Dawson was operational command.

"Roger will give you the intel background on all this."

"Good."

"Boss," McCord began, "you were the CENTCOM commander for three years, so I know I don't need to give you a primer about tensions there. The intelligence community has increased the number of analysts looking at this, but in essence, the centrifugal forces the Arab Awakening released are still having a ripple effect. The militaries in an increasing number of countries are having so much trouble dealing with internal unrest in their major cities that they're less and less able to deal with terrorist groups operating in the hinterlands."

"Yeah, got that," Williams replied. "Nothing we didn't see coming back in 2011, is it, Roger?"

"Maybe not in kind, but in degree," McCord continued. "In many ways, some of these countries—Yemen, Syria, even Egypt—are becoming almost like Lebanon, even Afghanistan."

"And you know how massively we've increased security at embassies in the region over the past several years," Dawson added. "Still, even at that, boss, you see why we're surging forces into the region as a precaution."

"No, I get all that," Williams replied. "I think you all have summed up the situation, and Brian, I know you know the tribal politics in the region as well as anyone. As you all continue to plan, let's factor in how we might get our JSOC cell into the region if we need to."

"Well, boss, I'm no Gertrude Bell," Dawson began, referring to the English archaeologist whose subtle understanding of tribal politics helped the British administer Iraq during the colonial period. "Even so, you're right. If we move in on the ground there, I'll need to reach out to the right tribal chieftains. Having them on our side will be crucial, especially once you get a few miles away from the cities and out into the deserts."

As the morning briefing continued, Chase Williams reflected on where Op-Center had been and where it was going. They had come out of the gate fast and made their bones in finding and taking out Azka Perkasa and Abdul-Muqtadir Kashif for the stadium bombings. It was an act of justice as well as revenge. Plus they had accomplished this while they were moving to a new location and before he had recruited and assembled his full staff.

If there was anything that had kept Williams centered during his long career of service it was to pause often to count his blessings. One of those blessings was the trust he had in the staff he had so carefully assembled. Another was the trust the president had continued to place in him.

After the serious business of eliminating Perkasa and Kashif was over, Op-Center had not been called into action again. Since then, Op-Center had been just been an expensive, but unused, asset. The president signaled his confidence in Williams by letting him and Sullivan continue to build the capability they knew they needed and train their team. Yet, they both had to admit, they didn't anticipate the costs of the Geek Tank Williams had promised the president he would create from whole cloth.

Williams was especially grateful for the fact that the president had never complained about the expense, or meddled as Williams got Op-Center up and running. Most of their interaction was through their POTUS/OC Eyes Only memos. Much of what Williams communicated to the president were reminders about the new, professional threat facing the nation. Without burying the president in details, Williams had carefully explained how Op-Center was organizing to defeat this new threat.

Half a world away, in his palace in Riyadh, Prince Ali al-Wandi was setting the wheels in motion to keep his dream of reaping the riches his position as "pipeline czar" for Saudi Arabia's multibillion-dollar oil pipeline was going to bring him from slipping away. Forces completely beyond his control had put the project in jeopardy, but he had found a solution. He had one more task to perform, and then he would go and see what his handpicked crew had created many miles to the northeast in the Saudi desert.

"Enter," he said as he pushed his 245-pound body from the expensive chair behind his smoke tree burl desk in his personal office. He moved around his desk to greet his visitor, pausing to catch his breath from this momentary exertion.

"Your Excellency!" the man said. "Thank you for agreeing to see me."

"You have done good work, and I thought it was time we met face-to-face. Sit, please," Al-Wandi said, motioning to one of the two chairs in front of his desk.

"It was an honor to be of service to a member of the royal family."

Al-Wandi knew that was a lie. The man had done it for the money, plain and simple. He had paid him a substantial sum up front, and promised him even more upon delivery. Now this man was here to collect.

"Remind me again how you were able to obtain this technology," the prince said, his voice conveying natural curiosity. He had acted through intermediaries to have the man do this for him, and he wanted to assure himself there were no loose ends—no trail that would lead back to him.

His visitor hesitated a moment. He didn't know whether he should share this secret, but Ali al-Wandi had paid him well. Now the job was done. All he wanted to do was collect his money. Perhaps there would be another job and another payday in the future if he told the prince what he wanted to know.

"Your Excellency, until recently, I was an officer in our Royal Saudi Air Force and worked at a base where the Americans operated their Global Hawk unmanned aerial vehicle. The Americans were in the process of selling us our own UAVs, and I was one of the officers picked to learn how to operate them."

"But, if you were just a UAV operator, how did you get hold of the technology?" the prince asked.

"It was easier than you think, Your Excellency. The United States was anxious to reduce its presence at our air bases and the contractors who taught us how to operate these UAVs were eager to sell these birds to the kingdom. In their zeal to ensure we kept our enthusiasm for these birds, they were . . . well . . . a bit careless in protecting their technology."

Prince Ali inquired, "So you were able to just walk off with the technology that controls these UAVs?"

"Not precisely. As is always the case in such matters, money changed hands, but I assure you what I paid, and what you are paying, is a small price compared to the capability that you now have."

"Indeed, indeed," the prince replied. "You have earned your money. My assistant tells me you delivered what we needed to him yesterday morning."

"Yes, Excellency, I did." The man had, in fact, taken risks, many risks, and this Saudi prince had an immense personal fortune. What he was getting for his efforts was really a pittance, he rationalized. He smiled as he watched al-Wandi open his desk drawer and fish around for his reward, undoubtedly an envelope stuffed full of even more riyals than he received when he first took this assignment.

Al-Wandi rose and his visitor rose, too. But the man's smile turned to a look of terror as he stared at the prince's hand. The hand didn't hold an envelope with riyals. He was looking at the ominously long barrel of a pistol!

"You have earned your reward, my friend," Ali al-Wandi said as he leveled his pistol at the man's head.

The silencer did its job and suppressed some, but not all, of the sound. The bullet hit him square in the right eye and he went down like a dropped sack, blood, bone, and tissue erupting from the back of his head.

Ali al-Wandi's bodyguard appeared moments later.

"It's done," the prince said. "Get rid of his body and clean up this mess."

Ali al-Wandi took no delight in killing. Actually, the act repulsed him, but obtaining this technology was the last step in an intricate chain of events the prince had conceived, and he could not leave anything to chance. With this man dead, nothing could be traced to him. Yet there was another issue. He operated in the shadows, but not in a vacuum. Those who did know of his business, like his bodyguard detail, had to fear him as well as obey him. The fact that he was not afraid to take a life, as well as to order it to be taken, would now not be wasted on those close to him.

His bodyguard bowed with a new measure of respect as al-Wandi strode out of the room.

"Three minutes till landing. Cinch down your seat harnesses, and tight!"

Laurie Phillips and her fellow passengers aboard the U.S. Navy Carrier-Onboard-Delivery aircraft needed no further urging from the COD's crewman. The 240-mile flight from Norfolk, Virginia, to USS *Harry S. Truman* had been a bumpy one, and Phillips had already filled up her "barf bag" with what was once her lunch. What seemed like a good idea months ago, furthering her career at the Center for Naval Analyses by taking an assignment as a CNA analyst aboard the *Aegis*-class cruiser USS *Normandy,* now seemed like a really bad idea.

"Can you see the ship?" Laurie shouted to the man sitting next to her as they both hunched down in their backward-facing seats. They were already bracing for what they knew would be a bone-jarring landing, actually more of a controlled crash, on *Truman*'s four-and-a-half-acre flight deck.

Her seatmate stared out the tiny window, one of only two windows in the entire cargo compartment, or tube, of the C-2A. He was unable to make himself heard above the deafening roar of the aircraft's two Allison T56-A-425 turboprop engines. So he turned toward Phillips, smiled weakly, and shook his head from side to side. *Truman* might be down there, but the dark gray clouds just below them completely obscured the surface of the Atlantic, to say nothing of the ship they were trying to land on.

Laurie saw the fear in the man's eyes and hoped she wasn't registering the same fear herself, but she knew she was. Why had she gotten herself into this mess?

"Arrughh," choked Laurie reflexively as the COD pilot chopped the throttles and the aircraft dropped from the sky like a rock. They hurtled down through the dirty, swirling clouds toward the *Truman*'s wet, pitching flight deck.

Deep inside *Truman*, the Tactical Flag Command Center, TFCC for short, was the hub where the flag officer responsible for the ships, aircraft, and eight thousand men and women of the

Truman carrier strike group directed the group's efforts. Admiral Ben Flynn had more important things to worry about than Laurie Phillips and her fellow passengers.

"Chief of Staff," he said to his second in command, "we did a damn fine job on our final joint training exercise. Hell, we hit it out of the ballpark. We should be pumped up, but the staff seems down. I know we're not getting our normal thirty days in port for predeployment rest and resupply time, but we've got a damned important mission to do."

"They're a little stressed, Admiral, that's for sure," his COS replied, "but it's not because we're deploying to the Middle East. They're all ready to do their duty, but everyone counted on this final period in port to spend some quality time at home. They all had to scramble to get a bunch of last-minute things done before leaving their families behind for six months."

The loud, persistent hum of the air conditioning allowed Flynn and his COS to have a private conversation in the corner of TFCC. Across the dimly lit space, the two officers and four sailors in the command center tracked ship and air traffic on their two seventy-two-inch large-screen displays and on multiple smaller workstations. Status boards displaying all manner of tactical and operational information competed for space on the steel matte-black bulkheads of TFCC. Transmissions from several radios periodically crackled from various speakers in the overhead.

"I know that, COS, but this crisis has reached its flashpoint. The president has always called on the Navy to be his first responders," Flynn replied. "Remember what happened in the

Mideast in 2011? All it took was for some damn street vendor in Tunisia, what was his name, Mohammed Bouazizi, that's it, to set himself on fire in December 2010, for God's sake, and that started a crisis that snowballed to a half dozen countries. And things haven't calmed down there since."

The COS nodded in agreement, knowing his admiral was right. Despite major diplomatic efforts by every American president stretching back to Jimmy Carter, the greater Middle East remained a strategic riddle and one that demanded constant attention. Now, in the aftermath of the Iraq and Afghanistan wars and in the wake of the forces unleashed by the 2011 Arab Spring, Mideast tensions were high. In Ben Flynn's professional experience, they were higher than at any time since Saddam invaded Kuwait and threatened Saudi Arabia in 1991.

Yet the immediate reason for the *Truman* strike group's rushed deployment was Iran. The theocratic government, now widely thought to be armed with nuclear weapons, had ratcheted up its rhetoric toward Iraq. The United States had spent enormous blood and treasure to oust Saddam, quell a long-running insurgency, and prop up the fledging Iraqi state. Virtually all U.S. ground forces were out of the Middle East. Now it was up to U.S. Navy carrier and expeditionary strike groups to deter Iran from moving against Iraq or threatening their other neighbors. If the United States had learned anything during its long history of trying to ensure stability in the Middle East, it was how counterproductive it was to put boots on the ground. All that did was enrage potential jihadists. No, naval presence was the answer and that was precisely what Flynn and the

Truman strike group were going to bring to the region—*presence.* As radicalized as the mullahs governing Iran were, they did understand the firepower a U.S. Navy carrier strike group could unleash.

Flynn turned to his operations officer. "Ops O, once we get that COD aboard, what's next?"

"Admiral, Fleet Forces Command gave us thirty-six hours to get all our people and parts flown out to the strike group before we put the East Coast behind us. Then it's a dash for the Mediterranean and through Suez. We're actually ahead of the power curve and still have about sixteen hours to get everything done."

"Then stay on it," Flynn replied. "I want those supply pukes to get us everything, and I mean *everything,* we need for this deployment."

"We're on the phone with them continuously," said his logistics officer, raising his voice to be heard as an F/A-18F Super Hornet came aboard. The screech of the jet smashing into *Truman*'s flight deck and the near deafening, grinding sound of the arresting gear drowned out the man's words. Reflexively, everyone in TFCC paused and looked up at the small camera monitor in the corner of the command center that showed the aircraft safely snared on *Truman*'s flight deck. Not all of those in TFCC were aviators, but they all knew the landing of a high-performance aircraft on a carrier was a crash landing—a safe landing, but nonetheless a crash.

"We've been fortunate so far, Admiral," the logistics officer continued. "If the weather holds, we'll be able to run our COD flights continuously, and with any luck we'll get all the gear we need."

On board the COD at that moment, Laurie Phillips felt anything but lucky. "What was that?" she asked of no one in particular as lightning flashed on both sides of the aircraft. The bird continued its rapid decent through the clouds as it was tossed about in the severe turbulence. Laurie flinched as the lightning flashed again and the booming thunder made it sound like they were inside a kettledrum. She watched the man next to her cinch his harness tighter and she followed suit.

"Forty-five seconds till landing," shouted the COD crewman as he waved his arms animatedly to ensure the eighteen passengers crammed into the COD's tube knew they were about to impact *Truman*'s flight deck. If they weren't terrified enough already, the crewman's crazed look and maniacal gesturing now put them over the edge of fear. As she screwed her five-foot eight-inch, 135-pound frame down into her seat and braced for the impact of the landing on *Truman*'s flight deck, Laurie began to dread what she suspected would be an equally harrowing helicopter flight onward from *Truman* to *Normandy*.

The *Normandy*. Once she got to *Normandy*, she had no idea of what to expect. She had never even been on the ship; the Center for Naval Analyses typically didn't have their analysts show up on their assigned Navy ships until a few days before a scheduled deployment. All she had to go on were sea stories from CNA colleagues who had had similar assignments in the past, and one e-mail from the ship's operations officer. *Normandy*'s ops officer had told her that she'd "enjoy her challenging assignment."

Her mind snapped back to the COD as it continued dropping out of the sky. *The challenge of staying alive in this rattletrap aircraft is more than enough, thank you.*

"WHACK!" The COD smashed into *Truman*'s flight deck at 120 miles per hour and Laurie prepared for what she had been told would come next, the aircraft jerking to a halt as the arresting wire snagged the bird—but they were still moving!

Up in the cockpit of the COD, the drama of the carrier-landing dance took a turn for the worse. "Bolter, bolter, bolter," shouted the landing signal officer, or LSO, the pilot on the platform jutting out from the port side of the flight deck who was in charge of coaching the COD down to the ship's deck. The LSO watched the Greyhound's arresting hook hanging down under the aircraft skip over each of the four arresting wires, or "bolter," and saw the plane continue hurtling down the carrier's deck.

"Power, POWER," shouted the COD's pilot to his copilot. The copilot needed no further urging; she had already fire-walled the engines, jamming and holding them into position to generate the power needed to get the lumbering aircraft away from the water a hundred feet below them.

"POWER, keep it climbing!" yelled the air boss from his perch in *Truman*'s tower high above the flight deck. The COD crossed the deck edge and begin settling toward the sea's looming surface, now less than seventy-five feet away.

The COD wallowed as it slid further below the level of the flight deck, its engines howling in protest as they strained to arrest the descent. The pilots pointed the gawky plane straight ahead, trying to minimize their control movements as the Greyhound clawed its way back into the air and away from the menacing water below.

"Oh my God," Laurie said, although no one could hear her.

Slowly, almost imperceptibly, the COD began to climb away from the water. The lighting flashed around them, and Laurie silently prayed to be delivered from what she was sure was going to be the aircraft crashing down into the swirling Atlantic below.

"Greyhound, the pattern is yours; when comfortable, turn downwind," the air boss instructed.

"What happened?" Laurie shouted to anyone who might hear her as her terror ratcheted up several notches, especially after catching a momentary glimpse *up* at *Truman*'s flight deck. No one heard her above the din of the aircraft noise, but the look in the crewman's eyes, a look of someone who had been through this harrowing experience many times before and was almost gleeful these poor devils were experiencing it, too, told her more than she wanted to know. This was a really bad idea.

"Here we go again, folks," the crewman shouted three minutes later, after the COD had lumbered around the landing pattern and lined up on short final for another attempt.

"Easy with it, easy with it," said the landing signal officer. This LSO was a pro. His voice was neutral, controlled, and even a little gentle. A bolter sapped any pilot's confidence, and he wanted to get the COD down on this approach before its pilots really started to clutch.

"Little power . . . you're a half mile from the ship . . . easy with the power . . . EASY . . . right for lineup . . . keep her coming . . . easy, *easy* with the power," he said in the most soothing voice he could muster, trying to coax the aircraft down onto the gyrating deck.

Lightning flashed again, and the booming thunder told them the developing storm was intensifying.

With only a quarter mile to go before impacting the deck, the COD wallowed like a drunk as its pilots struggled desperately to follow the soft-spoken commands. In the tube, there was complete silence, and even the crewman had lost some of his bravado. Laurie willed herself to keep her eyes open, although she didn't want to.

"Left just a bit . . . OK . . . don't settle . . . little more power . . . that's it . . . attaboy . . . power, more power!"

Faster control movements by the pilots now, seconds away from the moment of truth, the round-down, the curved, aft end of the flight deck, looming up at them, almost daring them to impale their aircraft on it short of the landing zone.

"Right for lineup, a little right, steady, easy with the power, *easy, easy with it*"—the LSO's commands were coming on now like a tape on fast-forward—"steady, steady, don't settle, a little power, *easy with it* . . ."

SLAM . . . SCREECH . . . the COD smashed into *Truman*'s deck, caught the number four wire, the last arresting wire, and was jerked to a halt in seconds, slinging Laurie and her terrified fellow passengers against their seat belts like rag dolls. Laurie Phillips took a deep breath. *My God, I'm alive—I think.* She didn't know what was ahead of her or what awaited her on board *Normandy*, but surely it couldn't be worse than this. Could it?

CHAPTER FIFTEEN

Op-Center Headquarters, Fort Belvoir North, Fairfax County, Virginia
(February 14, 1130 Eastern Standard Time)

One of the first things Chase Williams did after hiring Anne Sullivan was arrange their calendars to enable him to have lunch with his deputy once a week without fail. This was a carryover from his many command tours during his Navy career. He believed strongly if the relationship between the commander and the deputy wasn't rock solid the enterprise would fail, and fail spectacularly.

The National Geospatial-Intelligence Agency's atrium cafeteria wasn't gourmet, not by a long stretch, but it made a decent chicken salad. Two chicken salads, along with freshly baked croissants and two glasses of Diet Coke, were sitting on the small, round table in Williams's office in the NGA basement when Sullivan arrived at his door precisely at 1130.

"Mornin', boss. Still good for lunch now?" Sullivan asked. Wearing a Blue Akris suit and off-white blouse with Manolo black pumps and sporting a twenty-inch Akoya pearl necklace with matching earrings, Anne Sullivan looked the part of a powerful, but understated, professional woman.

"As always," Williams replied as he rose from his desk to greet his number two.

As Chase Williams seated Sullivan, he remembered why he hired her. He needed a number two who brought things to the table he did not. She did that in spades.

Anne Sullivan was a retired General Services Administration super grade who had made a career in Washington. She knew *all* about the government, including government contracting, hiring, firing, and funding, and how to sidestep the issues. These were things Williams never had to deal with, even during his multiple tours in Washington.

Unlike Williams, Sullivan came from money. Her father had fashioned a successful and lucrative career in finance with Bain Capital Ventures. Between that family money and her GSA pension, she was looking forward to a comfortable life as a retiree. She enjoyed the D.C. social and cultural scene and traveled often, primarily to Europe and especially to Ireland. That plan was interrupted when Williams recruited her—charmed her, really, she readily admitted—to be his deputy.

"So what's on our agenda today, Anne?"

"You wanted me to update you on how close we are to getting our Geek Tank fully up and running. As you know, they've been pretty demanding, and there's always some latest technology that they've simply got to have. Now that we've got their last server rack installed, I've just got to get them one more LCD display and I think they'll be pretty happy—for now."

"Still take some getting used to, don't they?"

"Ah, I'm OK with them, boss, but I'm afraid Roger is still struggling. Coming from where he spent most of his professional life, he still does a double take every now and then. Yet we agree on one thing: They are all incredibly gifted, and they don't mind working long after all the rest of us are done for the day. I can see why you recruited them."

"I promised the president we'd create something different, and they are the cutting edge of our intelligence operation."

"They're good alright, and Roger says they've mostly stopped griping about no surfing beaches nearby and having to wear grown-up clothes. Still, they come in every Friday wearing their T-shirts."

"T-shirts?"

"Yeah, boss, they had some high-end designer make them these gaudy T-shirts with a picture of the National Geospatial-Intelligence Agency's HQ building in the background and the words 'Geek Tank' in huge letters on top of that. It's kind of their fashion statement."

"Sounds like what we used to call unit cohesion in the military," Williams replied, smiling.

If there was one part of Op-Center that was completely different from anything that had ever existed before, it was the unit Chase Williams and Roger McCord dubbed their Geek Tank. Williams had promised the president he would build an intelligence organization with a collation architecture and algorithms that could electronically filter all raw intelligence data and distill the basic elements of a problem faster than even the best analysts. He drew great satisfaction that he had done just that.

On his first flag officer assignment, Williams had directed Deep Blue, the Navy staff's think tank. During that time, as well as during his subsequent tours, Williams had been a champion of innovation in the Navy. He had consulted frequently with the best minds in Silicon Valley and was on a first-name basis with many of its industry leaders. When he showed up years later, this time in a business suit rather than a Navy uniform, he found those CEOs still remembered him. When he asked for help in recruiting top talent for a classified national defense project, those same corporate leaders proved to be patriots. Far from being territorial and guarding their best talent, they helped Williams find those young men and women who were not only technically brilliant, but also welcomed the challenge of being involved in national security work. Aaron Bleich was his first hire and had already earned his spurs with the hits on Perkasa and Kashif. Now under McCord and Bleich's direction, they had built the capability Williams had promised the president.

It hadn't been an easy run, he had to admit. Some of his new geeks had not fully understood what they would be getting into and had asked to leave the project. He had also not anticipated the amount, and expense, of the equipment and software they needed to do what had to be done. Thankfully, as Sullivan had just briefed him, they were up and running, and most of the major expense was behind them.

"Think we ought to support that unit cohesion by getting

some of those T-shirts and showing up in the Geek Tank one Friday, Anne?"

"I'll see to it, boss," she added with a chuckle. "Pick your color carefully."

"I will. And to be honest with you, I find myself spending more time with those folks than with almost anyone else on the Op-Center staff. I see you snooping around there a lot. They seem to have piqued your curiosity, too."

"Ah, just want to see our biggest investment at work." Sullivan paused. "I'm not sure what it is, boss, but I just like being around them. They are so smart, but they are also simple, honest, and straightforward. It's refreshing. They don't have agendas," she said, smiling. "I guess that comes from being a career bureaucrat in this town, where *everyone* has an agenda—present company excluded," she added quickly.

Williams just smiled. Beyond the skills he knew she would bring to Op-Center, he found himself continuing to be struck by Sullivan's wisdom.

Anne Sullivan all but worshiped Williams. Never married, and with no significant other, she had a wide array of outside interests, especially theater and dance. She also had a large extended family, consisting of three older sisters and one younger one, as well as two younger brothers, and traveled regularly to Ireland, where she still had strong family roots. When it came to finding the right place and person to focus her professional passion and loyalty, she had found that in Chase Williams. Loyal as opposed to patriotic, she wanted, even needed, someone to be loyal to. Williams was the one.

"Anything else on your agenda today, Anne?"

"Yes. Let me give you the details of some of the new hardware and software we're installing in our command module. It's a capability Brian Dawson says we need, and I agreed with the purchase."

Their meeting continued, two seasoned professionals building what the nation needed and would come to call on again.

Half a world away, Prince Ali al-Wandi sat in his office in the Saudi Oil Ministry. He had now killed a man in cold blood. It bothered him at first but he told himself, this was business, both the doing and doing it himself. He realized, and not for the first time, he would do anything to see this project through. While al-Wandi was clearly the czar of Saudi Arabia's multibillion-dollar pipeline, he was still subservient to the head of the Oil Ministry, Prince Nayef. The oil minister was a lazy bureaucrat, and he was beginning to resent al-Wandi's fame. He reflected on a meeting with Nayef where he had had to work mightily to keep the project on track. Ali al-Wandi had surprised Nayef and asked for 80 million more riyals (about US$20 million) because his ambitious project was running over budget. Nayef had summoned him to his office on no notice.

"Enter," Nayef replied to the knock on the open door of his opulent office, not bothering to look up at al-Wandi.

"You wanted to see me, Minister," Ali began, barely hiding his annoyance. He was making things happen while this . . . this . . . bureaucrat did nothing but sit on his fat ass.

"Questions have come from the royal court," Nayef lied.

"They are beginning to have misgivings about this project, and there is even talk about terminating it." Nayef had no trouble with the big lie; he wanted to put al-Wandi off balance.

Al-Wandi was able to hide his shock, but his brain was spinning. What was this all about? Why now? He'd only asked for 80 million riyals. Didn't this pencil pusher get it?

"Minister, perhaps this is a good time to recap. Nothing has changed since you secured permission from His Majesty to undertake this project except the costs of labor and materials have gone up, not to mention the cost of security."

"As you say," Nayef replied. His tone and body language were all wrong.

"Here, I brought this just to refresh," al-Wandi continued, rolling out a large map on Nayef's desk.

The map showed the new pipeline at first taking the route of the old British Trans-Arabian Pipeline, abandoned decades ago. Then, instead of following the path of the old pipeline through Lebanon, it split off to the north through Jordan and Syria, then west to the Mediterranean at the Syrian port of Baniyas.

Nayef traced the dark red path of the pipeline, his hand stopping as it crossed into Syria and his finger tapping involuntarily.

"Yes," al-Wandi said, acknowledging that country's continued disquiet. "It's not Switzerland, but the Alawite military regime is firmly in control, and our money will help make sure they stay in power."

Al-Wandi didn't mind pandering to Nayef if it got him

what he wanted. Yet, just what was Nayef's game? Al-Wandi sensed there hadn't been any questions from the royal court, and certainly not from the king; he was in his mideighties and all but senile. No, Nayef just wanted to throw his weight around and show him who was boss. Fine.

"Doesn't the pipeline go through tribal lands from here . . . to here," Nayef said, tracing along the route al-Wandi had lain out.

"It does, and the tribal chieftains who control that portion of the desert will be paid, as will the central government officials."

Even though the pipeline was almost a year from completion, al-Wandi was already brokering multiyear oil futures deals throughout a Europe hungry for Saudi oil, and skimming considerable money off the top of every deal. All he had to do was to deliver the oil to cash in on hundreds of millions of riyals in personal wealth. He wasn't going to let Nayef screw that up.

"Yes, I can see all that," Nayef murmured, "but I don't see the return on investment here. Is there really going to be that large a payoff?"

"The riches that will come into the kingdom via this pipeline will dwarf the up-front investment. Our economists have pulled together substantial data, and paid handsomely for other information. What they have found is that the nations we once knew as Eastern Europe—Bulgaria, Romania, Poland, and the others—are at the beginning of a major economic expansion."

Al-Wandi paused for emphasis.

"Their thirst for oil is set to double or even triple, over the next decade and a half. It's a market Russia cannot begin to fill. We need to be first to market and have the ability to ship oil directly to them. And we can't be hostage to Iran, or anyone else who might choose to block the sea routes our oil must now take, who wants to keep us from getting our oil to market—"

"The United States would never let that happen!" Nayef exclaimed, interrupting him and challenging al-Wandi's logic.

"Ten or even five years ago, Minister, I would have agreed with you. However, the close bond we once had with the United States is fraying. The free rein we had when the House of Bush and House of Saud were figuratively joined at the hip is over. The relationship was never as good as it was when one of the Bushes was in office."

"Yes, I'll give you that."

"Then, as you know, our bond with the United States began to fray more when we clamped down on our people during the so-called Arab Spring in 2011, and when we rolled tanks into Bahrain to help quell their protests, that bond took a major hit. Add to that the fact that the United States has discovered enormous shale oil deposits and sooner or later won't be nearly as dependent on Gulf oil from anyone, and we can't count on the United States for anything."

"I see," Nayef replied, beginning to be swayed by al-Wandi's logic.

The conversation went on as Ali continued to lay out the facts and add his own spin, and eventually Nayef promised the additional 80 million riyals.

Ali al-Wandi smiled with satisfaction at how he had worked

Nayef, but that gratification was short-lived as he recalled a subsequent meeting. Now it was more than his reputation and status that were tied up in the pipeline; it was now part of his personal fortune. The meeting where Nayef had shaken him down remained a bitter memory. He replayed the meeting in his head, the bile in his stomach churning.

It was late afternoon in Riyadh, and Prince Ali al-Wandi was packing his Tony Perotti black leather briefcase when his assistant came in. "Your Excellency, Prince Nayef has asked to see you, and he says it's urgent."

Al-Wandi just rolled his eyes. He had had the man checking their construction account several times a day since Nayef had promised him the 80 million riyals, but thus far nothing had been deposited. "Have you checked the account this afternoon?"

"Yes, Your Excellency, nothing yet."

"He probably wants me to grovel some more," al-Wandi muttered.

Al Wandi brushed past his assistant and strode down the long hallway toward Nayef's office. He was getting tired of this lazy oaf making his life difficult. It was one thing if he felt the need to remind him who was boss from time to time. Fine. It was a relatively small price to pay for the fame, and access, he had garnered in his new role as pipeline czar, to say nothing of the fortune he was skimming off the top for each oil futures deal he made. Now Nayef was costing him money.

He needed the 80 million riyals to keep the pipeline project moving at the pace they had planned on. There were construction companies, suppliers, and security services to pay. Because of the lack of ready cash, a few of them had begun to withhold services and supplies.

As he entered Nayef's outer office, al-Wandi was steaming and made straight for Nayef's desk.

"Your Excellency, you asked to see me?" al-Wandi all but barked, almost spitting the words "Your Excellency" at Nayef.

"Yes, yes, please sit down."

Al-Wandi sat in one chair, facing Nayef just a few feet away.

"Yes, well, I suspect you know the funding you have asked for has not been deposited yet."

"Yes, I know that," al-Wandi answered abruptly.

"Well, there is a problem, you see."

"A problem?"

"Yes, a problem. I took this to His Majesty and the king is . . . well, to be truthful, he's not completely convinced we need to move forward this rapidly."

"Not sure?"

"Yes. Now hear me out, please. I know you are dedicated to this project, and His Majesty knows that, too. Yet you also must know what a drain this is on the kingdom's resources."

Oh, so this is what this is about. Nayef needs to plead poverty. Very well, I'll hold my tongue and listen, up to a point.

"Yes," al-Wandi replied. He didn't know where this was going, but he figured if he kept saying yes, Nayef would get to the point and get this charade over with.

"Well, as I'm sure you know, the US$60 billion commitment we made with the United States in 2011 to buy weapons has been a drain on the kingdom's treasury. You also know all too well the price of oil has not reached the levels we projected. Further, no one had anticipated . . ."

Nayef droned on, laying out the kingdom's financial woes. Yet al-Wandi still didn't know where this was going. His project was going to solve many of those woes. Was Nayef really that dense?

"So, in speaking with His Majesty, he is willing to add the additional eighty million riyals to the project's funding stream. However, he would like you to add some of your personal funds to the project, just to show good faith mind you. His Majesty was thinking in the neighborhood of perhaps thirty-five million riyals."

Al-Wandi's head was spinning. Was Nayef bluffing? Did the king really decide this? Did he dare call his bluff?

"That is vastly more money than I have. I'm just a humble servant."

"Well, no, that's not quite right. You see, we have examined your finances."

"Examined my finances!" al-Wandi exclaimed, pushing himself out of his chair. "Who are you to 'examine my finances'? This is enough. You say this is coming from the king. Then let's go see him—now! He can tell me this himself."

"Now calm down. It's not possible to see His Majesty; he is at the Intercontinental London Park Lane in his usual suite of rooms. He is in England for a medical procedure, but, I assure you, these are his wishes."

Al-Wandi sat back down. Examining his finances? Asking him to put up his own money for this project? Why?

Nayef broke the silence.

"I would have assumed you would not have to think about this. As you said a moment ago, you are a servant of the kingdom, and these are His Majesty's wishes."

Al-Wandi just sat mute. Nayef had put him in a box.

"So I must ask you again. Will you put up your own thirty-five million riyals to support this important project or not?"

"Yes," al-Wandi mumbled.

"Good. Then we are done. May Allah be with you and with our pipeline project."

Al-Wandi all but staggered out of Nayef's office and headed for the safety of his own office suite. He needed time to think.

After Prince Nayef had held him up for the initial thirty-five million riyals, he had come back to him three more times to put up additional money of his own, always upping the ante, and always as a "show of good faith for the king." Now he was personally invested in the pipeline to the tune of over 250 million riyals.

His accountants had worked feverishly to ensure he would be the first person paid when the oil revenues the pipeline would generate found their way to the kingdom. Al-Wandi smiled to himself. Then he would be a hero and there would be money for everyone. He seldom drank anything stronger than tea, but once the money began rolling in he would part with that established practice. He had already purchased two bottles of 2005 Dom Perignon White Gold Jeroboam to celebrate when the first tanker was filled with pipeline oil in the Syrian port of Baniyas. That was in the future, or what he hoped was the future.

That all changed in an instant, and Prince Ali al-Wandi's world was turned upside down. What was worse, he didn't see it coming.

With the pipeline nearing completion, disaster struck for al-Wandi. Fueled by the 2011 uprisings, and especially by the Assad family's brutal murder and repression of the Syrian people, Syria took a major lurch toward instability. The Syrian government, still dominated by the Alawites, was especially hostile to Saudi Arabia because of how ruthlessly the Saudis suppressed their own popular uprisings in 2011, to say nothing of how their autocratic state repressed its people today. When the dust had settled and some semblance of stability had been restored, the Syrian government reneged on the pipeline deal with Saudi Arabia and agreed to pay back the huge advance they had received "in due course."

Now the government in Syria was not only impacting the Saudi monarchy, it was impacting *him*! No amount of manipulation, cajoling, or outright bribery of Syrian government officials by Prince Ali had been able to sway their decision. He suddenly went from being the toast of the Saudi royal court to the scapegoat for everything wrong with the kingdom. How much effort had he put into working his way to a position of power near the top of the Saudi Oil Ministry bureaucracy? How much money, and part of his own personal fortune to boot, had he lavished on those ministers and bureaucrats in Jordan and Syria until they relented and allowed the Saudis to build the huge pipeline from the Saudi oil fields through their countries to the Mediterranean? And now it would go up in smoke? Not if he could help it.

He was working to turn things around, but he couldn't do it if the Saudi oil minister kept summoning him to his office to explain himself. Another beckoning. *What now?*

"So, Ali," Nayef began once Al-Wandi was seated in his office. "You told us this was a fail-safe plan. Now we have spent billions and your pipeline is almost complete and we will realize nothing from it!"

"We still can! Don't you see? Syria is the problem. The government is trying to consolidate power and doing it at our expense."

"Yes, of course, I see that, you fool!" Nayef shouted. "You said you could take care of that, but clearly you can't."

"I've used all the resources I could lay my hands on, but the Syrian government won't budge. There's no way I could have anticipated this when we started the project. Now we have no choice but to attack them and force them to let us complete our pipeline," al-Wandi continued. "We've paid the Americans tens of billions of dollars for the best military technology we could buy. If we strike while the current Syrian government is still trying to consolidate power, we should be able to reverse this setback. The new Syrian leaders know nothing about how to use their military. They'll sue for peace soon after we begin our initial attacks."

Nayef looked at al-Wandi as if he'd been shot. "Now, wait a

minute. Don't underrate the Syrians. We both know their military is vastly superior to ours," Prince Nayef retorted. "If we attack them, not only will they repulse our forces, they could well attack our oil fields, and then where would we be?"

"Our military has the strength to prevail against the Syrians," Al-Wandi persisted. The heated debate raged on, with Nayef and Prince Ali trading point and counterpoint. Finally, al-Wandi played his trump card.

"What if the Americans were to help us with this?"

Nayef was caught off guard. "What do you know that I do not?"

"I know the Americans are not happy with things in Syria. What if they were to become even unhappier?" al-Wandi asked furtively.

"Well, that would be to our advantage, but I can't worry about what the Americans may or may not do, and I don't think you should worry about that, either."

"I think there *is* a way to do this!" al-Wandi replied.

"Look, Ali, we're not getting anywhere with this discussion. I don't want to hear any more talk about our nation attacking Syria. Understood?"

"Yes, as you wish," al-Wandi replied as he left Nayef's office.

Ali was seething as he always was when he met with Nayef. Yet he knew the oil minister had a point. While Saudi Arabia possessed a great deal of modern weaponry, most of it courtesy of the United States and the result of a US$60 billion purchase order put in place while the Mideast revolutions were occurring in 2011, it was still not as strong as Syria militarily on the ground. They had the technology, but not the ground combatants. The Syrians had been hardened by years of fighting. They would swarm over the border and make straight for the Saudi capital. The kingdom could be crushed if it went to war with Syria. Their only chance, Ali al-Wandi reasoned, would be if Syria were somehow weakened militarily in a substantial way.

After al-Wandi departed, Nayef sat at his desk, deep in thought. *What does al-Wandi know that I don't? Have I let him have too much power? Where was this talk of war coming from?*

Price Nayef thought about it for a bit longer. He recognized Ali al-Wandi was an emotional man, while he himself was more clearheaded. He had told the so-called oil czar what to do and that was that. *I will just watch him more carefully now.*

Back in his office, al-Wandi knew he had but one course of action. *Now I must have the Americans attack Syria.*

Ali had spent many months working furiously, but surreptitiously, to ensure his dream did not slip away, and now he would redouble his efforts. Syria had to be weakened enough so Saudi Arabia could attack and be assured of winning a war. Or if that couldn't happen, at a minimum, the current Syrian government needed to be decapitated, eliminating those who opposed completion of the pipeline. Only then could al-Wandi complete the pipeline and gain the unrestricted access to the Mediterranean Saudi Arabia needed. He had pulled together a plan that could work, that should work. Now all he had to do was to wait for the Americans to react, but he could only wait so long.

Far to the west of where Prince Ali was trying to salvage his plan and his fortune, USS *Normandy* wallowed in the quartering sea. Captain Pete Blackman, *Normandy*'s commanding officer, sat in bridge chair, his patience wearing thin. Rain pelted the bridge's overhead and the windshield wipers on the bridge's thick, laminated, glass windows moved back forth almost spastically, but unsuccessfully, trying to push the water away. *Normandy*'s bow floundered in the confused seas, forcing the ship's head to vary as much as fifteen degrees from base course, and no one seemed to notice, or care. At least no one seemed to care but Blackman. He looked at the ship's nineteen-year-old helmsman and mustered some semblance of a smile.

"Son, I would appreciate it if you would hold a steady heading, and I know the inbound helo pilots would appreciate it also."

The young sailor grinned and responded, "Aye, aye, Captain, steady as she goes." The old man might be demanding on his department heads and be a bit rough with his junior officers, but he had a soft spot in his heart for his enlisted sailors.

Blackman sat in his leather-covered captain's chair, leaning against *Normandy*'s crest, stitched into the back of the seat cover. The crest featured a lion, an anchor, and other military symbols commemorating the Battle of Normandy, as well as the ship's motto, Vanguard of Victory, a motto Blackman had adopted as his personal slogan. He surveyed the officers and sailors making up the bridge watch team as they swayed from side to side, fighting to maintain their balance on the bridge's steel deck as the ship rolled in heavy seas. *Yes, they are improving,* he had to admit to himself, *but they are still a long way from where they need to be, especially going into a potential combat zone.*

As the young seaman fought to hold the ship on a steady heading, Blackman watched the flight deck TV monitor suspended from the bridge's matte-black overhead. The monitor showed the helo pilot fighting to bring his H-60 aboard *Normandy*'s gyrating flight deck. Above him and to his right, the voice of his landing safety officer blared from the red speaker as he tried to coax the helo onto the deck.

"XO!" he shouted to his executive officer. "We've been at flight quarters for over an hour and a half taking helos the carrier is sending our way. How much longer is this going to last?"

"Once the bird over our deck lands and takes off, our helo will be back here in about a half hour. Then we have one more bird from *Truman* landing here just before sunset. That final helo has a part for our gyrocompass, the last part we need to fix it," his XO replied, hoping some kind of good news would help ease Blackman's frustration over the way his bridge team was handling the ship.

"Great . . . and it's about time! What the hell are we paying those supply weenies for anyway?" Blackman groused to no one in particular.

His exec knew Blackman was always demanding. Now,

with this new Mideast crisis brewing, he knew his captain could almost taste launching salvos of *Normandy's* Tomahawk missiles at a new enemy. The U.S. Navy had pounded Libya with hundreds of Tomahawks in the spring of 2011, and Blackman was deskbound in a Pentagon job then. Now it was his turn.

Before his exec could reply, Blackman demanded, "Well, what's our helo bringing us?"

"Oh, our bird is bringing that Center for Analyses rep joining us for the deployment."

"CNA rep? What the hell are we supposed to do with a geek from some think tank?" Blackman asked, shaking his head in disbelief.

The XO had nothing to offer his captain. Nor was he in any mood to listen. He'd leave it to the CNA rep to tell Blackman why she was there.

Brian Dawson strode into Chase Williams office for their scheduled meeting with the staff international crisis manager, the N31, Hector Rodriquez, in tow.

If Op-Center had a de facto chief of staff, it was the operations director, the N3. Williams liked and needed Dawson, but he was certainly not your run-of-the-mill former Green Beret officer. Williams had recruited Dawson soon after he retired from the Army as a young colonel, based largely on his command tour with the 5th Special Forces Group and his proven ability to think outside the box to get things done. He had precisely the talents and experience Williams knew he needed in an ops director.

No one, in or out of uniform, had Dawson's unique skill set. He spoke all the "right" languages (Arabic, Dari, and Pashto). He was skilled in assignation, extortion, bribery, agent handling, and false-flag recruitment. He had a deep and abiding knowledge of tribal politics, and leaders from other cultures seemed to like and trust him as if he were almost one of them. He also had baggage. As a B-Team leader, he planned the takeover of a small Central Asian country, and was almost cashiered from the Army when he set *himself* up as the interim ruler. He had recovered from that miscue and had, at one time, been a strong candidate for general rank. Yet the Army didn't like controversy surrounding their general officers. Dawson decided not to put it to the vote of a promotion board. He decided to leave the Army following his last operational command.

Williams hired him conditionally, to a one-year-long tryout to see if he could play nice with others. If he passed that test, Williams promised he'd have broad authority as the ops director. Dawson had been with Op-Center for just over ten months, and while he was sometimes impatient and exacting in dealing with others, he had impressed Williams thus far and was on the road to fulfilling his expectations.

"Boss, you wanted to talk about our trip down to Fort Bragg next month to meet with our JSOC troop, so I asked Hector to come on in with me."

"Good call, Brian. Hector, how's it going?"

"Good, Admiral—"

The small man at Dawson's elbow froze as Williams narrowed his eyes. After thirty-one years in the Army, if anyone at Op-Center had trouble not addressing the director by his military rank, it was the former battalion sergeant major, Hector Rodriquez.

"I mean, good, boss!" Rodriquez corrected himself.

"Mets doing OK in spring training so far?"

"Naw, lousy as always, boss, but they'll bounce back come regular season."

Williams just nodded in agreement. He knew his international crisis manager was a passionate New York Mets fan. Unless there was an operational crisis, he made every Mets–Washington Nationals game and bought the highest-price tickets he could afford.

"I'll let Hector brief you on our plan," Dawson began.

If there was one Op-Center staff member Dawson wasn't impatient with, it was Rodriquez. As the international crisis manager, he was "Mr. Outside" and Op-Center's primary link to their JSOC troop. The entire special operations community had enormous respect for Rodriquez and always welcomed him as a brother, and with good reason.

Puerto Rican by birth, Hector Rodriquez was born and raised in New York City and enlisted in the Army right out of high school. He came out of boot camp as an infantryman and went immediately to the 75th Ranger Regiment. After eight years in the 75th, where he rose to E-7 platoon sergeant, he transferred to the Army's Delta Force, where he served for the next five years. As a senior E-7, he then went to the Q-course and into Special Forces, where he became a team sergeant, moved up to battalion sergeant major, and finally became command sergeant major for the 3rd Special Forces Group. Fluent in Spanish and Arabic, he finished his service career as the command sergeant major for the Joint Special Operations Command. Rodriquez knew everyone in the special operations community, and they knew him. Both Williams and Dawson knew he could open any door.

Chase Williams had gotten to know his international crisis manager well. Rodriquez was fifty-two years old, married with six kids. He lived for his family and for the United States of America. He was still fit and looked like he was thirty-five. His wife was twice his size and they were still in love. Their kids lived in fear of disappointing their father. For Williams, Rodriquez *was* America.

"So this is our agenda," Rodriquez began. "You'll see we're going to go over some Operational Plans with Major Volner and Master Guns Moore. Then we're going to review how the logistics worked out for that last surge we did."

The easy banter continued between and among the three men, mapping out their day with their JSOC troop. More so than any two members of his Op-Center staff, Dawson and Rodriquez had bent over backward to acquaint their boss with the special operations community and the Joint Special Operations Command. They knew that when the time came, it would be Williams who would send these professionals downrange into harm's way.

• • •

As Swampfox 248 approached the ship, the weather worsened, making *Normandy*'s flight deck appear small—that is, when Sandee Barron could see it at all. They were slipping below flight minimums, and she had a decision to make.

Ah, but Sandee, darlin', that's why they pay you the big bucks. Not many squadron pilots can do this, but you sure as hell can. She knew they'd be watching. *Read 'em and weep, boys.*

Then she went into the zone. It was part total concentration and part forced relaxation. She knew a part of her *had* to fly the helo, and another part of her *had* to let go in order to release all that muscle memory and experience from hours of flying in dog-shit weather like this. It was not unlike John Williams on the podium with the Boston Pops when he was really on his game—it was experience and technique, but it was also feeling and art.

Sandee Barron came by her confidence naturally. The only child of two Northwestern University college professors, Sandee had an idyllic childhood growing up in Evanston, Illinois. Her parents had visions of her following their same career path and becoming a tenured professor at Northwestern after receiving an Ivy League education. They enrolled her in only the best preschool and primary schools and carefully selected the exclusive Roycemore School as her high school.

Slight in stature, Sandee's focus was on academics and the arts. Always near the top of her class and a straight-A student, Sandee had after school hours that were filled with piano lessons and ballet classes. Her parents didn't wait until her late high school years to begin taking her on college trips. She visited her first Ivy League Campus, the University of Pennsylvania, the summer after her sixth grade, and the college trips—and parental pressure—to pursue an Ivy education only intensified from there.

Midway through her junior year at Roycemore, something happened to Sandee. Even now she couldn't put her finger on it, but it all became too planned, too predictable, too someone else's choice, not hers. She wanted something more, something different, and something she chose. Just what that would be eluded her. Then one evening, while she was laying out her clothes for the next day's classes at Roycemore with the TV on in the background, she heard the sonorous voice of James Earl Jones intoning "America's Navy—a global force for good." For Sandee, it was the solution, a life of adventure, not comfortable predictability.

Sandee's grades and her eye-watering SAT scores made her a competitive candidate for admission to the U.S. Naval Academy, and she easily secured an appointment from her congresswoman. At the Academy she was a good student and fit into the sports culture there by running cross country and was team captain of the women's varsity cross country team her senior year. Once she started running cross country and winning meets her confidence soared and any shyness she had as a younger girl disappeared. She was a blue-chip athlete at a Division One college; she was good—damn good—and she knew it. Call it confidence, call it attitude, but by her senior year at the Academy she had it. *Don't mess with me or I'll run you into the dirt.* Introduced to all branches of the Navy during the school's summer training programs, she chose Naval Aviation because it seemed to offer the best promise of high adventure. Now she was living that adventure. The landing safety officer's voice was insistent.

"Ah, Swampfox 248, LSO here. We're having difficulty holding a heading. Conditions are worsening. You want to abort?"

"Negative, LSO," Sandee heard herself say. She was so in the flow and one with the machine that a part of her neither heard nor registered the exchange with *Normandy*'s landing safety officer, one of her fellow pilots.

When she was in the zone, all her senses sharpened. She could feel the sweat that collected between her lip and her lip microphone; she could smell and taste the burning jet fuel; she could even, without glancing over at her copilot, smell the stench of fear that came from him. If it was his call, they'd be back on the carrier waiting for better weather, but more than all this, she could *feel* the helo—she was one with the machine.

"Ah, 248, you sure about this?"

"Affirmative."

Then, like John Williams during the adagio, she took the MH-60R to a hover over the ship's bucking and kicking landing area and held it there while the flight deck crew hooked up the recovery-assist cable. With the RA cable assisting, it was Sandee's task to finely maneuver the twenty-two-thousand-pound helicopter, with its eighteen-inch landing probe, into the three-foot-by-four-foot hydraulic jaws of the remote securing device—the "mousetrap"—attached to the ship's flight deck.

The LSO, the senior pilot on Sandee's otherwise all-male-pilot detachment, simply shook his head in awe. Only a fellow helo pilot could appreciate what he had just seen; only a helo pilot of immense skill could make that approach and hover in this kind of weather and make it look easy. On the one hand, it was pure, unbiased respect and admiration. On the other, it was a prayer. *Why, God, did you give her that much talent? Why not me?*

Now he knew it was his job to help her get her bird on deck.

"Left two, left one, steady. Land now! Down, down, down. Up, up, UP! Come left a little bit . . . easy with it . . . OK . . . steady . . . *steady!*"

Laurie Phillips couldn't hear the calls from the landing safety officer, and it was just as well. The swirling winds, pounding rain, and gyrating flight deck were forcing the LSO to make his calls loudly, insistently, and increasingly rapidly. With each jerk of the aircraft, Laurie was tossed about in her seat, either bumping into the aircraft's haze-gray soundproofing or knocking her knees against the helo crewman's console in front of her.

Her short conversation with the helo's commander right before they lifted off suddenly sounded prescient.

"All right," Lieutenant Sandee Barron had begun winking at Laurie, *"I'll be your captain today. No smoking. Fasten your seat belt. Turn off all electronic devices. All you have to do is sit back and*

enjoy the flight. Normandy is less than twenty miles away, out ahead of the carrier."

Then Barron's face had hardened a bit. *"Seriously, the weather conditions are marginal, and this will be a bit of a rough flight. But I've done this a lot, and I'm damn good at it. It'll be piece of cake,"* Barron had concluded with another wink.

Laurie, terrified after her COD experience, felt reassured. What was it about this pilot? She had been vaguely aware the Navy had a number of female aviators, but she had never *met* one. She didn't sound cocky, but she did sound confident.

Laurie willed herself to look out the window on her left and down at *Normandy's* pitching flight deck. She'd flown in Marine Corps helos and MV-22 Ospreys during her career in uniform, but they had been based on land, not on ships bobbing around like bathtub toys. Laurie was certain that at any moment their bird would crash on the pitching flight deck below. She willed her body to be transposed back to her warm office and tiny desk at the Center for Naval Analyses headquarters in Alexandria, Virginia, or anywhere else but here.

"Left one. Come left. You're drifting right. Stop right. Don't climb. You're hooked on! Easy, EASY with the power."

The LSO continued to talk, but Sandee Barron no longer heard him; it was just her, the helo, and the moving deck.

You're over the circle. Do it! The muscle memory, the thousand-plus hours of flying, the instincts, took over, and Sandee planted the MH-60R hard in the circle on *Normandy's* flight deck.

Laurie finally exhaled. She was totally disoriented as she found herself in her second completely unfamiliar environment in the last several days. The helo crewman unstrapped her from her seat, grabbed her right arm, and helped her climb out of the bird.

As she staggered out of the helicopter, Laurie's right hand was gripped by the outstretched, outsized hand of Captain Pete Blackman. "Welcome aboard, shipmate!" Blackman shouted over the roar of the helicopter's slapping blades and howling T700-GE-401C engines.

"Glad to be here," Laurie lied. It was the captain's custom to greet every new "shipmate" personally and administer a firm handshake. It let them know who was in charge right away.

As Blackman continued to pump Laurie's hand, the pilots chopped the throttles, applied the helo's rotor brake, and jumped out of the bird. Once out of the helo, Sandee Barron headed right for Laurie.

"Come on, I'll show you where our stateroom is. The flight deck guys will bring your gear down in a minute," her roommate-to-be said, rescuing Laurie from Blackman's handshake.

"Thanks," Laurie replied, as she tried to stand erect on wobbly legs.

Once inside the skin of the ship, Sandee Barron stopped.

"So, Ms. Phillips, looks like we're going to be roommates."

"So I'm told . . . and it's Laurie, please."

"OK, Laurie, fair enough. My name's Sandee."

"The captain seems . . . well . . . enthusiastic," Laurie said as Sandee led her down a ladder to the deck below the flight deck.

"Yeah, captain's a piece of work," Barron said over her shoulder as they continued walking, "but you didn't hear that from me. He won't say much to you on the ship, but get him on liberty and put a few beers in him and he'll open up and tell you more than you want to know. He was a big football star at the Naval Academy, a linebacker. You could probably guess just by looking at him."

"He does seem a little larger than life."

"Yep, but I think you'll find him a pretty straight guy. We're lucky, I guess. He grinds the ship's company officers, but leaves us Airedales pretty much alone. We just try to keep a low profile and do our mission."

The inquisitive look on her face told Sandee she ought to enlighten her new roommate further. She stopped walking, turned around, and looked directly at Laurie. "Look, you gotta understand something. The captain didn't grow up with a silver spoon in his mouth. He came from some small mill town in North Carolina, and he only got out of there because he was recruited by the Academy to play football. This is his big chance as captain of *Normandy*. If he does a good job, he'll probably get promoted and get his admiral's stars. If he doesn't, he's yesterday's news. He's a little rough around the edges, but a ship's CO has incredible responsibilities. If just one of us screws up badly, it's not only our career, but his, too."

Laurie nodded that she understood, but Sandee wasn't done.

"Best advice I can give you is to just give the skipper a lot of room. He's risen through the ranks because he gets the job done. Plus, whatever else happens, we've got to live with him for the next six months. We all just have to remember why we're here."

However, after two harrowing flights in the past several days, and in the foreign environment of a Navy ship at sea, Laurie Phillips had the profound sense of not, in fact, being quite sure why she *was* here. As Sandee led her through the maze of *Normandy*'s passageways and to their small stateroom, Laurie looked toward that future with some apprehension.

CHAPTER SIXTEEN

The Saudi Arabian Desert
(March 9, 1015 Arabian Standard Time)

Even in March, the Saudi Arabian sun was already baking the desert, the air shimmering in the heat, but Prince Ali al-Wandi was seemingly immune to the weather. He was single-mindedly focused and was in the process of shaping his future. He was far from Riyadh and in the vast Saudi Arabian Desert, but at a location well within range of his Sikorsky S-92 executive helicopter. Al-Wandi watched as his team of handpicked men put the finishing touches on their building project.

He had just left the nondescript blockhouse a few meters away. There, another group of handpicked men, all engineers, were working with the Global Hawk technology his now-dead minion had stolen from the United States. They had their part of the operation almost up and running. The prince conferred with his chief engineer, the man he used as his chief of staff and alter ego. He was a Pakistani named Jawad Makhdoom.

"Do you think the Americans will take the bait?" the man asked.

"I know they will," al-Wandi replied. "They can't leave anything in this region alone. Look how they bully our leaders into keeping oil prices at unreasonably low levels, how they meddle in our internal affairs with all this antiterrorism rhetoric, and how they incessantly scold our king with this human rights nonsense."

"I know," Makhdoom replied, "and they have been doing it for a long time. But now you'll make them do what we want them to do, in'shallah."

"It is more than Allah's will," Prince Ali responded. "You've explained why the position of this camp is an ideal one. The prying eyes of the Americans don't miss much and they won't miss this."

"Yes, but even if they see it, will it move them to action?" Makhdoom asked.

"I know it will!" al-Wandi replied emphatically. "Look, the government they have worried about for decades just took a huge jog in the direction of instability. The revolution the Syrians suppressed so ruthlessly in 2011 has continued simmering. The Americans will see what they see, and what they want to see."

They had planned this out so well. As much as he admired the man he had handpicked as his chief of staff, al-Wandi suspected the Pakistani expat did not share his faith that what they were doing would succeed. Yet the man didn't know everything that Ali al-Wandi did. Nor would he, ever.

"What about the prying eyes in our country? Do you think we're well protected from discovery here?"

"Oh, don't worry, we're completely secure," Ali al-Wandi

replied, surprise registering on his face that his man could think he hadn't taken care of this aspect of the operation. No, he had paid enough to ensure they would be left alone.

"Then you're certain the United States will act?"

"Oh, they'll act, and they will act soon!"

The prince knew he could order the man to do anything he wanted him to do. Yet he wanted to convince him what they were doing was the right thing to do for the kingdom, and not solely to continue to line his own pockets with bribes extracted from the oil deals he had cut. Further, he had not told his assistant about the money Nayef had extracted from him as a personal investment in the project.

"Look, if the Americans are friends of our kingdom shouldn't they want to intervene with Syria? All they need is an excuse. Look what they did to Libya in 2011, and that country doesn't have the strategic importance Syria does. If Syria explodes it will set their Mideast strategy back decades and if Syria threatens them, then it squares the circle. They'll be chomping at the bit, just wait."

"Yes, I think you're right," Makhdoom replied, though the look on his face showed he might yet be a bit skeptical.

Ali al-Wandi could see the man still had doubts. He wanted there to be none.

The prince looked the chief engineer dead in the eye. "Don't lose confidence now," he said as he laid his right hand on the man's shoulder to reassure him. "I've listened carefully to what the U.S. president has said and have paid close attention to U.S. security policies."

"Yes, Your Excellency, but they will have to act preemptively in this case, won't they?"

"They will. We watched the United States employ its doctrine of preemption against Iraq in 2003, in Libya in 2011, and on other occasions, too. I am confident they'll use that policy again if they feel they need to. Also don't forget how this president's predecessor was criticized for not intervening in Syria years ago."

For the most part, Prince Ali was doing all this for the power and the money, but at his core he was a Saudi. Geography didn't lie and he knew enough about history and geopolitics, and was shaken enough by the 2011 Arab Spring uprisings. So he was genuinely concerned for the future of his nation.

As a reasonably devout Sunni, al-Wandi's nightmare scenario was a region dominated by radical Shias in Iran and their proxies in Syria. No, he rationalized, he had to do this. More than that, he must do this. Not for himself, but for his nation and for future generations of Saudis. Get the United States to decapitate Syria, move in militarily, oust the current government, and put the Sunni majority in charge of the country. That would not only get the oil flowing, but would also wrest Syria away from Iran's embrace. He would not only be rich; he would also be a Saudi national hero. It was a beautiful plan. The United States would start the dominos falling and would help him achieve his dream. The Americans would do this, and it would be their own idea to boot!

His plan was as simple as it was clever. The Global Hawk would "see" a threat when it overflew what they were building, but it would be tricked into thinking that threat was in Syria. He shook his head in satisfaction. It was almost done and when he activated his plan things would move quickly.

Far from where Ali al-Wandi and the chief engineer were putting the prince's plan in motion, two hundred kilometers north of the Syrian oasis city of Tadmur two men were engaged in conversation. The older man sitting in the passenger seat of the four-wheel-drive Range Rover was Hibah Nawal. He was the mukhtar of the Rulawa tribe, the largest of the eight nomadic tribes that roamed Syria's half-million-square-kilometer desert. His driver, Feroz Kabudi, turned and said, "I don't know why we aren't moving this building to the next segment of pipeline. It does not make sense."

The mukhtar smiled. Feroz meant "fortunate" in Arabic, and Hibah Nawal reflected on how fortunate Feroz was, as indeed were the men of their Rulawa tribe who had elected him as the leader of their tribal council. While he had grown up in the desert doing what most of Syria's Bedouin population did, herd sheep, he had spent enough time in Tadmur to keep abreast of events in the nations surrounding Syria. The Bedouin tribes were insulated from most of the chaos of Syria's civil war because Syria's steppe and desert was considered of little value.

When Hibah Nawal learned of Saudi Arabia's intention to build their oil pipeline through Syria's desert, he saw opportunity. He jockeyed for position with the leaders of Syria's other Bedouin tribes and secured a contract to provide services and labor to the army of engineers and construction workers who were building the pipeline. The contract was extremely lucrative for the Rulawa tribe and secured the long-term loyalty of his kinsmen who had elected him mukhtar. It had also allowed him to skim money off the top and reward himself with perks like this expensive SUV.

"Feroz, this pipeline is a big project, and it is not our job to manage it. Our job is just to help build the temporary quarters for the workers, deliver supplies to them at each of these base camps, and when they need our help, assist them with some of the construction."

"Yes, I know that, Mukhtar. The pipeline is complete here and now we will be paid just to provide security, but the next segment of the pipeline is being built almost due north and we should be moving this temporary barracks north for the workers."

"You think too much, Feroz. Our instructions are to help build a brand new barracks to the north and just leave this one in place here. Now we need to drive over there," the mukhtar said, pointing in a westerly direction.

Feroz Kabudi just shook his head as he stepped on the accelerator and followed instructions.

Laurie Phillips and Sandee Barron sat in their tiny stateroom aboard *Normandy*, each chugging a Powerade sports drink, sweat dripping on the room's deck as they both recovered from a ninety-minute workout. A midafternoon respite from flight operations had opened up the ship's flight deck to joggers. After spending almost an hour running in endless circles on the flight deck they had hit Normandy's tiny weight room in the bowels of the ship. Even in March, the arid, ninety-degree temperature in the region had dehydrated them both.

"Didn't know if there'd be any way to work out on a Navy ship, Sandee. This isn't bad, though that flight deck isn't much of a track."

"No, it's not. It's easier when we deploy on an aircraft carrier like *Truman*. A four-and-a-half-acre flight deck makes it much easier for running."

"Didn't you tell me you were a runner back at the Naval Academy?"

"Yeah, back in the day. Cross country."

"Enjoy it there?"

"Nice place to be from. Hey, why don't you hit the showers first? I've got to slam out an e-mail to my hubby back in Norfolk. He needs constant reassurance the guys on the ship aren't hitting on me, or if they are, I'm ignoring them."

"I'll testify all you're doing is flying, working out, and sleeping. Tell him to send more pictures. Your two daughters are too cute!"

As the easy banter between the two women continued, Sandee Barron reflected on how different their backgrounds were and how liberally Laurie had shared her unique life experience with her.

Born and raised in Des Moines, with an IT degree from a junior college, Laurie Phillips enlisted in the Marine Corps after she was jilted in an affair with a married man. Smart and good with languages, she was accepted into the Marine Corps

Cultural Support Team program and trained to interface with local Afghani women in the battle space.

She did two tours in Afghanistan and was decorated for heroism, but an affair with a deployed Marine during her second tour went badly as he, too, was married. Sadly, a latent eating disorder forced her from the Corps when she was unable to control her weight, ballooning to well above Marine Corps weight standards and failing her semiannual physical fitness test. She continued on this bad eating path until finally converting to the South Beach diet and undertaking a workout regimen that she followed with near-religious regularity. She regained control of her life, and returned to school for a four-year degree in IT.

After graduation, she gravitated first to the National Reconnaissance Office (NRO), then to the Center for Naval Analyses (CNA) as places where she felt she could be recognized and rewarded for her skills and strong work ethic. When the CNA accepted her application for this important shipboard position, it helped provide that recognition she so wanted. Now it was her job to make it work.

Now fit and modestly attractive, she was working mightily to guard against her eating disorder, which, like an alcohol addiction, was always present. She vowed never to go back there, and she packed much of her own chow for this deployment. Every nook and cranny of their stateroom was jammed with food she brought aboard or had shipped to her.

While she didn't talk much about her personal life, she had revealed to Sandee she had a long-standing, on-again, off-again relationship with a techie friend from her days at NRO.

"So, Laurie, other than working out and sitting here e-mailing folks back home, we hardly see each other much."

"Hey, roomie, you've been flying your ass off day and night. Did that waiver to fly more than a hundred hours in a month ever come through for you?"

"Yeah, thanks for asking. It did, just last week. How about you, though? Things working out the way you wanted them to for you professionally here?"

"Yep, pretty much. The playbook for CNA analysts on ships like this is to park in the ship's Combat Direction Center for the deployment and take in as much data as you can. Some analysts I've talked with have had productive and satisfying tours doing this and some not so much."

"And for you?" Sandee asked.

"For me, so far so good. I think it helped that our ops boss, Lieutenant Commander Watson, served with a CNA analyst on one of his previous ships. He seems to have the big picture of where I fit into his operation, especially in the Combat Direction Center."

"Sounds pretty good. How's it working out with the captain? I know he's usually camped out on the bridge, but do you talk with him when he comes through CDC?"

"No, not really. He usually banters with the tactical action officer or the petty officer managing the Aegis tracks on the display. I'm pretty much below the noise. He says hello, but it's kind of perfunctory."

"With the captain, that may be a blessing. Hey, every time I come through there to get the flight brief I see you at one console or another doing what looks like interesting stuff."

"Yep, I'm learning a lot. The watch team leader usually slots me into either one of the track management consoles or the Global Hawk consoles and I think I'm getting pretty good at both."

"Global Hawk!" Sandee exclaimed. "Hey, you'd better keep those toy airplanes from T-boning my bird when I'm flying," she continued, only half in jest.

"Tell you what, roomie. Just keep that eggbeater you're flying below sixty-five thousand feet and you'll be just fine."

Laurie Phillips was, in fact, feeling accomplished in her work aboard *Normandy*. She just hoped it would keep up for the entire deployment.

CHAPTER SEVENTEEN

*Op-Center Headquarters, Fort Belvoir North, Fairfax
County, Virginia
(March 12, 0900 Eastern Daylight Time)*

Chase Williams sat at his desk catching up on paperwork,
e-mails, and other messages when his N5, or planning director,
arrived at his door for their scheduled meeting. "Morning, boss,
ready for our meeting or should I come back?"

"Let's do it, Rich. What do you have for me today?" Williams said as he motioned his N5 to a chair next to his desk.

"Well, I know you pay me to look way ahead, so I thought
I'd update you on some of the intelligence trap lines we've got
going. We're trying to anticipate what this surge of U.S. military
forces to the Mideast might precipitate."

The most essential quality a planning director brought to
any organization was to look beyond the immediate horizon, often way beyond. Someone had to anticipate what the organization would have to deal with in a distant future no one else was
looking at. Richard Middleton was the right guy for the job. It

was moments like this that reminded Williams why he hired this unusual and uniquely capable man.

Middleton was an Amherst graduate and a blue blood and had marched against the Vietnam War when he was in junior high. He went to CIA after a tour at State and was fluent in five languages. Middleton was far more cunning than anyone Williams had ever met. In the process of considering him for Op-Center Williams had learned Middleton was not well liked or terribly successful at the CIA until a supervisor at Langley saw in him the makings of a covert operator. There, and perhaps only there, he more than excelled, and became one of the best.

Manipulative and even Machiavellian, Middleton understood his role at Op-Center and loved planning. He was a classic big picture guy. Williams marveled at how his planning director could take a plan of operations and see around and ahead of the execution. Middleton had been the first to understand the shift to the terrorists-for-hire threat they were now dealing with and had helped the rest of the staff create the vectors that enabled the Geek Tank to ultimately finger Perkasa and Kashif.

He did come with baggage. Married and divorced twice, his longest monogamous relationship was with an expensive call girl who was now a little long in the tooth. Twice a month they met for dinner, the theater, and a sleep-over. He always paid her well.

"So what do you think we might need to anticipate?" Williams asked.

"I figured we'd want to look at the recent past and extrapolate ahead a bit, especially as it relates to domestic security."

"Good idea. What you got?"

"The way I figure it, a surge like this, with a focus on Iran's saber-rattling, isn't going to stir up any enraged masses. The intelligence community is standing by what we learned in the wake of the NFL attacks. You've also advised the president by memo about the terror-for-hire threat."

"And I appreciate you drafting those memos, Rich. I can tell you they resonated with the president."

"Thanks, boss. Roger's intelligence folks, and especially our Geek Tank, are all pretty much in line with what the intelligence community is saying—for the most part. The threat has changed dramatically. We can't ignore jihadists in explosive vests or some other low-end weapons, but that's not the way it's happening today. At least not here."

"We sure as hell saw that with Kashif and Perkasa, didn't we?"

"Sure did. Roger and his folks have a great flow of information from the intelligence community. Adam Putnam's people have delivered everything you've asked for and Aaron and his team digest it in real time. Looking ahead, while there are still groups like AQAP, Hamas, and the rest who just stay pissed off at us permanently, there doesn't seem to be any one leader of a stature approaching bin Laden who's got a master plan to do us harm."

"So it's going to be more random events? Is that what you're suggesting?"

"I wouldn't call it random, maybe more like episodic. You get one pissed-off Arab like Kashif with enough money who wants to poke us in the eye 'just because' and he hires a guy like Perkasa who's nothing more than a professional hit man, and he sticks it to us. As far as the IC is concerned, and Roger and I agree with them, that's the model we should anticipate in the future."

"That's a tougher one to deal with than just a dozen guys who want to get to paradise in a big hurry," Williams replied.

"You're right there, boss. So now that we know what our Geek Tank can do, Roger and the rest of his intel team think we should provide Aaron and his gang more guidance on where to focus most of their efforts looking ahead. They're good—but they can't cover everything all of the time. I have some thoughts on where they should be looking, but I wanted to run them by you."

"I'm glad you're doing that, Rich. So where do you think we ought to be looking, internationally or domestically?"

"Well, the easy answer is, both. However, the way my group looks at it, there's probably not going to be another successful attack like the one on the Marine Barracks in Lebanon, or the U.S. embassies in Africa or the U.S. consulate in Benghazi, or the Cole in Aden Harbor."

"You don't think so?" Williams asked. He didn't want to second-guess his planning director, but Middleton was raising important issues.

"No, I don't, and for a number of reasons. Number one, we've gotten a lot smarter. We've hardened targets like embassies and consulates, stopped putting our troops in barracks where they can get blown up, and stopped making dumb-ass decisions like refueling ships in Aden Harbor, no offense to the Navy, boss."

"No offense taken. My predecessor as CENTCOM commander when *Cole* was hit in October 2000 would tell you the same thing; it was a dumb move, one of our dumbest."

"Roger that, but the other big thing is this. With targets that hard, any professional hitter is going to walk away from that kind of assignment. Oh, he'll take the initial cash and scope out the target, but chances are he won't try to complete the mission. The risk-reward curve wouldn't be in his favor."

"OK, fair enough," Williams replied, "but what about domestically?"

"*Completely* different story. Something like those NFL attacks could happen tomorrow. As you know, we've turned up the gain in the intelligence community to focus on the kinds of things that have to happen to set those types of attacks up. In addition, now that we've got our Geek Tank cranked up and running on all cylinders, we should get intelligence and warning *before* the intelligence community does. Nothing's foolproof, but we're not defenseless, either."

"So what should we do next?"

"Next time you speak with the attorney general or the FBI director, you might want to ask them if they think the FBI's Critical Incident Response Group is staffed and ready to use the intel our folks provide. We can only push the intel to them; we can't make them use it. To be honest with you, boss, talking with the staff and especially our folks who've gone onsite at the CIRG command center, we're not sure they're able—or even willing—to use the intel we push to them. However, we're convinced Aaron's team can provide the best actionable intelligence on a domestic threat before anyone else does. Armed with that, the FBI's CIRG can intervene before we take a hit."

"That's a great idea, Rich. To be honest with you, I've had the same thoughts but haven't reached out to the AG or the FBI director on this issue yet—but I will."

Several days later, Prince Ali al-Wandi was again at his desert site. He was pleased. His men had done their job and done it well. The false ballistic missile site was in place, ready for the prying eyes of the Global Hawk. Now he walked the short distance from the mock-ups of missile launchers and canisters to the blockhouse to see what his engineers and technicians were doing.

"Come in, Your Excellency," Jawad Makhdoom began. "I think you'll be pleased with what you see."

"I know I will. You have done a great deal in an incredibly short time," al-Wandi replied. He had no particular love for these engineers, but they were loyal to him and were doing precisely what he wanted them to do. Right now that was all that was important.

Al-Wandi cast a sideways glace at a man, a white man, working in the corner of the blockhouse. "Is he doing what you are paying him to do?" the prince asked, his voice stern, his look hard.

"Yes. Yes, he is. We could not pull this off without him," Makhdoom replied in as reassuring terms as possible.

Like most Saudis, al-Wandi hated infidels, especially American infidels, on Saudi Arabia's sacred soil. However, Makhdoom had convinced him early on this man, an American engineer from Northrop Grumman, builder of the Global Hawk, was absolutely indispensable. He had patiently explained to the prince that try as they might—and even with the stolen technology he had obtained—his best technicians could not crack all of the security codes they needed to break. Without these codes, they could not make the Global Hawk do precisely what they wanted it to do.

Makhdoom had told the prince he had persuaded the man to leave Northrop Grumman and he would be paid handsomely for his efforts. He felt no need to tell him what he had to do in order to secure the services of this decadent American. The prince did not need to know he had to ensnare the man in a sex scandal. Had Makhdoom released the secret video he took of the American's escapades, it would surely have caused him to lose his security clearance. That would have ended his employability by Northrop Grumman or any other defense contractor. Sending the video to the man's wife, as he threatened to do, would surely have ended his marriage. The process didn't matter; the results did. This former Northrop Grumman technician now worked side by side with his men. The American was doing precisely what Makhdoom needed him to do, and the prince was pleased. That was what really mattered.

Al-Wandi was curious enough to go see what this infidel was working on. Makhdoom darted ahead to ensure the man showed the prince the proper respect. He failed.

"My man tells me you have expert skills," the prince began, his eyes narrowed and his tone harsh.

"I am doing what you pay me to do," the man replied, his tone anything but respectful.

"I would hope so. I'm told we are paying you enough money," the prince shot back.

"Look, you can't do this without me. What you're paying me is a pittance for what you're getting. Deal with it," the man replied, almost snarling as he looked up and down the prince's enormous bulk with clear disdain.

"So you say," the prince replied, seething, as he turned on his heel and walked away. He made a mental note to tell his body-guard to kill this infidel, slowly, once their operation was complete.

Jawad Makhdoom was eager to placate the prince after that encounter. Although Prince Ali didn't understand all of the technology, the chief engineer began to explain how they were able to do what they were doing. After a lengthy explanation, Ali al-Wandi was both pacified and pleased. His plan had come together and now he was ready for action.

"We picked this spot well," Makhdoom continued. "As we predicted, we're right on the flight path and under the footprint."

"Good, this is exactly where we want to be," Ali al-Wandi replied. "We are talking about the right footprint, aren't we?"

"We are," the man continued. "This location is far from civilization and the men grumble about that, but we are along the path of the standard route flown by the U.S. Global Hawk."

"Please assure me that it is the right one," the prince replied. He had too much riding on this and there could be no mistakes or oversights.

"Yes, it's the Global Hawk the Americans call Two Bravo," Makhdoom replied. "It flies from its small aerodrome near Central Command's forward base in Qatar, then over our desert in a roughly northwesterly direction, and then over Jordan and Syria to the Mediterranean where it reverses course and returns, covering the same route."

"That's good, and we'll soon have something to say about what it sees, won't we?" al-Wandi replied. The prince's soft brown eyes conveyed approval but his body language told the man his superior wanted it done right—or else.

Makhdoom knew the prince trusted him to do what was expected, but he felt if he explained how this all worked, Al Wandi would trust him even more.

"Your Excellency, what we're doing is really quite simple given the technology you've provided to us. When Global Hawk Two Bravo passes over this ballistic missile site it digitally records what it sees, just like everything else on its flight path. We've calculated the speed of the bird and given the size of the site, the time it appears on the Global Hawk's digital memory is precisely 26.47 seconds—"

"I had no idea you had it calculated that exactly," the prince interrupted.

"Oh, we had to be that accurate, Your Excellency. That is critical to know so we can put a 26.47-second time-jump in the digital recording so what the Global Hawk appears to capture is just a continuous picture of an empty desert as it passes over our site."

"I see."

"Your Excellency, I can't emphasize enough how precise our calculations must be. Hours later, when the Global Hawk is just where we want it to be, we insert that 26.47 seconds of video back into its digital memory. Then it 'sees' the site just where we want it to be seen, in the Syrian desert, not far from Damascus," Makhdoom concluded with a bit of a flourish.

Ali al-Wandi allowed himself a slight smile. He knew the Americans would be alarmed the Syrians had this missile, the DF-21D carrier-killer, operational. He just needed them to take action when they did.

"You have done well. I could not have hoped for better results. We'll put your system into action soon. Can you be ready at a moment's notice?"

"Yes, we can, Your Excellency, absolutely."

"Good. I will be back frequently to check your progress," the prince replied. He was pleased. It was all coming together.

As for the American contractor, he would deal with him soon enough.

Hibah Nawal leaned against the hood of his Range Rover watching his two-dozen kinsmen break down the former pipeline-worker barracks. As they disassembled one portion of the prefabricated building, they used forklifts and portable cranes to load it on the semis parked nearby.

As each semi was fully loaded it drove off in an easterly direction to a location just over forty kilometers away. At that site to the east, other members of the mukhtar's tribe were reassembling the building according to the specifications Nawal had provided to them. These men from the Rulawa tribe were being paid an extra bonus for this work, and the fact that the new "barracks" was in the middle of the trackless Syrian desert did not concern them. Nor was the fact that they also carried a truckload of camouflage netting to this new location. The mukhtar had given them a nearly impossible deadline to complete their work, and they had no time for wondering.

As Laurie Phillips had explained to her roommate, she was feeling a sense of accomplishment during her daily routine in *Normandy*'s Combat Direction Center.

Always shorthanded, the watch teams that manned CDC didn't take long to recognize Laurie's IT skills, the fact that she was a quick study, and her willingness to work hard. The officers, chief petty officers, and sailors laboring away in CDC looked at her as an increasingly valuable asset. As Laurie sat at the Global Hawk console looking up at the monitor, she reflected how things had come full circle since her days at the National Reconnaissance Office. She recalled her experience the first time she sat down at that console during her first week aboard *Normandy*.

Laurie had first entered *Normandy*'s CDC on that day and

had walked into a whole new world. Three weeks ago it was an unfamiliar and almost alien place. She was still battling seasickness then, as the *Truman* strike group had dashed across the Atlantic through the teeth of a howling winter storm. The storm had bounced *Normandy* around and caused substantial damage to many of the strike group's ships, but now CDC was home. She felt empowered, but more than that, she felt needed.

Laurie had quickly learned CDC was the nerve center of the ship. It had taken her a while to absorb all she was looking at in the sea of symbols on the four forty-two-inch by forty-two-inch paired projection screens on CDC's port-side bulkhead. She had also learned to make sense of the detailed information on the five ASTABs, automated status boards, on other bulkheads, as well as all the other screens displaying a wealth of information. She was no longer in information overload; she felt she was part of CDC.

The low, incessant hum of the air conditioning, the dim lighting that cast an eerie, almost sinister, glow throughout CDC, and the flickering green lights on the UYK-21 computers surrounding her had initially made Laurie feel like she was in another world. At first, her brain couldn't process everything she was seeing; but now it almost felt like second nature each time she sat down at a watch station in CDC.

She recalled the first time she had seen this console and monitor.

"What's this monitor for?" Laurie had asked, pointing at a small video monitor right above the radar console. "Oh, that's our UAV monitor," Brian Clark, *Normandy*'s CDC officer, had replied.

Laurie was cheered. She had worked on unmanned aerial vehicle projects at National Reconnaissance Office as well as at the Center for Naval Analyses for years and knew quite a bit about them, but her knowledge was based on what she did in a laboratory environment at NRO and CNA. Seeing this actual monitor on a ship might help put her work in perspective.

"I'll tell you, Laurie," Mike Clark had continued, "those unmanned aerial vehicles were huge stars during Operations Enduring Freedom and Iraqi Freedom. Real vacuum cleaners bringing in tremendous amounts of information while flying in places we didn't want to send manned aircraft."

"And we're using them now, right?"

"We are. Things haven't really calmed down in the wake of the major Mideast uprisings in 2011, and the United States needs situational awareness of what's going on here today more than we ever did. We use 'em all the time for ISR; that stands for intelligence, surveillance, and reconnaissance. We display the streaming video they send right here on this monitor, and on the Navy Tactical Data Consoles at other spots here in CDC. Between the UAV feed and our SPY radar we don't miss much."

"That's great," Laurie had replied, seeing the clear application of what she had worked on ashore. There, she didn't really understand how these things were used operationally. It was all just numbers to her, but she was fascinated seeing the big picture in CDC.

Now, weeks later, sitting at this console was providing her with the job satisfaction she sought. It wasn't her permanent station. Like the officers and crew who stood watch in CDC, she rotated between several watch stations, filling in where there was a need. She was an integral part of a team, something she hadn't felt since she was working village stabilization operations in Afghanistan as a member of a Marine Corps Cultural Support Team.

Mike Clark walked up and broke her out of her musing. "Don't forget to save any particularly interesting video and put it into the playback queue so we can look at it later."

"Will do," Laurie replied.

She thought of Charlie Bacon, the on-again, off-again boyfriend from her National Reconnaissance Office days she had told Sandee Barron about. She had worked with him on some of the early research on the technologies now used in the comms and sensor packages in these UAVs. Now some of that same technology was flying above the Gulf today. Laurie also thought about her growing friendship with Sandee. It had been a while since she had had a friend with whom she could share virtually everything.

However, this was no time for those thoughts or for her memories of Charlie and of a relationship they let fall apart for all the wrong reasons. Right now Laurie needed to just keep working. It cheered her when Mike Clark added, "You're doing a hell of a job, Laurie. We're lucky to have you here, and as things heat up, we're going to need you even more."

• • •

There was not much cheer, however, in the White House Situation Room, as a small group of the president's advisors joined him in one of the Sit Room's two secure conference rooms. The image of General Walt Albin, commander of the United States Central Command, or CENTCOM, covered the LCD screen at the front of the room.

"OK, General Albin, give us the lowdown," the president said.

"Mr. President, as you know, things never really are completely quiet in this region," Albin began. "The standoff between the Israelis and the Palestinians is as bad now as it's ever been, especially after that series of suicide bombings last month. Iran is threatening Iraq again, as they fear the new democratic government we put in place there more than they ever feared Saddam." Albin paused. "Mr. President, the level of tension has ticked up several notches over the past few weeks. As the new government in Syria tries to consolidate power, they are aligning even more closely with Iran as it jockeys for influence with the Saudis. As you know, Mr. President, Iran gives them massive military support, and, in turn, Syria aligns with them against Saudi Arabia—"

"And let me guess," Midkiff interrupted, "because they're pissed at the Saudis, lots of that splashes over on us!"

"Yes, sir," Albin replied.

President Wyatt Midkiff had gone to the University of Florida on a Navy ROTC scholarship and had done a stint as a naval surface officer right after graduation. He respected his military advisors and didn't like interrupting them, but his level of frustration with the continuing tensions in the Middle East was palpable.

Midkiff hadn't been a key player in defense or foreign affairs during his sixteen years in the Senate and four years in the House, but he had absorbed something. Hell, even he saw these heightened tensions between Syria and Saudi Arabia coming back in 2011. Wasn't anyone else smart enough to get it? Syrian President Bashar al-Assad was the most ruthless leader in suppressing his domestic democracy movement. Assad had slaughtered over one hundred thousand of his countrymen in the process. Even he eventually lost his battle for control and now the Alawite military controlled that country, and the Sunnis who had led the revolution were paying a terrible price.

The government in Syria, a cobbled-together alliance of Alawites, Shias, Druse, and even some Christians, didn't really have complete control of the country, at least not yet. However, if that government had a single organizing impulse, it was enmity toward Saudi Arabia for killing and continuing to oppress its Shiite minority. The Saudis, who had no love for Syria in the first place, were now especially hostile toward the regime as it continued to oppress its Sunni majority.

Oh, and all that talk about the United States weaning itself off Mideast oil. Ha! From Midkiff's perspective, that had gone down the tubes with the *Deepwater Horizon* disaster in 2010.

"Patricia, don't we have any damn friends over there?" the president asked. He knew the answer to that question, but had to ask it.

"We do, Mr. President," Secretary of State Patricia Green replied, "but this change in government in Syria, and particularly their hostility toward Saudi Arabia, is the worst possible scenario for us."

"How bad is it?"

"It's pretty bad, Mr. President," Green continued. "Because of our long-term support for the Saudis, we're getting the worst part of the guilt by association, and the Syrian government has now turned its venom on us."

"I know all that," Midkiff continued. "First Iran and Iraq, and now this. What are we doing about it? We can't just let things spin out of control!"

"We are increasing our presence in Central Command area of responsibility as rapidly as we can, Mr. President," Jack Bradt, his secretary of defense, reminded him. "General Albin is directing the build-up in-theater. We're sending the Iranians and the Syrians, and everyone else for that matter, a clear signal that our interests in the Gulf are long term and that we're prepared to defend those interests with military power."

Actions were being taken to do exactly that. General Albin had already moved his command headquarters forward from Tampa, Florida, to his Joint Command Center in Al Udeid Air Base, Qatar. A host of forces, including the *Truman* strike group, were now in the Central Command area of responsibility.

"We've had pressure on the Iranians for a long time, Mr. President," his national security advisor said, "and we'll send a signal to the Syrians loud and clear."

The president nodded that he understood.

"General Albin," the secretary of defense said, directing his focus to the large screen display. "We want you watching the Syrians like a hawk. I don't trust the bastards, and this isn't going to be the next administration to get nailed by an attack on the U.S. of A. You tell us about any indications they're gonna move against us and we'll preempt that. Do I make myself clear?"

"Abundantly clear, Mr. Secretary," Albin answered. "We're using all the overhead imagery assets, principally satellites and UAVs, at our disposal to blanket Syria. It would be helpful, though, if we did have some more UAVs—"

"Great, keep up the good work, General. We'll get you anything you need," the secretary of defense interrupted as he turned and looked at the president. "Mr. President, we have our forces moving as quickly as we can. I think General Albin knows he has your full support."

President Midkiff sat motionless and just nodded as he let the implications of what his advisors were telling him sink in. He recognized the gravity of the situation, but things were moving too fast.

CHAPTER EIGHTEEN

*Op-Center Headquarters, Fort Belvoir North, Fairfax
County, Virginia
(March 16, 0815 Eastern Daylight Time)*

Richard Middleton entered Chase Williams's office for the early
morning meeting wondering if there was a crisis brewing. Williams typically scheduled meetings well in advance and had a
smooth, relatively predictable battle rhythm under way at Op-
Center. Middleton had opened up his e-mail queue when he arrived at work that morning and found an e-mail from Williams
asking to see him ASAP.

"Mornin', boss. You wanted to see me?"

"Sure, Rich, come in."

Middleton sat down, searching Williams's face for clues.
There were none. "Anything wrong?"

"No, and I didn't mean to shake you up with an impromptu
meeting, but I have been thinking about our conversation several
days ago, the one where we discussed our support for the FBI's
Critical Incident Response Group. You were wondering how we

might support them more, given your observations about the potential for another terror-for-hire attack here at home."

"I'm glad you have, boss. The president's given you a pretty broad mandate and now that we've got our Geek Tank cranked up I think we have a unique and valuable capability. I give Roger and his folks all the credit."

As he sipped his coffee, Chase Williams thought about the relationship Op-Center had evolved with the FBI and the Critical Incident Response Group, the CIRG.

Op-Center's relationship with their JSOC unit was one of direct operational control. This was something all concerned were comfortable with given Chase Williams's extensive operational background as well as the military backgrounds of many of his core Op-Center staff. Williams could order his JSOC unit downrange and count on complete freedom of action.

Their relationship with the FBI CIRG was quite different, and there were strong reasons for that structure.

Americans were well accustomed to U.S. special operations forces working overseas in a covert manner and with the CIA operating in a covert, or even clandestine, manner. However, most U.S. citizens had a completely different attitude regarding what happened on American soil.

Having domestic forces under the full control of a shadowy agency such as Op-Center, no matter how well intentioned those leading Op-Center were, was not something most Americans were ready to support. Even if those actions would be designed to save American lives, that kind of freedom of action was something that moved well beyond the comfort level of most Americans.

So the Memorandum of Understanding, the MOU, between Op-Center, the White House, the Justice Department, and the FBI was crafted with great care. Boiled down to its essential elements, it stipulated that Op-Center would provide any intelligence it gained on international terrorists who could pose a domestic threat, as well as intelligence on any purely domestic threats, to the FBI Critical Incident Response Group. This notification would be made at the staff level and also by the Op-Center director directly to the attorney general or the FBI director. They, and only they, would direct the FBI CIRG to take action on American soil.

Middleton was worried this was not the most effective approach and he said so. "Boss, can you and the president revisit the relationship we have with the Critical Incident Response Group?"

"So you'd like us to have operational control of a CIRG element? Is that how I read what you're saying? You know the sensitivities regarding action on American soil."

"I do. Unfortunately, there is just too much at stake if the Justice Department can't, or won't, move fast enough. Shame on all of us if we don't try to fix that."

"I agree with you, Rich. You've laid out a good case. Test the waters with the FBI CIRG at your level and I'll take it up with the FBI director. If we do our jobs right, they may be accepting of our proposal."

• • •

Aboard *Normandy,* the watch teams had been at heightened alert ever since the ship passed through the Strait of Hormuz and entered the Arabian Gulf two days earlier. The dash across the Atlantic through a storm, through the Mediterranean, and through Suez and the Red Sea had been exhausting. The rough weather had taken its toll on people and ships alike. But morale aboard the ship had just hit bottom.

After evaluating the damage his ships had suffered during the sprint to the Gulf, the *Truman* strike group commander, Admiral Flynn, decided to pull most of his ships into port in the Gulf for badly needed repairs. *Harry S. Truman* had suffered the most damage, especially to many of her aircraft that had blue water crashing over them on her flight deck, and the ship was already pier side in Jabel Ali, near Dubai. Other strike group ships were in port in Bahrain and elsewhere.

Normandy was fortunate in that she had sustained the least damage, but it was a double-edged sword for the crew, as *Normandy* was assigned to remain at sea as the strike group's air warfare and missile defense ship. Rumors were sweeping the ship that Captain Pete Blackman, eager to impress his boss, had volunteered to stay at sea while all the other strike group crews enjoyed just a bit of time ashore. Like many rumors on Navy ships, it was not true. In fact, given the heightened tensions in the Gulf, from an operational and tactical point of view, keeping *Normandy* at sea to defend the other strike group ships from missile attack made sense.

Laurie Phillips was new to all this, and as they jogged

around the flight deck the previous afternoon she had asked Sandee Barron about all the grousing going on aboard the ship.

"Sailors bitching. Yeah, I'd say that's pretty normal," Sandee had reassured her.

"But they seem really upset," Laurie had replied. "I mean, my entire four-hour watch rotation in CDC, all I heard was them moaning and complaining about not getting to pull liberty while the crews of all the other ships are ashore."

"Listen, Laurie. First of all, if sailors ever *stop* bitching, then it's time to worry. It's just part of who they are. Hell, you've probably heard them say being on a ship is just like being in jail, except you can drown."

"Yeah, I have to admit, I had heard that, even before all this 'we're not getting any liberty' carping began," Laurie had replied.

"Just the nature of the beast, we roll with it."

Now at her watch station in CDC, Laurie reflected on the conversation with Sandee and how it had helped put things in perspective. What she also noticed was the increased tension and vigilance aboard the ship now that they were in the Gulf.

Weapons stations aboard *Normandy* were now manned constantly, extra watchstanders were stationed in CDC and on the bridge, and drills were conducted with more purpose. The captain's secret battle orders were read aloud by the tactical action officer, the TAO, at the beginning of every watch rotation. Laurie had been inserted in the watch rotation to monitor Global Hawk video. Now as a part of the A-team in CDC, she felt a great sense of pride. Despite that, the hours were long. As she viewed the hours of video, often showing nothing as the

Global Hawk transited seemingly endless desert expanses, she allowed her mind to wander. She reflected back to her earlier work at the National Reconnaissance Office and Center for Naval Analyses with UAV technology and recalled her relationship with Charlie Bacon, who worked on that technology with her at NRO. Their relationship ultimately crashed upon the rocks of professional competition. Bacon remained at NRO and she left for CNA. She knew he was still at NRO and had been promoted in the wake of her leaving. It was yet another relationship she had bungled. With a concerted effort she focused on her scope and put off thoughts of Charlie Bacon.

CHAPTER NINETEEN

Saudi Arabian Desert
(March 17, 1330 Arabian Standard Time)

"What is it?" Jawad Makhdoom asked as one of his assistants brought the satellite cell phone to him.

"It's Prince Ali," the man whispered, as he held his hand over the phone's mouthpiece.

Makhdoom took the phone. "Yes, yes. We will do it immediately, Your Excellency. Yes, we are ready in all respects. No, Your Excellency, we are ready right now," was all his assistant could hear as he listened to Makhdoom's end of the conversation. The man knew what was happening.

He knew the prince was telling them to take the camouflage netting off the site they had so laboriously built and to activate their system and begin sending time-delay and positioning signals to the sensors on the Global Hawk as it streaked overhead at sixty-five thousand feet above the Saudi desert. As the bird flew on its preprogrammed route, its cameras snapped continuously and recorded precisely what they saw, a ballistic missile site on the desert floor below.

However, when they activated the system, the Global Hawk received a signal, this one from the nondescript blockhouse near the mock DF-21D missile site. This caused the Global Hawk to put the 26.47 second time delay signal into its memory. When the missile site appeared on the monitors of anyone watching the Global Hawk video, it would appear not in the Saudi desert, but at a position east of Damascus, Syria, and hundreds of miles away from where the bird was. That position was where Hibah Nawal's kinsmen had just finished their assembly project.

Still at sea while the other strike group ships remained in port for repairs, *Normandy*'s watchstanders had remained at a heightened state of alert as the group's air warfare and missile defense ship. Captain Pete Blackman worked mightily to ensure his watch teams didn't lose their edge, but the new "eight-on, eight-off" watch rotation was beginning to take its toll.

It was five hours after the prince's chief engineer activated his system. Aboard *Normandy*, a senior enlisted watchstander in the Combat Direction Center saw it first and called out for Lieutenant Junior Grade Mike Clark.

"Lieutenant, come look at this," the man shouted, barely able to contain his excitement. Clark was quickly at his side.

"It's right here. I've played it back twice. This video is from Global Hawk Two Bravo, and it wasn't something that was there when it made its normal transit a day ago. It just sprang up out of nowhere," the man said, seeking reassurance he was not misinterpreting what he was seeing.

"TAO, we need you over here!" Clark said, calling for the tactical action officer.

Soon, almost every watchstander in CDC was huddled around the screen looking at the replay of the Global Hawk video. What the video showed was unmistakable; there was a DF-21D ballistic missile emplacement in the Syrian Desert east of Damascus. Not only that, but it was a missile no one knew the Syrians had, and there were buildings adjacent to the missile launchers that looked like they had been hastily constructed!

Maybe their captain was right about this region being a powder keg ready to explode. This put a new urgency on what they were doing, and on what they were preparing to do.

"Mr. Clark, call the ops officer and get him down here," the TAO said.

"Yes, sir," Clark replied.

Laurie Phillips was one of those huddled around the console. She wasn't on watch and didn't want to preempt a senior watch-stander, so she kept quiet as the entire CDC watch team stared at the Global Hawk video replay as if hypnotized by it.

"What have you got?" the ship's operations officer shouted as he burst into CDC.

"Sir, this video from the Global Hawk is troubling. Have a look, sir," the TAO said.

"Lemme up there," the ops officer said as he pushed past the others to stand right behind the senior watchstander. He sounded exasperated. *Normandy*'s junior officers had called him dozens of times on this deployment and it always was some false alarm or something they shouldn't have bothered him with. Still, it went with the territory as ops officer.

"OK, Chief, what ya got?" Watson asked as casually as he could. He'd show some interest, then leave and get back to doing what he was doing before they interrupted him. Everyone else in CDC was silent as the man patiently explained what he was seeing on the Global Hawk video while he replayed it for the ops officer. Watson showed no emotion as he looked at the video. Nevertheless, when he turned around and looked toward the assembled CDC watch team, his wide eyes betrayed his alarm.

"TAO, pass this to the battle watch staff on *Truman*, ASAP!" he nearly shouted.

"Mr. Clark, start writing that OPREP Three Pinnacle message now!" Watson commanded, referring to the highest priority emergency Operation Report naval message they could send, and one that "bumped" lower priority messages already in the queue. "I'm going to see the captain!"

Laurie's head was spinning. DF-21D missiles suddenly appeared in the Syrian desert and during one of the worst periods of tension between the United States and Syria? In any case this was happening at the same time U.S. Navy ships were in port and unable to defend themselves from ballistic missiles. *What did it all mean, and what were they going to do about it?*

Often accused of being bureaucratic and ponderous, the United States military is anything but that when passing critical information up and across the chain of command. The Global Hawk information captured in *Normandy*'s CDC was rapidly passed to Admiral Flynn's watch staff on *Harry S. Truman* in Port Jabel Ali; to the 5th Fleet Command Center in Manama, Bahrain; to the CENTCOM Command Center in Al Udeid Air Base, Qatar; to the National Military Command Center in the Pentagon; and then quickly to the White House Situation Room.

Without waiting to be called, the president's chief advisors—the secretary of defense, the secretary of state, the secretary of homeland security, the chairman of the Joint Chiefs of Staff, and others—began to converge on the White House Situation Room. In the Sit Room harried NSC staffers rushed to pull this alarming Global Hawk video up on monitors.

Roger McCord showed up unannounced at Chase Williams's office as he was going through his e-mail inbox.

"Roger?"

"Sorry to interrupt, boss. But we've gotten the same intel feed from several sources and we've got Aaron and his folks going into overdrive. I just wanted to plug you into a developing situation in the Middle East."

"Sure. What have you got?"

McCord walked Williams through what had transpired since the Global Hawk video first showed up on the monitor aboard *Normandy*. The admiral asked few questions. Processing what he was hearing was challenging enough.

"Whew, Roger, that's a lot to absorb."

"Sure is, boss."

"Let's get the planning cell cranked up."

"Will do, boss. We'll come brief you as·soon as we have more information."

Even though he was young, inexperienced, and often asked annoying questions, Hibah Nawal continued to use Feroz Kabudi as his driver. There was a reason and it was loyalty. Feroz's father was the kinsman who had pressed the hardest to have Nawal elected mukhtar of the Rulawa tribe and the man had asked Nawal to mentor his son.

As Feroz drove the Range Rover to the top of a short sand dune, the mukhtar looked down at the building his men had reassembled. As he looked around there was nothing else but trackless desert as far as the eye could see.

"Drive right down there," Nawal commanded, pointing to the building and to the group of men sitting in the shade of a large, open truck sitting adjacent to it.

"Yes, Mukhtar," Feroz replied, having finally been schooled by Nawal to do what he was told and stop asking about things that were none of his business.

As the Range Rover stopped in front of the truck the four men got up.

"It is time," Nawal began. "Pull all that camouflage netting out of the truck and cover the building completely. Use everything in the truck. I want at least three layers of the netting covering the building."

"Yes, Mukhtar," the group's foreman replied. With that, the four men sprang into action, and Nawal commanded Feroz to drive them back to their tents. The young man did as he was ordered to do, kept his mouth shut, but discreetly shook his head in disbelief.

Aboard *Normandy,* eight tense hours had passed since the ship sent its first streaming video of the Syrian ballistic missile emplacement and sinister-looking material surrounding a nearby blockhouse up the chain of command. Now the ship had settled back into its routine. For *Normandy,* already at sea, little seemed to change, but new messages continued to come in signaling the *Truman* strike group was increasing its level of readiness. Other ships were having their port calls abruptly cut short and *Harry S. Truman* would have only those storm repairs that could be completed in the next thirty-six to forty-eight hours done. The rest would have to wait.

Laurie had remained in CDC for virtually the entire time since the alert regarding the alarming Global Hawk video footage. She wanted to sleep, but she also wanted to remain in the battle rhythm of the ship so when she assumed her watch she would be as up to speed as possible.

"You ready to relieve me, Ms. Phillips?" the senior chief asked. As one of the A-team watchstanders in CDC, he had been monitoring his Tactical Data Consoles, keeping track of both Aegis radar contacts and the Global Hawk's video.

"Sure am, Senior Chief," Laurie replied. He wasn't typically in the watch rotation right before Laurie's, but as tensions had risen, *Normandy*'s senior watch officer had quietly pulled junior sailors out of the CDC watch rotation and replaced them with more senior people. Laurie was now included as a senior person.

"OK, then. Here's the tactical situation. We've been ordered to steam in this box anchored around this position here," the senior chief began, showing Laurie the center of the rectangular-shaped area *Normandy* was assigned to stay in. "*Mustin* has gotten under way from Bahrain and will be in our area in about ten hours. Other ships are getting under way just as fast as they can. *Truman* will probably take a little longer, maybe thirty-six hours or more, as their storm damage was more extensive. For now, our assignment is to just monitor air traffic in the area as well as keep track of what the Global Hawk is seeing."

"I think I've got it, Senior Chief," Laurie replied with as much confidence as she could muster. She was pleasantly surprised, no, come to think of it, she was stunned, she had been left in the watch rotation. Maybe her attention to detail and the extra effort she had made to learn her watch duties was paying off.

"Roger. You got it. Show's yours. You're going to get Global Hawk video pretty much continuously. Remember, there are three people in each watch section monitoring the video from that bird, but don't assume anyone else sees what you see. Report anything unusual to the TAO."

"Will do, Senior Chief. Any idea where the ops officer is? He usually spends a lot of time in here. I'm surprised I haven't seen him, given what's going on."

"Oh, word is he's been in the CO's cabin with the captain and the exec. Something big must be cooking for them to be behind closed doors for that long."

"Think it has anything to do with the Global Hawk video we saw earlier?"

"Yep. Things pretty much smoked up the chain of command as soon as the TAO saw that."

"Yeah, guess you're right, Senior."

"Need me for anything else, Ms. Phillips?"

"No, thanks, Senior Chief . . . and thanks for filling in the white space for me."

"No worries then. Gonna hit the rack myself."

As the senior chief left CDC and Laurie settled into her chair for the eight hours of the watch rotation, she could feel the tension aboard the ship. However, she forced herself to put that in the back of her mind so she could focus on the puzzling Global Hawk video she viewed eight hours ago. During those eight hours, while *Normandy*'s officers had been involved in a frenzy of activity, Laurie had had time to reflect on what she had seen and she had tried to make some sense of it. She knew something about the optics in the Global Hawk and about the "footprint," the amount of ground covered by its cameras as it streaked across the sky.

The Global Hawk video they had seen earlier was from the single bird that made its daily flight from Qatar to the Mediterranean and back, Global Hawk Two Bravo. It had to have been a profoundly lucky flight to have stumbled on this missile site all of a sudden, a discovery that had driven the level of activity aboard *Normandy*, and throughout the *Truman* strike group, from heightened, right through intense, to frenetic.

When she had viewed that video as one of a dozen people

crowded around a small screen eight hours ago, something had seemed a bit odd. She wasn't sure exactly what it was, just something different. She thought back to some of her work at the National Reconnaissance Office as well as at Center for Naval Analyses with UAV communications and optics packages and knew what she had seen on that footage wasn't quite right, but she couldn't put her finger on precisely what it was.

Now she had these displays to herself and a bit of free time, so she kept the current Global Hawk video, which showed nothing remarkable, on one screen of her UAV monitor. She used the playback capability of the system to display the video from eight hours ago on another screen. She played it back once, and then played it back again. She wasn't sure what she was seeing, but she was determined to keep watching it until she found out what wasn't right about this bit of video.

Seven time zones away, in the White House Situation Room, NSC junior staffers were scrambling to accommodate the president's most senior advisors in both secure conference rooms simultaneously. As they did, they continued to field questions from other officials too junior to be included in the top-secret meetings and secure video-teleconferences.

These more junior officials crowded into the tiny Sit Room watch floor both to monitor the action and to be close to their principals should they be needed immediately. Their demand for information and other support was nearly insatiable. Captain Joe Wexler was the Sit Room director, and his ops deputy, Rick George, had seen this all before.

"We're in a feeding frenzy again, Captain. This place is always a zoo at times like this. Don't worry; it will calm down eventually, it always does. What do you make of it anyway? We gonna pull the trigger this time?"

Wexler knew George's decades-long service on the NSC staff made him an invaluable asset. On the other hand, he also realized that after seeing dozens of crises and multiple tempests in a teapot, George took everything in stride, perhaps too much so. It was his job as Situation Room director to strike a balance.

"I don't know, Rick. We may. What that video shows us is pretty ominous. Put that together with the rhetoric coming from some groups in Syria and I think it spells trouble."

"Do you?" George asked.

"I do. The Syrians were never our friends to begin with. You remember the *Duelfer Report* said that Saddam probably transferred missiles and WMD to Syria right before Operation Iraqi Freedom? We also haven't forgotten that the Syrians weren't any damn help to us in the aftermath of that war; more insurgents got into Iraq across Syria's border than from anywhere else."

"You're right there."

"Yes, and now this new government in Syria isn't that warm to us to begin with and it's clear they don't have complete control of their country to boot. The intel we pick up from multiple sources tells us groups like Al Qaeda and Hezbollah are operating with near impunity and maybe even with a wink and a nod from the government."

"Sure," George said, "I get all that. Then again we're talking about just one missile site for God's sake, not an entire country armed to the teeth to attack us."

"No, you're right, but here's the thing. Those are Chinese-made DF-21D medium-range ballistic missiles. Remember when we first learned China was testing them back in 2006? DoD and Navy officials were catatonic and began calling it the first carrier-killer missile."

"I remember that, and I also remember it was some of their most jealously guarded technology."

"It was, but as China's economy continued to boom and their need for oil became nearly insatiable, they cut a deal with Iran. It was sweet deal for both parties. In return for selling Iran the DF-21D, China locked up some lucrative oil contracts with Iran."

"Yeah, but it's a long journey from Iran to Syria, how'd that happen?"

"Look, you've had an insider's view for years regarding what's going on in the Middle East. It's no secret that once this new government took over in Syria, Iran wanted to ensure its equities were advanced with the government as well as with elements in the country like Hezbollah. Hell, it's no stretch at all to think Iran put those DF-21D's directly in the hands of Hezbollah, knowing that group wouldn't feel any constraints using them where the new government in Syria just might."

"No, that all makes sense."

"And for all we know, those aren't the only DF-21Ds they have and we've got three carrier strike groups in the Central Command area of responsibility in range of them. Forget about worrying over what might happen to our friends in the area. Those missiles have a range of over 1,500 miles and can easily hit *Harry S. Truman* pier side in Jabel Ali and likely hit our other carriers and big deck amphibious ships in the area as well. We have to take action, and soon."

"We're worried about what they can put on them as a warhead, too, aren't we?"

"We sure as hell are," Wexler continued. "Those DF-21Ds can carry a nuclear warhead and the fact that the building at that site adjacent to the missile launchers has what appears to be fissionable material in canisters stacked up all around it is the worst possible scenario. We could be looking at ballistic missiles armed with WMD, most likely a radioactive dirty bomb."

"None of that was there as recently as a week ago."

"Right," Wexler continued. "The technology is pretty basic and there's little doubt Syria can put that all together in almost no time. If they lob just one DF-21D with a dirty nuke warhead and hit anywhere near *Harry S. Truman,* we'll lose hundreds, even thousands, of sailors instantly and the ship will be useless for years, maybe decades."

"So I get it, it's something we can't ignore, but . . . ," George continued, shaking his head, clearly unable to reduce their conundrum to an easy solution.

"The problem is, Rick, for all we know, the Syrian government may just be using the ruse they don't have complete control of their country. That way, they'll have plausible deniability if a missile gets launched from their territory."

"It still comes down to the question, is the threat compelling enough to make us act preemptively? Will the voices within the president's inner circle wanting action trump those urging caution?"

"Wouldn't shock me," Wexler replied. "We've been slow to deal with these kinds of threats in the past, and look what happened. Everything I've heard from the National Security Council principals coming in and out of here, including the national security advisor, tells me they don't want to be that slow again. No, my bet is we decapitate Syria, period."

George had to admit Wexler's arguments were hard to refute.

In the Presidential Palace in Damascus, Syria, Hafez Shaaban listened to his advisors' arguments, but said nothing.

"Excellency, the United States is an enemy of our government, don't you see?" the first man said.

"They didn't like the Assad regime, but they now complain more about the supposed chaos of our country," another advisor added.

"Something has caused them to issue threats against us, there's no doubt about that," the first man said.

Even though he was an Alawite, Shaaban had been an early leader in the uprising against the Assad dynasty during the Arab Awakening in 2011. Now he led the brittle, cobbled-together coalition of Alawites, Shias, Druse, and Christians that was attempting to govern the country. Unlike other new leaders in the Mideast, Shaaban had never lived abroad. In fact, he had never been outside the borders of Syria, save for regular religious pilgrimages to Saudi Arabia. Shaaban was focused on internal matters. He had much to do inside of Syria's borders to cure it of so many years of despotic rule.

Finally, he spoke. "The United States was never happy the Assad regime was close to Iran, and they thought when we replaced it, that would change. As you all know, we continue to get a great deal of support from Iran. The United States also thought we might move closer to Saudi Arabia but you know we continue to have issues with those responsible for Islam's two most holy sites, Mecca and Medina."

"But, don't you see," the second man said, "it's exactly because we are united with Iran to challenge their Saudi lackeys that the United States now poses a threat to our nation. The Saudis are alarmed and that has translated to their benefactors being alarmed."

"The Saudi Royal Court had become secularized and their moral leadership of Islam is weakening," Shaaban replied. "We will fill that void. What the Americans do is not my concern."

Hafez Shaaban did not want to be distracted by international events while he consolidated power within his country. He knew he didn't have complete control of all groups within Syria. He feared that the same revolution that brought him into power might be pulling apart his country and making it another Lebanon. He depended on his close advisors to keep track of external events for him. He would listen to them, and he would do what was necessary, but he felt with all his soul his primary focus needed to be within the borders of Syria.

CHAPTER TWENTY

USS Normandy
(March 18, 1615 Arabia Standard Time)

Aboard *Normandy*, Laurie Phillips was learning more by the minute, she just wasn't sure precisely what it was. Whether intuition, or a hunch, she knew there was something inconsistent about the Global Hawk video she had replayed a half dozen times.

Laurie reflected a moment on how different her perspective was from that of the officers, chiefs, and sailors aboard *Normandy*. They were operators, not analysts. They were used to reacting to a situation and taking action. They saw what they saw in the Global Hawk video and took that as ground truth. Now their focus was on informing their chain of command of what they had seen and preparing their ship to carry out the orders of that chain of command should they decide to act on this information. Laurie was coming to realize the officers and crew of *Normandy* seemed certain their chain of command would take action.

As an analyst, however, Laurie resisted the temptation to jump to the same conclusion the others had drawn from the video footage. She had trained all her post–Marine Corps professional life to do exactly the opposite. She was supposed to challenge every assumption, to look at things in an objective manner, and to put even the most compelling evidence to the closest scrutiny with the ultimate goal of discovering the real truth.

As she subjected the Global Hawk video to this examination, she sensed there was something wrong with the shadows on different parts of the video and with the latitude and longitude displayed in the corner of the streaming video. She hesitated to ask any of the sailors or officers in CDC about these anomalies, even though they were the people who respected her professionally. No, she would figure this out herself.

Where could she go for help to get more information? This was pretty esoteric stuff she was dealing with. The officers on board *Normandy* were operators and the nuances of how the video was captured, what it conveyed, and its overall validity was not their concern. Laurie knew a lot of the "why" behind the "what" and she had her suspicions about what she was seeing. She just needed to vet her thoughts and suspicions with a professional colleague with a better understanding of these comms and sensor packages. That would help her validate what she was seeing.

Laurie knew precisely who that person was. All it would take would be to simply type his address into the Outlook mail queue, but was that the only way to find out what she wanted to discover? Wasn't there a less risky way, one that wouldn't open up old personal and professional wounds? Laurie was oblivious to everything around her in CDC as she found herself frozen in inaction for a tiny eternity.

Seven time zones away, in the White House Situation Room, less than twelve hours since the Global Hawk video had hit the Sit Room staff, the president's small circle of senior advisors were trying to come to grips with what this all meant, and what, if anything, they could do about it. But their underlying core impulse was to do something. The Sit Room director, Joe Wexler, took little solace in getting it right in his discussions with his deputy, Rick George, the day before. The Sit Room staff had remained in place throughout the night orchestrating video teleconferences, pulling together intelligence reports, and preparing for the onslaught of action anticipated today.

President Wyatt Midkiff opened the meeting with his top advisors in the Sit Room's larger secure conference room. "All right, ladies and gentlemen. I know it's early, and we all are anticipating a long day, but this is something we need to deal with in real time. Adam, give us a recap, will you?"

The director of national intelligence, Adam Putnam, recapped what they all already knew. A DF-21D ballistic missile site had sprung up, seemingly overnight, in the Syrian desert, and there appeared to be fissionable material at hand that could be readily fitted into a warhead atop one of the four missiles at the site. Subsequent passes by the Global Hawk confirmed a great deal of activity by men in uniform, day and night, at the site.

The president turned to his secretary of defense, Jack Bradt.

"Jack, we know what we're looking at. Now what do we make of it?"

"Mr. President, as Adam has described, there's no new intelligence. We don't know anything we didn't know yesterday. We, Defense, and the intelligence community are moving to increase surveillance of Syria with various imagery and communications assets. We're reasonably confident there won't be any more surprises."

"Good, Jack. Good."

"I guess the only thing to add, Mr. President, and I hesitate to belabor the obvious, and I've conferred with State on this," Bradt continued, nodding toward the secretary of state, "but Syria *is* a sovereign country. They live in a pretty bad neighborhood, and the flip side of all this is perhaps it's just something that bears watching." Bradt knew what he was suggesting to the president was contentious. He just didn't know how much so.

"Jack, dang it. You're my SECDEF! If *anyone* is leaning forward on this, I need it to be you."

Bradt started to speak, but the president was in broadcast mode.

"Does 2009 ring a bell for anyone? Christmas maybe? Remember some guy named Umar Abdul Mutallab, a.k.a. the underwear bomber. We almost lost Northwest Flight 253 that day and do you remember why? Anyone?"

There was a nanosecond of silence in the Sit Room, so Midkiff plowed ahead.

"Because, as one of my predecessors in this office said, 'We failed to connect the dots.' He said it plain as day, and had we lost Northwest Flight 253 I'm pretty sure Barack Obama would have been a one-term president. Adam, I needn't remind you, one of *your* predecessors was hustled out of his job as DNI pretty quick over that episode, and nothing happened; the flight crew *did* stop the underwear bomber before he took down that plane."

No one spoke. The president's body language made it clear they shouldn't.

"So do we see any dots to connect here? We surge our forces forward to the Gulf as is our right in order to deal with threatening behavior from Iran. And just when we have five big deck ships within range of them, then what? Syria, who is *clearly* Iran's proxy in the region, just happens to roll out the one missile in the whole God-danged world that can hit a moving, let alone stationary, aircraft carrier or big-deck amphib. Do I really need to have State here give you all a tutorial on the long-standing tension between us and Syria? Or how that has ratcheted up in recent months?"

"Ladies and gentlemen, it's not just our job, it's our sworn duty to connect the dots. You can do it on your own, or I'll do it for you and drag you along kicking and screaming, but you *will* do it. Syria has demonstrated extreme hostile intent."

The president turned toward his attorney general.

"Judge, you spent your entire professional life in 'the law.' Do you know the difference between first-degree and second-degree murder?"

"I do, Mr. President."

"Then that's what we have here. Extreme hostile intent: The

difference between first-degree and second-degree murder. Adam, Jack, you have your folks turn up the gain on the intel side. I want an update this afternoon."

Prince Ali al-Wandi willed himself to be patient, but it was no use. He wanted to know what impact his actions were having and he wanted to know now. Too much hung on the outcome to just let things play out without him taking some measure of control. He would have to influence the final outcome. He needed to know the right time to put the next part of his plan in motion and he couldn't do that in a vacuum. He had paid enough money to and done enough favors for a few key people and now he was determined to call in those markers. Nothing would be traced to him.

How easy it was with e-mail. Here he was, a member of the extended Saudi royal family, soon to regain the respect of the Saudi king and move into the inner circles of the Saudi royal court. Yet in the Internet world he was a nameless, faceless address, savvy446@aol.com. He composed his e-mail to his associate in the Saudi Embassy in Washington, D.C. Oh, he was paid and paid well, but Ali liked calling him his associate. He was certain he would learn what he needed to know in short order.

Laurie Phillips and Sandee Barron were each hunched over laptops in their tiny stateroom going through work and personal e-mails. The two women had grown closer day by day. Although there were substantial differences in their upbringing, professional backgrounds, and current life-situations, they both looked at the world in basically the same way. Additionally, as two female professionals embarked in a male-dominated ship, there was a natural "we're in this together" alliance they had struck.

Laurie knew her roommate was in a foul mood, so she was careful about how she initiated the conversation as both stayed hunched over their laptops.

"Still no flying, huh?"

"Shit no," Sandee replied.

"Any idea when you'll start again?"

"Maybe when the powers that be figure out how to do more than one thing at a time, or when hell freezes over, whichever happens first."

"So what's the deal? The missions you all fly are important. Why did this video put the kibosh on that?"

"Like I said, and as you can probably tell, captain's pretty hyped up about being in the Gulf as it is. Now that we may have to be either chucking Tomahawk missiles at Syria, or knocking ballistic missiles out of the sky, or both, he just wants to just focus on one thing at one time. He says he doesn't want to deal with any 'distractions' like us flying."

"Not digging being thought of as a distraction, huh?"

"Nope. Not this aviator. I'm getting rusty just sitting on my hands."

"Yeah, I kind of get that, too."

"Look, maybe I'm just bitching, but hey, I'm a sailor too, it's my right," she replied, smiling. "But I figured we could be the eyes and ears of the ship while they're so focused on missile defense, that's all."

"No, I agree with you. Maybe he'll let up after a while," Laurie replied as cheerfully as possible. "Hey, you got time for a pretty serious question?"

That caused Sandee to stop typing and look right at Laurie. "Sure."

"Well, I'm kind of new at this. I've got to tell you, this Navy stuff is completely different from everything I experienced in the Marine Corps," Laurie began. "Anyway, now that you're not flying I see you coming in and out of CDC now and then so you know all this heightened tension is due to this Global Hawk video we saw yesterday."

"I'd say you're right about that."

"Yeah, well I think I told you, I've got a lot of experience with the optics and sensor packages on these systems from my previous work at Center for Naval Analyses and especially at the National Reconnaissance Office. I've got to tell you, there is something funny about this video of this missile site, something just not right . . ."

"Not right?"

"Yeah, Sandee, not right. I mean the shadows around the DF-21D missile site in the Syrian desert aren't the way I anticipated they would be. Not only that, but the lat and long displayed on the screen kind of jumps right before and after looking at the site. I just don't know what the problem is, but I'm convinced there is a problem."

"So what's the question? It seems like a lot is riding on that Global Hawk video. If it's not right, well . . ."

"So the question is, what I should do next? I've sort of off-handedly mentioned it to some of the watchstanders in CDC and they've just shrugged and kind of given me the 'it is what it is' salute. I think I need some validation of what I suspect. I'm thinking of reaching out to one of my former colleagues and ask him about it."

"You mean someone off the ship?"

"Yeah, a colleague back at the NRO."

There was a momentary pause as Sandee struggled with her roomie's question.

"If you're asking me for advice, Laurie, and I think you are, you might want to try running this up the chain of command on the ship first."

"Really? Everyone seems so busy they don't even have time to answer pretty simple questions."

"Yeah, but Laurie, you gotta understand. If there's anywhere in the Navy, hell, in all the services, where the control mentality prevails, it's on a Navy ship at sea. I know you served in the Marine Corps, which is the closest service to the Navy, but this is way different. The responsibility and authority vested in the captain of a Navy ship is like nothing in any of the other services. Like I told you when you first got here, if anything goes wrong on a Navy ship, it all comes back to the captain as far as accountability. Do I agree with the control thing all the time? Hell no. But I get it."

"No, I sort of see that."

"Look. It's like this. In the aviation world we kind of live by the motto 'It's easier to beg forgiveness than ask permission.' I guess you kind of lived by that in the Marine Corps from what you've told me about your career, but these guys are different, way different. And you have to understand, this captain is not like a lot of other people. No one has ever handed him anything. He's succeeded because he's always taken charge. Maybe the control thing is just part of it. Trust me; I've been burned before in my career when I've gone around the chain of command on a Navy ship. I've learned the hard way."

"I see."

"Didn't you tell me you had a pretty good relationship with the ops officer, Lieutenant Commander Watson? If anyone on the ship needs to know about your suspicions, it's him, and he can take them right to the captain. Why don't you start out with him?"

Laurie thought about it a moment and agreed. "I will, Sandee. I'll do that."

CHAPTER TWENTY-ONE

Saudi Arabian Desert
(March 19, 1530 Arabian Standard Time)

The phone in the blockhouse rang and Jawad Makhdoom picked it up on the first ring. He had been anticipating the call from Prince Ali and he was almost certain what the prince would tell him.

"Enough time has passed," the prince said. "Neutralize the site and let me know when you have completed your work."

"Yes, we will do it immediately."

Makhdoom rousted his men, shouting, "That was Prince Ali. Neutralize the site now. Let's get moving."

There was a frenzy of activity as his men swung into action. They had practiced this and they knew their roles. No other orders needed to be given.

Ali al-Wandi's call to the Saudi Embassy in Washington the day before had not been to some bureaucrat or minor diplomat. He had spoken with the man in the embassy who held the science and technology portfolio. He paid him enough to be responsive to his calls.

That man had served in the embassy for a number of years. As the S&T expert he had been instrumental in brokering the US$60 billion deal in 2011 in which the United States sold the Saudis platforms and weapons they sorely needed, many of them representing the cutting edge of American military technology.

The United States, and especially American defense contractors, had been eager to close this deal with the Saudis and had granted this man unusual access and information regarding the capabilities of key U.S. military technology. This Saudi was lavish with his gifts to important officials at some of the biggest defense contractors. They, in turn, had granted him unprecedented entree. The man often boasted, and with good reason, he knew the specifications of the best U.S. military equipment better than high-ranking generals and admirals did.

What Ali al-Wandi wanted to know, and what the man had readily delivered, was how long it would take the U.S. military to rush other overhead assets to the Gulf to confirm what Global Hawk Two Bravo had seen in the Syrian desert. He also wanted to know how long it would take the United States to redirect one of the military's satellites to peer down on the site.

Once he had his answer, al-Wandi had calculated how long he could leave his missile site in place before what Global Hawk Two Bravo was seeing was contradicted by another overhead asset. He knew how long it would take his men to disassemble and cover up the DF-21D missile site, added a few hours fudge factor just in case, and made the call to his chief engineer.

Now, minutes after his call, Jawad Makhdoom had his men disassembling the dummy missiles and fake missile launchers and putting them into the low-slung blockhouse. They then covered the blockhouse with roll after roll of camouflage netting and then for good measure used powerful blowers to blow sand over the blockhouse.

"What do you think?" his number two man asked Makhdoom.

"I think we've got it covered pretty well. Standing here, and maybe looking down from a few thousand feet, you can still tell something is here, but from the altitude the Global Hawk flies, it will just look like sand."

"Are we going to stop hacking the Global Hawk's sensors now?"

"Already done, and at the precise time we calculated."

"Then why does Prince Ali want us to stay here," the man asked. "Isn't our work over?"

"My friend, we must never question the prince. He may want us to activate the site again, and while it is true I don't need all of you here while I do this, the prince has instructed me to start playing the tapes he has prepared. For now, we wait."

"Tapes?" the man asked.

"Yes, tapes of some constructed conversations we want the Americans to overhear, but I've told you enough already. The prince doesn't want this information generally known."

The man feigned ignorance, but living in the tight quarters of the blockhouse, there really·were no secrets. The prince had paid someone to tape conversations that sounded as if they were coming from the Syrian army high command. The ominous-sounding exchanges were designed to make the Americans think

Syria had multiple DF-21D sites in its vast desert and that it was on the verge of launching her DF-21D missiles at U.S. Navy ships in the Gulf.

"All right then," the man replied, "but can we burn the Syrian army uniforms we have been wearing? The men are still angry they were made to wear them when they were outside the blockhouse."

"Not yet. Not yet."

On board *Normandy*, Laurie Phillips knew she hadn't done everything she needed to do, but she was on a mission to do just that. She had mustered the gumption to take her roommate's advice and go see *Normandy*'s ops officer and relate her concerns to him. Now, ten minutes after knocking on his stateroom door and having him listen to her worries about the video, she waited for Neil Watson to reply to her almost nonstop story.

"Ms. Phillips, you've explained what you've observed and related your suspicions. I've got to tell you, this is a lot to absorb. And you say you've shared this with some of my folks in CDC, and no one has a really strong take on this either way?"

"I think that about sums it up, Commander. I'm just not sure, but I *am* concerned something's not just right."

"All right then, we need to take this to the captain. He'll make the call."

"Captain, a moment?" Neil Watson asked as he appeared at the doorway of the captain's at-sea cabin with Laurie Phillips in tow.

"Sure, Ops O, what you got?"

"Captain, well, it concerns the Global Hawk video showing that DF-21D missile site in Syria. Ms. Phillips has some concerns she shared with me and we wanted to bring them to your attention."

That wasn't the affirming introduction Laurie was looking for, but it would have to do.

"Concerns, Ms. Phillips?"

"Yes, Captain," Laurie began, trying to be as respectful and diplomatic as possible. She certainly hadn't rehearsed this, and if she had she might not have had the courage to say anything at all.

"Captain, we have looked repeatedly at the Global Hawk video, or I should say I have, and well, sir, it appears this video may not be what we think it is. What I mean is, well . . . it could be presenting false information, and since it is information that seems to be sending the strike group into overdrive, we should give it a second look." This wasn't coming out precisely the way Laurie wanted it to. She tried to regroup. "Sir, I've looked at the video many times, and there appear to be some issues with the location of what it is taking pictures of. I mean to say, sir, well, it doesn't seem that based on the scenes shot earlier in the flight and the scenes shot later in the flight that the location of the DF-21D missile site is where this video is saying that it is."

Laurie tried to keep eye contact with Blackman as her words poured out, but occasionally she also cast a furtive glance at Neil Watson for support. However, the ops officer just looked at his shoes.

"In any event, Captain," Laurie continued, "since it appears the evidence we have against Syria is based solely on this video, perhaps we ought to tell our leaders there might be some issues with it." Laurie mentally kicked herself for letting her voice trail off a bit as she finished her last sentence.

Captain Blackman stared at Laurie as if he had been shot.

"Well, Ms. Phillips," Blackman began, "thank you for that . . . that . . . what is it you told us you came here to do? . . . that *analysis*."

"Yes, sir, Captain. Not analysis, not yet, anyway, just a suspicion."

"Do any of my other professionals in CDC share your suspicions? Mr. Watson, do they?"

"Well, not really, Captain; we wanted to tell you first."

Laurie jumped in. "Captain, the point is there appears to be so much riding on this video, maybe even us attacking Syria, that I just think we ought to take a better look at this before acting."

"Anything else, Ms. Phillips?"

Blackman's tone and body language weren't necessary hostile; they conveyed astonishment more than anything else. Yet they weren't friendly, either.

"No, Captain."

"OK, look. Let me tell you just a few things about the geopolitics here, Ms. Phillips," Blackman continued, his tone almost tutorial. "These folks don't really like us to begin with. They don't like our form of democracy and they don't like us telling them how to run their countries. Now, a long time ago we decided these repressive regimes were a hot bed for Wahhabi radicalism and a breeding ground for terrorism, a lot of it pointed toward us."

Laurie worked mightily to keep eye contact with Blackman.

"So you see, Ms. Phillips, it's perfectly logical to think the leadership in Damascus, a leadership who's clearly taking orders from Tehran, has it in for us. When they stood up to the Assad regime we didn't give them the same degree of support we provided to the rebels in Libya. They know we don't like their alliance with Iran and they know we sure as hell don't like them threatening our friends in Saudi Arabia. But they may be dense enough to think we'll just stand by and let them have their way. Trouble is, they didn't reckon with the United States of America or the United States Navy!"

Blackman was now becoming agitated.

"Now, about this video, we *do* know what the hell we're looking at and we *do* know what the hell we are supposed to do with it. I don't need anyone, and I mean *anyone*, second-guessing what we're doing, especially someone who is a guest on my ship. And I want to be clear on this Ms. Phillips; I don't need anyone trying to foist some cockamamie theory on us in the middle of a war zone."

Blackman paused to frame his thoughts, but not long enough for Laurie to jump in.

"Look, Ms. Phillips, I give you credit for coming forward. You're from CNA so I also give you credit for knowing a little bit about the Navy. There are only two ballistic missile defense ships in the strike group, us and *Mustin*. However, *Mustin* has a casualty to her SPY radar that might not get fixed for days; the part has to come all the way from the United States."

Blackman paused again.

"That leaves us aboard *Normandy* as the only defense against those DF-21Ds should Syria decide to lob just one of them at *Truman*, or any other Navy ships within range. So right now, Ms. Phillips, I gotta tell you, I'm a little preoccupied with ensuring that *Normandy* does her job and protects American lives. You get that, don't you?"

"Yes, Captain, I . . . ," Laurie stammered.

"Then help me do my job, OK? Just do your job. We're way past the analysis stage here. We may be in a fight at any moment."

Blackman's tone had softened a bit, and Laurie began to get it. It wasn't that he was a jerk or that he didn't respect civilian techies or didn't respect her because she was a woman. It was that what she was suggesting was so far outside the box of his background and experience that he couldn't fit what she was saying into his worldview.

"Captain, thank you. I think Ms. Phillips gets it. We're sorry to have bothered you."

"No bother, Ops O. I thank you both for coming forward, but you know what our orders are."

"Yes, sir."

"Ms. Phillips?"

"Yes, sir, Captain."

Laurie's head was spinning as she and the ops officer left the captain's at-sea cabin. He needed proof. OK. She would get him proof.

CHAPTER TWENTY-TWO

USS Normandy
(March 19, 2030 Arabia Standard Time)

Sandee Barron was sitting at her desk going through her e-mail queue when the door to their stateroom flew open and Laurie Phillips stormed in.

"Hey," Sandee began, but caught herself. Something was wrong.

"Well, that went over like a fart in church."

"What?"

"Just came from seeing the captain about the Global Hawk Video—"

"Lemme guess," Sandee interrupted. "He didn't see it your way?"

It had been Sandee's idea for Laurie to take this up *Normandy*'s chain of command. She felt invested in what Laurie was trying to do. She had evidently given her a bum gouge.

"That's an understatement! I got 'schooled' in how things work around here. He didn't chew me out or anything, but I gotta think any creds I've built up with him just went all to hell. I got patted on the head, dismissed and sent away to be a good girl."

"Was it that bad, really," Sandee asked, trying to be a good listener, but also trying to help her roommate work through this. She could tell she was steaming.

"I'm just pissed I didn't have my shit together. I was stammering and stuttering. I can see why he didn't buy what I was saying."

"Look," Sandee replied, slamming her laptop closed. "Let's work through this together. Tell me the whole story from the beginning."

Laurie poured out the details of her encounter. After a heated fifteen minutes, they were of like mind. Sandee said it first.

"You were right the first time, Laurie. You need to reach out to your friend at the National Reconnaissance Office."

"Boss, you ready for us?"

"Come in, fellas."

Roger McCord, Brian Dawson, Hector Rodriquez, and Aaron Bleich entered Chase Williams's office. Williams rose and motioned for them to sit at the small conference table.

"Well, you all have my attention. Let's hear it."

"Bottom line up front," McCord began. "Based on the flow of intelligence we have, we think we need to surge our JSOC team forward. Things were hot enough in the Middle East to begin with and now this Syrian missile thing has everyone going high order."

"Think this could be the real deal? Is it something where we'll need to give the president options?" Williams asked.

"It might be, boss. Brian and I have already engaged our logistics director and we want the N4 to start looking into this, and I've asked Aaron here to get the Geek Tank to focus their algorithms, anticipatory intelligence systems, and decision support software more intently on the Middle East. However, we wanted to bring this to you before going much further."

"I appreciate it, boys. Aaron, your folks ready to wet their beaks on this one?

"Yes, sir, we are."

If there was one person at Op-Center Chase Williams was still working to warm up to, it was McCord's networks assistant and Geek Tank leader, Aaron Bleich. He was McCord's "wunderkind" and he wanted to give his intelligence director the autonomy to run his own shop, but Williams had to admit to himself he still found Bleich to be an odd duck. He knew Bleich was McCord's MVP and de facto number two, but for the love of Mike, this kid was only thirty-two years old. Nevertheless, Williams had to admit that Bleich was just flat, scary brilliant.

Recruited via a gaming company front at San Diego's annual Comic-Con International Convention, Aaron Bleich grew up as a math and computer science prodigy. He skipped several grades in grammar school, attended the exclusive Francis Parker High School in San Diego, and won a full ride to Stanford. There, he dazzled Nobel Prize–winning professors with his computer and network skills.

On the surface, he was Op-Center's point man for protecting Op-Center's networks from external attack or internal compromise and also leader of the Geek Tank. Known only to Williams and McCord, he was also their chief hacker; he could get deep into any foreign or, for that matter, domestic network for information—or do irreparable damage. Bleich's skills were so prized that McCord was able to convince Williams and Sullivan to hire him on as a contractor and pay him deep into six figures. Williams had to admit that because Bleich was so smart, the kids in the Geek Tank respected his brilliance, and he had somehow molded them into a cohesive team.

During his many visits to the Geek Tank, Williams had learned Bleich was unmarried, with few friends except a small circle of gamers with skills like his, and that he lived alone in a third floor Capitol Hill walkup. His only indulgence was a 200-gallon exotic fish tank he surreptitiously had installed in his rental apartment.

"You're not going to ask Ms. Sullivan to buy you a whole new rack of servers just to take on this mission, are you?" Williams asked with a smile.

"No, sir," Bleich replied, "but we are going to have to crash a bit and tune up some of our algorithms to alert us to what's important and what's not. There's already an overwhelming amount of intel coming from that theater, as I'm sure you know, sir. Despite that, we'll get it done, no problem."

Confidence, Williams thought. *This kid has confidence.*

"I appreciate that, Aaron. OK, let's get to it. Brian, I'd like you and the logistics director to brief me soon on your surge plans. I need to send a POTUS/OC Eyes Only memo to the president and we need to bring the combatant commander into the loop."

"Will do, boss."

Laurie Phillips felt empowered after her talk with Sandee Barron. She was several years older than Sandee but she found herself continually drawn to her. What was it? Her presence and her confidence, that's what it was. Laurie didn't feel she had a great deal of either of those attributes and she looked to Sandee for those qualities. She knew what she needed to do, and she didn't have a lot of time to futz around thinking about it; things were moving too fast. However, this was bringing back bad memories. What was it? Was it a mixing of the personal and the professional that made her hesitate? Her relationship with Charlie had been great, and it was vastly more than just sex, though she admitted to herself that had been especially good.

Laurie had worked on some of the same projects Charlie did at the National Reconnaissance Office. The primary focus of their efforts was working with sensor and communications packages for UAVs. She smiled as she remembered how they had begun working together as colleagues, and how over time their collegial relationship had blossomed into much more. Yet there came a point when the projects they were working on began to compete for the same funding. There had been a major blowup between the two of them in front of their division director—and he had sided with Charlie.

As more of her most important projects lost out to Charlie's, and as he continued to move up at the National Reconnaissance

Office, she became more and more marginalized. The friction caused them to stop dating. He didn't want to stop. She called it off. Her professional pride and her ego had gotten in the way.

Laurie's thoughts turned back to the present. Now she needed Charlie's help. Would he help her? She had to find out.

The mood was grim as the president's advisors sat around the table in one of the Situation Room's secure conference rooms.

"All right, Jack, you talked with General Albin a few hours ago. What's his latest assessment?"

"Mr. President, as you've been briefed already," Midkiff's secretary of defense, Jack Bradt, began, "Syria took down that DF-21D site a few hours ago. We suspect, and the communications intercepts we've gotten support that suspicion, they knew we had seen it with our overhead assets so they took it down and moved it."

"Moved it where?" the president asked.

"We're still assessing that, Mr. President," Bradt continued, "but those same communications intercepts strongly suggest this wasn't the only DF-21D site Syria erected. We are rushing all the overhead assets we can to the Gulf right now, Mr. President, and we're giving General Albin everything he's asking for."

"Good, good," Midkiff replied.

"The other thing, Mr. President, as we've briefed you before, this might not be the Syrian government doing this at all. Our alternative theory is their government simply has to know that given tensions in the region, the United States would not sit idly by while they put DF-21D missiles in the field, missiles that directly threaten U.S. forces in the area, let alone U.S. allies. They're not that stupid."

"Maybe they are," the president groused.

"Maybe, Mr. President, but the problem is, we just don't *know*. As you're aware, since the civil war in that nation, Syria has become almost as closed a society as North Korea so there is no one on the ground there, not even international news media, who can confirm what the Global Hawk sees."

"I take your point, Jack."

"Thank you, Mr. President, and as you know, there have been strident denials by the Syrian government that it even has these missiles, let alone has them deployed in a threatening manner. One possibility is that President Shaaban is truly not in control of all of its territory. It may be that in some ways Syria is becoming like Lebanon, and a rogue group has placed the missiles there and intends to use them to at least threaten Western interests."

"I don't discount anything you say, Jack, but I'm worried about our forces right now, not what President Shaaban can or can't control in his own country."

"But what about *Truman*?" Midkiff's national security advisor, Trevor Harward, asked. "Can't General Albin get the carrier under way sooner? She's the biggest, most inviting, target."

"He, and the Navy, are working on it," Bradt replied, "but once they started tearing her apart to repair the storm damage, they found more hidden damage. They are only making the most essential repairs, but even working 24/7, it will be a good forty-eight hours before they can get the ship under way."

"Get me more intel on Syria, Jack, and get if for me ASAP," the president said.

As she typed her message, Laurie Phillips felt her eyes welling up. It had been the best relationship she had ever been in. Recalling it was more painful than she had imagined it would be.

If there was any ray of sunshine in this, she had unburdened herself to Sandee, telling her everything about the relationship with Charlie. She didn't know what quality it was: Empathy? The ability to walk in her shoes? Just being a friend? Whatever it was, she had needed Sandee and she had come through.

She looked at the message in her e-mail queue and considered it for a final time.

Charlie. Hi. It's been a while. My spies tell me you're still knocking it out of the park at NRO. I don't think I told you, but I have a new assignment with CNA. As I write this I'm aboard USS *Normandy*, an Aegis cruiser in the Arabian Gulf.

Since you're at NRO I suspect you know at least as much as I do, probably lots more, about the crisis here that got jacked up when our Global Hawk saw those DF-21D missiles in Syria. Who would have thought not that long ago when we were working on Global Hawk technology that here I'd be, seeing Global Hawk video in real time.

But I've seen the video the Global Hawk piped us from Syria and well, I'll just say it. I think something is wrong, maybe really wrong. I can't put my finger on it exactly but the shadows, the time hacks, a lot of things just don't add up.

There's a limit to the analysis I can do with the systems we have on the ship, but I know you have much more sophisticated gear at NRO. If I sent you a file on the high-side with this suspect video would you just look at it to see if my suspicions are correct or if I'm just imagining things? I think you know how important this video is. From what I can tell here, it's a major factor that might cause us to go to war with Syria.

I'll understand completely if this is something you can't do, but I sure hope you can.

Warmly,

—Laurie

She had reread the e-mail multiple times, and especially the last line, but she knew she needed to move forward—and quickly. She pushed SEND.

His advisors had to persist, and then persist some more, before Hafez Shaaban had relented and agreed to fly to Teheran and meet with Iran's Grand Ayatollah Seyyed Ali Hosseini Khamenei. What they needed to talk about had to be done in person.

Shaaban knew the grand ayatollah was a religious man who had renounced wealth, but the limo that had picked him up at Teheran's Imam Khomeini International Airport was something fit for a Saudi prince. Now he stood outside of the grand ayatollah's office in the Niavaran Palace, which was opulent by any standard. Shaaban began to understand why Iran had been able to bankroll Syria for so many years.

"Hafez Shaaban, my brother, may Allah's blessings be with you," Grand Ayatollah Seyyed Ali Hosseini Khamenei said as he walked up to Shaaban and embraced him in the traditional manner.

"And with you, Grand Ayatollah, thank you for agreeing to meet with me, and on such short notice."

"How may I help you?"

"First, Grand Ayatollah, you know I have been in office for but a short time, but I am aware of the long history of your country helping ours. We are in your debt and we remain your most loyal ally here in the region."

"And we yours. Go on, please."

"You know well our long-standing quarrel with the Saudis, but now their patrons, the Americans, are threatening us. I am afraid I must come to you for help."

"Whatever we can do, with Allah's help."

With that, Hafez Shaaban poured out what his intelligence services had told him about America's threatening moves against Syria. Of course, Ali Hosseini Khamenei's intelligence sources were vastly superior to his, but he let the younger man pour out his story. The more Ali Hosseini Khamenei listened, the more he saw opportunity in the issues raised by Shaaban. Yes, some of what he was prepared to do would help take American pressure off Iran's proxy, but more importantly, it would put Iran in a position to be the most powerful nation in the Gulf. It was something the Americans and their Saudi lackeys had denied them for far too long.

Laurie had been cheered when Charlie had gotten back to her, but she was pleasantly stunned by what he said in his reply.

> Laurie, it was great to hear from you. I've had my spies out, too, and I know you're a rising star at CNA. I've heard from people I trust they don't usually send analysts out on assignments like yours until they've been with the company for at least a decade or so.
>
> Your suspicions sound valid. I'm happy to help in any way I can. Send me what you have on the highside as soon as you can and I'll make it my number one priority.
>
> Miss you,
> —Charlie

Laurie headed for CDC and for a SIPRNET terminal, a node the Department of Defense and Department of State Secure Internet Protocol Router Network of interconnected computer systems used to transmit information up to the secret level. She wanted to get this suspect video to Charlie—and fast.

Miss you. Wow.

PART III

CALL TO ACTION

CHAPTER TWENTY-THREE

Op-Center Headquarters, Fort Belvoir North, Fairfax County, Virginia
(March 20, 0830 Eastern Daylight Time)

Chase Williams made it a practice not to ask his Op-Center staff to work overtime or into the night. He didn't have to; if they knew something vital to national security needed to be done they rallied and did whatever it took. However, a quick reading of time stamps on the e-mails that populated his queue that morning told him what none of his professionals would say. They'd been at it late the day before.

Brian Dawson and Williams's logistics director, the N4, Duncan Sutherland, entered his office.

"Brian, Duncan, come on in and make me a lot smarter than I am now on what you've got cooking."

"Duncan's done all the heavy lifting, boss. I'll let him start," Dawson said.

Chase Williams considered the diminutive man standing next to Brian Dawson. *A study in contrasts,* he thought. Dawson towered over the five-foot six-inch Sutherland, but God, was he lucky to have the man with the thick British accent on Op-Center's team.

A street urchin from Liverpool, Sutherland had lied about his age and joined the British army at fifteen. He gravitated to the British Special Air Service, the SAS, and served as liaison with the Gurkha regiment in Brunei. Williams knew perhaps more of Sutherland's history because he had to admit to himself, the man was so different from anyone he had ever worked with before. Sutherland was married to a wealthy New York socialite and had managed, through her connections, to be transferred to the American Army. A seemingly vanilla kind of man, still several years shy of forty, Sutherland was both shrewd and intelligent, just the qualities Williams wanted, and needed, in a logistics director. Sutherland knew the British army, the American Army, and by extension, all armies. Williams knew Sutherland could finesse any system, get anything, and never failed to have the right material at the right place at the right time. That's why he recruited him the day he qualified for his Army pension.

"Mornin', boss," Sutherland began, his thick Liverpool accent still part of his persona. "The boys said you want to surge JSOC into the Mideast, somewhere where they can range into Syria and maybe some of the surrounding countries. Got that about right?"

"You do, Duncan, and we need to get them there quickly."

"Well, that's good, then. Knowing you might not want to wait, I scrambled them last night aboard a sanitized JSOC Gulfstream—an extended range G-5. They packed out with a light-infantry load for a long-range desert patrol and an urban battle kit." He looked at his watch. "They'll be on the ground in Incirlik Air Force Base, Turkey, in about an hour. We have a hanger reserved for them and two de Havilland Otters standing by to take them south as needed. Brian here's been talking with some of the tribal leaders he's still friendly with. Here are one or two spots we can jump into for a forward operating base," Sutherland said as he rolled out an area map to explain his plan to Williams. "We can move as soon as the gear is transferred or lay up in Incirlik until needed."

"Hector was able to get down there and get aboard with the team," Dawson said as the three of them poured over the map. "Major Volner has a full suite of comm gear, but Hector took along some iridium encrypted phones, so we can talk to him whenever we like, in real time."

Williams looked from Dawson to Sutherland and back. Then he smiled broadly. "How'd you know?"

"That's why you pay us the big bucks, boss," Sutherland deadpanned.

"If there's no need for them," Dawson said with just a trace of a smile, "we can recall them anytime. And it's good flyaway training."

In Chantilly, Virginia, at the National Reconnaissance Office's headquarters, Charlie Bacon was glad Laurie Phillips had reached out to him. He was, above all else, a patriot, and he knew since NRO was the U.S. intelligence agency that designed, built, and operated U.S. spy satellites and coordinated the analysis of aerial surveillance and satellite imagery from several intelligence and military agencies, NRO was the right agency to look at the suspect video Laurie had sent him. While he tried to be humble about it, he had to admit he was just the right analyst to review this video. He'd been with NRO for just short of a decade, he knew he was the best, and his bosses did, too.

Charlie had elected not to share this with his management chain, at least not yet. They hadn't come up the hard way like he did through the imagery branch. They'd moved laterally from elsewhere in NRO and, in the case of the Senior Executive in charge of his division, from outside the office. *What the hell did she know except how to screw with my budget?* he found himself thinking.

Charlie had sequestered himself in the corner of the vault and reviewed the short clip Laurie had sent him a half dozen times. He reached the same conclusion each time.

"Hey, Aaron, come here!"

Aaron Bleich walked up behind Maggie Scott, who was monitoring one of the screens in the Geek Tank. Not yet thirty, Maggie had been one of Op-Center's early hires. Five feet seven inches tall and, in her words, a "fluffy" 170 pounds, with flaming red hair and a penchant for wearing whatever the latest Goth fashion was, Scott had made her bones at Amazon before Chase Williams hired her away.

"What ya got, Maggie."

"You know how we altered our programs to pretty much zero in on intel coming from the Middle East, right? Well, they've had a while to churn now and we've got a confluence of information. We got comm intercepts coming out of Syria about what they are going to do with those DF-21D missiles, some communications between a Navy ship in the Gulf and NRO on SIPRNET, and some feeds out of Iran. The programs tied them all together and this is what it's pointing to. What do you think?"

Bleich studied what was displayed on the screen at Scott's workstation.

"This looks promising. Let's run it through the decision support program. How long will that take."

"Dunno. Maybe thirty or forty minutes."

"Good. Holler when it's done and if it confirms what you suspect, we'll take it to Roger."

Laurie was monitoring her SIPRNET e-mail queue while she stood watch in CDC when Charlie's message hit her screen.

> Laurie. I gave your video top priority and ran it through some of our most sophisticated analysis and I have an answer for you. Your suspicions were right. This video is hosed up.
>
> You remember when we were doing some of the early work on Global Hawk? There were issues that were raised about the links going to and from the bird from the UAV's ground station being susceptible to intercept and maybe even hacking?
>
> Not sure if you were still here when that all got resolved, or not, but some of us here felt the contractors who manufactured the Global Hawk swept those

concerns under the rug because they were worried the Air Force wouldn't buy it because of those issues. However, that's all in the past and none of us can fix that now.

Bottom line, what you suspect is absolutely right. I found a time-delay that had been inserted in the bird and did some calculations and that missile site isn't in Syria, it's in Saudi Arabia. The attachment to this e-mail has the latitude and longitude and the grid co-ordinates of where I think it is. I'm no expert on Saudi Arabia, but it looks like it's definitely in the desert away from civilization.

Yet here's the thing, Laurie. You're right, but you're going to have to do whatever you feel you need to do through your chain of command. Not to tell you too much, but we had a security inspection here at NRO about eight months ago and we didn't do so well. As a result, security here has been jacked up to an unbelievable level. I can't tell my bosses I did this or I'll get slammed. Wish I could do more, but I just can't. I hope you understand.

You're right, Laurie, and I'm sure when you show them what I've got in the attachment the folks you work for will understand you're right. Go get 'em, Laurie.

Be well,

Yours,

Charlie.

Laurie sat bolt upright in her seat. Now she had it. She'd go see the captain again, but this time armed with proof!

Trevor Harward was in a foul mood as he sat at the end of the table in one of the Situation Room's two VTC conference rooms. Some of his senior National Security Staff populated other chairs around the table for this hastily called VTC with the Central Command commander, General Albin. Harward didn't want the president at this VTC. He wanted Albin all to himself.

"Good morning, Mr. Harward," Albin began.

"General, know you're mighty busy so I'll get right to it. I've been reading the reports you've been sending us and I just don't get why things aren't moving faster. We've got a threat to your forces in theater. We all agree we need to do something about it, but things need to move!"

"I hear you, Mr. Harward, but we are redeploying our forces as fast as we can. There are a lot of moving parts to getting this done. We're proceeding as rapidly as possible to ensure we have all the forces we need in place before we move."

"General, we're not attacking China, or even Iran. This is a shithole that has been turned inside out by a years-long civil war, for God's sake. This isn't Desert Storm, either, and while we're at it, why is it taking so God-damned long to get *Truman* under way? I asked for every-six-hour updates, and your last up-date had the time to get under way longer than the report before that one! Are we moving backward or what?" Harward was let-ting his exasperation get the better of him, and finally Albin had had enough.

"Mr. Harward, respectfully, let me address *Truman* first. As you know, the Navy rushed the *Truman* strike group here, but in doing so, they drove it through one of the worst Atlantic storms of the last decade. I've been aboard *Truman*, sir. The ship's a mess and as the Navy digs into it to fix one thing, they find other issues with the ship and the aircraft. I can put my 5th Fleet commander or the *Truman* strike group commander on an aircraft today and one of them can explain this to you in person with more granularity than I can."

"That won't be necessary," Harward snapped.

"Sir, we have moved USS *Normandy*, our missile defense ship, into position to protect *Truman* from missile attack as it undergoes repairs. I'm confident the ship is safe for now."

"It had better be!"

"Now, Mr. Harward, about Syria and these missiles, as you are well aware, the site the Global Hawk discovered is no longer there or else it's been extremely well camouflaged. We have the Global Hawk flying the same route and there appears to be nothing where there previously was a missile site."

"Nothing?"

"There's a limit to what we can see from sixty-five thousand feet, sir. While there certainly aren't missile batteries at that latitude and longitude, there may be a building, but one that has been well camouflaged."

"But what about satellites? I've been briefed on how many satellites we have covering the region, surely we can get some sort of confirmation," Harward groused.

"Sir, we can't be sure with only Global Hawk or satellite imagery. They just don't have the granularity, but based on the comms intercepts we've received, we believe the Syrians have moved these missiles anyway, and that they have additional missile sites we haven't located yet. Right now our overhead assets are so scarce we don't know whether they have additional missile sites elsewhere in the country or where they are."

"General, they are not ten feet tall!" Harward interjected. "Get some manned aircraft over the country and get eyes on. I'd have thought you'd done that already and I wouldn't have to fight this war for you from here in the Sit Room!"

The national security advisor was becoming agitated and General Albin paused before continuing. "Mr. Harward, this is a bit out of my wheelhouse, and I'd suggest your European Command commander would know vastly more about this. However, when the Arab Spring was churning in 2011 and NATO made the decision to attack Libya, there was intense criticism for NATO not going into Syria as well."

"There was a reason for that, General, and I don't need a history lesson from you on Libya. That was then and this is now. This is Syria, not Libya. It's on my watch and yours, and we have to deal with it. Are we clear on that?"

"We are, sir, but I know Syria. That's my job. I suspect I needn't remind you, Mr. Harward, Russia has sold Syria the S-300 missile. That's one of the best—if not the best—air defense missiles in the world; it's better than our Patriot missile system. Our initial intelligence has told us the A-300 is deployed throughout the country, and in substantial numbers. Sending aircraft over Syria is just too risky a proposition. I'm not going to send my pilots on a one-way mission."

"Yes, I know that, General. No one is asking you to do that; there are always risks in war."

"Sir, we need to get more information on where other missile sites may be located. I've just got an additional Global Hawk moved into theater and another one arrives the day after tomorrow. I am increasing overhead coverage of Syria as fast as the other combatant commanders can send me more assets. Nevertheless, Mr. Harward, regardless of what we can see, we have to believe what the communications intercepts we are getting are telling us. Syria has multiple DF-21D missile sites deployed throughout there desert. It's a huge area, sir. It may take us days to find them, no matter how many overhead assets we have. For right now we need to move more forces into the area to support *Truman*. One hit from one of those DF-21D missiles and my aircraft carrier will look like the Marine barracks in Beirut. I'm sure you don't need a history lesson from me on what happened there."

"No, General," Harward said tightly, "I do not."

The VTC continued, with both men standing their ground, and the National Security Staff staffers around the table were becoming more and more uncomfortable.

Laurie had printed out what Charlie Bacon had sent her, found Lieutenant Commander Watson in CDC, and laid out her case to Normandy's ops officer. Watson absorbed what she presented and they went to see Captain Blackman on *Normandy*'s bridge.

"Ops O. Ms. Phillips," Blackman began, wary that they might be approaching him on the same subject they had bothered him about in his cabin the day before.

"Captain," Watson began. "After our meeting yesterday, Ms. Phillips decided she needed to get some additional help interpreting what the Global Hawk video was showing, so she reached out to a colleague at the NRO—"

"The NRO?" Blackman interrupted.

"Yes, Captain, the National Reconnaissance Office—"

"Neil! I know what NRO stands for," Blackman interrupted again. Then turning to Laurie, his face hardened. "Ms. Phillips, I thought we settled this yesterday in my at-sea cabin. Did you tell anyone else you were going way outside our chain of command to 'reach out to someone' at NRO?"

"No, Captain, I didn't."

"Both of you, my at-sea cabin, now," Blackman said as he pushed himself out of his bridge chair. He turned toward his officer of the deck. "OOD, I'll be in my at-sea cabin for a few minutes."

"Captain's off the bridge," the bos'n mate on watch chimed as the pair followed Blackman out the door at the aft end of the bridge and back to his at-sea cabin a deck below on *Normandy*'s port side. They entered the cabin; no one sat down. "Ms. Phillips, Mr. Watson has been with me since I took command, so he knows why we just came back to my at-sea cabin. I'll ask you, why did we move off the bridge?"

The question threw Laurie off-guard. "Well, so it would be quieter, Captain?"

"No. How many people were on the bridge?"

Another off-guard question. "I'm not quite sure, Captain. A half dozen maybe?"

"Eight to be exact. Ms. Phillips. Now I have the class to try not to have disagreements, or to be disagreeable, in front of a crowd of people. I'm not sure you share my view."

"But, Captain, this is important and I wanted to inform you, sir."

"Ms. Phillips, before you 'inform' me, can you tell me first what you think you were doing communicating with the NRO without informing me or anyone in your chain of command?"

Blackman looked toward his operations officer. "You know about this, Mr. Watson?"

"No, sir."

"Did you tell anyone else, Ms. Phillips?"

"No, Captain."

"I see. We'll deal with your flagrant disregard of professional courtesy later. To show you that, as opposed to you, *I* have good manners, what is it you came to so urgently tell me?"

Still off-guard a bit from the captain's initial questions, Laurie plunged forward, going back to the original Global Hawk video received aboard *Normandy*. She segued seamlessly to her prior work on UAV comm links and sensors at NRO and the Center for Naval Analyses. She told the captain about Charlie Bacon's expertise but didn't reveal his name. Finally, she laid down the attachment Charlie had sent her on the small, gunmetal gray desk in the captain's cabin.

Pete Blackman picked up the paper and studied it. He looked at Laurie. Then he looked at Watson.

"Well, Ms. Phillips, thank you for coming forward. This is a lot to absorb. Now, I think you told me you are on watch in CDC so I'll let you get back to that. That will be all right now. Mr. Watson, stay behind a moment, will you?"

"Captain?" Laurie said, now completely off-guard, wanting to hear Blackman's verdict.

"Thank you. That will be all right now."

Laurie staggered out of Blackman's cabin, not knowing what to do next.

Aaron Bleich stood behind Maggie Scott and looked at what their decision support software displayed on her screen. He leaned over, took control of her mouse, scrolled down, then up again, then relinquished control.

"Whew, this is something," Bleich said.

"We going to see Roger?" she asked.

"You bet." The pair headed for Roger McCord's office.

The senior chief walked up behind Laurie, who sat at her watch station in CDC. She was still stunned and didn't know what to think of the encounter in the captain's cabin. Even three hours after the meeting she was still trying to make sense of what happened.

"Ms. Phillips?"

"Yeah, Senior Chief, what's up?"

"Ma'am, Commander Watson requests you meet with him in his stateroom."

"Ah, sure. Can you get someone to cover my station?"

"Already done, ma'am."

Laurie made a beeline for Watson's office. She was cautiously optimistic that, in spite of his reservations, her proof had carried the day with Captain Blackman.

"Commander, you wanted to see me," Laurie said as she knocked on his open stateroom door.

"Yes. Please come in and sit down, but close that first, would you?"

"Yes, sir."

Laurie sat with her hands on her knees, leaning toward Watson, her anticipation growing.

"Ms. Phillips, first of all, let me say I respect your professional ability and what I think is your wanting to do the right thing, but it's my duty to present this to you and ask you to sign it."

Watson slid a piece of paper across the small table in his stateroom. As Laurie began to read the paper her jaw dropped. She finished reading it and slid it back toward Watson.

"With respect, sir, are you shitting me?"

"I assure you, I'm not, Ms. Phillips. The captain drafted the language himself and had our legal officer review it. You're to have no other communications, via e-mail or any other means, with anyone off the ship, other than your immediate family members, for the duration of *Normandy*'s time in a war zone."

"But the communication with my contact at the National Reconnaissance Office was crucial. You saw, and the captain saw, that the Global Hawk had been hacked and video of the missiles in Syria wasn't from Syria at all!" Laurie exclaimed.

"Yes, well, about that. I'm afraid the captain didn't find your arguments and your proof compelling, and to be honest with you, Ms. Phillips, I'm afraid I didn't, either. This is clearly the opinion of just one person in one agency, and I don't see any reason why we should believe what he alleges."

"Commander, I think if you'll let me walk you through what I received from my contact at NRO, perhaps in more detail, you'll change your point of view. You have got to do this. You have got to do the right thing!" Laurie shot back, feeling this was her last chance to convince Watson.

The ops officer sat silently for a few moments. Finally, he spoke.

"Anything else, Ms. Phillips?"

"Well, no. I do think you'll change your point of view. Now, look at this—"

"Stop!" Watson interrupted. "My point of view, as you call it, doesn't mean a goddamn thing on this ship, and yours means even less, Ms. Phillips!" he continued, his voice now betraying his anger. "The only, and I mean *only*, point of view that matters on this ship is that of Captain Peter Blackman. He's our commanding officer. He has twenty-two years of Navy experience, seagoing experience. That makes him the most knowledgeable person on this ship, *and* if that weren't enough, there's a ream of

United States Navy regulations that gives him paramount authority over everyone on this ship. That means everyone, military and civilian, embarked in *Normandy*."

"Yes, sir, but—"

"NO, Phillips! I heard you out, now you listen and listen good! You may be a hotshot civilian analyst and think you can run your own little show here. My officers have gone out of their way to make you feel welcome and make you feel useful, and to your credit, most everyone says you're trying to do a good job. However, you are *way* out of line challenging Captain Blackman on something like this. He takes his orders from Admiral Flynn, and from a long chain of command going up to the commander in chief. So the captain showed you enormous courtesy just by letting you come up to his cabin and give your little show, and I stuck my neck out by going with you. Now we are way past the point where everyone can just chime in with their personal opinion."

"Yes, I know, but we may be making a terrible mistake. That video—"

"Phillips, you're not hearing me!" Watson interrupted again. Now there was real venom in his voice. "We are in a *war zone*! You are on a U.S. Navy *warship*! The captain says jump, the only question we ask is 'how high?' Don't compound your problems by trying to change anyone's mind after the decision has been made. Time to get with the program, Ms. Phillips."

Laurie opened her mouth to speak but Watson put up his hand.

"Look, Phillips. You don't know what the hell you're doing

'or what the hell you're talking about. You have some pet rock theory about this video. You presented it to the commanding officer. You had your day in court. He heard you out. Now we're moving forward, and you're moving out of my stateroom, damn it; because I've got little enough time to do what I need to do on this warship! Clear?"

Laurie rose without a word and stormed out of Watson's stateroom.

CHAPTER TWENTY-FOUR

USS Normandy
(March 20, 2115 Arabia Standard Time)

Sandee Barron took one look at Laurie as she slumped into their stateroom and knew something was wrong, really wrong.

"Laurie, what's the matter?"

"Oh God, I've failed, I've failed miserably," Laurie said, tears welling up in her eyes.

"What, what happened?" Sandee replied. She could see her roommate was about to lose it.

"Oh, I don't know what to do. I don't know what to do," Laurie continued, beginning to sob.

"It's OK. It will be OK," Sandee said as reassuringly as she could as she put her arm around Laurie. "Look, sit down, tell me what happened."

Laurie sat, the sobs coming more freely now, and poured out her story to Sandee. The younger woman tried to be a good listener, but what Laurie was telling her wasn't making sense. How could they not believe her? It was so unfair. She was trying to do her duty, but she was being stonewalled. At the same time, she had never felt so powerless. Laurie was pouring her heart out to her and she couldn't do a thing about it. Finally, Laurie was finished.

"Look, Laurie, we'll figure this out together, I promise," Sandee said as reassuringly as possible. "How can I help?"

Laurie made no reply, her sobs now turning to sniffles. *How could anyone help her?*

Roger McCord had complete confidence in Aaron Bleich, but what he was telling him was so off-the-chart he had trouble getting his brain around it. But once he did, he knew they had to take it to Chase Williams. The Op-Center director responded to McCord's call by telling him to come to his office immediately.

"Boss," McCord began, once he and Bleich were seated in Williams's office. "Aaron has had the Geek Tank churning to get this intel. I'll let him lay it out to you."

"Aaron?" Williams began.

"Well, it's like this, sir. Once you asked us to focus on the Middle East to the exclusion of almost everything else we were able to dedicate the bulk of our resources, including all of our high-performance computing assets, to what is coming out of that area. Naturally, we put the most intense focus on these Syrian missiles."

"I appreciate that, Aaron, and I know you and your folks have been burning the midnight oil to do this."

"Not a problem, sir. Well, I'll just give you the bottom line up front. We are certain these missiles are not in Syria—"

"Not in Syria?" Williams interrupted. "If not there, where are they?"

"Well, we're still working on that and expect to have an answer in a few hours. For now, the fact they are not in Syria, *and* that someone was able to hack into our Global Hawk downlink to make us think they are in Syria, tells us something really fishy is going on."

"It's a preliminary analysis, boss," Roger McCord added, "but we wanted to bring you this much right away."

"You did the right thing, Roger, but what about our JSOC flyaway team? We have them forward now, but are they in the right place?"

"I was thinking the same thing," McCord replied. "My guess is that they're probably close to where they'll be needed if they're needed. We'll know soon."

"I agree. Aaron, great job, please come in and update me as soon as you have more information. Roger," he continued, "Brian and I talked about him going downrange with the team if things heated up. I think the kettle's boiling. Tell him it's time to saddle up and ask Duncan to get him to Incirlik ASAP."

It took the nation's intelligence agencies, all of which worked in the world of secret, top secret, and higher levels of classification, a bit of time to get and absorb the news, as it was gathered by the CIA's Open Source Center. Nevertheless, the fact that it had come from a completely open source made it all the more stunning.

The Islamic Republic News Agency, or IRNA, the official

news agency of the Islamic Republic of Iran, posted the broadcast on its Web site without fanfare at 2230 Arabia standard time on March 20:

> *Iraq has demonstrated criminal intent and proven that they are lackeys of Western governments by once again stealing oil from the Islamic Republic of Iran's oil reserves. They have been tunneling horizontally to reach our oil, something they clearly could do only with Western help. At this moment they are shipping this oil from their facility at the Al Baṣrah oil terminal.*
>
> *This thievery is not only contrary to Islamic law, but it is an affront to the peaceful people of the Islamic Republic of Iran. The Islamic Republic has no recourse but to state that until this criminal activity ceases, not one barrel of any nation's oil will leave the Arabian Gulf. Furthermore Iraq must acknowledge its illegal acts and compensate the Islamic Republic of Iran for the stolen oil.*
>
> *Any attempt to stop the Islamic Republic of Iran from preventing this wanton thievery will be met by appropriate force.*

Prince Ali al-Wandi trusted his chief engineer above all others, but he wanted to see the operation for himself. He was pleased when it took him and his pilot a second look from only two miles away to find the mostly obscured blockhouse. Once the S-92 helicopter landed and the prince got out, Jawad Makhdoom was outside to great him. The prince waved his helicopter away. "Come inside quickly," he said to the chief engineer. "We don't know what other prying eyes the Americans have."

Once inside, Prince Ali looked at the large audio apparatus and computer monitor they had set up. "So you have been alternating these communications as we discussed," the prince began.

"Yes, I have. We have six tapes and I have been playing them according to this schedule," Makhdoom replied, moving his mouse and clicking an Excel spreadsheet on his computer desktop. "We are running the conversations you had taped that sound like Syrian army officers and other officials talking about making these missiles ready for launch. We are broadcasting this on the frequencies you gave us, the ones you said the Syrian military uses for high-level communications."

Al-Wandi knew Makhdoom wasn't questioning his judgment, but just needed reassurance. "Yes, it wasn't difficult to get those frequencies or the kind of jargon their military uses. After all, you know how many of their military went over to the rebel side during their civil war. Even soldiers need to feed their families."

"I understand, Your Excellency. Listening to them myself they sound convincing. It sounds like Syria has multiple DF-21D sites throughout their desert and a command center somewhere else, probably in Damascus, that is trying to coordinate between all the sites so when they launch the missiles, they make a coordinated attack against the American aircraft carrier."

"You listen well, my friend. So tell me, what are the communications saying as to why they haven't attacked already?"

"It appears the Syrians are having technical issues at several of their sites and the people in the command center are angry about it. In several cases they talk about sending technicians to the sites to fix things."

"Good. You are hearing just what we want the Americans to hear. Yet still no action from them yet?"

"They may be taking action, but we just might not know about it yet," Makhdoom said, trying to reassure his boss.

"You may be right. But we need to get them to move faster. Here, here are two more tapes I want you to load up, put in the queue, and start playing."

"Mr. President, thank you for seeing me on such short notice," Jack Bradt said as he entered the Oval Office. "Trevor," he continued, acknowledging the national security advisor.

"No, Jack, thank you for staying on top of all this. We've got a hell of a mess in the Gulf, don't we?"

"Mr. President, we've now basically got a two-front crisis. I think we need to move and move quickly."

"All right. I've been getting information from Trevor's National Security Staff throughout the day, so pull it all together for us from your perspective, would you?"

"Certainly, Mr. President. Now that we've got the three-letter agencies focused intently on Syria we're getting more and more communications intercepts. Syria, or groups working from Syrian territory, is talking about doing a coordinated DF-21D strike on U.S. assets in the area. We're giving General Albin all the overhead assets we can as fast as we can, but . . . well, Mr. President,

Syria is bigger than Florida, and you know how big your home state is. That's a hell of a lot of ground to cover."

"No, I get it."

"And now we've gotten this message from the Islamic Republic News Agency about stopping the flow of oil out of the Gulf."

"And we think they're serious?" the president asked.

"We do, but not for the reasons they state. Iraq's not stealing their oil, that's just a ruse they're using, a similar one to one they've tried before. We know Syria's leader traveled to Iran and that Iran is desperate to prop up their one remaining friend in the Gulf."

"So this is a threat against us, to prevent us from doing anything to Syria?"

"That's our consensus assessment, Mr. President. It kind of is in line with what one of our Central Command commanders, General Mattis, said back in 2013."

"Oh, you mean his Senate testimony?" Harward asked.

"Yes. He told the Senate the collapse of the Assad regime would be the biggest strategic setback for Iran in twenty-five years. That got a lot of people's attention. Yet it's as true today as it was then. Regardless of who's running Syria, Iran needs that government to be aligned with them, maybe more so now than they ever have."

"So they'll do what they need to do to keep us from moving against Syria?"

"In a nutshell, yes, Mr. President. If we look at just how Iran might do this, the only logical conclusion is they'd do it by mining the Strait of Hormuz. They don't have the naval assets to seriously threaten oil tankers transiting the Gulf, not with as many ships as we have there to provide tanker escort."

"So what are you and the Joint Chiefs suggesting we do?"

"Mr. President, we need to move against Syria and this missile threat, and soon. Once that's done, we need to turn our attention to Iran. If they mine the Strait of Hormuz we know how to sweep those mines. We've got to put our mine-countermeasures forces, our Navy MCM folks in Bahrain, on alert now. We also need to get additional MCM helos moving from Norfolk because it will take them a week to get there, and we need to bring other assets to bear to protect the minesweeping forces while they do their job."

"All right, Jack. I understand it's not a simple operation. Then what's our next step?"

"I'd like to get the Joint Chiefs over here to the Situation Room as soon as possible to lay it all out for you and Mr. Harward. However, above all else, I need to emphasize the need for us to move quickly."

CHAPTER TWENTY-FIVE

USS Normandy, *Southern Arabian Gulf*
(March 21, 0930 Arabia Standard Time)

Laurie had slept fitfully the night before, trying to convince herself that there was some other way. She had yet to think of one. She and Sandee had been back in their stateroom for only a few minutes following their workout, when Laurie decided to ask her friend for help.

"Boy, that feels a whole lot better, doesn't it?" Sandee asked.

"Yeah, guess if there's any upside to you all not flying, it's that the flight deck is always open for running."

"Small upside," Sandee replied, smiling. "But, hey, that changes tomorrow, finally! That part for *Mustin*'s radar arrives in Bahrain later today, and they want us to fly in and get it. *Mustin*'s helo is down so we have to make the delivery."

"I know, I heard folks talking about it in CDC." *Now or never*, Laurie thought. "Sandee, you were a good friend to listen to me yesterday. Sorry to come apart like that; it's really not like me. God, I'm a little embarrassed I was sobbing like that."

"Don't be. It's because you care and because you're up against a brick wall. To be honest with you, I feel kind of like I'm letting you down because I can't help. Hell, I wish there were some way, anyway, that I could."

"Sandee, I think there is, but it involves a risk, a big risk, and I don't know if I have the right to even ask you do to it."

"Ask away," Sandee replied. "Remember what I told you the other day, 'It's easier to beg forgiveness than ask permission.'"

"I'm afraid this would take that to a new level."

"Look, we're both trying to do the right thing here. Just spit it out, OK?"

"OK. You read the intel reports just like I do. It's as clear as day the United States could attack Syria at any moment and, who knows, throw this entire region into a senseless war. We also have proof something is not right about this. I'm telling you, I know the intel the ship and everyone else is looking at is completely bogus."

"I know, I know," Sandee replied, "but you gave it your best shot with the captain. Maybe he'll change his mind. Or maybe you could prevail on your friend at NRO to go forward up his chain of command."

"Neither of those things is going to happen, Sandee."

"No, I guess you're right, but how can *I* help you?"

"Sandee, later today, or maybe tomorrow, you're going to go get that part for *Mustin*. You've told me before that on one of these, I think you called them, 'gedunk runs,' you could take me up in the left seat of the helo as a qualified observer. Could you take me on this part pickup mission? It's a pretty simple mission, right, and one that doesn't require an experienced pilot in the other seat?"

"I suppose so, Laurie. Heck, yeah, I'd be happy to take you flying. It would be a good mental health break for both of us. But why now?"

"Here's why," Laurie replied as she reached over to her pull-down desk and grabbed the SIPRNET e-mail and attachment from Charlie Bacon as well as a navigation map of the Arabian Gulf.

"What am I looking at, Laurie? You've shown me all this before, but I still don't see how I can help?"

"I'm getting to that. Do you see here on Charlie's attachment? The DF-21D site that everyone thought was in Syria is really here in Saudi Arabia."

"I remember when you told me that originally. I didn't look at the map that closely, but yes, now I see that."

"Do you see how close it is to the coast?"

"I do, yes. Why is that important?"

"If someone could fly over the site and show this was where the Global Hawk saw the DF-21Ds, that would prove they weren't in Syria. Then, maybe we could keep this thing from spiraling out of control."

"I suppose if that happened it would . . . ." Sandee stopped short, the full impact of what Laurie was suggesting hitting her like a two-by-four. "Laurie, wait a minute. Are you suggesting we fly there? You want me to overfly that site in Saudi Arabia? That's why you wanted to fly with me?"

"Yes, Sandee." She gave her a helpless shrug. "I know it's asking a lot—maybe too much."

"Laurie, I know you're not an aviator, but do you have any idea what kind of international incident it would cause if we flew over Saudi Arabia without permission?"

"I know there would be risks, Sandee. Believe me; I had a hard time making myself ask you to do this, but there really isn't any other way."

"Whew. I need a minute, OK. I'm gonna hit the shower. I just need a minute," Sandee said as she grabbed her towel and robe and made for the officers' head.

Duncan Sutherland had worked wonders redeploying them from Incirlik Air Force Base and the JSOC team was on site at an unused airfield in western Iraq. Volner and his team had taken their operational, logistics, and communications gear from the initial Gulfstream lift into the remote strip and had all but gone to ground. They were in camouflaged tents and the only creature comfort was the generator for the comm gear. They could wait at this remote location for a week to ten days and be ready for any operational tasking. Their footprint in the western desert was small and only the most discerning satellite imagery would reveal their presence.

The assets Volner and his team were most focused on at the moment were their air assets, both manned and unmanned. They were netted to hide them from airborne surveillance. They knew their first step was to get eyes-on of the site, or sites, in

Syria where the DF-21D missiles were located and then if ordered to, go in and neutralize the missiles.

They had been surged forward before, in various theaters, only to have the crises they were anticipating not evolve to a situation that required direct triage. As professionals, they viewed these situations not as a waste of time and resources, but as opportunities to rehearse their support and logistic procedures. Each time there were lessons learned, ways to do it better the next time they rolled into their kit bag.

For Brian Dawson, Hector Rodriquez, Mike Volner, and his men, this time it felt more like the real thing than on previous flyaways. As soon as Dawson made his check-in call, that feeling surged.

"Hector, Major Volner," Dawson said. "Here's the secure message that just came in from Op-Center. What we're looking for isn't in Syria; it's in Saudi Arabia! The mission just changed. Let's get the planning cell assembled now, and Hector, get ahold of Duncan. I want those Combat Talon aircraft on standby alert in al-Asad, Iraq, and I'll want them there within fifteen minutes of making the call."

Like his predecessors before him, President Wyatt Midkiff's schedule was handled by a bevy of aides and his days were scheduled almost to the minute. There was little or no time for "pop-up" events or drop-ins by anyone, except for a select few. Chase Williams was one of those and as he entered the Oval Office at 0900 the president rose to meet him.

"Chase, your POTUS/OC Eyes Only memo this morning

certainly got my attention, so I had my calendar adjusted to meet with you. Tell me more now that I've had a moment to absorb what your memo said."

"Mr. President, I'm dialed in to what your national security team is doing, and I fully understand what Secretary Bradt, Mr. Putnam, and others are telling you. Believe me, armed with that intel I would be ready to move against Syria immediately."

"And now," Midkiff offered, "we have Iran threatening, and maybe moving forward, to mine the Strait of Hormuz."

"I understand, Mr. President, but as I alluded to in the memo, we have intelligence the Global Hawk was spoofed, and the missile site isn't in Syria, but in Saudi Arabia."

"Chase, what are you saying; that can't be!"

"It is, Mr. President. The other thing is this. All of the communications our intelligence agencies have been picking up that are ostensibly coming out of Syria threatening to strike our ships and bases in the area are false, a ruse, likely orchestrated by whoever erected this site in Saudi Arabia."

"That's a hell of a lot to process."

"There's more, Mr. President. Evidently someone on a Navy ship in the Gulf has seen the video we've all seen back here, the Global Hawk video that started this chain of events, and that person sent it to someone at the National Reconnaissance Office. We're still pulling the string on who that person is, but anyway, this person at NRO is convinced the site is not in Syria but in Saudi Arabia and we've read what the NRO analyst has sent to the ship and it looks convincing to us."

"Chase, I needn't remind you, other than Israel, Saudi

Arabia is our strongest ally in the region. It's . . . it's . . . just beyond belief they would do this."

"You're right, Mr. President, but when we were convinced these missiles were in Syria we admitted to ourselves Syria didn't have complete control of her territory and a terrorist group could operate there with near impunity."

"Yes, I know, but Saudi Arabia hasn't had to deal with a civil war. They don't have any issues controlling their own territory, and they certainly aren't harboring any terrorist groups."

"True, Mr. President, but Saudi Arabia is more than ten times the size of Syria. Most of the country is trackless desert. Other than where the oil fields are, much of that desert is someplace no one in the country ever cares about, let alone flies over or drives through. Our analysis tells us someone—we don't know who yet—could set something like this up in Saudi Arabia for reasons that still elude us."

"Well, Saudi Arabia is our ally. I can ask the king to send his forces to that area to resolve this. He could do that right now."

"Mr. President, respectfully, sir, you know the Saudis have a long history of being less than candid with us about their actions."

"Yes, I'm aware of some of that history."

"Sir, I saw that in spades during my years as CENTCOM commander. Also now, in the wake of the United States criticizing the Saudis for suppressing their own people during the Arab Spring and their sending troops to Bahrain to squelch protests there, we have to recognize relations between our two nations may be at an all-time low. Even if the king agreed to do what you asked him, and he might not, he could slow roll you and not move out quickly enough. You also have to remember, the Saudis have their pride. Would they even admit some rogue element could erect a site like that on their soil?"

"I see your points, but I'm going to have to take this to my national security team. The stakes couldn't be higher and we've got to think about protecting American sailors on our ships like *Truman*. I know this is more than a hunch on your part, and I realize you wouldn't have come to me if that's all it was, but I'm reluctant to call a halt to all the plans and forces we've put in motion."

"I'm not asking you to do that, Mr. President. I understand your position completely, but I *am* aware the CENTCOM commander, General Albin, is still moving assets into position and there is flexibility in when he makes his move."

"Maybe some, but not that much, Chase. You say there's an analyst at the National Reconnaissance Office who says this site is in Saudi Arabia. This is a lot to put on what one analyst says."

"Fair enough, Mr. President, but as you know, I've surged my JSOC team into western Iraq. They're operational. Give me eighteen hours to allow the team to get eyes-on and boots on the ground where we suspect this site is in Saudi Arabia. If it *is* there we can stop what is about to happen with Syria."

"You understand the logistics of getting ready to strike Syria are just too intense to completely stop, then start again. We have to keep moving forward, and eighteen hours is a long time to wait given the dire situation."

"My team is trained and ready to go, Mr. President, and if

we can pull it off in less than eighteen hours we'll certainly do that."

"You also know we've got this threat of Iran moving to mine the Strait of Hormuz."

"I'm not asking you to hold back on anything General Albin needs to do to stop the Iranians. We all know how catastrophic that would be, especially since it would trap so many Navy ships inside the Gulf. Believe me, Mr. President, as a former CENT-COM commander, I fully appreciate his situation."

"All right, Chase. Get your JSOC team moving to resolve this. We don't have any time to lose."

Sandee Barron had indulged herself with a "Hollywood shower." She took a shower that at home was considered normal, but on a Navy ship, where every ounce of fresh water has to be distilled from salt water, was considered excessive. It was a waste of a precious asset.

Yet she needed it, just this once. As she thought about what Laurie was asking of her, the full magnitude of it hit her as hard as the hot water that pounded down from the shower head. It was nothing short of putting her life and her career on the line. How could Laurie ask her to do this? It was beyond the pale—or was it?

Sandee turned off the shower. She reflected on her first day at the Naval Academy, standing in Tecumseh Court with 1,100 other new plebes on that steamy June day in Annapolis. They all had their right hands raised as the Naval Academy superintendent swore them in as midshipmen and future Navy or Marine Corps officers. That oath now played back in her brain's frontal lobe. In light of that, there really was no decision to make; there was only her duty and only one right thing to do. She looked at her watch, the plan forming in mind. *So, let's get this thing done.*

The president was still absorbing what Chase Williams had just told him when Trevor Harward entered the Oval Office. While Williams had insisted on the right to communicate solely with the president when necessary, this was not one of those times. He knew Harward would be key to slowing down moves against Syria, so he back-briefed the national security advisor immediately after leaving the Oval Office.

It had not started out as a pleasant meeting. Harward had gone on the offensive and given Williams a half dozen reasons why the forces put in motion to neutralize Syria's ability to use her DF-21D missiles against U.S. forces in the region had to adhere to a strict timeline. He told Williams General Albin had used another hastily deployed Global Hawk to fly over the suspected missile site in Syria at a lower altitude and that flight had revealed a covered-up and camouflaged blockhouse, a clear sign that Syria once had a missile site there but had evidently redeployed it somewhere else. Williams had listened, and listened intently, and then carefully used his three-plus decades of military experience, and especially his years as CENTCOM commander, to explain to Harward how what he was proposing to the president would in no way derail General Albin's preparations. At the end of the meeting all the two men could agree on was they saw things differently, perhaps vastly so.

Now Harward stood in front of the president's desk, having declined the president's invitation to sit down. Wyatt Midkiff could tell he was seething. He let him pour out what was on his mind. Finally, his national security advisor stopped talking.

"Trevor, I don't need to remind you I have complete confidence in your judgment. You also know that I respect the counsel of Jack Bradt and Adam Putnam, to say nothing of General Albin and the rest of our military. I know you are firmly behind the plans to move against Syria immediately—"

"And then Iran, Mr. President," Harward interrupted. "We've got missiles in Syria that are clearly getting moved around like a peas under walnut shells. You also know if Iran does even a half-assed job of mining the strait we've got a dozen ships and somewhere north of fifteen thousand sailors trapped there. We've got to move, Mr. President."

"Trevor, before we agreed to stand up Op-Center again and put Chase in charge, you told me above all else, I needed to trust him. I need to trust him on this. He's going to either find out, or rule out, whether those missiles are in Syria."

"As you wish, Mr. President," Harward replied. There was an uncomfortable silence before Harward turned and left the Oval Office.

Wyatt Midkiff made no attempt to call Harward back or assuage him. He needed his national security advisor to do that himself. For now, he was putting his chips, and maybe his presidency, on Op-Center.

• • •

Sandee Barron didn't consider herself especially "religious." She preferred to call herself spiritual. Yet after she had showered and dressed, and knowing Laurie was on watch in CDC, she had locked the door of their stateroom, gotten on her knees, and prayed like she had never prayed before. She wanted—no, needed—God to help her do the right thing.

Still, what is the right thing? It's beyond just putting my life and Laurie's life on the line, to say nothing of my career. I'll have to lie to my squadron mates, to the ship, and to everyone else for that matter.

In addition to that, what about her husband and their two daughters? What if something happened to her? Would it have been worth it? This would in no way be a victimless crime.

God hadn't told her what to do. She had to make the decision herself.

Once Sandee decided she needed to help Laurie do what she wanted to do to prove the threatening missiles were in Saudi Arabia, not in Syria, the rest was execution. She told her immediate boss, the helo detachment officer in charge, she had been promising to take Laurie up on a familiarization flight for the longest time and that a parts pickup for *Mustin* was as simple a mission as there was. He had agreed. Next, she had used the information Laurie's National Reconnaissance Office contact had sent to plan the fastest ingress/egress route to the suspected missile site. She had also spent some time on the SIPRNET Intel-Link learning all she could about Saudi radar coverage in that area. Finally, she reminded herself of her oath and told herself, firmly, the decision had been made and she wouldn't look back. *OK, Sandee, you fancy yourself the best pilot on the detachment, maybe in the entire squadron. Here's your chance to prove it.*

Ayatollah Seyyed Ali Hosseini Khamenei considered himself a man of infinite patience; it was something Allah expected of him. He had made his decision with due diligence and it was, he reminded himself, in the best interests of the Islamic Republic of Iran. However, his patience had worn thin when advisor after advisor had come to Niavaran Palace to try to convince him to change his mind. Change his mind? Rescind a decision he had come to after earnest prayer and contemplation? Perhaps he ought to reconsider who he had chosen to be his advisors. He would attend to that later. For now, he had a solemn duty to do what he was about to do.

"Swampfox 248, winds are twenty-five to port, fifteen knots, gusting to twenty, you're cleared for takeoff. Beams open. Green deck. Lift."

Sandee Barron pulled a bit of collective, kicked the rudder pedals, and pivoted the nose of the MH-60R to the left. Once pointed directly into the wind, she pulled an armload of collective, pushed the helo's nose over, and flew away from the ship.

"Box Top," she began, using *Normandy*'s daily changing call sign, "Swampfox 248 is away, three plus one-five hours on the fuel, two souls aboard."

"Swampfox 248, Box Top control, Roger. Your vector to Delta Whiskey is 262 for forty-four miles."

"Roger vector, Box Top control. Swampfox 248 out."

Sandee was on her way to Bahrain, identified by the daily changing call sign, Delta Whiskey, to pick up the critical part for *Mustin*'s SPY radar. "Here we go," she said, looking to the aircraft's left seat.

Here we go, Laurie heard herself thinking.

For Sandee, there was still time to back out. They could just get the part, take it to *Mustin*, then return immediately to *Normandy* as she said she would. Sandee's mind was in overdrive. In the helo's left seat, Laurie Phillips was also conflicted. Had she asked for too much?

Almost due east of where Sandee Barron piloted Swampfox 248, Islamic Revolutionary Guard Corps Navy sailors loaded mines onto dhows in the Iranian ports of Chabahar and Shahib Rajaee. Soon they would head south, bound for the Strait of Hormuz. What they did not know was that American satellites had been watching from the time the mines had been taken out of their underground bunkers and had followed them as they were taken to the mine assembly area buildings in the port areas and then to the loading docks in the ports.

At the Niavaran Palace, Grand Ayatollah Seyyed Ali Hosseini Khamenei had made his decision. The mining operation was under way and he had turned that over completely to Rear Admiral Jamshid Rostami. He had given Rostami explicit instructions to mine the Strait of Hormuz as a show of strength. He wanted to show the Americans and the west what Iran *could* do if the United States attacked Syria.

Rostami would carry out his instructions and seed just a few mines at strategic points near the Strait of Hormuz. That harassment mining would be enough to panic Western nations and drive the price of oil to unprecedented levels. Also it would be something the Americans could clear in fairly short order. The grand ayatollah knew a mine clearance effort would take months if Iran sowed a larger portion of the more than five thousand sea mines in its inventory. That was not his game. This would be a precision operation and he counted on Rostami to carry it out flawlessly.

His mind cleared of that for the moment, Ali Hosseini Khamenei turned to his next task, ensuring the United States would not retaliate against Iran for any of her actions. What he had decided he wanted to be prepared to do needed be done with care and therefore it needed to be done professionally. He had contacted his man, a Bahrainian national, several days ago. The Bahraini had assured him he could hire just the right person to do exactly what he asked and do it just the way he wanted it done. Now that hired man, an American of Russian extraction, was holed up in his hotel suite in Silver Spring, Maryland, with his supply of sarin gas and a do-not-disturb sign affixed to his door. The man's orders were to do nothing—yet.

CHAPTER TWENTY-SIX

Western Arabian Gulf
(March 22, 0845 Arabia Standard Time)

Laurie had ridden in the back of the MH-60R when Sandee had picked her up on *Truman* and delivered her to *Normandy*, but riding in the left seat of the MH-60R was a completely different experience. It was all but sensory overload, looking at the multiscreen display in the Seahawk's all-glass cockpit, peering down on the crowded blue waters of the Arabian Gulf populated with all manner of dhows, coastal freighters, enormous oil tankers, and the like. She watched the broad Saudi coastline, all the while trying to make sense of the chatter over the radio.

The part pickup in Bahrain had been routine, although the Navy logistics people who loaded the part, along with several bags of mail for *Mustin*, wondered why the MH-60R didn't have a crewman in the back. There were the same puzzled looks when they had made an uneventful landing on *Mustin* and then had *Mustin*'s flight deck crew unload the part and mail. *Mustin*'s landing safety officer had been mildly inquisitive as to why they needed fuel for the short trip back to *Normandy*; but they had been refueled nonetheless. As they lifted off *Mustin*'s deck, Laurie saw Sandee put the sun on the bird's right side and turn north, not back south toward *Normandy*. She felt she had to say something.

"Sandee, I know we talked about this. I know you are doing this for all the right reasons, but if you want to head back toward *Normandy*, I'll understand completely."

"We decided, Laurie. We're going."

"I appreciate it, Sandee, I—"

"Laurie!" Sandee snapped. "We're *way* beyond talking about this. What I need for you to do now is to be a good copilot and focus on the mission. We're going into Indian country and I need you to help me. I can't do this alone."

Properly refocused, Laurie replied, "What would you like me to do?"

"Look at the right-hand display in front of you. You can see the coastline of Saudi Arabia on the left-hand side of the display, right?"

"Yes. Yes I can."

"Fine. We're going to head north until that way-point up here," continued Sandee as she leaned over and pointed her gloved-finger at a spot on the display. "By that time we'll have descended to below fifty feet. Once we hit that way-point we turn west and head directly for the latitude and longitude your friend at the National Reconnaissance Office gave us."

"Is that this symbol here?" Laurie asked, pointing to the display.

"Yes. I put the latitude and longitude of this suspected site into the bird's navigation system. The nav system will take us right there."

"Got it."

"Now, as we approach the coast, we'll drop down to twenty feet off the deck. That's really low and it will feel uncomfortable to you, but we've got to do everything we can to keep Saudi radars from picking us up. We'll stay down at twenty feet as we cross the desert. Based on our speed and where this point is, I think we'll reach it about twelve to fifteen minutes after we cross the coastline."

"I think I've got all that."

"I'm setting the radar altimeter to fifteen feet. If we drop below twenty feet and get down to fifteen, we'll both hear a steady 'beep, beep, beep' tone in our headsets. Don't assume I'll react to it fast enough. You hear that beep-beep and you yell at me to pull up."

"Got it. What else can I do?"

"Keep a sharp eye out on the left side of the aircraft. I can't see much on that side from my seat. You're my eyes out there."

"I can do that. What else?"

"When we get about five miles from the site, I'll pop up to about five hundred feet. I don't think the Saudis monitor their desert with radar, just their coastline and their borders with other countries. As we get close to that final way-point we'll look for this missile site. You told me you've read in intel reports the missile launchers have been taken down, so all we're looking for is a building, right?"

"Yes, and a building that's likely been camouflaged."

"Got it. Five hundred feet is a good visual search altitude. There's only so much you can camouflage. If there's a building there, we'll see it."

"And then we look for the pads?"

"Yes, and that's where I'll need your help the most. You told me that your knowledge of all this tells us those missiles can't be set up in sand, but need to be put on concrete pads. I'm guessing those pads are still there but will be way harder to see than a building. So keep a sharp eye out."

"And once we have those located?" Laurie asked.

"Then I put our tail to the sun and use our FLIR to take a picture of what's there," Sandee continued, referring to their Forward Looking Infrared Imaging System. "The building and the pads will be all the proof we need that something was there. Once we do that, we're dropping back down to the deck and getting our asses out of there!"

The two women continued north. Meanwhile, USS *Normandy* set flight quarters anticipating Swampfox 248's imminent return.

At Forward Operating Base Tiger, as the JSOC team named the small strip in western Iraq, Brian Dawson gathered his planning team in the air-conditioned comms van. Around a small crowded table, he began by relating his conversation with Chase Williams.

"OK, team, listen up. Just got off the secure net with the boss. The situation with Syria is heating up and now Iran is moving to mine the Strait of Hormuz. The president gave him only eighteen hours to find this missile site in Saudi Arabia, otherwise we'll be attacking Syria and doing who-knows-what to Iran."

"Got that, sir," Mike Volner said. "Is the plan we have in place still good?"

"Not quite. It looks as if this is going to have to be more than a special reconnaissance mission. We now have to give the president ironclad proof this false missile site is on Saudi Arabian soil, not in Syria. Just looking at it from the air or getting stand-off photos won't be good enough. We're going to have to go in and physically inspect the site. It will be a full-on sensitive site exploitation—that's the mission. We have to be certain the missiles are at that location."

"How about the extraction?" Volner asked. "The Black Hawks are still coming for us, right?"

"Correct. The two MH-60Ms will launch and head southeast. Just before they leave Iraqi airspace the Combat Talon birds will top them off so they have a full bag of gas."

"And we'll have no trouble with the Saudis detecting us?" Volner asked. He was the one leading the special reconnaissance mission, and he needed to ensure they had covered every possible contingency.

"No. Just before the two MH-60Ms cross into Saudi airspace, Aaron Bleich back at Op-Center is going to take down the Saudi military air traffic control system—"

"He's *sure* he can do that?" Volner interrupted, knowing the Saudi Air Force would knock any intruders out of the sky first and ask questions later.

"He is. He's already experimented by taking down a portion of their air traffic control system over their Red Sea port city of Jeddah. He knows he can cripple the entire system, and he knows about how long it would take the Saudis to bring the system back on line. We won't have a lot of time for the extraction, but we'll have enough."

"So when do we go, sir?"

"Master Guns Moore, the boss says we go as soon as it's dark and your team is ready to saddle up and jump."

"We'll meet here two hours before sunset for our prelaunch brief," Mike Volner said. "We'll be ready, sir."

OK, Sandee, this is it. Let's see what kind of aviator you really are, Sandee said to herself as she turned west, pushed the collective down, and pointed the nose of the aircraft toward the fly-to point now thirty-four miles dead ahead on the nose of her aircraft.

"Sharp eyes, Laurie. Sharp eyes."

The bird streaked along near its redline speed of 135 knots, more than 150 miles per hour, making a beeline for the missile site.

God, please let us get in and out quick, and get this done.

Chase Williams stood in Op-Center's command center looking at the array of large-screen displays and status boards and reminded himself why they had trained for so hard for so long. His watch team was quiet, composed, and there was no hint of concern or frenetic activity. It was business and nothing but business as they communicated with the JSOC team on the ground in

Iraq, as well as with Aaron Bleich's Geek Tank, while monitoring a half dozen feeds that kept them plugged into the activities of the military forces in the Central Command.

Williams had been on the phone with General Albin from time to time and was provided with status updates. Albin, for his part, had provided logistics support for Forward Operating Base Tiger, but it was more than that. As a former Central Command commander, Williams had experience that paralleled and even exceeded Albin's. The general had on several occasions sought Williams's advice on theater-specific issues, and he trusted that counsel.

"JSOC team is ready and they're going to jump tonight," his watch team lead began.

"Very well," Williams replied. "Your people ready?"

"Yes, sir. Aaron and his team are standing by to neutralize the Saudi military's air traffic control system any time."

Williams nodded. "All their aircraft up and ready?"

"All's green, boss. They're ready to go. All we're waiting for is nightfall."

"There it is, Sandee, there it is!" Laurie Phillips exclaimed as they approached the coordinates of the missile site. It was right where Charlie Bacon had said it would be.

They had climbed to five hundred feet several minutes earlier and slowed their airspeed to eighty knots.

"Where? Where is it? I can't see it."

"Down there, about ten o'clock," Laurie replied. "About two miles away. Come left just a bit to put it on your nose."

Sandee did as Laurie asked and pressed forward, scanning ahead, slowing her airspeed further, down to sixty-five knots now.

Finally, after a tense thirty seconds, Sandee saw it.

"Yes, yes, I have it. God, it looks like they have layers of camouflage netting over it. I'm not surprised. Do you see any concrete pads yet?"

"No, but I think I will as we get closer."

After another fifteen seconds, Sandee all but shouted, "There, there at one o'clock. I think I see one of the pads! Anything on your side yet?"

"Looking . . . looking . . . are you going to slow a bit?"

Sandee pulled back slightly on the helo's cyclic stick, slowing the bird further. Time seemed to stand still.

"Down there, I see another pad. Right on the nose, Sandee. Can you see it?"

Several seconds of searching, time now on a slow crawl. "Yes, yes, I do!"

"This proves it, Sandee. This proves it. We were right!"

"You were right."

"What now? Are we going to get the FLIR picture?"

"Yes, but this angle is lousy, and I'm too low. Just keep a sharp eye out, OK?" Sandee replied as she maneuvered the aircraft, setting up a small circle around the blockhouse and pads as she tried to line up for good FLIR shots. They were only doing this once. She wasn't coming back again. She had to get it right the first time.

· · ·

In the blockhouse below, Jawad Makhdoom had heard a helicopter approaching from several miles away. He knew the prince wasn't coming to the site today. He went outside to see what it was.

Seconds later, he was back in the blockhouse and rushed up to his second in command. "It's an American helicopter circling us!"

"Are you certain?" the man asked.

"Yes. I think it's from their Navy. It's matte gray and I see a star on the side of the fuselage."

"Call the prince. Call him now!" the man exclaimed.

"Sandee, I can't be sure, but I think I just saw someone come out of the blockhouse, and then run back in again."

"I figured there would be someone in there. They probably weren't going to leave those missiles just sitting out here in the desert unattended, and they probably don't have helos flying over their building all the time, either."

"Can I do anything?"

"This FLIR is acting a little finicky today and I'm having trouble bringing it on line. My head is going to be mostly in the cockpit while I circle the blockhouse. Just keep a sharp eye out."

"Will do, Sandee." *I know we're doing the right thing, but I can see Sandee is beyond nervous. Oh God, please let that FLIR work.*

Minutes passed as Sandee Barron continued to circle the blockhouse and work with the FLIR.

"Sandee, I see two men coming out of the blockhouse

now, and one of them looks like he's holding some kind of long cylinder."

"Where?" Sandee asked, popping her head up.

"What!" Sandee shouted as she saw a flash of light at her four o'clock position, a flash that came from where the two men were standing. Seconds later, a thin trail of smoke connected the two men on the ground with the helo.

"BANG!" A loud explosion rang out from the back of the helo.

"Sandee?" Laurie exclaimed.

"God, we've been hit!" Sandee cried out.

The sound of the explosion when the rocket-propelled grenade hit them was ear-splitting, and now the sounds coming from the tail boom of the MH-60R were deafening.

"What's going on, Sandee?"

"We've been hit. I think it was an RPG!"

"Master caution light. Warning lights. Tail rotor gearbox, oh shit!" Sandee yelled out.

An eternity passed in a second. Sandee Barron knew what was happening. Whatever had hit them had struck near the tail pylon of their MH-60R. Either the drive train leading to the tail rotor had been severed, or the tail rotor gearbox itself had been hit. As the tail rotor slowed down, Sandee pushed harder and harder on the left rudder pedal trying to keep the bird pointed straight ahead.

Finally, she jammed the rudder pedal to the stops. It was no use.

"I've lost tail rotor authority . . . no, wait . . . I've totally lost thrust!" shouted Sandee. *All right, Sandee, you think you're such a hot shit pilot. Get through this. Get through this. Get on the deck in one piece.*

As the vibrations increased in intensity, the helo started to turn to the right more rapidly, now deprived of the antitorque normally provided by the tail rotor. No matter how many times she had practiced this in the flight simulator, the real thing was a hundred times worse. Reflexively, Sandee bottomed the collective, taking torque off the blades and entering an autorotation. This stopped some, but not all, of the helo spinning.

"MAYDAY, MAYDAY, MAYDAY, Swampfox 248 hit by an RPG. Crash landing in the desert," Sandee said as she instinctively keyed her radio.

The MH-60R dropped out of the sky and plummeted toward the desert floor below. In the left seat, Laurie was gripped with fear and held on to the glare shield in front of her for dear life. As Sandee rode the mortally wounded bird toward the ground the nose of the MH-60R wandered up and down and kept drifting to the right more rapidly now that the tail rotor had completely stopped. The vibrations increased in intensity and the two women were getting bounced around in their seats. As the helo continued to head toward the desert floor looming up below, Sandee pulled the power control levers and killed the bird's two engines, trying to take as much torque off the rotor blades as possible and stop the helicopter from spinning. The vibrations increased as Sandee fought to keep the nose from drifting farther right, but her efforts were futile.

Laurie was transfixed on the desert floor now filling their

cockpit window. She wanted to help, do something, *anything,* rather than just sit there, but she was in a completely alien environment when the helicopter was operating normally. Now that it was plunging to the earth she was in sensory overload. She just prayed.

Sandee's focus was now completely outside the aircraft, measuring their rate of descent by how fast the ground was coming up at them, following her procedures as best she could, and praying silently she would do this right.

Now the moment of truth, just feet above the desert floor, Sandee pulled the nose of the aircraft up progressively, first about ten degrees above the horizon, then fifteen degrees, and ultimately to thirty degrees up as she slowed the MH-60R's progress over the ground to near zero. At the last moment, she rocked the nose forward so the helo was level and yanked the collective up into her armpit, slowing their rapid rate of descent as much as she could.

Still it wasn't enough. The bird hit hard. The landing gear struts stroked all the way but the G-forces on the aircraft were too great and the landing gear collapsed unevenly and the helicopter started to tilt to the right. Laurie just hung on. Once the helo had tilted far enough, the rotor blades hit and started chewing up the desert floor, shaking the helicopter violently. Finally, all motion stopped.

Jawad Makhdoom couldn't believe what they had just seen. He had called the prince as his number two man had suggested, and Ali, without hesitation, had told him to grab the rocket-propelled grenade launcher they kept at the blockhouse to deal with this threat. "Shoot the American spy helicopter out of the sky!" the prince had ordered. They had trained with the RPG and taken a few practice shots months ago, but Makhdoom was surprised by his good fortune to have actually hit the bird with one shot.

However, there was no plan for what to do next. He didn't know if the people in the helicopter were dead or alive, but he did know Ali al-Wandi was on the way to their site. He knew he had better get answers before the prince arrived.

Hasan Khosa was standing watch in the Geek Tank cell. He picked up the transmission, then played back his tape to hear it again. Then he called out, "Aaron, I need you."

"Whatcha got, Hasan?" Bleich asked as he walked up behind Khosa. If Bleich had one member of his Geek Tank who he counted on the most, it was Khosa. Just twenty-eight years old and a former wunderkind at eBay, Hasan Khosa was rail thin and barely 140 pounds dripping wet, with shaggy black hair and a wardrobe that might charitably be called early Goodwill. He was second-generation Pakistani and deeply devoted to his immigrant parents, who had sacrificed to send him to Columbia University. He was easygoing and prided himself in doing whatever Bleich asked him to do faster and better than his boss asked for.

"Got this from the DIA net," Khosa began, referring to the Defense Intelligence Agency. "There's been a Mayday call from a U.S. military aircraft in the Gulf. I'm putting the latitude and longitude of the report on my screen now. Here, have a look."

As Bleich looked at the screen in front of him and did some quick mental math, he realized instantly the lat and long on Khosa's screen matched the location of the suspected missile site in Saudi Arabia.

"Great work, Hasan, I'll get Roger in here ASAP. He needs to see this!"

The MH-60R sat there, tilted almost thirty degrees to the right, its huge rotor blades dug into the sand and serving as a prop to keep the aircraft from tumbling completely over on its side. Only a few indicators powered by the aircraft's battery were still alive. An eerie silence settled over the helicopter and its two occupants.

I'm alive—by God, I'm alive! Laurie thought as she looked over in the right seat and saw Sandee moving her head from side to side and heard her moaning.

As the commander of a military aircraft, beginning with the sound of the RPG hitting her bird, Sandee Barron had experienced the classic range of emotions that accompanied such events. First disbelief, then actions based on training and on instincts, then bargaining with God, more actions, concern she had somehow screwed up, more actions, and finally, fear. *We're on the ground and I'm alive, but is Laurie?*

"Laurie? Are you OK?" Sandee asked. Somehow her neck wouldn't turn to the left, so all she could do was to ask it out loud.

"Yes, I think so."

"We've got to get out of this bird, now. We may have ruptured the fuel tanks and this thing could go up like a torch any minute."

•   •   •

Jawad Makhdoom didn't fancy himself a hero. He proceeded cautiously. He had gathered all of his crew from the blockhouse and armed them with the rifles and pistols they kept there for security. Now he had them walking with him as he cautiously approached the crashed helicopter.

He struggled with his decision. He knew the prince would want to know precisely what was going on, but he didn't want to become a casualty doing it. He knew all too well American helicopters had a penchant for carrying SEALs or other special operators and even a crashed helicopter might disgorge a half dozen armed and angry men at any moment. For now, his team remained huddled behind a sand dune about fifty yards from the downed bird.

As Sandee continued to assess the situation, her most intense focus was on getting Laurie out of the aircraft and then getting out herself.

"Laurie, I know it's uphill, but can you open your door? Just push it hard, unstrap and then drop onto the ground. My door is stuck and I'll need you to come around to my side of the bird and pull it open from the outside. I can't get any leverage on it sitting in my seat and my right arm is pretty bunged up, I can hardly move it. Hurry, I see a bunch of men, and they look like they're armed, behind that sand dune at my three o'clock."

Laurie did as she instructed and soon was on the ground. Meanwhile, Sandee unholstered the pistol she was armed with and put it in her left hand.

Laurie came around to right side of the bird, twisted the door handle, put two hands on it, and pulled with all her might. It opened!

"Great, Laurie, you did it," Sandee said. "Here, before I get unstrapped and drop out, take this," she continued, handing Laurie her pistol while warily eyeing the men behind the dune. "You probably have some experience with these from your Marine Corps days."

"Just a bit," Laurie replied. "Here, let me help you get unstrapped and get out."

Laurie leaned in and began helping Sandee. Suddenly, Sandee cried out.

"Ouch! Oh shit. I think my right arm is broken."

"Are you sure?"

"Here, grab my left arm and let me lean against you and I can drop out," Sandee said, grimacing with pain.

As gingerly as she could, Laurie helped Sandee out of the aircraft. She could see she was in tremendous pain and her right arm hung limp at her side. "Here," Laurie said. "Let's move toward that small dune over there. It's far enough from the helo and it will provide us some cover if those guys start shooting."

Once behind the dune and at least momentarily safe, Sandee had a moment to collect her thoughts. They were not good thoughts. *I've lied to my detachment OIC, I've lied to my fellow pilots, I've lied to the ship, and I've almost gotten us killed. I've destroyed a $30 million helicopter and we're in the Saudi desert and we're screwed*, Sandee told herself. *Now I just have to get us the hell out of here.*

She keyed her PRC-90 survival radio and made the call she knew she had to make.

As Roger McCord and Aaron Bleich walked up to Chase Williams in the command center, the Op-Center director could tell that something was wrong.

"What's up?" Williams asked.

"Boss, looks like the mission's changed."

"How so?" Williams had been focused on the JSOC team's preps and hadn't been dialed into anything the Geek Tank had been doing for the last few minutes.

"Well, boss, Aaron's team picked up a DIA feed that a U.S. military aircraft in the Gulf made a mayday call. Then they picked up an indication a U.S. Navy ship in the Gulf, USS *Normandy*, had declared their helo overdue. Not only that, but there's a U.S. military aircraft emergency crash beacon going off at that location. And, well, the coordinates track to where we think this missile site is located in Saudi Arabia."

"Wow. So we think some Navy helo stumbled on the site that our JSOC team is about to investigate?"

"I'm not sure 'stumbled' is the right word, boss," McCord replied. "There's nothing out there but sand and it makes no sense that a U.S. Navy helo would just drive thirty-five miles into the Saudi desert."

"We know if the crew is still alive?"

"Unknown, boss. You want to call General Albin and see what he knows?"

"Good idea, Roger. In the meantime, get ahold of Brian

and the JSOC team. You're right. Our mission has changed—or maybe just gotten bigger."

Jawad Makhdoom looked through his binoculars, alternately looking at the helo, waiting for heavily armed Americans to emerge, and looking at the two figures who had taken cover behind the small sand dune. His men sat with him, armed and ready, but ready to do what, they didn't know yet. Besides, they were technicians, not infantrymen.

He turned toward his number two and handed him the binoculars.

"Here, have a look, and tell me if those two pilots aren't women."

The man grabbed the binoculars and stared at the two huddled figures.

"By Allah's will, they are. And one of them looks wounded."

"Let's move toward them. We can find out everything we need to know before the prince arrives."

CHAPTER TWENTY-SEVEN

Western Iraq
(March 22, 1530 Arabia Standard Time)

Brian Dawson huddled with Hector Rodriquez, Mike Volner, and Charles Moore. He had briefed them right after talking with Chase Williams and Roger McCord.

"And we still don't know what that Navy helo was doing there?" Volner asked.

"No clue at all," Dawson replied. "However, in a way, they did our job for us. About ten minutes after the mayday call, the Navy pilot on the ground there made an emergency radio call asking for help. As part of that transmission she said she was certain they had found the missile site that was supposedly in Syria there in Saudi Arabia."

"Did you say 'she'?" Hector Rodriquez asked.

"Evidently two 'shes,'" Dawson replied. "The other person in the aircraft was a female CNA analyst from *Normandy*. At least that's how they IDed themselves."

"This is stranger than fiction," Moore added.

"Tell me about it, Master Guns," Dawson replied. "Now,

I've talked with Op-Center. There are a lot of moving parts to what's going on around us, but for right now, our mission is to go extract these two ladies ASAP and confirm the missile site. Here's what I'm thinking."

The men formed a small circle around Dawson as he brought up a display on his iPad and began to lay out their plan.

Jawad Makhdoom finally came to the conclusion he was not dealing with a squad of SEALs, but only two Americans, and two women to boot. He cautiously led his team toward the enemy. He knew how long it would take the prince to make the trip from Riyadh in his Sikorsky S-92. He wanted to take control of these two unwanted visitors before Ali al-Wandi arrived. He wanted to be in charge.

"Laurie, it looks like they're coming to get us and they're all armed."

"I know; I can see them."

"I don't have the kind of combat experience you have. Plus I can't do shit with my arm the way it is. What do you want to do?"

"You made the distress call on your emergency radio, right? I gotta think help is on the way. If we can just hold them off a little bit, I think we can get ourselves pulled out of here somehow."

"I agree, but I don't have any extra ammo on me; it's all in the helo. What you have in that clip is all we've got."

"Then that will have to do. If this is all the ammo I've got, I have to wait till they get closer to start firing. Maybe I can hold them off."

•   •   •

Major Mike Volner and Master Guns Moore led their small squad up the ramp of the CH-130H Combat Talon II aircraft. Volner was proud of the fact it had only been fifteen minutes since Dawson had initially huddled them together to tell them their mission had changed. Most of what a Tier One JSOC element did was tied up in their well-practiced tactics, techniques, and procedures. They knew what to do. A change in mission was no more difficult than an orchestra conductor passing around a new set of sheet music. With American lives at risk, the mission might be more dangerous and possibly more complex than a pure special reconnaissance mission, but that meant little in the calculus of these men. They were ready. Once buckled into their troop seats, Volner turned to Moore.

"Master Guns, the good news is all the planning we did for our original mission translates pretty well to this one. The only exception is the fact now we can't wait for nightfall."

"Got that, sir; the boys are ready."

"Good. We still don't have comms with the Americans on the ground so we don't know if they're injured or if they're in enemy hands. We're going to do a low altitude jump about six miles from the site. Our planners think that with the blowing sand this time of year that will get us on the ground undetected. Then we hump it over to the site, and while we're doing that, we'll send the Raven over it to collect as much intel as we can."

"Got it, sir. Op-Center gonna mess with the Saudi air traffic control before we cross the border?"

"Negative. They want to save that for the helo extraction. They figure if we go in low enough and follow the route the

Combat Talon pilots have laid out we can sneak in pretty much undetected."

"How much time are they giving us on the deck before the extract birds arrive?"

"That's our call. Once we get eyes on the site we can call for extract. With refueling and all they'll be about an hour and a half out."

"That's a lot of time waiting on the deck, sir. It could create problems."

Volner grinned at his team chief. "And that, Master Guns, is why they pay us the big bucks."

The dhows were loaded with a total of about eighty mines and then pushed out of port and headed toward the Strait of Hormuz. The nondescript vessels blended in with the hundreds of others like them in the Gulf as they made their way south.

The grand ayatollah had spoken with his naval commander, Rear Admiral Sayyari, and ordered him to have his naval vessels escort the Islamic Revolutionary Guard Corps Navy dhows toward the strait. Sayyari had bristled at the order. "Grand Ayatollah, our navy is mighty and we can certainly complete this mission, but should we?"

"Why do you question this, Sayyari?"

"Grand Ayatollah, the West, and especially the Americans, know our Islamic Revolutionary Guard Corps forces often operate independently from the rest of our military."

"Yes, but what is that to us, and to this mission?"

"Just this: If the Revolutionary Guard vessels go alone and

the Americans or others decide to retaliate, we will have deniability that our nation was involved at all. However, if our navy escorts them, then it is an act with national intent. Imam, it is an act that only you yourself could order," the admiral had replied.

The grand ayatollah had paused, but only for a moment. "I understand your concerns, Sayyari, and it is not the way of a righteous, sovereign nation. I do not intend to cower behind some false front and say we don't have control of our Revolutionary Guard Corps naval vessels. The world must know, just as it knew in early 2013 when you took your 24th Flotilla to the Pacific and visited China, we are a powerful nation. We are not to be bullied. We gave the world a reason why we are mining the Strait. It is the Islamic Republic of Iran, not just the Revolutionary Guard, that stands by our Syrian allies. We will not make believe someone else, who we don't control, is taking that action." Ali Hosseini Khamenei paused. "Will there be anything else, Admiral?"

"No, Grand Ayatollah, nothing else. It will be done."

It didn't take the president long to assimilate the information from his advisors and to issue orders to his national security team. He now sat in the Oval Office with Trevor Harward.

"Mr. President, we've seen a hell of a lot of change in the last twenty-four hours, haven't we?"

"Almost more than any of us can absorb, Trevor, both good and bad."

"Yes, sir, but on the good side of the equation, we now are all but certain that Syria is not going to move against us and we are not going to attack them. And that is a great relief."

"It is. We came damn close to doing just that."

"I know we did, Mr. President," Harward replied. "Chase Williams's counsel was spot on. We owe him and his organization a great deal."

"Did you listen in on my call to President Shaaban of Syria. I hope I handled it properly. We didn't want to come across as overly apologetic."

"No, sir, I think you handled that well. We were misled. You conveyed that without surrendering our right to protect our forces in international waters. Also I think putting Secretary of State Green on an airplane to Syria as early as you did will go a long way toward mending that fence."

"I'd be a damned sight better off if we knew why this ruse got pulled in the first place. When we actually get inside that blockhouse where we think the missiles are and get our two people out of Saudi Arabia, I'll breathe a lot easier."

"I know, Mr. President, Chase has briefed me on their operation to rescue them." Harward paused to look at this watch. "His JSOC team will be on target soon. We'll know more shortly, but until then, there's nothing we can do but focus on what the Iranians might be doing."

"Tell me again why we don't have our forces stop the Iranians from mining the Strait of Hormuz."

"They haven't done anything yet, Mr. President. If we blasted those Islamic Revolutionary Guard dhows in their ports, Iran would just say they were conducting an exercise."

"I'm not sure that's a good enough answer, Trevor."

"That's the Central Command commander's assessment,

Mr. President. Would you like me to set up another VTC with him?"

"Yes, but not yet. One thing at a time; let's hold off until Chase's people are on the ground and we have some resolution in Saudi Arabia."

For a moment, it didn't look like it was going to happen. Laurie had waited until the Saudis were within forty yards of their position before she took her first shot. *That* got their attention. The fact that at least one of the two women was armed caused Jawad Makhdoom to change his strategy. Caution was now the watchword and he deployed his men in a large circle around the women, preventing any chance of escape as well as dividing their attention.

Laurie had fired several more times. She never scored a hit, but the men now advanced more cautiously. The fact that she didn't hit them frustrated her. *Every Marine a rifleman* was the mantra she had lived by in the Corps. However, it had been years since she had fired a weapon, and at the range she was dealing with, a rifle was the weapon of choice, not a pistol. The armed men crawled and dashed toward the two women as one or the other of them provided covering fire. Laurie rose again to fire but all she heard was *click*. She was out of ammo, and she thought they knew it.

The CH-130H Combat Talon II streaked across the desert floor at one hundred feet at its top speed of three hundred miles per hour. The terrain-following radar kept the SPECOPS aircraft off the deck, but it was a rough ride. Volner and his team were alternately pushed into their seats or lifted into their restraints. They had just crossed into Saudi airspace and were trying to stay under the prying eyes of the Saudi's radar warning system.

Volner was on the aircraft's internal comm system and heard the pilot tell him they were ten minutes out. He turned to the sixteen men, eight strapped to each side of the aircraft's cabin just forward of the tail ramp, and keyed his KY-152 team radio. "Ten minutes. Ten minutes!"

Each man held up ten fingers, indicating they knew and understood.

Jawad Makhdoom was no hero. He was anything *but* heroic. However, he was close enough to where Laurie and Sandee crouched behind the sand dune to see Laurie rise and aim her pistol without firing. He had also seen the panicked look on her face. He stood, raised his right arm, moved it in an emphatic circle, and as he did, charged the small dune. His men followed suit.

It wasn't a fight; it was little more than a scuffle. Seven armed men against two unarmed women, one of whom had a broken arm. Soon Laurie and Sandee were bound, gagged, and being marched at gunpoint toward the blockhouse.

My God, Laurie thought as she felt the muzzle of a rifle dig into her back, *what have you done now?*

CHAPTER TWENTY-EIGHT

Over Eastern Saudi Arabia
(March 22, 1730 Arabia Standard Time)

Mike Volner's men lined up in two files of eight, both facing the rear of the Combat Talon II C-130H. On command they clipped their static lines to the wire cable that ran down each side of the aircraft. The C-130H had climbed to nine hundred feet, as low as they dared to safely make the jump with their modified, low-altitude parachutes.

"Check equipment!" shouted the Combat Talon jumpmaster above the din of the aircraft's four Allison T-56-A-15 turboprop engines. Each man checked the man in front of him.

The top door and lower cargo ramp at the rear of the C-130H yawned open. As they did, the howling wind competed with the bird's engines to envelop them in ear-splitting noise. The sixteen men inched forward toward the end of the ramp, awaiting the jump order.

"GET READY!" the jumpmaster shouted. Then he yelled, "GREEN LIGHT! GO! GO! GO!"

The two files of jumpers raced toward the open bay of the

aircraft and leapt into space, each jumper in a tight body position. In the wake of the Combat Talon, two strings of parachutes blossomed above the desert floor below.

Inside the blockhouse, Jawad Makhdoom and one of his men, the only other man who spoke English reasonably well, were trying to extract information from their two captives. "I will ask you again. Why were you flying over our desert?" Makhdoom barked at Sandee Barron. He was sitting just inches away from where she was bound in a straight backed chair.

"I told you already. We got lost on a flight back to USS *Ship*."

"What is the name of this ship," shouted the other man. "What ship is it?"

"I can't tell you that," Sandee replied, determined to hold her ground. "As you can see from my flight suit, I am a U.S. Navy pilot and our country is allied with yours. In the spirit of friendship and our alliance, I demand you contact the American embassy."

Sandee had determined the "name, rank, and serial number" answer prescribed in the U.S. Code of Conduct wasn't the right response for this situation. She would give them something, but not everything.

"You demand! You had no right to fly over our country," Makhdoom shouted, and as he did he slapped Sandee, hard, across her face.

"And you had no right to shoot us out of the sky!" Sandee shot back.

"We have every right. This is our country; now tell us what we want to know. Why were you flying over us?"

"Are you a Saudi soldier? Do you serve in the Saudi armed forces? If so, I demand to speak with your commanding officer."

Makhdoom paused a moment, not knowing how to answer this, then hit her hard across the mouth. "My commanding officer will be here very soon," he spat, and hit her again.

The Saudis were not trained interrogators and clumsy in their demands, but Jawad Makhdoom wanted to extract as much information as he could before Ali al-Wandi arrived, and the prince could only be minutes away. Makhdoom knew Sandee's right arm was broken. He grabbed her just above the right elbow and squeezed. "Tell me!" he shouted. The pain nearly overwhelmed her, and she bit her lip to keep from crying out. A thin rivulet of blood ran down her chin and onto her flight suit.

"Hey, leave her alone. Are you out of your mind, you asshole?" Laurie shouted, trying to draw attention away from Sandee as best she could. "We are Americans."

Makhdoom jumped up from his chair facing Sandee and leaped at Laurie. "Shut up, you woman!" he shouted as he slapped her hard, knocking her, and the chair she was bound to, onto the floor.

The other men laughed, but from her position on the floor Laurie shot back, "Oh, big man, big man!"

The enraged Makhdoom began kicking her chair, sending Laurie lurching along the concrete floor of the blockhouse. The abuse continued, but they were getting nothing from either of their captives, and Jawad Makhdoom became more worried. The prince would not be pleased.

"Feet dry, en route, over," Volner radioed to the Combat Talon II as it banked sharply back to the west and dropped down to one hundred feet.

"Copy, feet dry, and en route. Good luck, out."

Volner's team quickly assembled, buried their chutes and set out in an extended patrol formation. They carried a light combat load of about forty pounds per man. They moved quickly at an easy jog-trot. There was no need for conversation.

"Team's all up," Moore said, moving up to Volner's elbow. Neither man was breathing hard. "Point man has us nine clicks from the target."

"Roger that, Master Guns," Volner replied. "I have a good iridium uplink with Op-Center control. No indications our jump was detected."

"I didn't figure it would be, sir. This blowing sand makes it hard to see more than a few miles."

"But we can still run to the sound of the guns, right, Master Guns?"

"You got that right, sir," Moore replied, mirroring his team commander's tight smile.

By any standard, Ilya Gorbonov was not an attractive man, at least not now. In fact, on seeing him, most people looked away quickly, not wanting to stare. That was just the way he wanted it, or the way it had to be. Gorbonov was born and raised in Brighton Beach, Brooklyn, and was third-generation Russian mob, with "was" the operative word. He had maintained a quiet profile in his neighborhood, serving as a mid- and low-level functionary, not yet a soldier in the organization. He was moving up the ranks, but not as fast as he would have liked. He was ambitious; he wanted more.

But Gorbonov's rise was stopped, abruptly, when he beat his girlfriend, Maria Domeshev, one too many times, sending her to the hospital with a broken jaw. Unfortunately for Ilya, Maria was the daughter of Leonti Domeshev, a powerful and dangerous Russian mob boss. Knowing the father's promise that he would kill him slowly was no idle threat, the thirty-four-year-old Gorbonov left town. When he slipped out of Brighton Beach, he was six feet tall, trim, blond, dark complected, and fit. Women, including Maria, had found him attractive. He traveled by bus and put as much distance between himself and Domeshev as possible.

In Salem, Oregon, he had found a plastic surgeon whose practice was failing and who, for the right amount of cash, was willing to transfigure him into a stooped, late-middle-aged man, looking easily like he was in his fifties. Gorbonov now sported unruly black hair, an overgrown beard, and was pushing 220 pounds. Thanks to his surgeries, his skin looked like leather and he had the old-aged shuffle of a man who had been ridden hard and put away wet.

Ilya had not been able to flee Brooklyn with much money,

and he had spent much of it on his surgeries. He needed to make a living in the only way he knew how. A former contact in Brooklyn's tight-knit Lebanese community agreed to keep discreet contact with him via e-mail. Gorbonov had done business with him before, and he had paid him well. That same man contacted him via e-mail when Ali Hosseini Khamenei was looking for a "professional to take care of some necessary business."

Now living in a small, remote town in Tennessee, Gorbonov had carried out the first part of his instructions. He had checked into a hotel in Silver Spring, Maryland, and there he babysat a supply of sarin gas. He had not asked the Lebanese intermediary how he obtained the sarin he had had delivered to him. He suspected it came from a supply of sarin Syrian officers defecting from Assad's army had sold on the black market. Gorbonov had also bought a franchise selling costume jewelry from carts in some of the major shopping malls in the greater Washington, D.C., area. Now he waited, but his patience was wearing thin. The Lebanese in Ali Hosseini Khamenei's employ had paid him a large sum up front, but he wanted his final payday.

At Forward Operating Base Tiger, two MH-60M helos lifted in a tsunami of swirling sand. They would head southeast toward the far southeastern corner of Iraq, rendezvous with the Combat Talon II aircraft, and refuel. There they would wait on high alert for the order to dash across the border into Saudi Arabia to pick up Mike Volner and his team, and, hopefully, the two American captives.

.   .   .

Prince Ali al-Wandi's helicopter kicked up its own tsunami of sand as it landed close to the blockhouse. Jawad Makhdoom was outside to greet him.

"Have you found out why they were here yet?" the prince barked at his chief engineer.

"Not yet, but we know they are from the U.S. Navy. They have admitted they flew off a ship in the Gulf, but they won't tell us why they flew over us."

"But what do they say?"

"They say they were lost."

"Do you believe them?"

"No, Your Excellency."

As the prince entered the blockhouse he was seething. How could his brilliant plan have come so undone? The United States had not attacked Syria, nor did it appear that it would. Worse, now some Americans had discovered this site. Had they radioed anyone about it? He needed to know this and he needed to know it now.

Al-Wandi burst into the building. He saw the two women bound in their chairs with their faces bloodied and swollen. Their hair and flight suits were soaked with sweat and blood. One, he had been told, had been knocked to the ground and kicked around and was drifting in and out of consciousness. He walked up to Sandee and stood towering over her.

"So you are the pilot in command?"

"Yes, I'm the command pilot," Sandee replied. She was clearly in pain, but her eyes flashed with hatred.

"Why were you here, flying over our country?"

"I told your bullies, we were lost. Now, I demand you release us and take us to the nearest American consulate."

"You demand?"

"Yes."

Now the prince was enraged. His men had done little to soften these women up, other than stupidly beating them senseless and making them thoroughly angry. That wouldn't get him what he wanted.

He stepped away from Sandee and looked around the blockhouse, taking a moment to compose himself. Then he walked up to Sandee and began again.

"So, as the command pilot, you make the decisions?"

"I do." Sandee replied, determined to shield Laurie as much as possible.

"So this other woman is your responsibility?"

"Yes," Sandee replied, but now a bit off balance as to where al-Wandi was going with this.

"I see. I ask you again, why were you here, flying over Saudi Arabian sovereign territory? I know your military has rules against that."

"I told you, we were lost."

"Don't lie to me!" al-Wandi shouted as he slapped Sandee across her face. She shook it off; her eyes were still defiant.

Al-Wandi looked toward Jawad Makhdoom. "Do you see that board over there? Bring it here, along with some of the bindings you are using on these two women. Then bring me two or three blankets from the living area and put them all down on the floor right here." He again turned back to Sandee.

"So, command pilot. My wives no longer interest me and I haven't been with a woman for far too long. You say your friend is your responsibility. Let's see if you really mean that." Turning toward Makhdoom, he continued. "Once you have the board, bindings, and blankets down on the floor, strip that other one and tie her down. Then leave the three of us alone. This . . . this . . . *command pilot* is the only one who will watch me satisfy myself."

Master Guns Moore looked through his Fujinon 16x40 S1640 stabilized binoculars as the JSOC team crouched on a large sand dune about a half mile from the blockhouse. They were on a slight rise with good visibility of the site.

"That's definitely a U.S. Navy helicopter, sir," Moore began. "Can't make out the tail numbers yet, but it's a Navy Seahawk. I don't know how anyone survived that crash. Guess we'll find out once we get down there. That other helo is most certainly an executive bird."

"See any other activity?" Volner asked.

"No, sir, just the crashed helo, the executive helo, and the blockhouse. The executive bird must have brought someone here and they're probably inside."

"Can you see if there's a pilot in the executive bird?"

"Not from this angle, sir."

"All right." Volner keyed his 152 intersquad radio. "OK, fellas. We'll angle around to the right and come up from behind the helicopter, and set up a sniper overwatch when we're about four hundred meters out. If there is someone in that bird, we'll detain him. If he sees us or makes a move—kill him. Then we move on the blockhouse. We need to bring our two Americans out alive, so hostage protocols are in effect." He was answered by a series of squelch breaks. "Let's get it done."

Standing on the wide bridge of USS *Ponce*, Commodore Joe Armao was focused on his mission: preparing to clear the mines U.S. intelligence had told them the Iranians were about to sow near the approaches of the Strait of Hormuz. Armao was a twenty-four-year Navy veteran and had been training for this his entire professional career. Now, as the Navy's forward-deployed Mine-Countermeasures Squadron commander, Armao was ready to do his job. *Ponce* was a ship that was almost as old as he was. She was decommissioned, laid up, and later brought back into naval service to be the Navy's only Afloat Forward Staging Base. She was his flagship and he loved her. Since July 2012, *Ponce* had been moored pier side in Manama, Bahrain. She put to sea only occasionally, waiting for missions worth the significant cost and effort of bringing her back to life. The Navy no longer officially referred to ships as "she," but Armao was of a time when they did, and he was not about to change now.

Now she had that mission, and Armao was the mission commander—the squadron commodore. Three enormous MH-53E Sea Dragon helicopters sat on *Ponce*'s flight deck. Behind the flagship steamed six small mine-countermeasure ships. Armao called them his ducklings. The skyline of Manama receded in the distance as the little flotilla made best speed toward the Strait of Hormuz. Speed was of the essence. Mines laid in the water near the Strait of Hormuz would completely stop shipping in and out of the Gulf.

The first MH-60M Pave Hawk slipped back from the C-130H Combat Talon II, its belly full of fuel, as the second helo pushed closer, its long fueling probe inching closer and closer to the Combat Talon II's towed refueling basket cone. A combination of the downdraft from the Combat Talon's four engines, the up-drafts from the desert floor three thousand feet below, and the helo's rotor wash made for a bumpy ride. It was a complex but well-practiced piece of airmanship. Once refueled, the helos and the C-130H would continue to orbit north of the Saudi Arabian border, waiting for the go order and for Op-Center's Geek Tank to take down the Saudi air traffic control system. Then the two helos would begin their eighty-five-mile dash to where Volner and his team were working to extract the two American hos-tages. Meanwhile, the special operations Pave Hawks and the Talons would maintain an on-call orbit.

CHAPTER TWENTY-NINE

Eastern Saudi Arabia
(March 22, 1900 Arabia Standard Time)

Mike Volner's team had made their way to the blockhouse without incident and on the way had surprised the prince's pilot. They bound him with nylon cuffs, gagged him, and stashed him out of sight in the back of the executive helicopter. To the west, the sun was just setting over the Saudi Arabian desert. One element of the team had arrayed themselves along a shallow dune line to serve as a security element and blocking force. Two snipers had the area under their muzzles. Volner and the assault element were now pressed against the outside wall of the blockhouse. The lead assaulter carefully put a small linear breaching charge on the door while a teammate held on the door with his M-4 rifle. The third man in the stack, also camped over his M-4, had two flash-bang grenades at the ready. Volner nodded to the breacher as the line of assaulters flattened up against the wall.

"Fire in the hole," he said in a low, conversational voice and pulled the plunger on the Nonel firing system.

WHAM! The door handle was cleanly defeated and the door hung by a single hinge. Then the number two man kicked the door aside and went in. The rest of the assault team, save for Volner, poured through the door like a ballet troop rushing on stage. Volner, as the ground-force commander, would remain in a control position outside while his team lead would run the fight inside—but there was no fight. The assault element quickly took charge of those inside without firing a shot.

The prince, the chief engineer, and his half dozen men were quickly overwhelmed by Volner's squad. It was over in forty seconds. What the Saudis could not know was the two Americans they held may have saved their lives. Without them, the JSOC team would shot anyone who was armed or even near a gun.

"Clear!" The lead assaulter called out from the rear of the blockhouse.

"Clear!" Moore repeated. "Building secure."

"Building secure," Volner echoed over the 152 net. "Security element, collapse in and hold on the target area." After the security element leader rogered up, Volner moved to the door of the blockhouse. "Coming in," he called to his team inside.

"Coming in," Moore yelled back. Only then did Volner enter the building.

The Saudis, including the prince, who was half dressed, were all seated against a wall, their hands bound behind them with snap cuffs. All had bags over their heads. One of the assaulters was carefully helping Laurie back into her flight suit.

The team medic was tending to Sandee. The sensitive site search team was about their tasks, collecting computer hard drives and documents, and photographing everything.

"Team lead," Volner called.

"Right here, sir."

"Get these guys into that back room. Then bring the fat, half-dressed one outside and put him on his knees."

"Roger that, sir."

With a gun to his head, the prince's helo pilot identified the man kneeling by the blockhouse as Prince Ali al-Wandi, the deputy minister for energy for the Kingdom of Saudi Arabia. Volner stepped over to his communicator, who had a satellite antenna rigged to his PRC-147 radio and a secure channel with Op-Center.

"Major Volner, here."

"Major, Brian Dawson. You hear me all right?"

"Five by five, Colonel," Volner replied, referring to Dawson's military rank.

"OK, Mike, give me a status."

"Sir, we are secure with two live pilots and seven EPOWs—if you want to call them enemy POWs. No friendly casualties, but one of the pilots needs medical attention. This looks like the Syrian site recorded by the Global Hawk. We're processing the site now and will have data transmission to you in five mikes. Oh, and we have a senior member of the Saudi Oil Ministry and a member of the royal family in tow."

"You what!"

"Stand by, Colonel, and see for yourself."

Within minutes, Op-Center was receiving imagery of the site and head shots of the captured Saudis. There were two of the prince, one head shot and one of a half dressed, very overweight Arab with a bag over his head. Moments later, Dawson was back on the net.

"You still with me, Mike?"

"Right here, sir."

"OK, we're about to take down the Saudi military's air traffic control system and send the helos at best dash speed. Probably take them less than thirty mikes to get to your posit."

While the MH-60Ms streaked across the desert to the site, Volner and his team found DF-21D missile mockups and launchers inside the blockhouse. All were recorded digitally and uplinked back to Op-Center. They set charges on the crashed Navy helicopter.

Brian Dawson came back on the net just as Volner and his team were finishing their site exploitation. "Mike, I have your extraction birds about twenty minutes out."

"Roger that, Colonel, we've rigged the wrecked helo with explosives for command detonation, and we've swept the site. What about our fat prince and his friends?"

"Question them, but don't hurt them. We have most of what we need."

Per their standard field interrogation, the team separated and politely questioned their captives—in English. The prince refused to speak at all, Jawad Makhdoom babbled on about doing what he was told, and the Northrup Grumman engineer spilled his guts. The technicians spoke among themselves in rapid, heated Arabic. Two on the team, ostensibly on guard duty, stood in the background and said nothing. Both spoke fluent Arabic and Dari. They learned a great deal about the site and the instructions given to these men by the prince through the chief engineer. When the extraction helos were a minute out, the captives were freed and told to start walking west. The team marked a landing zone some hundred meters from the blockhouse. Before he left, Volner turned to where the prince was still seated by the blockhouse. He dropped to one knee and spoke in his ear.

"Listen, you fat sack of shit," he said in a low voice. "My orders are to leave you here unharmed. Otherwise, it would be a bullet to the back of the head, after I castrated you. Now that broken helo over there is going to explode about five minutes after we lift off. If you and your helo are still here, then you go up with it. I hope you don't make it. And by the way, your American contractor told us everything, and I mean *everything*, about your little operation here. I guess you didn't pay him enough to buy his loyalty."

Volner turned and followed his team to the LZ. A short while after they were collected by the Pave Hawks, a sharp explosion consumed what was left of the wrecked Navy MH-60R. Jawad Makhdoom watched from the cover of some desert scrub and contemplated what to do next. His technicians looked to him for direction, but he had none. Then a Sikorsky S-92 swooped low overhead with a fat man in the copilot's seat wearing a set of headphones and very little else.

•   •   •

Night had fallen in the Arabian Gulf as *Ponce* and her ducklings made their way toward the Strait of Hormuz. "Evening, Commodore," *Ponce*'s commanding officer, Captain Jackson Bowling, said as Joe Armao appeared on *Ponce*'s starboard bridge wing. Bowling was sporting a light windbreaker, a *Ponce* ball cap, and was holding a mug of steaming coffee.

"Hello, Captain, beautiful night to be at sea."

"Amen to that, Commodore. How'd your conference call with the head-shed go?"

"Like always, lots of gratuitous advice."

The two men were simpatico—of an accord. They were sailors at sea doing what they loved to do and potentially going into harm's way.

Ponce was operated jointly by Navy officers and sailors and government civilian mariners from the Military Sealift Command. As the ship's captain Bowling had all the challenges of operating a Navy ship at sea with the additional task of molding Navy officers and sailors and his complement of civilian mariners into a cohesive team. *Ponce*'s captain was a former mustang, an enlisted Navy sailor who had then moved into the officer ranks. This assignment was a difficult one and one that would not lead to a promotion for him. Yet he had taken the job for one reason. He loved being at sea.

"Yeah, I figured that," Bowling replied. "A lot of folks ashore are wanting to tell you how to do your job. Any change from what we were originally briefed on back in Bahrain?"

"No, not much," Armao began, looking around to ensure they were still alone on the bridge wing. "Pretty straight-stick mine countermeasures operation and one we've practiced many times. The intel folks are saying it looks like the Iranians loaded up somewhere between eighty to one hundred mines, tops, on their dhows and there were damn few moored acoustic mines in the lot. Looks like we'll be dealing primarily with shallow-moored contact mines."

"Not rocket science, huh?"

'No, not really, Jackson, but you know the biz, so it will be slow going and there are always risks in this game. If we go about it methodically with the assets we have, we may even be done before the other Sea Dragon helicopters they're flying in from Norfolk get here."

"Sounds like a plan, Joe. Anything more, anything you're allowed to tell me, that is, as to why this was such a pissant effort by the Iranians? I mean, they have way north of five thousand mines, including some pretty sophisticated stuff. This is little more than a nuisance."

"Well, we'll see how we do clearing these bad boys before we declare victory and say it was only harassment mining. With what we've learned so far, and believe me, the intelligence community has been in overdrive on this, Iran is desperate to have us lay off Syria. Back when they were laying these mines, we were making it pretty clear we were going to go into Syria. So the dhows dumped the mines. My best guess is this mining effort was a 'look what we can do if you mess with us' ploy by the Iranians. I figure by now the diplomats are working overtime to sort this out."

"Meanwhile, we got a mission," Bowling replied. "I figure

I'll have you in the vicinity by daybreak. We can start our clearing operations at first light."

"Chase, that's good news indeed," Wyatt Midkiff said as Chase Williams called him with his initial report.

"Thank you, Mr. President, now that we've actually put eyes-on those DF-21D fakes in that blockhouse, and have imagery, I suspect we're ready to completely stand down against Syria." The cryptic reports from the downed pilots about the fake site were one thing, but the documented evidence collected by the JSOC team was the clincher.

"That's correct. Jack Bradt is talking with General Albin as we speak. You pulled us back from the brink on this one, Chase. I'm also cheered your JSOC team has rescued our two American captives. I'll be anxious to hear from you once your extraction helos have them and your team out of Saudi territory."

"The extract team is outbound as we speak, and I'll call you immediately when they're clear of Saudi airspace."

"Excellent. I understand your team got some information from the Saudis they interrogated as to why they did all this in the first place."

"They did, Mr. President. I understand that you have some of the story in that regard. I may ask to brief you again in person, assuming we get any significant additional information."

"Thank you, Chase."

"Anything else I can help you with at the moment, Mr. President? I know General Albin's got a big task ahead clearing those mines in the Strait of Hormuz."

"No, thank you. I think we're good for now. I'm told the mine-clearing operations should be fairly straightforward. Iran has even reached out to us via the Swiss and is telling us rogue Revolutionary Guard Corps Navy elements dumped those mines in the water."

"You don't believe that, do you, Mr. President? Our communications people have compelling evidence this is not the case."

"No, Chase, I don't believe that for a minute, but the fact they're apologizing is a good thing. With the Iranians you never know, but maybe this will allow us to begin a broader dialogue. They even volunteered to send their navy to retrieve the mines, but we turned them down. They don't have the capability or the capacity to clear mines quickly. I want our Navy ships to be able to move freely in and out of the Gulf. I don't like having a carrier strike group trapped in there. It's good for the Iranians and the world to see us do this."

"I understand, Mr. President. I'll let you know when I have more information for you."

The two MH-60M helos streaked low and fast across the desert. There was no time to waste leaving Saudi territory and Saudi airspace as it was unknown how long it would take the Saudi military air traffic control system to get back up and running after Aaron Bleich and his team had taken it down.

Volner conferenced with his two Arabic speakers and they pieced together much of al-Wandi's plan. This information, along with the ramblings of Jawad Makhdoom and the Northrup Grumman engineer, were passed by secure comm link to Op-

Center. All this made it quickly up the chain and diplomatic fences between the United States and Saudi Arabia were already in the process of being mended.

It was several hours before dawn and Joe Armao's forces were reviewing their hunting and clearing plans. Armao had asked the 5th Fleet commander for an escort ship to accompany his scantily armed mine-countermeasures force as they moved into the Strait of Hormuz and close to Iranian waters. *Mustin* was detached from the main body of the fleet in the northern Gulf to accompany them. At that moment, the *Arleigh Burke*–class destroyer was streaking south at thirty knots from her position to join the MCM flotilla.

Ilya Gorbonov was in a foul mood. He was getting weary of living in a hotel, and he hated Washington and especially the D.C. traffic. He needed to visit his costume jewelry carts, however, from time to time so when he made his final delivery of sarin gas to each cart, disguised as a box of costume jewelry, the salespeople he had hired to manage the carts would be accustomed to him coming by.

He had been to his carts at Union Station, the Pentagon City Mall, the Crystal City Underground, and White Flint Mall, and now he trudged up to his cart in Tysons Corner's large food court. "Hello, Allison."

"Hello, Mr. Wilson," she replied, using the name Gorbonov had selected for his new identity.

"So how is business today?"

"Good, Mr. Wilson. It's spring break, so this place is swarming with high school kids and with visitors from out of town. This stuff is cheap enough that it sells pretty well."

"That's good, Allison, and how are your night classes at George Mason going?"

"Oh, they're going OK; thanks for asking. I'll have my associate's degree by the end of June and then go on for my bachelor's degree."

"Well, keep up the good work, Allison. And remember, no matter how many degrees you have, life is all about selling. What you're learning here will stand you in good stead even after you have your PhD."

As Gorbonov trudged away, Allison reflected on what a nice man he was.

Gorbonov, now known as Mr. Wilson to all his young employees, knew some of these young people would die horribly. Exactly who died would depend on who was working at the time the explosive device he would rig to the canister of sarin gas he delivered to each cart went off. It troubled him little.

CHAPTER THIRTY

Niavaran Palace, Tehran, Iran
(March 23, 0830 Arabia Standard Time)

Grand Ayatollah Seyyed Ali Hosseini Khamenei had summoned Iran's president, Sarosh Madani, to the Niavaran Palace shortly after morning prayers. There was a great deal they needed to talk about.

"Grand Ayatollah, good morning, and may Allah's blessings be on you."

"And with you also, President Madani. Please, sit. There is much we need to discuss."

Sarosh Madani was on guard, as he always was in the grand ayatollah's presence. Now in his second year as Iran's elected president, Madani was already wearying of being a mere puppet to Khamenei. He was a veteran Iranian politician, and had anticipated the grand ayatollah's meddling in everything he did. Yet, somehow he hadn't thought it would be this bad.

"This has been a great victory for our nation, President Madani, don't you think so?" Khamenei asked. "We have honored our pledge to Hafez Shaaban and the Americans have not attacked Syria. Our ally is now secure and will continue to help us achieve our long-term goals in the region."

If those long-term goals include remaining an international pariah and having Iran's citizens continue to suffer because of Western economic sanctions, then your goals are being more than met, Grand Ayatollah. Madani thought all this, but dared not say it.

"Yes, Grand Ayatollah, that is certainly a good thing."

"Now the Americans are going to meekly sweep the mines our Islamic Revolutionary Guard Corps Navy forces sowed near the Strait of Hormuz. I think the West now has the message not to trifle with us."

This mining fiasco had enraged Madani. He was not even consulted before Khamenei had ordered Revolutionary Guard Corps Navy forces to mine the Strait of Hormuz and had browbeat Admiral Sayyari to have Iranian navy corvettes escort the mine-laying dhows. This alone destroyed any chance of the Iranian regime having plausible deniability. *And then saying that the Revolutionary Guards had done this on their own. What was behind that? Was Khamenei that stupid he thought the Americans would believe that?*

"Grand Ayatollah, yes, I think you, we, have more than made a statement to the United States and the West. Once the Americans finish sweeping these mines we will have accomplished what we set out to do, and then we, too, will be able to ship our oil to market." Madani couldn't help but glance around Niavaran Palace where Khamenei continued live in near-Western luxury no matter how much or how little of Iran's oil made it through the strait.

"President Madani. I know you have been in office only a short time, so I must remind you this is also a matter of ensuring the West, and especially the Americans, respect the Islamic Republic of Iran and the great Persian nation. Anything less is unacceptable."

"Yes, I understand that, Grand Ayatollah."

"Then you also understand that we sometimes must insist on that respect and take action if it is not given. We must also demand the West respect our right to develop nuclear capabilities. Yet the West, led by the Americans, has put economic sanctions in place and has tried to make us yield by crushing our economy, but they have failed."

So you say, thought Madani. *You aren't an average Iranian whose standard of living has been set back by a decade.*

"So we are *allowing* the Americans to sweep these mines," the grand ayatollah continued as he raised a finger to call for attention to his point. "The Revolutionary Guard Corps put them in the water and we will allow the Americans to remove them, so long as they respect our territorial waters and our laws as they do so."

"Yes, Grand Ayatollah, I have heard those announcements from the Islamic Republic News Agency." *Just one more thing you didn't consult me on, you idiot. Have you no idea how zealously the Americans guard their rights regarding freedom of navigation?*

"Good, but what you might not know, since you are young, President Madani, is that for decades the United States has been harassing us about our supposed illegal maritime claims and our sea boundaries. I needn't remind you of the claims the great

Persian nation has had for centuries, since what is now America was still wilderness."

Now you are lecturing me, old man. What is it you are planning?

"I see, Grand Ayatollah. So you have warned the Americans and I hope they will heed your warnings."

"If they do not, I have told Admiral Sayyari, whose ships are now shadowing the American mine-clearing forces, to enforce our territorial claims and our maritime boundaries. He has been instructed not to allow the Americans to enter our territorial waters without permission."

"Grand Ayatollah, I believe we need to make sure the West, and especially the Americans, respects the Islamic Republic of Iran. Yet we may not wish to anger the Americans more than we have, at least not right now. May I suggest that since we now have our victory, we not press them further. Should they decide to retaliate we could suffer greatly."

"President Madani, these matters are not your concern. If the Americans dare to attack us I have already put events into motion that will cause them to be more concerned with their own affairs and less with ours."

Madani knew this could only be a terrorist strike against America. "But Grand Ayatollah," Madani said, trying to keep his voice even, "there are risks to this, especially now. Perhaps we should rethink this?"

"Again, President Madani, this is not your concern," Khamenei said. He rose to suggest that the meeting was over. "Now, I am sure you have many important matters of state to attend to. May Allah's blessings be with you as you go about them."

Sarosh Madani left the grand ayatollah's office more worried than he had ever been in his life.

Seven hundred miles south of where the grand ayatollah and President Madani were having their conversation, Commodore Joe Armao's forces had already been at work for several hours. They were preparing to sweep the mines the Iranian dhows had dumped in the approaches of the Strait of Hormuz. This would not be high-tech, sophisticated work, but some of the most blue collar of all the tasks performed by the U.S. Navy. It would be backbreaking work that involved hauling on lines and working in concert with heavy mechanical devices. Armao knew he would need to balance the need to clear these mines quickly and reopen the strait against the toll it would take on his men and women.

Ponce's captain, Jackson Bowling, saw Joe Armao working his way up to the starboard wing of the bridge.

"Commodore on the bridge," he called to his bridge crew.

"As you were," Armao said. "We about set, Captain?"

"Yes, sir, I hold us on station and in a good position for you to control the operation."

"Perfect. Thank you. We had good overhead imagery of where the Iranian dhows laid their mines so we think we know where most of these mines are planted. There's no danger to your ship if we operate right here. We don't have to worry about any tanker traffic while we do our job."

"No, I guess not," Bowling replied. "That Notice to Mariners 5th Fleet issued stopped ship traffic cold."

"Here's an update with the latest mine-laying intelligence," Armao continued, opening the navigation chart he had folded up under his arm so Bowling could see the chart with its overlays. "We've got the bulk of them right here in a more or less straight line, beginning at the eastern tip of Quesm Island. The mines then string south past Larak Island and all the way down to the vicinity of Ras al-Khaimah near the northern tip of the United Arab Emirates."

"Looks like just the way we anticipated they'd do it," Bowling said. "And just the way we've always trained on how we'd clear them."

"But with far fewer mines than we ever thought, so that's a break."

"That's good. My surface-search watch team is keeping an eye on that Iranian *Bayandor*-class corvette that's steaming right over the horizon near Larak Island. You've assigned *Mustin* to keep an eye on her, too?"

"I have. *Mustin*'s here, about five miles southwest of Larak," Armao replied as he stabbed the map with his forefinger. "She'll be in position to take action should that corvette move our way."

"Pretty old ship though, isn't it?"

"It is. Actually it's an old U.S. Navy PF-103 class corvette we gave Iran back when the Shah was in power. Now it's been armed with C-802 antiship missiles and a reasonably capable 76-mm Fajr-27 gun. They could do some damage." Armao paused a moment to frame his thoughts. "However, with *Mustin* accompanying us, we should be in good shape. Still, we're not that far from the Islamic Revolutionary Guard Corps Navy bases. They could send a swarm of fast boats out here pretty damn quick."

Bowling nodded in agreement and understanding. "I think we'll be all right. 5th Fleet has their intel folks keeping an eye on those bases and we'll get enough early warning if something's up. Our ace in the hole is the high-energy laser the Office of Naval Research put on *Ponce* a few years ago. We tested it last year on some unmanned surface vessels and it burned right through them. Turned 'em into toast. I think we'll win any dustup."

The two men ducked reflexively as one of MH-53E Sea Dragon helicopters approached *Ponce*'s flight deck to refuel. The Sea Dragons had been airborne since before dawn using their AN/AQS-24 mine detection sonar to confirm the Iranian mines were where the initial intelligence said they would be. That task was still under way, but the location of enough mines had already been confirmed to enable the *Avenger*-class mine-countermeasure ships to begin clearing operations. One Sea Dragon, the one now refueling, would be fitted with the Mk 103 Mod 2 mechanical mine sweeping system to begin sweeping the moored mines.

Armao's attention lingered on the Iranian corvette and the C-802 cruise missiles she carried. "That Iranian corvette is no match for *Mustin*," he concluded. "Let's hope she's not stupid enough to try anything."

They stood on the wing of the bridge in companionable silence before Bowling spoke. "So, Commodore, now that we're a half day into it, any guesses as to how long this operation is going to take?"

"If we keep up progress like this, I think we can get traffic moving through the strait in maybe two days and then finish up by clearing the mines closer to the coast in three or four days after that. I figure we're here a week, tops."

As he spoke, Armao directed Bowling's attention to the chart. They were beginning their mine-countermeasure efforts in the center of the navigation channel on the Arabian Gulf approaches to the Strait of Hormuz. Once those mines were cleared and at least a narrow ship channel was restored, they would press out north and south and clear those mines closer to Quesm Island and in the vicinity of Ras al-Khaimah, respectively.

"That's good news," Bowling replied, smiling. "My wife's birthday is next month, and I need to do some shopping in the gold souk in Bahrain."

Aboard the *Bayandor*-class corvette *Naghidi*, Lieutenant Qaisar Ghorbani was not smiling. His was the only Iranian warship between Iran and the American ships. He nervously paced *Naghidi's* narrow bridge as he steamed his ship east and west north of Larak Island as ordered. Only two months into his first sea command, Ghorbani was still trying to figure out what he was doing, and more to the point, what he might be asked to do. His commodore, based in Bandar Abbas, had relayed Admiral Sayyari's vague orders to "ensure the Americans respect the Islamic Republic of Iran's territorial waters."

Ghorbani had history with Admiral Sayyari. He had been Admiral Sayyari's aide in early 2013 when the admiral had taken the Iranian navy's 24th Flotilla to the Pacific and the historic naval visit to China. Ghorbani had done everything the admiral had asked, even some things, terrible things, he was now ashamed of and regretted. Now he was known as Sayyari's golden boy, and the powerful admiral had used his considerable influence to get Ghorbani an at-sea command. A good many more qualified officers had been passed over so that Ghorbani could command the *Naghdi*. He had very little time at sea and had never heard a shot fired in anger. Now he was supposed to take action if an American ship strayed into waters Iran considered their own.

As he paced the bridge, he nervously fingered the script he was to use to demand that American ships leave Iranian waters. Ghorbani had read the scripted text over and over until he nearly had it memorized. He prayed to Allah that he would never have to use it.

CHAPTER THIRTY-ONE

Central Arabian Gulf
(March 26, 1330 Arabia Standard Time)

Commodore Joe Armao was again on the *Ponce*'s starboard bridge wing where the ship's captain sat in his bridge chair surveying the mine-clearing operation.

"Afternoon, Commodore. Quite a little operation you have going here. Fifth Fleet commander must be pleased. How'd the call with him go?"

"Reasonably well, thanks. There's obviously some relief we've cleared the main navigation channel and ships are flowing in and out of the Gulf, but I think he expected more to have been done after three-plus days at it."

"Well, you have to understand that he's an aviator, and what they know about mine countermeasures would fit in a thimble."

"You're spot on there. He did direct us to start to go after the shallower mines up near Quesm Island, as well as in the vicinity of Ras al-Khaimah, and try to get it all done in the next two to three days."

"Doable from your perspective?"

"It is, as long as that Iranian corvette doesn't give us any trouble. He's stayed on station around Larak Island for the past three days. I don't know what his orders are other than to shadow us and report on what we're doing. Still, having it there is annoying. You never know what these Iranians might do."

"We'll find out soon enough. You sending one of the Avengers up there to work?"

"Two, actually—*Scout* and *Ardent*. *Mustin*'s going to escort them into shallower water and keep an eye on that corvette."

"Good idea. I'll just enjoy it here from the cheap seats."

Aboard *Naghidi*, Lieutenant Ghorbani was no less nervous than he was when he first arrived on station, but now he was bored. Listening to the radio chatter from the American ships and aircraft as they slowly and meticulously cleared mines was like watching paint dry. What was he really doing here? Surely *Naghidi* was there only as a show of force. The day before he had watched the first tanker steam cautiously through the strait's main navigation channel and now he was seeing one after another sail past. Clearly whatever Iran's leaders wanted to accomplish with this nonsense was not working. He was brought back to the present when one of his seamen approached.

"Captain, the lookout reports the American destroyer and two smaller vessels are moving north toward us!"

"Where? How far off are they?" Ghorbani asked, grabbing his binoculars.

"There, right on the horizon," the seaman replied, pointing in the direction of the American vessels.

"Very well. Sound battle stations. I want us ready to engage and defend ourselves as necessary. Have the communications officer meet me up here."

"Yes, Captain," the seaman replied.

Was what Ghorbani feared about to happen? Was he going to have to carry out his orders?

USS *Mustin* led the ducklings, *Scout* and *Ardent,* slowly toward Larak Island. Commander Jennifer Sullivan had already brought her ship to general quarters. Nearing the end of her thirty-month command tour, this was Sullivan's third time in the Gulf as commanding officer of *Mustin,* and she knew these waters well. She also knew her mission: Don't show any hostile intent toward the Iranian corvette, but ensure *Scout, Ardent,* and *Mustin* were not threatened. Before leaving Bahrain, the 5th Fleet lawyer and operations officer had come aboard *Mustin* and briefed her wardroom on Iran's maritime claims. They were not the same as those recognized by other maritime nations. Sullivan wasn't looking for trouble, but if she were challenged by the Iranian navy she knew what was authorized in the way of force and what wasn't. Her ROE, rules of engagement, were clear. She just hoped the Iranian commanding officers' were, too.

Lieutenant Ghorbani had left *Naghidi*'s bridge, gone to his stateroom, and locked the door. He rolled out his prayer carpet and prayed to Allah to deliver him from what he feared was about to happen. He was not a coward, but he knew he was outgunned and outclassed by *Mustin,* to say nothing of the armed Seahawk helicopter she carried. Now, back on the bridge of his ship, his white uniform blouse was wet with perspiration. He was beyond fear. In his hand, he held the papers his commodore had given him. Numbly, he prepared to carry out his orders. Though they were still about five miles from *Naghidi, Mustin* and the other two vessels had finally entered waters Iran claimed as its own. Reluctantly, he keyed the microphone and read from his script.

"American naval vessel entering the territorial waters of the Islamic Republic of Iran, identify yourself."

Aboard *Mustin,* Commander Jennifer Sullivan was ready. "Iranian naval vessel, this is USS *Ship.* We are conducting innocent passage through your waters and our mission is to remove hazards to navigation. We mean no harm to the Islamic Republic of Iran."

Ghorbani froze. His communications officer, who stood next to him, pointed to the phrase on the page he was supposed to read next.

"American naval vessel, you are illegally trespassing in the territorial waters of the Islamic Republic of Iran. You will turn your vessel around and leave our waters immediately."

Sullivan was ready with her reply. "Iranian naval vessel, this is USS *Ship.* We are conducting innocent passage through your waters and mean no harm to the territorial integrity of the Islamic Republic of Iran."

Aboard *Naghidi,* all eyes were on Ghorbani, but he did

nothing. "Captain," his communications officer pleaded as he pointed to the piece of paper he held in front of Ghorbani. "Here is what the admiral ordered. We must fire a warning shot across the American ship's bow."

"I will determine if and when we fire!" Ghorbani said. He was petrified. He looked down toward *Naghidi*'s poorly maintained 76-mm Fajr-27 gun. *Can my gun crew even fire in the right direction? I have never taken them to sea and trained them. No one had told me to do that, and I've always worried that something bad might happen if I ever had them fire the gun. It might even blow up, and then where would my career be?*

Ghorbani scanned his paper for the right phrase. "American naval vessel, you are illegally trespassing in the territorial waters of the Islamic Republic of Iran. You will turn your vessel around and leave our waters immediately. I say this again. American naval vessel, you are illegally trespassing in the territorial waters of the Islamic Republic of Iran. You will turn your vessel around and leave our waters immediately."

"Captain!" his communications officer pleaded. "If we are going to use our gun then we at least have to light off our fire-control radar and train it toward the American ship."

Ghorbani was sweating more profusely now and kept removing his ill-fitting battle helmet and mopping his brow with his sodden handkerchief. He knew he looked ridiculous, battle helmet and starched whites. He considered the communications officer for a moment. The man was at least ten years older than he was and had served in the Iranian navy since he was a naval cadet. He had to trust someone.

"Yes, yes, go ahead and do it!"

Sullivan was warily eyeing *Naghidi* when her ops officer called her from *Mustin*'s Combat Direction Center.

"Captain, Ops. The Iranian's lighting us up with his fire-control radar."

"Roger, Ops."

Ghorbani was near panic. Now he shocked his communications officer when he snatched the microphone out of his hand and shouted into it, "American ship. Stop and turn around now or I will be forced to fire on you. Make no mistake; you will not violate the territorial waters of the Islamic Republic of Iran!"

Mustin's motto, emblazoned on the ship's crest, was *Toujours L'Audace*, "Always Be Bold," and Commander Jennifer Sullivan did not intend to become the first *Mustin* commanding officer to soil that crest. *Mustin* continued to plow ahead and Sullivan pointed her bow directly at the Iranian ship, presenting a bow-on aspect, the smallest target should the Iranian vessel, now less than three miles away, carry out its threat. She had spent enough time in the Gulf to know sometimes the Iranians were long on bluster and short on action, but she was taking no chances.

She called her ducklings on the UHF radio. "*Scout* and *Ardent*, fall into my wake in loose trail. Remain at general quarters and prepare to take evasive action."

Sullivan mashed the button on her control panel that connected her to *Mustin*'s CDC. "TAO, light her up!" she commanded. Her tactical action officer in *Mustin*'s Combat Direction Center did the rest. Around CDC, officers and sailors went through their well-rehearsed procedures, engaging the fire-control radars for *Mustin*'s RIM-66 Standard medium-range antisurface missiles as well for her five-inch Mk 45 Mod 4 gun.

Inside *Mustin*'s Mk 41 Vertical Launching System, six RIM-66 missiles spun up, while on her bow, her five-inch gun moved imperceptibly in *Naghidi*'s direction.

Sullivan punched another button on her radio panel. "Papa Tango, this is Yankee Oscar. I need to speak with Alpha Bravo now!"

Within seconds, Commodore Joe Armao was on the line. "What you got, Captain? We've been listening to the VHF nets and your conversation with the Iranian ship."

"Roger, Commodore. My rules of engagement tell me I can engage this guy if he fires at me or at *Scout* or *Ardent*, but you're the mission commander, sir. You can override me."

"No override, Captain. Follow your ROE. Alpha Bravo, out."

Sullivan slowed her approach toward the Iranian ship from ten to five knots. She needed time and she somehow knew her opposite number aboard the Iranian corvette also needed time. They were now firmly in Iranian territorial waters. It's not an issue of who blinks, she told herself, but I have no choice but to protect my ship.

Aboard *Naghidi*, Ghorbani's communications officer, still at his side, picked up the phone, listened for only a few seconds, then slammed the receiver down and said, "Captain, the Americans are lighting us up with their fire-control radar!"

Ghorbani stood frozen. Time stood still. All eyes were on him.

"Captain!" the communications officer pleaded. "We have our orders . . . from the admiral!"

The word "admiral," knowing the man was referring to his patron, triggered something in Ghorbani. He looked directly at the communications officer, deepened his voice as much as he could, and commanded, "Fire a shot across the American's bow."

The order went from the communications officer, to *Naghidi*'s combat center, to the gun officer on the bow, to his lead gun crewman. There was a frenzy of activity as his gun crew trained the gun on *Mustin*.

On *Naghidi*'s bridge, Ghorbani became agitated when he saw nothing happening. "Fire, fire, fire!" he shouted. The order was passed again. Seconds passed. Still nothing. "Fire, by all that is holy, fire, fire, fire!" Ghorbani shouted at the top of his lungs.

Suddenly, a shot rang out and a puff of smoke followed closely behind the 76-mm projectile. Fifteen seconds later, another shot and another puff of smoke. Another twenty seconds, another shot. The panicked gun crew, hearing the order to fire passed multiple times, tried to comply with what they thought their captain's wishes were.

Aboard *Mustin*, Commander Sullivan had her bridge glasses trained on the Iranian ship. She saw the smoke from *Naghidi*'s gun and the splash from the fall of shot of the first shell, well to starboard. Sullivan was considering her options when she saw the second puff of smoke.

"Take him with guns," Sullivan commanded.

Naghidi was presenting its beam to *Mustin* as *Mustin*'s five-inch Mk 45 Mod 4 gun began to spit seventy-pound shells at the Iranian ship. The first round took the corvette amidships. The Mk 45 Mod 4 gun can deliver five-inch projectiles at its maximum rate of twenty rounds per minute. In that first minute, fifteen rounds hit *Naghidi*. In three minutes, it was racked with explosions and reduced to a smoking hulk.

"Cease fire," Sullivan commanded. "Officer of the Deck, steam ahead and look for survivors. Order *Scout* and *Ardent* to do the same thing. Get the RIB ready for survivor pickup."

"Aye, aye, Captain."

Then an eerie silence fell over *Mustin*'s bridge. It had been a one-sided fight and everyone knew it. They also knew there would be few survivors.

The engagement and *Mustin*'s sinking of *Naghidi* made international news for several days. This battle was linked to Iran's closing of the Strait of Hormuz, and ultimately, a justified action on the part of the United States to keep the waterway open. However, at sea there was work to be done. *Mustin, Scout,* and *Ardent* had recovered almost two dozen Iranian sailors. Medics aboard those three ships, as well as doctors aboard *Ponce* and *Truman*, did what they could for those critically injured. As these sailors were released from medical care they were flown to Bandar Abbas and turned over to Iranian authorities. The rescued crewmen were treated with great courtesy and respect. Less than twenty-four hours after the incident, IRNA, the Islamic Republic News Agency, had broadcast a report, saying, "The captain of the *Naghdi* acted completely without authority and in contravention to the peaceful intentions of the Islamic Republic of Iran." Commodore Joe Armao had the remaining Iranian mines cleared within three more days and *Ponce* steamed back to Bahrain with her mine-countermeasures ships. The *Truman* strike group and other U.S. Navy ships steamed out of the Arabian Gulf and into the Gulf of Oman.

Brian Dawson entered Chase Williams's office with Roger McCord and Aaron Bleich in tow. The N3 was usually an island of calm, but as soon as he walked in, Chase Williams could see the urgency in his body language.

"Morning, boss," Dawson began. "Thanks for seeing us on such short notice."

"No problem, Brian. I'm assuming this has something to do with the shootout in the Gulf."

"It does," he replied. "Roger and Aaron and my folks have talked this over and we're anticipating a reaction—probably a strong one—from the Iranians after this dustup. We've already asked General Albin's people to loop us in with all the SIGINT they get from Iran," Dawson continued, referring to signals intelligence Central Command would collect from multiple sources monitoring Iran.

"I agree. That sounds like the prudent thing to do."

"That's not all, boss. We're also watching our forces in and around the Gulf. General Albin's still got a lot of combat power concentrated there and while no one has said anything officially, we think the U.S. might retaliate for this mining of the Strait of Hormuz. We don't know if or when or how yet, but if *that* happens, then the next move the Iranians make could be something that ups the ante even more."

"Roger, I assume you and Aaron and his team are sharpening their focus on what the Iranians might do to retaliate."

"We are," McCord replied. "Intel community is in overdrive on this and we're mining all their feeds, and Aaron and the crew are already working their anticipatory intelligence algorithms. We're not certain precisely what we're looking for, but I'm pretty confident we're doing everything we can."

"Good," Williams replied. "Aaron, you and your team need anything, just let us know."

"Got that, sir. We're good for now, but if we do I'm sure Ms. Sullivan has an open checkbook," Bleich replied with a wry smile.

"Good luck with that," Williams replied, "but I'll be sure to let her know." His team was working on all cylinders and his gut told him they might need to pull a rabbit out of the hat.

Laurie Phillips and Sandee Barron had been flown to *Truman,* where they were treated for their injuries. Both were then brought back to Washington for debriefings and follow-on medical attention. As a serving naval officer, Sandee was still bound by the constraints of her service. Laurie, a government contractor, had similar though less binding restrictions. Their experience and collective information was of interest to a number of agencies as well as the United States Navy. Individually and together, they endured a series of debriefings. Some were amiable and sought information about the events in Saudi Arabia. Others were along the lines of an inquisition as to why they were where they were, and what regulations and conventions they had broken in making the journey.

CHAPTER THIRTY-TWO

The White House Oval Office, Washington, D.C.
(April 8, 1000 Eastern Daylight Time)

President Wyatt Midkiff sat in the Oval Office considering what had happened over the past month. He had reason to be satisfied, but he also had reason to be concerned, gravely concerned.

Yet another war in the Mideast had been averted, but only by the narrowest of margins. He was happy Chase Williams and his Op-Center team had been there to assist during a time of crisis. More than that, they had been able to respond rapidly and execute their mission without mishap—a mission that changed in midstream. The president was still receiving congratulations from the heads of state of allies and partners for not only averting war in the Mideast, but for opening the Strait of Hormuz so quickly. The price of oil was back down to precrisis levels and financial markets had begun to stabilize.

Over the past week he had attended a seemingly endless series of meetings with his National Security Staff. Now Trevor Harward entered his office for yet another of their scheduled meetings, this one between just the two of them.

"Mr. President."

"Trevor," Midkiff said to his national security advisor as they moved to the conversational area in front of the president's desk, "we know why we're here so let's get to it. Please have a seat."

"Thank you, Mr. President." Midkiff waited expectantly, so Harward plunged ahead. "Sir, we've had our meetings, and General Albin has had a chance to position his forces where he feels he needs them. The 5th Fleet commander has the *Truman* and *Vinson* carrier strike groups both ready and steaming in the Gulf of Oman. We've stepped up our monitoring of the Iranian networks, and we are confident they are not at a heightened state of alert."

"So you are saying we're ready to move forward."

"Yes, Mr. President."

Midkiff had conferred with two former presidents, one from each of the two parties, and asked them for their counsel. He had also spent time with several individuals who were both career politicians and personal friends. Yet he was as conflicted as he had ever been in his life, and he still couldn't decide. After a long moment, he turned to his national security advisor.

"Trevor, I still need some time."

"Mr. President?"

"I said I need more time."

Harward paused for a few seconds, then rose. "Yes, Mr. President." He left the Oval Office without another word.

Rear Admiral Jack "Stinger" Smith, the commander of Naval Air Forces Atlantic, sat quietly in his office. He, too, was conflicted.

He had a decision to make, and it was one that troubled him. He had read the report multiple times, and had consulted with his senior staff, but the decision was his and his alone to make. There was a sharp knock on his door. "Enter," he barked as he rose to stand behind the podium that had been placed next to his desk. Lieutenant Sandee Barron and her commanding officer, Commander Rick Kennedy, walked quietly in. Both were attired in their Service Dress Blue uniforms.

"Commander Kennedy and Lieutenant Barron reporting as ordered, Admiral," Kennedy said.

Admiral Smith, who loved his pilots only slightly less than he did his twin granddaughters, did not put them at their ease. Both Kennedy and Barron read this as not a good sign.

"Lieutenant Barron, please step forward." She did. Then, without preamble, the admiral began reading from the script his legal officer had prepared.

"Lieutenant Barron, you are standing before me, the commander of Naval Air Forces Atlantic. I am the first flag officer in your chain of command. Do you understand why you are here?"

"Yes, Admiral."

"Do you understand that these are not legal proceedings and that a potential court-martial case is being brought against you for numerous violations of the Uniform Code of Military Justice?" He looked up at her for confirmation.

"Yes, Admiral."

"You are appearing here for one reason only, and that is for me to determine if you are to retain the privilege of wearing your naval aviator's wings."

"I understand, Admiral."

"Commander Kennedy, what can you tell me about this lieutenant?"

Commander Rick Kennedy had anticipated the question and was ready. Kennedy spoke for ten minutes, often passionately, about Sandee Barron's fine qualities as a naval aviator. He, without qualification, said that she was the best pilot in the squadron and that she had a bright future in naval aviation. He ended by describing in some detail her remarkable feat of airmanship in getting Swampfox 248 on the deck after the RPG had taken out its tail rotor, describing for the admiral, who was not a helicopter pilot, the extreme difficulty of maintaining control of a helicopter in that situation. Finally, he was done.

"Will there be anything else, Commander?" Smith asked as his eyes narrowed. Kennedy was not making this easy on him, nor had he expected him to.

"No, sir, Admiral, only that I'd be proud to have Lieutenant Barron keep flying with the Swampfoxes."

"I respect that feat of airmanship, Skipper, as well as your inventory of Lieutenant Barron's fine qualities. However, the fact remains, she would not have been shot down if she hadn't broken every rule in the book. Furthermore, she violated the trust of her nation and her Navy in doing so." Then he spoke directly to Barron. "Lieutenant, regardless of how any legal proceedings turn out, you're done flying in this admiral's Navy. I take no pleasure in this, but I want you to remove your wings from your uniform and hand them to your skipper."

Sandee hadn't expected this to turn out well, but the admiral's final pronouncement made it reality. *I can fly that helo and the box it came in—I know it, the skipper knows it, and I'll just bet the admiral knows it—but if he says I'm done, I'm done.* Her hands were shaking as she reached inside her blue coat and pulled the two backings that held her wings to her uniform. With that done, she handed her wings to Kennedy.

Smith reached across the podium, his palm up. "Give them to me, skipper." Kennedy did as he was told.

"Now, I'd advise you to exercise a bit more leadership in your squadron so your pilots don't pull any dumb-ass stunts like this again. Next time, I'll have your wings as well." Smith looked from Kennedy to Barron and back. He was in pain, and both pilots knew it. "I want you both to get out of my office."

Kennedy and Barron left Smith's office and stood in the long hallway outside the command spaces. Sandee's emotions ran from rage to disappointment to disillusionment to frustration—and sadness. She truly loved flying and she loved military aviation. Now it was gone. Above all, she had let people down including her squadron mates and her commanding officer.

"Skipper, I am *so* sorry. I don't know why I didn't think this through better. I let you down and now your career is on the line." She bowed her head. "I wish to hell I had this to do all over again. If I did, I wouldn't have let you down."

"You stopped a war, Sandee, and no one can take that away

from you. I'd fly with you any day, and you can take that to the bank."

"Thank you, skipper." On an impulse, she hugged him, something she had never done with any male in uniform—until now. Now she had to go home and tell her husband and her girls her career was over. Once that was done, she had one more call to make.

Ilya Gorbonov had been in the extended-stay hotel for almost a month, and he was getting tired of it. He couldn't let the maids clean his room because they might get curious and open one of the fake boxes of costume jewelry and discover the sarin gas and explosive timers he had rigged for delivery to his carts.

Gorbonov wasn't a neat man, not by a long shot, and now he was living in complete squalor with the stench of old pizza, beer, and dirty laundry permeating the room. He wanted his payday. He desperately wanted to get back to Tennessee so he could spend time with the woman who serviced him. He paid her well, and now he would be able to keep that up for a long time.

They weren't telling him anything, other than he was not to communicate with them. *To hell with that!* He typed an angry e-mail to his Lebanese contact in Ali Hosseini Khamenei's employ demanding to know when he would be given the go-ahead to execute his mission.

When Sandee Barron had called Laurie Phillips at home the evening after her dressing-down by Admiral Smith it was a difficult conversation for both of them. They had briefly discussed career options for Sandee, who had already decided she'd not stay in the Navy if she couldn't fly. Laurie had offered to help her with a job search in the Washington, D.C., area. Sandee and her husband currently made their home in Mayport, Florida, an area with limited job prospects for her. Sandee's husband was a consultant with KPMG, and he enjoyed good career mobility. They agreed to talk again soon and to meet in D.C. as soon as feasible to discuss career possibilities.

What Laurie didn't tell Sandee as she reviewed her career options with her was that she, too, was making a career move. She would tell her later, when the time was right. For Laurie, there was no formal hearing in front of a senior person or anything like it. She had come into work three days ago and found a sealed white envelope with her name typed on the front on her desk. She had opened it and found a short letter on Center for Naval Analyses letterhead:

Ms. Laurie Phillips:

I regret to inform you that, due to your actions aboard USS Normandy *while in our employ we have decided to terminate your service with the Center for Naval Analyses. Your actions, while they may have been well intended, contravened Navy rules and regulations.*

Given the Center's long and fruitful association with the United States Navy, we can no longer have you in our employ. Out of consideration of your previous service in the United States Marine Corps, and in deference to the injuries you have sustained, we will give you two weeks to turn over your assignments to your immediate supervisor. Additionally, you will be entitled to two months' severance.

> *(signed)*
> *Malinda Duffy,*
> *President*
> *Center for Naval Analyses*

It was cold, final, but not totally unexpected. She read the letter quickly, only once, folded it, and put in her desk drawer. Then she quietly left the office. She'd return after working hours for her personal things. Her ongoing work would fit into a single file box, which she would leave on the desk.

The mood was considerably better at Op-Center. Duncan Sutherland had worked his usual magic getting Volner, his team, and all their equipment back to the United States. Following the debriefings, Chase Williams had told his JSOC team to take some well-deserved time off.

Williams believed that victories should be celebrated, so he had reserved the National Geospatial-Intelligence Agency's atrium cafeteria for a quiet, late-afternoon celebration. He and Anne Sullivan served as bartenders while the caterer they had engaged served heavy hors d'oeuvres. Both Williams and Sullivan looked on their staff with a mixture of pride and ownership. After everyone had wine, a beer, or a cocktail—Sullivan prided herself on her killer mojitos, heavy on the rum—Williams released Sullivan from her duties to mingle with the others, something she rarely did. Aaron Bleich and some of his Geek Tank misfits, as they called themselves, were becoming uncharacteristically gregarious. He didn't want to break this up with a long speech, but he wanted to say something to capture the moment and celebrate their first major success.

"Ladies and gentlemen," Brian Dawson boomed. "Gather around, would you? The boss wants to have a word." There was almost instant silence as the staff queued up in front of the bar and Chase Williams walked in front of it.

"You all have made me enormously proud, and more importantly, you have taken an important step in knowing how critically dependent we all are on each other. You've shown me, and this administration, how you can bring your diverse talents together in a common effort. We've accomplished a great deal in a short time, and I'm proud to serve with each and every one of you."

The senior staff knew Williams was a big fan of the writer Daniel Pink; in fact, he had given his department heads a copy of Pink's book *A Whole New Mind* as Christmas gifts. So they anticipated what he would say next.

"They say that people come to work and, more importantly, keep coming to work at the same place for three reasons: for autonomy, for mastery, and for a sense of purpose. I think you would all agree that no organization in government has more autonomy than Op-Center, and as you've all just demonstrated, along with our JSOC team, you all are masters at your craft." He paused for a moment. "Now, with this success behind us, I hope you all feel, and feel deeply, a sense of accomplishment and purpose. No one else could have done what you all have just done. Thank you and well done."

With that, Chase Williams came to attention, raised his right hand, and rendered a crisp salute.

The staff broke out in spontaneous applause. Williams glanced over his shoulder to where Anne Sullivan had stepped back behind the bar.

"Ms. Sullivan, would you like to add anything?"

"Yes, sir, I would." She raised her voice to be heard and said, "The bar is still open, so why are all these cowboys just standing there?"

More applause, this time for Sullivan, as the staff surged toward the bar.

CHAPTER THIRTY-THREE

Gulf of Oman
(April 11, 0445 Arabia Standard Time)

The predawn silence was broken as the first Tomahawk missile emerged from *Normandy*'s bank of vertical launchers. Dozens more came out of the launchers of the other cruisers, destroyers, and submarines steaming with the *Truman* and *Vinson* carrier strike groups. The first wave of these precision missiles targeted the underground bunkers where the Islamic Revolutionary Guard Corps Navy stored their mines near the Islamic Republic of Iran naval bases at Bandar Beheshti, Bandar Abbas, and Jask.

The second wave of Tomahawks, launched only minutes after the first, headed toward the railways and roads connecting these bunkers to mine assembly area buildings in the port areas. They also hit the buildings themselves, large structures where the batteries, sensors, and firing circuits of the most sophisticated mines were stored and where the Islamic Revolutionary Guard Corps Navy made the final assembly of their mines before loading them on the nondescript dhows that planted them. The Tomahawks also hit the roads leading from the assembly buildings to the port areas as well as the docks where satellite imagery had shown mines being loaded onto dhows.

Immediately after these two waves of strikes, analysts at the CENTCOM Command Center at Al Udeid Air Base, Qatar, scrutinized imagery from a variety of sensors to determine battle damage assessment of the targets singled out for attack. They then compiled a short list of targets for reattack. Ninety minutes later, a third and final wave of Tomahawks roared from their launchers and finished the job. Iran's mine inventory and mine-laying capability had been destroyed.

The command center at Op-Center was normally manned by three-to-five watchstanders in the daytime and two in the evening. More staff could be called in if events or current intelligence warranted. Chase Williams had just turned in when his watch captain called him at the Watergate.

"Sir, turn on CNN, and I think you'll want to get in here right away."

The early morning news shows were just beginning their broadcasts when the announcement intoned, "We interrupt this broadcast to bring you an important address from the president of the United States."

Wyatt Midkiff sat behind his desk in the Oval Office with a single sheet of paper in his hand. He had finally given the order Trevor Harward had urged him to give. He had no regrets, but he did not know what would happen next.

"My fellow Americans. Early this morning, at my direction,

United States Navy ships conducted a coordinated attack on mine bunkers, mine assembly areas, and mine transport railways and roads near several naval bases of the Islamic Republic of Iran Navy. These attacks were in retaliation for the Iranian navy mining the Strait of Hormuz in contravention to all norms of international law and freedom of navigation. Iran has long maintained they could and would close this important waterway should they choose to do so. They recently demonstrated that intent. While they may still have that intention, they no longer have the means to do so.

"The Iranian navy and their associated Islamic Revolutionary Guard Corps Navy forces were responsible for these mining operations, and we concentrated our attacks specifically—and surgically—on this mine-laying capability. We regret any unintended harm done to the long-suffering people of Iran as collateral damage from these attacks and will work with the International Red Cross and the Red Crescent organizations to provide relief and medical supplies to those civilian victims of these attacks.

"I congratulate our brave Navy men and women on this successful operation. May God bless the men and women of our armed forces and may God bless the United States of America."

With that, the camera faded out in the Oval Office, and on all the networks, the talking heads took over. As U.S. networks were broadcasting the president's address, Al Jazeera was broadcasting live video of grieving and weeping Iranian adults carrying horribly burned and mangled children to Bandar Abbas's Khalij e Fars hospital.

•   •   •

Chase Williams reached Op-Center thirty-five minutes after being called by his watch team. Other senior staff soon followed. After a summary briefing by his watch captain, he had asked to not be disturbed while he kept up with the news on the multiple nets he monitored. By noon he was ready. He asked his N2 and N3 come to his office.

"You wanted to see us, boss?" Brian Dawson asked as he stood in the doorway of Williams's office.

"Brian, Roger, come in and give me an assessment."

With that, his intelligence director and operations director repeated much of what he already knew. They also added their personal appraisal of the strike and what it meant going forward. Their assessment was not unlike his own.

"All right. Thank you, both."

"Also, boss," McCord replied, "as we briefed you two weeks ago, Aaron and his team have been running their anticipatory intelligence looking for what Iran might do. Now that we've attacked Iran he's going to focus in even tighter on communications coming out of the Iranian military command and even the Niavaran Palace. The algorithms he's run so far suggest Iran is going to retaliate. We're just not sure where yet."

"Got it, Roger, thanks. Keep the press on. Brian, let's ensure the command center is manned appropriately to monitor the situation. Other than North Korea, Iran's probably the most unpredictable nation on the planet. Like both of you, I don't think Iran can let this go without a response. We need to be prepared for just about anything."

"Got it, boss."

Turning to his intelligence director, Williams continued.

"Roger, several weeks ago we had a conversation about having your Geek Tank start to look at bit more inward, more domestically. That got overtaken by events. I think we need to ramp that up immediately, don't you agree?"

"Sure do."

"OK, fellas, we've a nation to protect. Let's get to it."

In the Niavaran Palace, Grand Ayatollah Seyyed Ali Hosseini Khamenei had spent the morning getting reports from his naval commanders about the damage done to Iran's mine bunkers and buildings as well as to the port areas of the three Iranian naval bases. Other advisors briefed him regarding casualties to Iranian citizens. One of his staff had a rebroadcast of the American president's address earlier that day piped into Khamenei's office. Nothing was lost in the dubbed translation. He watched it without comment and seemingly without emotion.

Now he was alone. He picked up the phone and called the Lebanese agent in his employ.

Aaron Bleich was on edge and paced around the Geek Tank watching his eclectic band work. They combed the airways with their algorithms and decision-support software, sifting data and generating screen displays. The trouble was, he didn't know *what* he was looking for. He had scrambled to reprogram their systems for domestic anomalies, but he still didn't know what to look for. Later that afternoon, Maggie Scott and Hasan Khosa approached him.

"Aaron, we're looking at some strange stuff and trying to make sense of it. Can you take a look at it?"

"Sure. Where?" Bleich asked.

"Maggie's machine," Khosa replied. "This way."

The Lebanese had e-mailed Ilya Gorbonov at 1500 Washington, D.C., time, right before the start of the rush hour. The e-mail said simply, "Deliver your equipment to the prearranged locations and set it to activate at noon tomorrow, Washington, D.C., time."

Finally, Ilya rejoiced. Then he felt something approaching panic. It was rush hour. He had to drive to multiple spots and get this all delivered before closing time in the malls where his carts were.

Couldn't this idiot tell time? What was he supposed to do, fly to these places? He started slamming the keys on his laptop. Once he hit SEND, he pulled out his Northern Virginia map and started tracing out what he thought would be the best route to reach each of these malls given the area's soon-to-be-gridlocked afternoon traffic. His efforts were interrupted when his e-mail binged. His contact had replied sooner than he had anticipated.

He began to mutter and then curse as he read this e-mail. Who did this asshole think he was, ordering him around like some coolie and not the professional he was? He typed furiously, his fingers flying over the keys, and then hit SEND. Ilya leaped up and started pacing around the room. He didn't need to be treated like this. He would do it, but he would do it his way.

Less than three minutes later, his e-mail binged again. Ilya read it and began banging his fist on the desk in rage. He slammed his laptop closed and went to the closet to begin loading the boxes labeled "costume jewelry" into his SUV, still debating what route he should follow to make his deliveries without getting stuck in Washington's late-afternoon traffic.

The meeting had begun with just Bleich, Scott, and Khosa in Roger McCord's office. Then McCord had asked Brian Dawson to come in with James Wright, his domestic crisis manager. After much spirited discussion, Brian Dawson tried to sum it up.

"OK, first of all, Aaron, Maggie, and Hasan, outstanding job. This would have eluded most electronic search teams. We clearly need to take this to the boss, but just so I get it right and we're of an accord, would you sum it all up, Aaron?"

Bleich looked to Roger McCord, but McCord just nodded, so Bleich spoke, "Well, it's like this. We've had a stream of e-mails going back and forth from a foreign entity and someone here in Washington. They're talking around what they are doing, but our system parameters are strongly suggesting they are planning an attack somewhere in the Washington, D.C., area."

"And these attacks are supposed to happen soon?"

"Yes, sir," Bleich replied. "Noon tomorrow."

"Your team thinks these attacks are going to be mainly against civilians, right? Not on any instruments of national power, or on the government or the military? And this is all somehow connected to the attacks on Iran?"

"From the looks of it, yes, sir," Bleich replied. "They're talking about trying to achieve maximum casualties."

"Are we're still trying to source the location of this e-mail account?" McCord asked.

"That's right," Bleich replied. "So far, the process of elimination is pointing to somewhere outside of the District, and not west or south into Virginia, so we're thinking somewhere in Maryland, most likely."

"I see. Is your decision-support software suggesting anything regarding where they are going to try to get mass civilian casualties?"

"We're still working it, but nothing yet."

"All right, I think we have enough to take this to the boss now."

CHAPTER THIRTY-FOUR

Washington, D.C.
(April 12, 0700 Eastern Daylight Time)

Chase Williams had called the FBI director in the early afternoon following his team's report. He offered to send James Wright, his domestic crisis manager, along with his intelligence director and part of his team, including Aaron Bleich, to the Hoover Building to brief him in person. The FBI director had listened to Williams, thanked him, but declined a personal briefing. He promised he would look into the matter.

When Bleich and the Geek Tank called Williams later in the afternoon and told him they had tracked the e-mail account to a six-block-square area in Silver Spring, Maryland, Williams had again called the FBI director. He urged him to have the FBI's Critical Incident Response Group position themselves to be ready to act once the exact location was nailed. Once again, the director thanked him and told him he had contacted the attorney general and they would respond appropriately. When Williams again called him late that afternoon, he was told the director had gone to see the attorney general. Chase Williams knew and trusted both men. He had done all he could, but he couldn't go home. He had headed to where Bleich and his team were doing their analysis and remained there all night.

Ilya Gorbonov had not returned to his hotel room until almost 2230, drained from dashing around the Capitol Beltway to deliver his sarin gas to the selected locations. He had chosen well, he reminded himself. He also smiled when he thought of the money. He was being paid a fixed fee, as well as a bonus for each dead American. The Americans were very good at counting their dead, which would make his accounting that much easier. This cheered him. What didn't cheer him was the $260 parking ticket. He had placed the box in his cart in Union Station, his last stop, only beating the mall's closing time by five minutes. He had parked in a fire zone right in front of the station. *A parking ticket— just you wait!*

He had set the explosive timers to go off precisely at noon when the malls would be full of regular shoppers, and the food courts would be full of people on their lunch breaks. He had told his salespeople at each cart that the boxes were not to be touched until April 15, Income Tax Day. That was when the new company he had purchased this jewelry from was going to have a Tax Day promotion. He assured them all there would be a nice bonus if they moved a lot of this jewelry on Tax Day.

His Lebanese contact had promised to transfer the money to his offshore bank account electronically the next morning. He was to remain in his hotel until then, at which time he was free to leave Washington forever. Gorbonov had his one bag packed, his SUV gassed up, and had paid his hotel bill in full in cash. He was ready to leave.

Chase Williams was back in his office by 0900, having shaved and showered in the National Geospatial-Intelligence Agency's gym. His patience with the FBI director was wearing thin. He called the director's office, got his EA, and was told the director was with the attorney general and could not be reached.

At precisely noon, eastern daylight time, there was a loud explosion in carts selling costume jewelry in Union Station, the Pentagon City Mall, the Crystal City Underground, the White Flint Mall, and the Tysons Corner's food court.

As the sarin gas cloud filled the air, people began to drop to the ground, choking with severe asphyxia as their breathing muscles ceased functioning. First dozens, then hundreds more, dropped to the tiled mall floors, clutching their throats. Death came quickly after that.

CHAPTER THIRTY-FIVE

Op-Center Headquarters, Fort Belvoir North, Fairfax,
Virginia
(April 16, 1030 Eastern Daylight Time)

Chase Williams had pulled his senior staff together immediately after the sarin gas attacks and had charged them with one mission: Find out who had conducted this attack on America. He had his suspicions, but he wanted to let Roger McCord, Aaron Bleich, and his Geek Tank find the answer.

At 0900 that morning the FBI Critical Incident Response Group team had finally gone to where the suspicious e-mails had emanated from, the hotel Op-Center's intelligence algorithms had nailed as the precise location. All indications pointed to just one person, a Mr. Wilson, who had been a long-term guest. However, Mr. Wilson was gone when they got there and they had no leads as to his whereabouts. They had interviewed salespeople who had not been at work at the time of the explosions and had learned that Mr. Wilson had delivered a special box of costume jewelry to each cart the evening before the explosions.

Bleich and the Geek Tank did not disappoint. Anticipating the U.S. attack on Iran's mine-laying capabilities would elicit a response, they focused their intelligence gathering and their sensitive search engines on the Iranian high command and that led them to where they thought it might—directly to the Niavaran Palace.

While Chase Williams followed his "POTUS/OC Eyes Only" memo up with a personal visit to the president hours later, the memo said it all. "Mr. President, over the last four days, using the analysis feeds your intelligence community has continued to so generously share, we have determined the reason for, and the source of, these sarin gas attacks on America. This order was issued directly from the Niavaran Palace by Grand Ayatollah Seyyed Ali Hosseini Khamenei. The grand ayatollah used an intermediary, but there is no doubt he ordered this deadly attack on our citizens immediately after our attack on Iran's mine-laying capabilities."

During his visit with the president Williams was careful not to criticize the president or his national security advisor for ordering the attacks on Iran's mine-laying capabilities. It should have been clear to them those attacks would have elicited the deadly response they did, but that was in the past and revisiting it would serve no purpose now. Nor was it Williams's place to ask the president what he intended to do armed with the intelligence he had just given him. That would all be taken care of in due course. The president asked Chase Williams to maintain 24/7 intelligence on one specific target.

• • •

Thirty-six hours later, cruisers, destroyers, and submarines steaming with the *Truman* and *Vinson* carrier strike groups launched a massive barrage of Tomahawk missiles toward the Islamic Republic of Iran. Dozens of missiles emerged from their launch tubes and headed downrange, but this time instead of hitting multiple targets, those missiles all had the same geographic coordinates dialed into their guidance systems. The coordinates were those of the Niavaran Palace in Central Tehran.

The timing of the attacks was precise. Aaron Bleich's people had provided a direct feed into the CENTCOM Command Center in Al Udeid Air Base, Qatar. Bleich and his team had determined Grand Ayatollah Seyyed Ali Hosseini Khamenei had just retired for the evening. The strikes were launched moments later. When the dust had settled the entire Niavaran Palace complex was little more than a smoking, smoldering hole.

However, Bleich's team had provided more. They had learned the Iranians mine-laying operation had not been—as the Iranians had alleged—a rogue operation by the Islamic Revolutionary Guard Corps Navy. Rather, it had been a coordinated operation with regular Iranian navy ships escorting the mine-laying dhows.

Hours after the devastating attack on the Niavaran Palace complex, the cruisers, destroyers, and submarines steaming with the *Truman* and *Vinson* carrier strike groups fired more of their Tomahawk missiles. The first wave of these precision missiles targeted the air defense facilities and Iranian military air bases, cratering their runways and making aircraft takeoffs impossible. The second wave headed north toward the Islamic Republic of Iran naval bases at Bandar Abbas, Jask, Bandar Beheshti, Kharg Island, Qeshm, and Larak Island. A total of nine ships, five from the *Truman* and *Vinson* carrier strike groups, and four others, rushed to the Gulf of Oman from station off the Horn of Africa, producing the biggest U.S. Navy Tomahawk barrage since Desert Storm.

Missiles were still coming out of their launchers when the first F/A-18E and F/A-18F Super Hornet strike fighters roared off the catapults on *Truman* and *Vinson* bound for those same ports. Their mission was to turn the Iranian navy into scrap metal. They singled out Bandar Abbas for special attention and destruction as it was home to the Islamic Republic of Iran naval headquarters as well as the base for its three Russian-built Kilo class submarines.

The initial Tomahawk barrage was so effective that there was almost no air defense. What little remained was handled by F/A-18G Growler electronic jamming aircraft accompanying the strike. The F/A-18E/F Super Hornets were now free to rake the ports and ships with their SLAM-ER Standoff Land Attack Missiles, their AGM-154 JSOW Joint Standoff Weapons, and their AGM-84 Harpoon antiship missiles. The *Truman* and *Vinson* carrier strikers returned to refuel, rearm, and reattack. The devastation was both appalling and complete. By nightfall, there was little evidence the Islamic Republic of Iran navy had ever existed.

• • •

The president's Oval Office address was shorter than the one he had given eight days earlier. He was brief, almost cryptic, in telling the nation the attacks on America and its citizens had been avenged and the "coward who had ordered the sarin gas attack had been found and eliminated."

CHAPTER THIRTY-SIX

The White House Oval Office, Washington, D.C.
(May 2, 1030 Eastern Daylight Time)

Almost fifteen hundred Americans had died in the sarin gas attacks, and President Wyatt Midkiff had been overwhelmed with trying to restore calm and reassure the nation.

Chase Williams had thought long and hard before requesting a meeting with the president. He wanted to give him time to deal with and get through the worst domestic crisis in the United States since the NFL attacks. Williams had prided himself throughout his career on never speaking badly of a colleague, but too many people had died. This could have been prevented. He had done his best to work through the FBI director and the attorney general. It was simply unacceptable. As Williams entered the Oval Office he noticed Wyatt Midkiff looked years older. This crisis had drained him. "Mr. President."

"Chase, come in. You're a sight for sore eyes. Please sit."

The two men sat in the president's conversational area.

"Now what's on your mind, Chase?"

"Mr. President, I'll get right to the point. I think Op-Center should take a stronger role in dealing with potential terrorist attacks on our soil, and here's why."

Wyatt Midkiff listened intently as Chase Williams went through his detailed analysis and rationale.

Sandee Barron had prevailed on her husband to take a few days off from work to look after their two daughters so she could fly to Washington, D.C., to spend a few days with Laurie Phillips.

Laurie had told her about her termination at the Center for Naval Analyses and Sandee had formerly resigned her commission, so they were both officially unemployed. Washington was arguably the most recession-proof city in America. They both decided they would look for work here, and Sandee's husband had already secured a promise from KPMG they would transfer him to Northern Virginia when the time came. They had agreed to meet for beers at Clyde's in Georgetown, one of Sandee's old haunts from her Naval Academy days. Laurie knew the bar as well.

They sat in a booth talking about job prospects and a million other things. Sandee was staying with Laurie and they had arrived by taxi. They intended to cab it back once they closed down Clyde's, or were thrown out. The beer flowed freely.

Neither were heavy drinkers but this occasion was unique. Immediately, they fell into a conversational world of their own. They talked of the crash, the capture and interrogation by the prince and his men, and their abrupt career terminations. All this brought them closer, closer than sisters. It was talk, more beer, and more talk. They were so engaged they failed to notice the large man who was watching them from the bar until he appeared at the end of their booth. They looked up together, mildly annoyed at the interruption.

"Ms. Phillips, Ms. Barron, good evening."

"How do you know our names?" Laurie asked.

"Oh, I know a great deal about you two, as does my employer."

Now on guard, Sandee replied, holding up her left hand, "Hey, I'm married, see? And you're not my friend's type."

"Forgive me, ladies; it was not my intention to make you uncomfortable. I understand that you are both looking for work, and I have something that might interest you," Brian Dawson replied. "Mind if I sit down?"

Sandee and Laurie were surprised enough by Dawson knowing their names they sat in stunned silence as he pulled a chair up to the end of their booth.

"Have either of you ladies heard of an organization called the National Crisis Management Center?"

Silence.

"I didn't think so. I can't tell you much here in a restaurant, we need a secure space for that, but I can tell you the gentlemen who snatched you out of Saudi Arabia belonged to our JSOC cell. We operate internationally, and now, domestically, and we like to recruit people who don't mind throwing the rule book away when it's absolutely necessary. You two seem like our kind of people. Interested in learning more?"

Laurie and Sandee just gaped at Dawson, then at each other.